The Heart of a Lion

Other books by Kathy Hawkins

The Heart of a Stranger
The Desires of the Heart

The Heart of a Lion

Kathy Hawkins

kregel
PUBLICATIONS

Grand Rapids, MI 49501

The Heart of a Lion

Published by Kregel Publications, a division of Kregel, Inc.,
P. O. Box 2607, Grand Rapids, MI 49501. Kregel Publications
provides trusted, biblical publications for Christian growth and
service. Your comments and suggestions are valued.

For more information about Kregel Publications, visit our
web site at http://www.kregel.com.

Cover Illustration: Ron Mazellan
Cover Design: Alan G. Hartman
Book Design: Nicholas G. Richardson

Library of Congress Cataloging-in-Publication Data
Hawkins, Kathy.
    The heart of a lion / by Kathy Hawkins.
        p.   cm.
    1. Bible. O.T.—History of Biblical events—Fiction.
    2. David, King of Israel, Family—Fiction I. Title.
    PS3558.A823165H42   1998   813'.54—dc21   98-33822
                                                         CIP

ISBN 0-8254-2872-6

Printed in the United States of America
1 2 3 / 04 03 02 01 00 99 98

To my three children,
Karen Justice,
Donna Hancock,
and Brent Hawkins

I want to thank my children, to whom this book is dedicated. My daughters have been firm in their insistence that I can tell a good story. My son has shown infinite patience in teaching me to use my computer and rescuing mc from many disasters.

I am ever grateful to Betty Norton (Aunt Betty), for painstaking proofreading and words of encouragement. Two of my friends gave their time and valuable opinions to *The Heart of a Lion*. Kris Beckenback lent her help when I was tired and out of ideas. Frieda Thompson, longtime friend and English professor, added her literary insight as well as encouragement.

I appreciate the assistance of Rachel Derowitsch, Dave Lindstedt, and the editorial staff at Kregel, who polished a rough work until it was ready to publish.

And I can never adequately thank my life partner, Don, who contributes to all my work in too many ways to mention.

Historical Notes

$\sim$

No portion of Scripture has more danger, adventure, pathos and suspense than 2 Samuel 13–18. The sheer drama of Absalom's attempt to usurp his father's throne makes fascinating reading, but God intended this story to be more than just a good read. His mercy, justice, and everlasting love for his imperfect children shine through in every line and give us hope.

The numerous characters and plot twists found in this story can be confusing. The following are some observations that may be helpful.

Chileab was King David's second son, born to Abigail, the widow of Nabal. Nothing is mentioned of this child but his name and parentage, even though, after Amnon's death, he would have been the heir apparent to David's kingdom. Because he is not mentioned as a contender for the throne, most scholars believe he died in infancy, or that he had some debilitating disease or condition that excluded him from the line of succession. In *The Heart of a Lion,* Chileab is portrayed as mentally impaired as an answer to this scriptural mystery.

There is another intriguing mystery that remains part of the story of Absalom's revolt, and that is the question of whether Mephibosheth, the crippled son of Jonathan, really turned traitor against David when the king had treated him like a member of his own family. Ziba, Mephibosheth's servant, tells one story in 2 Samuel 16:1–2 and Mephibosheth another in 2 Samuel 19:20–24. Who was telling the truth?

Mephibosheth had lived in the palace and doubtless knew Absalom very well. He would have observed Absalom's murder of Amnon, who was in line of succession before him. As the grandson of Saul, the former king, Mephibosheth could have been a contender for the throne, and it would not have been wise for him to trust Absalom, who had a penchant for killing his competition.

Ziba, on the other hand, was presented with a perfect opportunity for self-promotion when the revolt occurred. By lying to David, he would lose nothing if the king lost, and if David won the war with Absalom, he stood a chance of having everything that had belonged to Mephibosheth. Like Gehazi, the greedy servant of Elisha (2 Kings 5:20–27), it appears that Ziba lied to enrich himself.

The main female character in this book is named Shoshanna, which means "lily" in Hebrew. While there is no Bible character with that name, people in Bible times, as people today, named their daughters after beautiful things. For instance, the name "Esther" means "star." It stands to reason that some parents would have named their daughters after a beautiful flower. Even though the word *shoshanna* does not appear in Scripture as a woman's name, it does appear in the superscriptions of Psalms 45, 69, and 80 ("to the *shoshannim*"), and in reference to flowers numerous times, especially in the Song of Solomon.

The Hebrew word *Rab* means "great man" or "chief," and is closely connected to the Aramaic word *Rabbi* used in the New Testament.

Ahmi and *Ahbi* are transliterations of what may have been familiar forms of address for "mother" and "father" in ancient Hebrew.

The word *Gibborim* means "mighty ones" in Hebrew. David

used this designation for the greatest warriors in his army. They also were referred to as "the Thirty," because their ranks were apparently kept at that number. It appears that the *Gibborim* who either retired or fell in battle were replaced to keep the number at thirty. A total of thirty-seven are listed in 2 Samuel 23 and 1 Chronicles 11.

In Job 39:19, there is a unique rendering of the Hebrew word *ramah* (thunder). While the KJV reads, "Hast thou given the horse strength? hast thou clothed his neck with thunder?" modern versions have rendered *ramah* as "a flowing mane." This is why the horse is named Ramah in *The Heart of a Lion*.

Archaeologists have discovered pieces of pottery from around Solomon's time that are stamped with a royal seal that includes the name of the city where the pieces were made. Scholars believe that the pottery from these places were given this "royal seal of approval" because they met exacting standards for size and volume. The village of Ziph was one of those pottery works so designated.

The lion found in Israel during Old Testament times was smaller than the African lion of today and had a shorter, curlier mane. Three men in the Bible are said to have fought and killed lions: Samson, David, and Benaiah.

My desire in the *Heart of Zion* series is to turn the reader to the Scriptures. I have endeavored to include in this book all the information found in the Bible in 2 Samuel 14–16. In addition to what the Old Testament tells us explicitly, I have drawn some conclusions that I believe to be based on implicit information that can be found in a careful examination of the biblical story coupled with deductive reasoning—in other words, a little detective work. But the conclusions I have drawn are fallible. My hope is that the reader will study the Word of God carefully, and discard any assumptions that are found to be contrary to it.

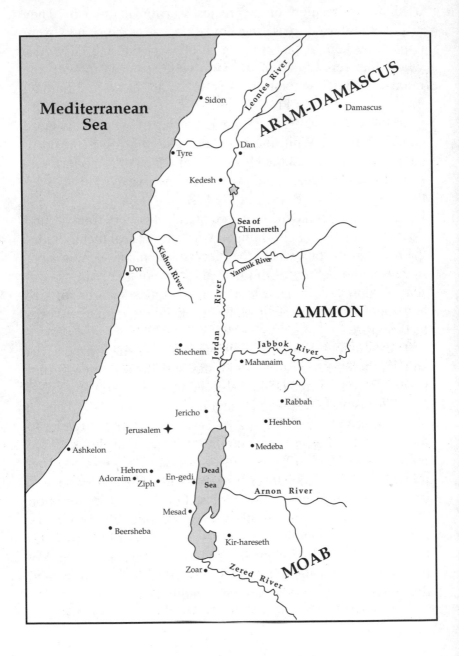

Characters

~

Fictional

AILEA (eye LEE uh), Aramean wife of Jonathan, son of Shageh
   of Ziph
IGAL (IGH gal), young warrior from Ziph
JERUSHA (jih ROO shuh), daughter of Jonathan and Ailea
MARAH (MAH ruh), Shoshanna's widowed mother
MICAH (MIGH kuh), son of Jonathan and Ailea of Ziph
SHOSHANNA (shoh SHAN uh), granddaughter of Ahithophel;
   cousin of Bathsheba

Historical

All of these characters are found in 2 Samuel 15–17, except
for Jonathan and Shageh, who are found in 2 Samuel 23.

ABIATHAR (uh BIGH uh thar), co-high priest with Zadok
ABISHAI (uh BISH ay eye), David's nephew and one of his
   generals; brother of Joab
ABSALOM (AB suh luhm), David's third-born son, whose
   mother was Maacah, princess of Geshur
AHIMAAZ (uh HIM uh az), son of Zadok, the high priest

AHITHOPHEL (uh HITH oh fel), King David's counselor; grandfather of Bathsheba

AMASA (uh MAY suh), David's nephew; became Absalom's general

BARZILLAI (bar ZIL ay eye), wealthy Gileadite, loyal to David

HUSHAI (HYOO shay eye), loyal friend of David, from the town of Archi

ITTAI (IT ay eye), a Philistine who was one of David's generals

JOAB (JOH ab), David's nephew; commander of Israel's army

JONATHAN, son of Abiathar, the high priest

JONATHAN, son of Shageh; one of David's mighty men

MEPHIBOSHETH (meh FIB oh sheth), lame son of Prince Jonathan, David's friend

SHAGEH (SHAY geh), the wise Rab of Ziph

SHIMEI (SHIM eye), a Benjamite who cursed David

SHOBI (SHOH bigh), son of Nahash, the Ammonite king; vassal of David

ZADOK (ZAY dahk), co-high priest with Abiathar

ZIBA (ZIGH buh), servant of Mephibosheth

Pronunciations are from the book *Pronouncing Bible Names* by W. Murray Serverance, Broadman and Holman Publishers, © 1994.

"And even he who is valiant, whose heart is like the heart of a lion, will melt completely. For all Israel knows that your father is a mighty man, and those who are with him are valiant men."

—Hushai's advice to Absalom in 2 Samuel 17:10

Prologue

~

*A*bsalom impatiently paced the length of the porch of his mountain retreat in Baal Hazor in Ephraim, some five miles north of Bethel. From time to time, he would stop and search the valley below for any sign that his invited guests were coming. His hazel eyes, flecked with amber, green, and blue, squinted against the brightness of the midday sun, but he could see no movement on the road, which lay nearly a mile below. He clenched his fists in frustration as he continued to pace.

He had built his mountain retreat and furnished it lavishly some years before, and he returned there often, especially at the time of the sheep shearing in May and June, because he kept large herds nearby. Usually he came to escape the heat of Jerusalem, and to enjoy the feasting that went hand-in-hand with the shearing. He had won the adulation of the people of Ephraim, and always welcomed them to a celebration feast after the shearing was done.

The inhabitants of the small villages had been celebrating for three days, and tomorrow Absalom would invite many of them to the feast he would give in honor of his brothers. As yet there was no sign of the royal entourage that would bring his brothers from Jerusalem. Had his father, or, more likely, Joab, become suspicious of his motives? After all, Absalom had never invited any of his brothers to this retreat before. But this year, there was a reason—a good reason.

As his eyes swept the valley once more, a movement caught his eye. It was his sister, Tamar, picking wildflowers in the high meadow that fronted the villa. Tamar spent much of her time picking the flowers that formed a blanket of color in the spring. There were poppies and wild lilies and meadow saffron with its lilac-colored flowers. His sister's beauty was hidden behind the veil she now wore whenever she was outside her room, and her shoulders drooped in a perpetual state of despair that Absalom had been unable to alleviate.

His lips thinned in bitterness as he thought about his sister, disgraced and humiliated beyond her ability to cope, and sentenced to a life as a recluse in his home—only a shadow of the loving, happy, and beautiful girl he once knew.

But very soon now, Tamar would be avenged. Her attacker would be seated at Absalom's right hand tomorrow night, reassured by the welcome Absalom intended to give him. Then, when the other guests were too far gone in drink to come to Amnon's defense, Absalom's half-brother would see justice.

Absalom rubbed his hands in anticipation of carrying out the vindication due his sister, justice that should have been meted out by his father two years earlier. Absalom had waited all this time for David to bring vengeance on the man who had raped his daughter. That Amnon was the king's own son didn't matter. David should have seen that he was executed, but he hadn't even banished Amnon from court.

Instead, he had treated Tamar as if the incident were somehow her fault. The king had not once visited his daughter to comfort her. When Absalom thought about the travesty, it was all he could do to keep from going to the palace and slaying his father as well as his brother. But no, he would bide his time. First, Amnon would pay, then David would be made to suffer for all the times he had slighted him and Tamar, and their mother, Maacah.

He called to his sister, and she turned toward him with a smile. Though she was veiled, her beautiful eyes—exactly the color and shape of his—crinkled at the sight of the only person in the world she now trusted.

"Stay where you are," he called as he hastened to join her. She was having a good day. There were few of those, and Absalom always did his best to make them memorable for her.

∽ ∽ ∽

An hour later, they returned to the porch, Absalom carrying Tamar's basket, now full of flowers, and Tamar laden down with more. She would place them in vases situated throughout the house. It was one of her few pleasures. Absalom dropped his gaze once again to the valley, and spied his guests in a long procession, just now turning off the main road onto the winding path that would bring them to his estate. His lips thinned in a grim smile.

"They are coming, Tamar. I told you they would come." Tamar's eyes followed those of her brother, and she dropped her flowers with a gasp.

"Oh, no, no! They are here. Oh, no."

Absalom put a reassuring hand on his sister's shoulder. "Yes, Tamar, it is our brothers, but you needn't be afraid. No one will hurt you. I'll protect you. You may stay with me all day."

"But they will ask for me and I don't want to see them."

"Not any of them?"

Tamar hesitated for a moment. She loved her other brothers, but had refused to see any of them since the rape. Absalom hoped for her sake that she might have recovered enough to once more visit with her siblings, but she shook her head, her eyes brimming.

"Then you may go. You do not have to see them if you wish not to. I will escort you to the kitchen. You can help with the baking that has to be done for the feast tomorrow."

"I don't want to go to the feast, brother. I can't do that."

"You don't have to go to the feast, Tamar." But Tamar wasn't cheered by her brother's promises. She began to weep softly as he led her to her suite in an upper corner of the villa, with a view over the meadow of wildflowers that she loved. He left a servant with her and went to await his brothers' arrival.

≈ ≈ ≈

Absalom was smiling when he greeted his brothers, though his greeting to Amnon was restrained. Absalom had given careful thought to his actions, and had concluded that feigning affection for his older brother would cause Amnon and the other princes to become suspicious. Absalom was known for his vanity and pride, so he decided to pretend that pride in his mountain retreat had motivated the invitation.

"When I realized that none of you had been to Baal Hazor before, I decided to invite you. I want you to see what I have built here." As he showed them through the house, except for the rooms used by his family and Tamar, Absalom silently congratulated himself for his skill. They all thought they were here to be regaled with their brother's accomplishments. They relaxed more with each hour, as Absalom worked diligently to appear pleasant. The only sign that a strained relationship remained between David's sons was that no one asked about their sister. Their silence stoked the furnace of Absalom's hatred, but he continued to smile.

≈ ≈ ≈

The next day, as the sun sank low in the sky, Absalom sought out his sister in the kitchens at the rear of the mansion. Tamar was occupied, carefully shaping the "heart cakes" he had requested for the feast. He had asked her to prepare the special confection in part to keep her busy so that her fears would not overcome her, but also as part of an ingenious idea for revenge on his brother that would incorporate the sweets. Tamar gave them to the cook to place in the oven that stood against the outer wall of the kitchen, below the hole in the roof that allowed smoke to escape.

"These look delicious, my sister," Absalom remarked as he put his arm around her shoulder and hugged her affectionately. "They will be the favorite at the feast tonight."

At his mention of the feast, Tamar stiffened. "No, Tamar, don't be afraid. You do not have to attend. I will serve the cakes. Have you eaten anything?" When his sister shook her head, Absalom ordered the cook to bring some choice lamb and fruit, and coaxed his sister to eat, feeding her from his own hand. He often had to coax or even order her to eat when the dark moods descended on her.

An hour later, Absalom carefully dressed for the feast. After greeting his brothers yesterday, he had not spent much time with them, claiming he would give them a chance to settle into their chambers and rest from their journey. He had sent word this morning that he would see them at the banquet.

As his thoughts drifted back to Tamar, Absalom's hands shook in anticipation of his revenge. Since she had come to live with him, his sister had made almost an obsession of baking and giving the heart cakes to members of the family, his wife, daughter, and son. She even baked for the villagers and servants. It was as if she were trying to prove to herself that generosity and kindness should not have the outcome it had had with Amnon in the palace two years before.

"Absalom, the baby is sick again today. Please make my excuses to your brothers. I cannot leave his side to attend the banquet." Absalom's beautiful, fragile wife had entered his chamber silently. *She flits about like some wraith,* he thought, *and her whining sounds like the moaning of the wind.* He regretted very much having married her. She had given him three sickly sons, two of whom had died in early infancy. The third, who was now in his fourth year, was not likely to live to see his fifth.

But he kissed her, mentally granting her one great accomplishment. She had given him a little daughter of surpassing beauty. He had named her Tamar after her tragic, beautiful aunt, and she was the joy of his life. "I understand, my dear. Don't worry. I will explain to my brothers." As his wife left the room, Absalom thought that everything was going perfectly. His wife would be out of the way tonight.

≈ ≈ ≈

The eating and drinking had been going on for hours. Most of the princes were well under the influence of the strong wine Absalom had ordered served. They had been wary of their brother at first, and had watched carefully to see what kind of interchange would take place between Amnon and Absalom. Absalom had seemed a bit cool in his greeting to his older brother, but had given him the same kiss of greeting as the others. And he had accorded him the place of honor at the feast that was due Amnon as the elder brother.

All the older sons of David were there, except Chileab. Absalom had worried about the son of Abigail, second born of David. Though Chileab was in his late twenties, his mind was that of a child, and Absalom would not have wanted him to witness the violence that would take place tonight. Tamar used to include her half-brother in their play when they were children. Some of the other royal children teased him, but Absalom and Tamar had been his champions. It occurred to him that Tamar might be comforted if Abigail could be persuaded to allow Chileab to visit Baal Hazor.

He shook his head to clear his thoughts. Of course that would not be possible. After tonight, he would be an outcast in Israel. He would have to flee Baal Hazor as soon as the deed was done. His plan was to take Tamar to Geshur, where their grandfather, Talmai, would give him refuge. Geshur, a desert kingdom east of the Sea of Chinnereth, was a vassal state of Israel, but Absalom had no doubt that his mother's father would fight, if necessary, to protect the grandchildren he doted on.

David's other older sons, who had been born when he ruled from Hebron, were present—Adonijah, Shephatiah, and Ithream. Ibhar, born shortly after David's installment in Jerusalem, was also there. The other princes born in Jerusalem were too young to attend. It was a pity the sons of Bathsheba, especially Solomon, were still small children. Absalom hated the adulteress who had taken his mother's place in the king's affection, and he hated Solomon, who was now the favored prince of the palace. He sensed that the winsome child would one day challenge him for the throne, but that problem could wait. In time, Absalom told himself, he would take care of Solomon. Tonight he would take care of Amnon. He smiled at his brothers and motioned to his servants to replenish their wine.

Absalom stayed the hand of Amnon, who sat on his right side, before he could raise his cup to his lips yet again. He wanted his older brother to be fully aware of the events that would occur in the next few moments. He forced a warm smile to his lips as he spoke. "Hold a moment, brother. I have had a special dish prepared especially for you, and I wouldn't want you to be nodding off before you can enjoy it."

Amnon laughed. He had finally decided that his brother no longer held a grudge against him. *After all, as a man, he should understand that sometimes a man's needs overcome him and . . .*

Amnon deliberately forced the image of his half-sister from his mind. He would not allow himself to feel remorse. After all, the girl *had* come to his rooms. She should not have come, beautiful as she was, if she had not intended what had happened. . . .

Absalom's voice intruded on his guilty reminiscence. "I have been absent from all of you these past two years, and I wish to give each of my brothers a gift befitting him, to show my regard for each of you." He had stood to make his announcement.

His brothers were seated on plush cushions around the thick, round leather mat that served as the table for this meal, which was served outside on the wide verandah where Absalom had stood earlier. Absalom gestured to a burly servant who had been serving them throughout the feast, and the man began to hand out beautiful little brass boxes, each containing a different exotic spice, most of them from Africa and very expensive. All received a gift, except Amnon.

The royal princes, who had been admiring their gifts, fell silent one by one, as they realized that their elder brother had been slighted. Absalom smiled at Amnon. "I have left your gift for last, my brother, as it was specially prepared for you just this day."

He nodded to the servant, who picked up a silver tray from a side table and placed it in Absalom's hands before moving to stand directly behind Amnon. Absalom held the tray in front of his older brother, where each of the princes could see its contents—four honey-colored, heart-shaped little cakes.

"These are the best heart cakes in the kingdom," he proclaimed with a strange gleam in his eye, "as sweet and tender as our sister, Tamar, who made them. You remember the last time you had them, don't you, my brother? It was when you lured the innocent girl to your room on the pretext of illness. Did you taste of them before or after you helped yourself to my sister?"

Absalom's voice rose as he spoke, and his brothers grew alarmed before he was halfway through his speech. Amnon turned pale the moment he saw the cakes. He started to rise, but Absalom nodded to the servant who stood behind him, and a thick, muscular arm covered with black hair grasped Amnon around the throat. With a lightning-quick thrust, the man's other hand swung forward, plunging a thick-bladed knife into Amnon's heart.

"May the same thing happen to any man who dishonors his own family in such a disgraceful way!" Absalom shouted the last statement, but only his servants heard. The royal princes were running for their mounts, certain that their brother intended to slay them as well. Amnon heard nothing. He was face down on the eating mat, his blood forming a widening pool around him.

Chapter One

~

*T*he Rab was dying. Everyone in the small village of Ziph waited in hushed expectation, anticipating the loss of their most venerated citizen. A large number had gathered in the courtyard of the Rab Shageh's house. Periodically, Ailea of Damascus, the Rab's daughter-in-law, brought news of his condition, which had steadily worsened over the last several days. The rest of the time she spent trying to comfort the other family members, who kept a silent vigil in the corridor outside the dying man's chamber, waiting to be called to his deathbed.

Ailea felt bereft at the thought of losing the Rab, who had been her only friend when she had first been brought to Ziph as a captive bride. Her father-in-law had been a buffer between her and his son, Jonathan, during the first tumultuous months of their marriage. He had taught her about Adonai, the God of Israel, whom she had come to embrace as a result of the Rab's patient teaching of the Torah.

She felt an almost uncontrollable urge to go to the Rab's side. But Jonathan, his only son, deserved these private moments with his father. Ailea knew that Jonathan would call the remainder of

23

the family to gather around the Rab when the end came. She waited patiently, fighting the urge to wail her grief as loudly as a child. Once in a while she would relate an amusing or touching story about her father-in-law. The others keeping watch seldom commented on her stories, but that wasn't important to Ailea. She just needed to talk about Shageh.

The Rab's daughter, Ruth, who was two years older than Jonathan, sat on a three-legged stool on Ailea's right, wiping an occasional tear from the corners of her eyes. When her father had taken ill, she had come from the nearby village where she lived in order to help. She was not a person of strong emotion or many words, but there was no doubt she was already grieving the loss of her father.

Jerusha, Jonathan and Ailea's young daughter, had certainly not taken after her aunt. She felt all her emotions strongly and was never hesitant to share them with others. Whether angry, happy, frightened, or sad, Jerusha never left any doubt as to how she felt. Now she sat on her brother's lap and sobbed brokenly.

"It isn't time for grandfather to leave us, Micah. He has hardly begun to teach me from the Torah. Oh, how I wish I had gone to the teaching rock with him last week instead of taking the sheep to feed in the hills. Now I may never have another chance to learn from him, and no one else would bother to teach it to a girl," she cried. Micah stroked her hair with his large hand and held her close, not denying her words, which he knew were true.

The Rab was truly a unique and irreplaceable teacher. Micah remembered his grandfather's response when one of the men of the village questioned him about his willingness to teach the girls of the village as well as the boys. "The Law of the Lord brings light into the life of the one who hears it. What man of reason would want his wife or his daughter to remain in darkness?" That had effectively silenced his critic.

No one would have guessed that Jerusha and Micah were siblings. She was delicate and her hair was black as pitch, while he was muscular, with brown hair streaked with golden highlights.

Though he was a dozen years older than his sister, even a casual observer would have noticed their deep affection as Micah comforted Jerusha, and her complete trust in him as she poured out her grief.

≈ ≈ ≈

Inside the room where the sick man lay propped up on a mountain of pillows to ease his breathing, Jonathan held his father's bony, parchment-like hand and spoke in low, soothing tones. The gentleness he showed the old man was incongruous with his fierce countenance and huge stature. As one of the *Gibborim,* or mighty men of King David, Jonathan ben Shageh had earned his status as one of the greatest warriors of Israel. Though he had recently turned fifty, few men in the kingdom could equal his strength, cunning, or strategic grasp of war.

But at this moment Jonathan was not the feared warrior of Israel's victorious armies. He was the son of the most beloved and respected man in the hill country of southern Judah, and he was remembering the times his father had held him, taught him, gently reproved him, and judiciously praised him. As he remembered, his eyes misted with tears. Soon, he must call the remainder of the family in. The time had come for the Rab, the wise man of Ziph, beloved father and grandfather, to utter his last words and give his final blessings to those he would leave behind. But it was hard, so hard, to let him go.

"I will call the others, Father," Jonathan said softly as he leaned over the old man.

"Just Micah. I must talk to Micah first."

"But Ruth will want to . . ."

"I will say my good-byes to my daughter afterward, but I would see Micah before I grow any weaker. There is . . . much I . . . need to tell him." The Rab's chest wheezed with difficulty, and Jonathan worried that he didn't have enough breath left to talk to his grandson, much less his other loved ones who waited in the hall. But he reluctantly went to fetch Micah. Few people failed to disregard the wishes of the Rab; certainly not his only son.

"I will be but a moment," Jonathan promised before slipping from the room. As soon as he opened the door his older sister came to him. She was in her late fifties, but her excellent health had always made her appear much younger than her actual age. Not today. Jonathan noticed the dark circles under her eyes. The lines in her face were prominent. Ruth looked old and haggard. Jonathan heaved a sigh. He supposed he looked old as well. Why were they all so stricken when they had expected this for months now? After all, Shageh was ninety years old!

"He still lives?" Ruth's eyes held a mixture of hope and anguish. When Jonathan nodded, Ruth started past him to the door of their father's room. He stayed her with a hand on her shoulder.

"Wait a bit, Ruth dear. He has asked to speak to Micah first."

"But I'm his daughter," she wailed in an almost childlike voice.

With a glance down the hallway at the other family members, Jonathan lowered his voice to a whisper. "And he is asking for you, but he has something to say to Micah first. This will be harder on the boy than on any of the rest of us," he reminded his sister, hoping her love for her nephew would allow her to put his interests first. She did not disappoint him.

"Yes. That is true. Of course, Micah must go in to him first. I will wait. But do you think he might die before . . ." She couldn't finish the sentence, and Jonathan hastened to reassure her.

"You know the Rab, sister. He has willed himself to live until he has bid us all good-bye. He won't disappoint us." He gave her a sad smile, and Ruth returned a wobbly one. Then Jonathan motioned to his son and Micah joined him at the doorway.

"He wants to speak privately with you, but don't take too long. He is very weak, and the others will be heartbroken if they don't get their chance to visit him once more." Micah nodded grimly and closed the door. Crossing the room to his grandfather's bed, he noticed that the Rab's eyes were closed. He leaned over and kissed each of the old man's wrinkled cheeks. "I am here, Grandfather."

Shageh opened his eyes slowly, as if they were very heavy, but managed a smile for his grandson. "Sit," the old man commanded, motioning weakly for Micah to sit on the bed beside him.

"I would give you my blessing, Micah, before I leave this earth. You must not grieve long at my death. I will always be with you, Micah. You will remember the things I have taught you when you are tested. There is much of me in you, as well as much of your father, and you will learn to reconcile the two natures as you grow older." The dying man's voice had grown stronger as he spoke his last words to his grandson, as if he knew how important they were to Micah.

The long fingers of the dying Rab clasped his grandson's with surprising pressure, and Micah grasped at this false hope. "You will get better, Grandfather. It is not time yet for you to leave us. We need you too much."

The old man gazed directly into his grandson's eyes, which were the same clear amber as his own. "No, Micah, you do not need me any longer. You are a man now. You have been a man for several years, and you will be greatly used of Adonai, for you have a heart for him. I want to talk to you about the vow you made to me when you were a lad. You know the one of which I am speaking."

Micah nodded and clasped the old man's hand more tightly. "I vowed I would never strike or harm another person as long as I live."

"It was a good vow you made, in many ways, Micah. But it is not one that is possible to keep for all time in all circumstances, so I release you from it."

Micah's frown revealed his confusion. "Grandfather, I'm not sure I want to be released from my promise. It has served me very well for all these years."

"Micah, you are about to enter a new season in your life, and for that you need to be free of all that would hold you back. I allowed you to make the vow to me, and not to Adonai, so I could release you from it when the time was right."

"I remember you stopping my words with your hand over my mouth and telling me that I must never make a vow to Adonai in the heat of the moment, or out of guilt, or pride, or anything else. You said that a man must make vows to the Lord most sparingly, but that you would allow me to vow it to you, and you would hold me accountable to keep it."

"That is right, Micah. A man should only vow to Adonai to serve only Him, to care for his wife and family, and very little else. Now you are at a crossroads, and need to decide the path your life will take. You must only follow the same path your father has chosen as a warrior if it is the right path for *you*. Speak honestly with Jonathan about your doubts. Never deny what you are, Micah."

"But that is the problem, Grandfather. I don't really know what I am—Hebrew or Aramean, warrior or teacher."

Shageh opened his mouth as if to respond, but his words subsided into a low, rasping wheeze, as though the very breath of life had begun its final journey across his lips. He closed his eyes and rested his head on the pillows.

Alarmed, Micah pleaded with Shageh not to die, but the old man only shook his head weakly and told him to call his Aunt Ruth. As Micah went to summon his aunt, he knew he had spent his last hour with the Rab.

A few minutes later, after her special time with her father, Ruth motioned the entire family into the room. "Come near, Little One," the old man rasped. His eyes were fastened not on Jerusha but on her mother. "Little One" had always been his pet name for Ailea.

As she leaned close to the dying man, Ailea could not keep the tears from flowing, and the Rab reached up with a shaking hand to brush them away. "Hush, Little One. I am tired, and it is time for me to join my fathers. You are strong and will continue to be. The God of Israel will be with you. Do you remember your first prayer to him, and how amazed you were when he answered it?"

Ailea smiled through her tears. "I asked him for a friend and he sent me Judith. I remember how anxious I was to tell you about it. I thought it such a wondrous thing. But you weren't surprised at all when I told you."

The Rab's lips curved into a smile. "I am never surprised at the power and lovingkindness of Adonai, Little One. That is why I am happy to go to him. Do not grieve too much. You have given me great joy because you give joy to my son. And you have given me my heritage in Israel, my precious grandchildren. They may struggle, or falter, but be assured. . . ." He gathered his remaining strength. "Their righteousness will shine as the stars. . . ." The Rab's voice trailed off and he became very still.

Jonathan laid his hand over his father's heart, expecting to find it had ceased beating. But though faint, its pulse remained steady. A few minutes later, the old man opened his eyes once more and whispered his granddaughter's name. In her typical, impetuous way, Jerusha climbed up on the bed, cupped her grandfather's face in her small hands, and planted several kisses. "Your heart is brave and your spirit is free, precious one," he told her in a surprisingly clear voice. "Guard you heart carefully and commit your spirit to Adonai. Do not let it turn to rebellion. If you do these things, the Lord will reward you."

As Jerusha enveloped her grandfather in a warm embrace, the Rab's eyelids fluttered and he fell into a deep sleep. Sensing the time was near, the family slowly moved back into the outer rooms.

Several hours later, Jonathan made his way to the courtyard where most of the villagers were keeping a vigil, though darkness had fallen, necessitating the lighting of torches. His announcement that their beloved leader was dead started the process of mourning that would last for many days.

EIGHT MONTHS LATER

Micah awoke early. He had to make the journey to Jerusalem today. He didn't want to go back, but his father couldn't make the trip himself—or so he had claimed. He had insisted that Micah must go in his place.

It had come as somewhat of a surprise to Micah that Jonathan would choose him as his representative. After all, just a few weeks ago Micah had been sent back home to Ziph in disgrace—dismissed by Joab, the general of Israel's army, accused of cowardice and under suspicion of treason. It must have been a blow to Jonathan's pride as a military man that his son had failed as an army recruit.

Despite his grandfather's dying words instructing him to tell his father that his heart was not in it, Micah had enlisted in the army at twenty, the age the Law specified a young man to be eligible for the draft. In David's kingdom, however, there was no need for a draft; the volunteer army had won victory after victory during his reign, and now all the surrounding kingdoms had been brought under the domination of Israel.

Jonathan had pointed out to Micah that during peacetime it would not be unpatriotic to choose to stay home, gradually taking over the spiritual leadership of Ziph and the other small villages in the southern hill country, teaching young boys the Torah as Shageh the Rab had done.

But Micah was convinced that his father was wrong. He felt he had to prove himself first as a warrior before the people would accept him as leader. Despite Jonathan's stature among the most loyal and powerful warriors in the kingdom, Micah had never been completely trusted or accepted. After all, he was not a full-blooded Israelite. His mother was an Aramean from Damascus, and though the villagers had eventually accepted her, they still treated her and her children with the polite restraint that marked them as outsiders.

Micah felt he had something to prove, not only to the village, but also to his father, whom he admired above all men. He wanted to prove himself as a warrior to make his father proud, even though his father assured him he would not be disappointed if Micah did not choose a military career. Besides, life in the village was not the same without the Rab, and Micah had felt that maybe a change would help him deal better with the grief of losing his grandfather.

Micah had gone to Jerusalem to train directly under Joab himself. His father had been uneasy about that. There was no love lost between the general and Jonathan. Never had been. Jonathan had warned Micah that the general would likely be more demanding, more critical of him because he was Jonathan's son. But in truth, the general had been scrupulously fair.

The accusation of cowardice had come from the ranks of Micah's unit, where he had been challenged from the first day. Certain other recruits had mocked and goaded him from the very beginning. Because of his size—he was taller and heavier than any man in his unit, perhaps in Israel's entire army of nearly one hundred thousand—he had been taunted almost daily to fight some fellow who wanted to prove himself. Because of his sanguine nature and tendency to negotiate rather than fight, some had branded him a coward, mistaking his peaceful nature for weakness. They secretly feared him, but covered their fear with animosity. When they saw that Micah had chosen to live a chaste life, they taunted him constantly about women.

A warrior in the standing army was guaranteed to be sought after by women, and most of the young men took full advantage, with little concern about impurity. They would chide Micah as they left the barracks for a night of debauchery. "When will you be old enough to go with us, son of Jonathan? Are you yet a lad?"

"Aye, he's a lad. Not full grown yet," someone else would respond. They would all laugh mockingly, but Micah laughed right along with them until they gave up goading him and went their way. Even when they made veiled hints that Micah was somehow unnatural because he wasn't licentious, he didn't retaliate.

Their fear and guilt remained a barrier to his acceptance. Still, his ability with weapons of war, in which Jonathan had tutored him well, and his sheer size made Micah a candidate for leadership, and Joab had appointed him a squadron. The men followed his orders well enough until one day when their assignment was to chase a group of desert bandits during a training mission in the Transjordan.

Many of the men were anticipating their first taste of victory in battle, ready to spill the blood of the outlaws. Instead, when the robbers were surrounded, Micah did not allow his squadron to use their swords. He ordered his men to simply confiscate the stolen goods and let the bandits go.

Micah's show of mercy angered his men, and some complained directly to Joab. Micah was called before the commander and asked pointedly whether he had let the outlaws escape because they were Aramean, and thus had greater claim on his loyalty than the king. Micah flushed at the insult and clenched his fists in anger. He knew why the general had asked the question.

His parents had told him many times how Joab had opposed Jonathan's marriage to Ailea when he had brought her back to Israel as a captive. Joab had suspected her of spying for her brother, Rezon, who had become a raider and a guerrilla fighter against Israel after the defeat of the Aramean alliance more than twenty years ago. The general had never trusted Micah's father after his marriage to Ailea, and now he thought the worst of the son.

Micah patiently explained the incident to Joab. "Those raiders were not Aramean, though if they had been, I still would have let them go. They posed no threat to Israel. They were from a poor village near the Jordan and were only raiding to feed their families. I confiscated their booty and sent them home."

"Is it true that you sent your own unit's food rations with them as well?" Micah admitted he had sent enough bread to feed the tiny village for a week. Joab shook his head in disgust and mumbled something about it being a pity that a giant as big as Goliath should have a heart as soft as a woman's. He gruffly ordered Micah to return home while he contemplated whether he was worthy to be trained as a soldier.

Micah groaned at the memory and rose from his bed. He stretched, able to flatten his hands on the ceiling of the room, so great was his height. Micah ben Jonathan certainly did not look like a man who was either soft or cowardly. The truth was, Micah did not fear anyone, but not everyone knew that—including, apparently, Joab.

Micah shook off his unpleasant thoughts as he walked to the window, opened the shutters, and gazed out on the prosperous village of Ziph. "Oh, Grandfather, I wish you were still here." Micah's grief over the loss of the Rab had hardly abated over the past months. In order to escape it, he had joined the army only one week after his grandfather's funeral. But his home-sickness in Jerusalem only made him sadder. His grief had been particularly acute when he had come home in disgrace and had to confess to Jonathan that he had been at least temporarily suspended from the army.

Though Jonathan had been angry on his son's behalf, he showed no sign of being ashamed of him. Still, Micah couldn't help but feel he had disappointed his father sorely. Grandfather would have understood how he felt.

Micah turned from the window to a small table nearby. He picked up a scroll tied with a scarlet cord. It was a copy of the Torah, a gift to the Rab from King David years ago. Upon Shageh's death, it had passed to Micah, who had not once failed to follow his grandfather's instruction to read it daily. After reading a passage, he prostrated himself in front of the window and began to praise and thank Adonai for life, for material blessings, for his family and health. He prayed for forgiveness of his sins, and finally, for wisdom. His devotions finished, he felt up to facing the unpleasant journey before him, and went to break his fast. It took a lot of food to fuel the massive frame he had inherited from Jonathan. But his other characteristics were the legacy of his grandfather, especially his height and his clear, amber eyes. Shageh had towered six inches above his son's six-foot height. So did Micah.

Not only did Micah resemble his grandfather physically, but everyone said his personality was uncannily like the Rab's. Both of them had a great reverence for Adonai, and for all creatures that he had made. Each had a calm, contemplative nature, and a disconcerting way of assessing people that saw beyond their facades. They had been as one in spirit, and although he loved his parents dearly, he was convinced that no one would ever understand him like Shageh had.

As he left his room, Micah heard someone moving about in the courtyard. He knew it would be his mother, drawing water from the cistern for the day's needs. She had already fired up the oven, and he smelled the enticing aroma of baking bread. Micah smiled as he remembered all the times his father had insisted that his wife had no business tending to such mundane chores.

Jonathan was a wealthy man, after all, and had provided his wife with several household servants to see to such things. But Ailea always rose before anyone, even the servants, and had much of the household work underway before anyone else could help. Micah always suspected that Ailea did this to irritate his father. The tiny woman seemed to revel in any opportunity to stand up to the mighty warrior she had married. It was possible also that his mother wanted to prove to the other women of Ziph that though she had been raised in the privileged home of Eliada, a powerful general in the city of Damascus, she did not think herself above them. The respect they accorded her had been hard won.

Ailea smiled at her son as he entered the courtyard, craning her neck to look up at him. People often remarked how amazing it was that tiny Ailea had borne this giant of a son. After greeting him and motioning for him to sit, she brought him crusty bread and goat's milk and commanded him to eat. When he sat, she still wasn't quite at eye level with him.

"I baked early so you would have fresh bread to take on your journey."

His response was interrupted when his scrap of a sister appeared. The girl was the exact image of her mother and the apple of her father's eye. She was also a handful, as stubborn as a goat, shunning the attributes of a proper young lady for the freedom of the hills as a shepherd girl. This seemed to scandalize their provincial little village, but Habaz, the chief shepherd, could hardly protest. Jonathan had provided him with most of the stock for his herds.

She was barefoot, as usual, and in the process of wrapping her hair up in a haphazard turban. Somehow her green eyes looked twice as large without her hair framing her face. "Is that bread almost done, Ahmi? It smells wonderful! Do you mind if I take some for Reuben? And the cheese as well?"

Micah knew the answer before his mother spoke. She had a soft spot in her heart for old Habaz, raising his grandson alone. The boy's mother had died giving birth to him, and his father had died of a fever not long ago.

Micah brought his thoughts back to the moment at hand. "Thank you, Mother. You take good care of me—of all of us."

"You are the joy of my life," she answered simply.

He watched her bustling about, and thought with pride that she was as beautiful as a young girl, with her long black hair that had hardly a sprinkling of gray. Her form and energy were that of a much younger woman. She often drove her husband to distraction. Jonathan's father had warned him teasingly never to marry a woman a decade younger than himself, else she would run him ragged. Micah knew that his father's plaints were made affectionately. Jonathan loved his wife more than anything.

"Good morning," a voice boomed, and Micah looked up to see his father descending the steps that led to his parents' rooftop apartment. Over the years, Jonathan had improved and added to the compound until it was now twice the size of any other home in the village. "I see you are ready to travel," Jonathan commented as he accepted food and a kiss on the cheek from his wife.

"Are you certain you want me to go?" Micah asked again, as he had over the past several days.

"You know I do. I want to send you to the feast in my stead so everyone will know I am proud of you and count you worthy to receive this honor on my behalf. You have done nothing to be ashamed of, and the sooner you go back to Jerusalem to face these groundless accusations, the quicker everyone will know that."

"Some of your friends in the army wouldn't agree," Micah commented as he bit into another piece of the fragrant, rich bread. He remembered the mumbled comments and sly remarks that had circulated in the barracks in Jerusalem, both from officers and recruits.

"Those who are my friends would agree. Those who don't are no friends of mine. When you return, I will demand to know the names of any who would dare slight you."

Jonathan's eyes took on a hard, cold look, and his brows beetled together as he spoke. "Father, you can't come to my rescue. It would only make matters worse. We've spoken of this before."

Jonathan growled his reluctant agreement. "Just don't forget that the king is our friend. Appeal to him directly."

Micah shook his head. "I will appeal first to Joab. I know you don't trust him, but he is giving me the benefit of the doubt, even though he thinks I acted foolishly. But I will compromise and ask that I present my case to Joab in the king's presence. I am partially guilty of the accusations. I did allow the bandits to go free, but certainly not because I believed them to be Rezon's men. Joab really had no recourse but to send me home after several men asked not to serve in my unit because they didn't trust me."

"But you know you are neither a traitor nor a coward, Son, and so do I."

"No, but my reasons were just as bad in the eyes of some warriors. I'm afraid I don't have the stomach for slaughter. I can fight to defend myself, and I will gladly attack in battle for my king, and for Adonai, but even then the killing haunts me."

"You are much like your grandfather, Micah, and that's nothing to be ashamed of. Do not think that because I am one of the *Gibborim* you must follow in my steps. In truth, there are nights when the eyes of those I have slain haunt my dreams, and on some days, when your mother puts her soft hand in mine, I feel unworthy because these hands have shed blood. No, I would be just as happy if you decide that the military life is not for you."

"But *look* at me, Father. Has not Adonai expressed his will in how he made me? You know that one such as I will never be accepted as anything but a warrior. Both my size and my Aramean blood proclaim that I must be a warrior to prove my worth. You don't know how many times I have wished I were as short as Perez next door. He has more friends than he can count because no one either fears or envies him."

"You will come to peace within yourself, Son. Do not worry. I am proud of you, no matter what you do. Go to Jerusalem and offer your services to the king. As peaceable as the kingdom has been in recent years, it is possible that David may send you as his emissary on a diplomatic mission."

Jonathan often forgot to speak of the king in formal terms. After all, he had joined David's band when Israel's sweet singer had been a fugitive from King Saul, hiding in the caves of Adullam. Jonathan had earned the position of Mighty One when barely into manhood. Now, decades later, he still served on active duty as one of David's war counselors, making trips to Jerusalem several times a year to train new recruits and lead forays to the border between Israel and the Philistines, to make sure they stayed close to their coastal cities of Ashdod and Ashkelon.

"Father, I wish you would at least come with me. You and Mother haven't been to Jerusalem for some time, and you deserve the honor the king will bestow on you. I have done nothing to deserve recognition. Are you not afraid that your name as a great warrior will be sullied by bringing attention to a son deemed unworthy?"

Jonathan's eyes flashed in anger. "You are not unworthy. I have instructed you to go in my stead so that all may know that I believe in you. I will not go with you. I will not embarrass you by intervening in these ridiculous accusations that have been made against you. I know I would not restrain myself if someone slighted you, and it would wound your pride if I came to your defense.

"And your mother! Well, you have not had as many occasions to have her fury unleashed on you, but believe me, if someone were to offer insult to her only son, she would attack immediately, whether in the streets of Jerusalem or inside the palace itself. Unless you wish to witness such a scene, I suggest you leave the two of us here and head to Jerusalem alone. Of course, you are welcome to take Jerusha with you."

The look of horror that crossed Micah's face caused Jonathan to double up in laughter. Micah soon joined in. Ailea, who had overheard the conversation, complained, "You two may think it's amusing, but you both have to help me do something about that child! She is running completely wild."

"I will help, Mother, I promise, as soon as I return from Jerusalem."

"It might not be such a bad idea to take her, Micah. She needs to see that there is more to life than these hills and the animals she loves so dearly."

Jonathan chuckled again at the look of dismay Micah gave his mother, and took pity on him. He patted Ailea's cheek. "Her love of animals she got from you. I remember sleeping with a smelly goat a few times when you thought the weather was too wet for your pet to stay outdoors. We will take Jerusha to the city for Passover, but Micah has too many distractions to look after her this time."

Ailea gave her husband a disgruntled look. "Amal wasn't just another goat, Jonathan, and you know it. I haven't had another pet since he died."

Jonathan laughed. "Well, I know he wasn't just another goat. He was trouble. That's why I named him 'Trouble.' And even though you haven't had a pet of your own since he died, you have seen to it that Micah and Jerusha have always had one. Let me see if I can remember them all. There was the badger, the ferret, the owl, not to mention a handful of sheep and goats that avoided the oven by currying favor with either you or the children."

"The sheep and goats provided us with milk and wool! And as for the other creatures, what was I to do when the children brought home abandoned or wounded animals—break their hearts by telling them the creatures had to die?"

"Father is only jesting, Mother. He was as fond of those pets as we were. He only feared it would make him appear less fierce if he showed it, and thus weaken his position as a warrior." Micah took the last bite of bread, drained his cup of milk, and stood. "I had better start my journey, or else I'll arrive in Jerusalem too late to find lodging."

Chapter Two

~

*I*n the neighborhood of exclusive homes that dotted the upper city of Jerusalem, a tall, slender young woman stood at the open window of her chamber, drawing in the sweet fragrance of the blooming almond tree that grew right outside the window. It was midafternoon in early spring and the sun warmed her skin pleasantly.

The comfortable dwelling was one of two that belonged to her grandfather. The other was located in the southern hill country of Judah. The country home in Giloh, to the south, was much simpler and less opulent, but Shoshanna actually preferred it to this one with its whitewashed walls and floors of quarried stone and a bathing pool large enough to swim in.

She was a contemplative, quiet young woman, not overly enamored of her large home, or jewelry and fine clothes. These were things that, in her opinion, held too high a value in the minds of most of the women in Jerusalem society. She was not overly impressed by appearances.

But today, Shoshanna planned to take more time than usual over her appearance. After all, she had been invited to dine at the king's table. She had been to the palace many times but rarely attended the royal banquets. Predictably, Shoshanna's mother had refused the invitation, but Shoshanna was to go anyway. Her grandfather, Ahithophel, had insisted. He was one of King David's most important advisors and would have a place near him at the banquet that had been planned to honor the Thirty, David's most renowned warriors.

Absalom, the king's son, would sit at his father's right hand. Her grandfather had proposed to the king that the Thirty pledge their loyalty to the prince as well as to David. Absalom had been out of favor with his father for several years, but recently the rift between them seemed to have finally healed.

As she looked out on the spacious courtyard, she saw a servant in the livery of the king's household come to the gate and knock. Marah, her mother, answered the young man's knock. Shoshanna hurried down the flight of stairs to the courtyard. It was the formal invitation to tonight's feast, she was certain. Custom demanded that even though his guests had been invited several weeks ago, the host—in this case, King David—must send a servant on the day of the feast to formally request the presence of his guests. The servant would wait for a response so that he could tell the royal cooks which guests would be unable to attend. Shoshanna knew the invitation would include her mother, and she hoped to persuade Marah to go.

Her mother turned and smiled at her daughter. "Shoshanna, I expected you would be dressing for the feast already. I have just told this young man that you and your grandfather will be there. I have asked him to convey my regrets to the king."

"Oh, Mother, won't you reconsider? Grandfather will be at the head table, and I will have to sit alone if you don't come with me." Shoshanna looked pleadingly at her mother. Marah's eyes were large and round and a rich brown color like her daughter's. But unlike Shoshanna's, which snapped and sparkled with curiosity and humor, Marah's eyes had a wounded, doe-like quality that reflected a life of sadness. Her black hair was generously sprinkled with gray. She was not beautiful in the classic sense, but everything in her manner reflected the dignity of her patrician ancestry.

"I really cannot, Shoshanna. Now we must let this poor man go. You have many more stops to make, don't you?" she said to the servant. Shoshanna was not really surprised at her mother's reply. She didn't argue further or delay the servant's departure.

Marah saw the disappointment on her daughter's face and tried to explain. "Darling, I am sorry, but you know that I don't like these events, especially if they are held at the palace. It just upsets me too much to see Bathsheba with the king." She paused and sighed deeply. "Oh, I know it is not worth speaking of after all these years, but I just can't forget the way my niece disgraced this family and hurt your grandfather."

"But, Mother, can't you . . . ?" Shoshanna's voice trailed off. She knew it was useless to try to convince her mother to forgive Bathsheba, so she merely kissed Marah and told her she would say good-bye before leaving for the palace.

Shoshanna looked forward to seeing her cousin Bathsheba. Marah and Bathsheba's father, Eliam, had been brother and sister. Eliam had been killed in battle years ago, before Shoshanna was born. The scandal had disgraced the family when Shoshanna was four years old.

Bathsheba had betrayed her husband, Uriah, by lying with King David. Much worse, David had deliberately ordered Uriah into a battle that meant certain death, in order to conceal that Bathsheba was pregnant by the king. Joab, David's general of the army, had aided David's cover-up. The thought of the tall, cruel, beak-nosed general made Shoshanna shiver. Her grandfather did not trust the powerful nephew of the king, whose opinion the king regarded above all his counselors, even Ahithophel's.

Of course, no one would have ever known for certain that David had ordered Uriah's death if the king himself had not publicly confessed it after Nathan the prophet had confronted him in the king's court. Instead of having Nathan executed for his audacity, David had admitted his own guilt. Shoshanna had always admired the king for that.

Shoshanna had been too young to understand why her older

cousin no longer came to visit her. She remembered only that her mother became very upset whenever anyone mentioned Bathsheba, and that her grandfather had been sad for a long time. In her childish way of thinking, Shoshanna felt that somehow it was her responsibility to make them both happy.

Ahithophel was the only father she had ever known, because her father, Cheron, a rich merchant much older than Shoshanna's mother, had died when Shoshanna was only a year old. Marah and Shoshanna had lived with Ahithophel after Cheron's death, and the family had divided its time between the ancestral home in Giloh and Cheron's richly appointed house in Jerusalem. Several men had offered to marry Marah after her husband's death, but at first she had been too heartbroken to consider remarriage. By the time she recovered from her grief, the offers for her had ceased; she was no longer young enough to assure a man she could bear him heirs. She remained a widow in her father's household, seeing to his needs.

"Child, have you not even begun to prepare for the feast? What are you doing, standing there with your hands idle, your thoughts flitting who knows where?" The chiding voice brought not a frown, but a smile to Shoshanna's face. Anah was her nurse, brought in to care for her from the day of her birth. In some ways, Anah was even closer to her than her own mother. She was past her prime years now, but full of vigor as she moved her considerable frame about in the performance of her duties.

"Well, come here, child, and bring the comb so that I may untangle your hair."

Shoshanna sighed as she picked up the beautiful mother-of-pearl comb her grandfather had given her. She sat obediently as Anah ran the comb through her knee-length black hair.

Shoshanna's excitement over being invited to the palace had been dampened by her mother's refusal to go. She told herself that she shouldn't feel guilty for wanting to go to the feast at the palace. Marah had hardly spoken a civil word to Bathsheba since she had married the king. She believed that the name of her brother,

Eliam, had been sullied by his daughter's adulterous behavior. But Ahithophel had not cut off contact, and Shoshanna did not see any reason why she should either. Grandfather had taken her side, insisting that she visit her cousin from time to time.

Many people had been surprised when Ahithophel continued to serve as a counselor to David after his family's shame, but David came to honor the wisdom of Ahithophel above all others, with the possible exception of Nathan the prophet and Joab.

Anyway, Shoshanna told herself, it had all taken place many years ago—fourteen, to be exact. The first child of David and Bathsheba had died, an obvious punishment for their sin. But two years later their second son, Solomon, had been born. Now he was almost twelve. Shoshanna held a special feeling for her cousin's child, and always spent time with him when she visited the palace.

In addition to her fondness for Solomon, Shoshanna especially loved two other children of the king. She had traveled several times with Ahithophel to Absalom's country home at Baal Hazor, near Ephraim, several miles north of Jerusalem, where Absalom's sister, Tamar, and half-brother Chileab lived. Despite some obvious flaws in Absalom's character, Shoshanna had always admired his open love and compassion for his two tragic siblings.

Chileab was the offspring of David's marriage to Abigail, the winsome widow of Nabal, whom David had taken as his wife while he was still a fugitive from Saul. He had been born with the physical beauty of all of David's children, but it became evident when the prince was still in his boyhood that his mind would remain that of a young child. Absalom treated his brother, who was several years his elder, as though he were a cherished child. Recently, Absalom had brought Chileab to his home at Baal Hazor, to be cared for by Tamar.

Tamar and Absalom were the king's children by Maacah, the princess from Geshur, a woman David had married not for love but for political expediency. Absalom had taken in Tamar soon after her defilement by her half-brother Amnon. The disgrace had so horrified the beautiful young girl that it had unhinged her mind. Most of the time she kept to her quarters in her brother's house, sometimes mumbling to herself, and often bursting into tears for no apparent reason. Sometimes Tamar would refuse to eat. When Shoshanna would visit, often she would sit with the young princess and coax her to eat a little bread or some vegetables.

Shoshanna's grandfather had remained friends with Absalom, even during the years when the king had banished him from Jerusalem for killing Amnon to avenge Tamar's disgrace. Shoshanna did not quite understand the friendship between the two. Most of the king's friends and advisors had been in total agreement with David's anger and banishment of his son. In fact, most believed that David should have pursued and punished Absalom for the murder of Amnon. But Ahithophel went once to visit Absalom in Geshur, and had taken Shoshanna with him to visit Absalom in Baal Hazor. There was a strong bond between the older man and the prince.

Something about their friendship bothered Shoshanna. It seemed to have grown in intensity lately, and there was a furtiveness about it. Although she had often seen the gentle, admirable side of Absalom, she knew him to be exceedingly vain and able to manipulate others with his skillful charm. She suspected that he resented King David and coveted the throne for himself. Although she respected the way he treated his siblings, at least those he liked, she did not trust the prince.

"Now stand up child, so I can help you dress." Anah shook her head at Shoshanna's daydreaming. Drawing her thoughts back to the business of getting ready for the banquet, Shoshanna crossed the room to a mirror made of polished brass that hung above her clothing chest. Atop the chest, various grooming items had been arranged—combs for her long hair, a necklace set with a large amethyst, and a few cosmetics, though Shoshanna seldom used these.

She picked up a small pot of kohl, applying a bit to her eyes, which were large and fringed with thick, straight lashes. After highlighting her eyes, Shoshanna splashed on a bit of expensive perfume—a gift from Bathsheba on one of her visits to the palace.

One of the benefits of attending a palace function was the possibility of being seen by someone of importance and wealth. All the young women of Jerusalem society coveted an invitation to such an event, in hopes that an offer of marriage might eventually result. Ahithophel had full responsibility for choosing Shoshanna's husband. She knew her duty was to produce a great-grandson so that Ahithophel's line would not pass out of existence. And she knew that her grandfather loved her more than he had ever loved anyone except for his son. Somehow Ahithophel conveyed a sense of disappointment in his daughter; probably because she had never produced a son. Shoshanna's mother had never been able to earn Ahithophel's wholehearted love and respect, though she had spent her life trying.

Shoshanna felt a pang of pity for her mother. She had virtually withdrawn from life, and no matter how hard Shoshanna tried, she could not persuade her mother to do anything other than run Ahithophel's household. She sometimes resented the fact that Ahithophel allowed it. He seemed to take it as his due. Shoshanna wished he had insisted that Marah wed again after the death of her husband.

Anah began to chide her again. If she kept daydreaming like this, she would never be ready in time. Shoshanna allowed her nurse to help her slip on her long-sleeved undergarment, then topped it with a sleeveless purple cloak that she fastened at the waist with a girdle wrought with gold thread.

She returned to the mirror to try to decide what to do with her hair. "Don't ask me to braid that thick hair of yours at this late hour," Anah grumbled.

"You are right, Anah. It will have to be simple." Shoshanna picked up the gold combs and secured her hair back from her face on either side, leaving the long mass of it to flow down her back. She secretly felt that her shiny, thick hair was her best feature, and she knew it would gain attention tonight.

She grinned to herself as she thought of Absalom, who usually wore his auburn tresses in a long braid down his back. When he trimmed it once a year, on the anniversary of his birth, the weight of the hair he cut off often exceeded four pounds. Absalom would then distribute four pounds of gold among the poor of Jerusalem. No wonder the people loved him so much, despite his excessive vanity.

Should she risk making the prince angry by displaying her own hair tonight? No worry. Absalom was so sure of his own beauty that he wouldn't think to be jealous. *And I'll try not to be jealous of his,* she thought with a smile. She brought the length of her hair across the front of her shoulder, to keep it from getting tangled up or snagged on obstacles as she walked. Then she hurried to the courtyard.

Her grandfather was waiting for her, of course. He was never late. Shoshanna thought he looked very dignified in his dark brown mantle over a beige tunic. His soft leather girdle was secured with a large brass buckle. He held out his hands to her and she grasped them.

"You look beautiful tonight, my dear."

"As do you, Grandfather." The compliment was sincere. Her grandfather was a tall man of regal posture with long, white hair and beard. His nose was long and straight, and his dark eyes were bright with intelligence. Shoshanna loved her grandfather more than anyone else on earth, except her mother.

"You will not be able sit beside me tonight. The king wishes me to sit near him. He and your cousin have reserved a place for you next to Nathan and Prince Solomon. They would feel more at ease knowing that the boy is in your company. Though he is a good boy, his inquisitive mind sometimes lands him in trouble."

Shoshanna laughed. "I would be honored to sit beside Solomon. You may tell Bathsheba I will keep a close eye on him."

Ahithophel took his granddaughter's face in his hands. "You are my joy and my treasure, Shoshanna. Now let us go and bid you mother good-bye before we leave for the palace."

Chapter Three

~

*T*he massive doors swung open to the great room in King David's palace and heads turned to see a man with tawny, sun-streaked hair and piercing eyes. His huge frame crowded the doorway. Micah was arriving late at the banquet. He had planned it that way, hoping he would be able to slip into the room unnoticed by the crowd. It didn't work, of course. Micah stood head and shoulders above any other man there. He stood out in any gathering.

As though his size were not enough to draw attention, Micah dressed differently than most of the cultured city crowd. He wore a short, plain tunic made of fine wool and cinched at the waist with a leather girdle. The only article that bespoke his family's wealth was a copper armband etched with a pattern of palm leaves. His mother had given it to him several years ago, and he always wore it.

He stood at the back of the banquet hall, trying not to notice the heads that turned in his direction, or the conversations behind hands raised to lips. He wondered whether people really thought the gesture disguised their gossip.

Micah's eyes swept the hall, looking for a place near the back where he could take his seat unobtrusively. He noticed an empty space near the front, but he would have to walk the entire distance through the hall. People would gawk. Many of the military men present knew about the incident that had forced his return to Ziph. Micah felt a stirring of resentment that his father had coerced him into coming here.

He resigned himself to sit near the front. He would kneel before the king eventually, and this way he would be closer to the dais when the time came. He saw that Benaiah, third in command of David's army and longtime friend of Micah's father, was sitting next to the open seat. He started forward, assured of Benaiah's acceptance, and saw that Solomon, the favorite son of David, sat on the other side of the empty chair. He paused when he saw an unfamiliar woman sitting next to Solomon.

Surely he would have remembered meeting her, because her beauty was stunning. As she sat at the table, her shiny, straight hair hung down her back all the way to the floor. In the less urbane society of smaller towns, even the young, unmarried women often wore a head covering when in public. Until a woman married it was perfectly respectable for her to show her hair, but many conservative Israelites deemed it somewhat immodest for a maiden to flaunt her hair.

This young woman obviously was not concerned with others' opinions. Micah was not certain if he admired or resented her audacity. Though many of the women present displayed their hair, the richness and length of hers was extraordinary and enticing.

He lifted his eyes to study her face and saw that she was studying him. Her large eyes widened when she realized she had been caught staring, then her lashes immediately dropped in embarrassment. Her pale skin suffused with a deep pink he could see even from a distance. So, she wasn't a temptress after all. Micah found himself smiling.

The girl covered her chagrin by lifting her goblet, pretending to give all of her attention to its contents as she drank. She would not look at him again, he knew. At that moment, he saw Benaiah raise his hand and gesture for Micah to take the empty place beside him. At first Micah shook his head, but the veteran commander only motioned more effusively. Micah went to join him.

Out of the corner of her eye, Shoshanna saw that the awesome young man was now approaching her. Had he taken offense at her bold stare? *He looks as I have always imagined the Angel of the Lord would look if he appeared to me,* she reflected, then felt guilty for her thought. It was probably idolatrous to liken a mere man to an angel. Still, his larger-than-life stature and the golden glints in his hair did put her in mind of— Shoshanna froze as the man stopped next to her.

Micah had meant to speak to Benaiah, but he gazed down for a long moment at the regal young woman who had been staring at him. Now, in a gesture that belied her earlier interest, she kept her head lowered, giving great attention to a huge arrangement of pomegranates, dates, and figs in the center of the table. Micah looked at the glossy tresses, held away from her face with two gold combs. He sighed. She wasn't going to look at him again, so he might as well speak to the warrior who had saved him a place.

"Are you certain this seat is not taken?" He tried to focus his attention on Benaiah.

"It *was* taken, by Nathan the prophet. He tutors Solomon and the other children of the king, you know. But he was called away to attend to a family crisis, so feel free to take his place."

Micah had heard that Nathan acted as the royal tutor. Many thought it amazing that the man who had confronted King David about his adultery was now entrusted with the education of the royal children. Even more amazing, David and Bathsheba had named one of their sons Nathan in honor of the prophet. "Faithful are the wounds of a friend," the old Hebrew proverb said, and there was no greater testament than the relationship between David and Nathan. Micah would have liked to have met the prophet. He was surely a man of courage and conviction.

"I feel as if I am overreaching myself to be seated in such august company," he remarked to Benaiah as he struggled to tuck his long legs under the banquet table. He much preferred the way they sat at home in Ziph, around a thick leather mat, on cushions, with their legs folded.

"Your company is as august as anyone else's, son of my friend. More so, actually, because of your great size." Benaiah laughed and slapped Micah on the back as he made this observation.

"Indeed, Benaiah, he can sit anywhere he chooses, and who would stop him?" The eyes of the young prince on the other side of him sparkled with humor and admiration. "Except a giant even larger than he. You must be the largest man in the land!"

Micah smiled at Solomon. "Not quite, my prince. I feel quite in awe at the privilege of meeting you. I am Micah, the son of Jonathan, one of your father's *Gibborim*."

"And I am Solomon, and here tonight as a reward for my recitation of the Torah. In a matter of months I will become a man in Israel." Micah smiled at the pride in the boy's voice. He remembered his own passage into manhood, when he stood between Shageh and Jonathan, reciting a passage from Moses, and heard himself proclaimed *bar mitzvah*—son of the covenant— by his grandfather.

Of course, by the time he was twelve, he looked at least fifteen, and most people had held him accountable as they would a much older lad—all except his grandfather and parents. One of the drawbacks to his great stature was that people had expected him to act with a maturity far beyond his years, which was one of the reasons Micah had grown up to be unusually serious, even somber.

The girl laughed. "You are prone to exaggeration, young cousin. It will be nearly two years before you are declared a man." Solomon blushed but took the teasing graciously.

"This is my cousin Shoshanna, first cousin to my mother." Solomon leaned back a little in order to make the introduction, something done only in the more permissive atmosphere of the court. Micah again looked into the face of the fascinating young woman. Her rounded eyes, a warm, liquid brown, glanced at him for a mere second or two before dropping again to the table.

She nodded her head in polite acknowledgment, as any well-bred young woman would do before a man who was a stranger. It disturbed Micah somewhat that she seemed shy of him. Did she find his size intimidating, like so many others did? Was she timid? Something told him that it was not timidity that had made her lower her gaze.

Meanwhile, Shoshanna was wrestling with her suddenly tumbling emotions. At first, his great size had awed her, but when Micah was close enough for her to look into his eyes, she felt that he could see right into her soul. She could not bear the intensity of his amber gaze. It was unlike anything she had ever experienced.

This man was not just another of David's fighting men. She sensed about him a rare depth of spirit and absence of guile. It was all she could do not to stare, though many of the other guests were openly eyeing him. She could tell by his demeanor that Micah was not pleased to be the center of attention. *This is a man who will always draw people's attention wherever he goes,* she told herself.

Micah engaged in conversation, equally dividing his attention between the king's son and Benaiah. He wished Shoshanna would look his way, but she had ignored him since the introduction. He found himself wondering if she was staying at the palace, and if he could arrange to see her the next day.

The formal introductions of the dignitaries began with Sheva, the court scribe, calling out their names and cataloguing their accomplishments. Benaiah's name was called and the older man went to stand on the dais, to receive the accolades he had earned by his service.

Some time later, Micah's name was called, and as he rose to go forward, he sensed the girl's attention fastened on him. He stopped to look down at her. Their eyes locked for a moment and Micah's breath was taken. She was not beautiful in the traditional sense; her face was a bit too long, and her nose a little too pronounced to be considered classically pretty. But her large eyes and long neck, and her regal bearing, arrested his attention as more conventional beauty could not.

Though he had not yet seen her standing, Micah had the impression that she was tall for a woman. He found himself hoping she was. He always felt self-conscious around small women, with the exception of his mother. Dainty women emphasized his unusual size. And they fluttered around, like brightly colored butterflies. Some were afraid of him. Others were attracted by the disparity of their size to his. Micah smiled to himself. This woman would neither flutter, nor show any fear, of that he was certain. But did she find him as interesting as he was finding her? He hoped he would have an occasion to find out before leaving Jerusalem.

As Micah made his way to the front of the room, Sheva was explaining his status to the guests. "Jonathan ben Shageh had urgent business in his hometown of Ziph, and has sent his son in his stead. Jonathan, who joined the king at the cave of Adullam thirty-five years ago, is one of the *Gibborim*, and a faithful friend to the king." Micah was cheered as enthusiastically as the rest, but it was for his father's sake, not his own. He joined the line of men as they knelt before the king and Absalom in homage.

The prince, as was his habit, wore rich clothes befitting royalty. As he stood beside his father, their resemblance to each other was unmistakable. Both had perfectly sculpted masculine features. Each displayed even, white teeth when they smiled, and both had beautiful eyes. But David had spent his youth as a hardworking shepherd boy and his early manhood facing hardships as a fugitive. It had given him a strength and character that his son lacked. Absalom had been brought up in luxury and ease, which was evident in his choice of richly embroidered garments and silver diadem encrusted with rubies. On his hands were numerous rings. David, on the other hand, wore no crown and no ring except his signet. True, his scarlet tunic was made of fine linen, but it was simply made, and belted only with a woven leather girdle, which held a jewel-encrusted ceremonial dagger.

There was not much, other than the force of his personality, to distinguish him from the other honored guests.

When the king came to Micah, he smiled warmly. "Micah, you have grown into a fine figure of a man. I know your father is proud of you." Despite the kind words, Micah could tell that the king was taking his measure as a man. The king must be aware of the incident with the raiders. Did he wonder whether Micah could be trusted? "I was saddened to hear that Shageh sleeps with our fathers," the king continued. "He was a great Rab. I trust he did not suffer."

"No, my lord. We found him one morning, slumped over the copy of the Law that you gave him years ago. After that, his condition deteriorated quickly, and he was no longer able to hold the scrolls, but he never tired of having them read to him. It eased his passing." The king nodded and asked Micah to convey his greetings to his parents.

When Micah returned to his place, the young prince teased him good-naturedly. "You looked as exposed and uncomfortable as a freshly sheared sheep up there, son of Jonathan. I have noticed that large men are often shy, and you have shown my theory to be true. It must be a blessing from Adonai that he makes most giants gentle, or else the rest of us would live our lives in fear." When Micah's face grew red, the boy relented. "I'm sorry if I make you uncomfortable with my jesting, and I promise I won't do it anymore. Try some of the lentils with barley. It is delicious."

Micah tore off a chunk of the crusty bread set at his place and dipped it in the common bowl of food. Shoshanna happened to be dipping hers at the same time, and their hands touched. Both of them froze for a moment, then jerked back their hands as if burned. "Pardon me," Micah muttered, embarrassed. Solomon looked at each of them and smiled.

Neither Micah nor Shoshanna talked much as the banquet continued, course after course. Both were exquisitely aware of the other, though. When the feast came to a close, and Micah stood to leave, he had to step to the side to make way for a very portly court official to pass. As he did, he heard a gasp and looked down. He was mortified to see that he had stepped on Shoshanna's hair, which pooled on the floor where she sat. He stepped back quickly.

"Oh, I beg your pardon! I didn't mean to do that. Are you all right?"

He bent his knees to kneel beside her, but she rose as swiftly as a frightened quail. He had been right. She was tall, and it pleased him. She only had to tilt her head a little to talk to him. Somehow, the incident seemed to cause her to unbend a little. She gave him a smile. "You didn't hurt me. I should really have my hair trimmed anyway. It has become a hazard."

"That would be such a crime that I am sure the king would punish you severely. You are to do nothing to your hair. It is beautiful." Micah was well aware that his speech was quite immoderate given the fact that they were no kin and had just been introduced. But strangely, he felt he knew her.

"Perhaps it is an occasion to vanity, and I would be more blessed if I followed the example of our prince and polled it. I would then give its weight in silver to the poor, since I could never afford to give gold, as is his custom."

He admired the black waves, clenching his hand to keep from reaching out to feel its texture. Instead, he made a light remark. "Does your father have that much silver?"

She laughed, a rich, full-bodied laugh; not the tittering, silly laugh that some women affected. "My grandfather, Ahithophel, has that much silver, but he would agree with you that I shouldn't cut my hair, and he would not give me silver if I did. More likely he would lock me in my chamber and not let me out until it grew back."

"Ahithophel is your guardian?"

"Yes. My father died when I was a young child. I must go now and seek out my grandfather. He will not admit it, but he needs his rest these days, due to his advanced age."

Micah wished he could think of something to delay her departure, but he had already stretched the bounds of propriety with his attention to her, and he did not want to anger her grandfather. He had a feeling that in the future he might want to make a good impression on the man, once he cleared his name. He watched her thread her way carefully through the crowd to the place of honor where Ahithophel sat. He would not forget her.

~ ~ ~

Out of the corner of his eye, Ahithophel saw his granddaughter approaching from across the crowded room, and he realized that if he wanted to speak privately to the prince this evening he must do so before she joined him. He hoped Absalom would see him leave and follow. He slipped into an anteroom near the dais. It was dark, with only a little light from the banquet room filtering through the heavy drapes that covered its entrance. The counselor waited for only a short time before a hand drew back the curtain and the prince stepped inside.

"I didn't know whether you saw me leave," the older man said.

"I saw you. The time draws near, and we need to find a way to plan without interruption. Jerusalem isn't the place to do that. We will meet at Baal Hazor. I have sent word to others."

"What if word of our meeting comes to the king's ears?"

"Let it be known that you are bringing Shoshanna to visit my sister and brother. My father feels guilty that he neglects them. He will be happy enough when he hears you are performing a duty he should be doing himself."

~ ~ ~

Before she was near enough to the dais to get his attention, Shoshanna saw her grandfather slip through the arched doorway of an alcove to the side. She hesitated, uncertain whether she should follow him or make her way back to the company of Solomon,

Benaiah, and the fascinating young Judahite she had just met. Before she could make up her mind, Bathsheba was at her side.

"Shoshanna, you look so beautiful tonight. I'm sure our grandfather will double his wealth with the bride-price he will get when you marry." She had placed her hands on Shoshanna's shoulders and punctuated her remarks with a kiss on each cheek. Her eyes shone with genuine pleasure at seeing her cousin, and Shoshanna returned her cousin's greetings sincerely.

"Compared to your beauty, my looks are disappointingly average, but thank you for the praise." The comment was sincere. Bathsheba was dressed in a sleeveless tunic of pale blue. A train of deep scarlet was secured at the shoulders by two large ruby broaches. A strand of rubies was worked into the elaborate braids atop her head. She looked every bit the queen.

Though David had many wives and concubines, he had never had another at his side in public since Bathsheba had been brought to the palace after the death of Uriah. However sordid the beginning of their relationship had been, there was no doubt that David and Bathsheba were deeply devoted to each other.

"Is Aunt Marah well?" Bathsheba asked. Shoshanna saw the hurt in her cousin's eyes as she spoke of the relative who had snubbed her for years. Shoshanna wondered, not for the first time, why her grandfather had not insisted that Marah be civil to her niece. For him she would have put aside her grudge.

She tried for a diplomatic answer. "Mother is well enough, Bathsheba, but she is rather reclusive these days. We can hardly get her to venture from the house. But she sends her greetings and regrets." Shoshanna felt guilty for the lie, but she wished to make up for her mother's snub.

Her cousin smiled. "Tell Marah that I missed her this evening, and that I hope to see her soon."

"I will. Now I suppose I should go and seek out Grandfather. It's growing late."

"But we have hardly had a chance to speak! Won't you consider staying at the palace tonight? We could go upstairs now and have a good long talk. David will be hours longer with his courtiers. And in the morning you could visit the children. They all love you so."

Bathsheba had asked many times over the years for Shoshanna to be a lady-in-waiting at court. Ahithophel was inclined to allow it, but Marah had adamantly opposed it. "The palace is a wicked place, Father. Do you want another granddaughter corrupted? Just look what happened to poor Tamar! I would never get a night's rest if you allowed her to live at court." Ahithophel had given in to Marah. She made so few requests of him, after all.

Shoshanna well knew that her mother would be upset if she spent even one night at the palace, and so she answered, "I would like to, but I think it's best I go home with Grandfather. However, I will return in the morning, if it would suit you."

Bathsheba smiled. "I would like that very much, and so will Solomon and the other children. Oh, here is Grandfather." Bathsheba smiled at Ahithophel. "I didn't get a chance to speak to you during the banquet, Grandfather. Are you well tonight?" She kissed the old man on the cheek, then patted it. Shoshanna couldn't help but notice that their grandfather didn't respond to Bathsheba the way he did to her. Even though he returned her kiss of greeting, his eyes didn't twinkle in that special way, as they did when Shoshanna greeted him. Bathsheba didn't notice though, or pretended she didn't. Ahithophel politely answered her questions about his well-being, then told Shoshanna they must say good night. But before she let them go, Bathsheba suggested hopefully, "Tell my aunt that the invitation to visit in the morning includes her as well. Maybe she will feel more at ease if there is no formal occasion to attend." Shoshanna agreed to ask.

～ ～ ～

Hours after the banquet ended, Ahithophel stood at the window of his room, looking out at the night sky. He was pleased with the night's progress. There had been a perfect opportunity to speak with Absalom, and for the first time, the prince admitted openly that he would welcome an opportunity to take the kingdom from his father.

As they held a secret conversation under cover of the noise from the banquet, there had been some risk of being overheard, but it was better, at least in this stage of their plans, if they could arrange to meet at events where both were expected to attend. Absalom's suggestion about using Shoshanna to cover their real purpose for meeting at Baal Hazor was perfect. Ahithophel had assured Absalom tonight that there were many in Israel who would rally to him. And he had promised to organize the dissenters into a force that would defeat David. Evidently Absalom had already obtained a commitment from others, because they were to be at the prince's retreat.

Ahithophel drew a deep breath as he contemplated the revenge he had planned for more than a decade. He would see David punished. Finally, the man who had murdered Uriah would pay. The man who had disgraced his family and slept with his granddaughter would know the shame of disgrace himself. The person responsible for turning his granddaughter into an adulteress would meet destruction.

His plotting could get him killed if he were found out, but it would be worth it to have his revenge. Uriah had been like a son to him. He had always believed that Adonai had sent Uriah to take the place of Eliam, his son, an honored member of the *Gibborim,* who had been killed in battle so many years ago. Their family had been united and happy until the king seduced his granddaughter. Now he had only Marah and Shoshanna, really, even though he had pretended to forgive Bathsheba.

It was all he could do to pretend everything was forgotten, and serve the king as advisor, but he had put on the pretense for so long that it came easily now. Soon now, everyone would know what he really thought of his king. And more importantly, David himself would know. Ahithophel smiled as he contemplated the look David would have on his face the moment he realized that his most trusted advisor had betrayed him.

~ ~ ~

In her own room at the corner of the spacious home, Shoshanna also stood at the window; her thoughts, like her grandfather's, were too many and too disturbed for sleep. Only her thoughts were not of hate and vengeance. Far from it. She thought of Micah, the man from Ziph. She couldn't seem to draw her mind from dwelling on him. She had even ventured some cautious questions of her grandfather about the son of Jonathan, asking him what he knew of the family.

Though Ahithophel had seemed preoccupied, he answered readily enough. "Jonathan, his father, is one of the king's most trusted warriors. I have sat beside him at the council table. The family is a respected one. Unfortunately, Jonathan married a captive Aramean maiden, which caused a scandal at the time. I know nothing of the son, but when he was called forward tonight, I heard whispers that he has fallen out of favor with Joab for being afraid to fight. But I can hardly believe that, given the way the king honored him. And what would a man as powerful as the son of Jonathan have to be afraid of? His arms are like tree trunks! I think it was simply envy that caused the murmurs I heard."

Shoshanna had managed to hide her disappointment that her grandfather had added little to her knowledge of Micah and, after thanking him for taking her to the banquet, made her way to her room. There, she rehearsed every nuance of the evening, remembering how the top of her head barely reached his shoulder, how his hand dwarfed the goblet as he drank, and how his eyes softened like warm honey when he looked at her. He had the respect of Benaiah, one of Israel's most famous veteran warriors, so surely the gossip about him was false. How could she arrange to see him again? Would Solomon help? Or maybe her grandfather? *Oh, stop it,* she told herself time and again. *He is just a man. You will probably never see him again.* But even when she slept, she dreamed of him.

Chapter Four

~

*T*he morning after the banquet, Micah made his way through the corridors of the palace and entered the king's gardens. He had not planned to stay the night at the palace, but Jehoshaphat, the king's chief of protocol for the palace, insisted there was a room prepared for him. Now that many of David's offspring were grown, most of them had other homes in or around Jerusalem, so there was more than enough space in the sprawling palace to accommodate any number of guests and dignitaries.

David's home had been a work in progress from the time he made Jerusalem his capital. In the process of obtaining seven wives, more than sixty children, and more than a hundred concubines, the king had kept builders busy for years. When his friend Hiram became king of Tyre, David was able to acquire the cedar he preferred for building. The palace was luxuriously rich, but exuded warmth that it would not otherwise have if marble or granite had been used exclusively. The air was filled with the fragrance of the cedar floors and walls as Micah made his way downstairs. There were tables and couches at intervals in the long corridors. Vases made of gold or ivory adorned the tables.

He found his way outside and looked around the equally impressive garden. Flowers of all colors were blooming already, even this early in the spring. Bright red poppies and orange anemones—how did the royal gardeners manage it? He sat down by a lily pond and watched the small, colorful fish dart about.

Today he would try to gain an audience with the king. He would ask for an assignment that would exonerate him and prove his loyalty. He had an idea of a mission that might be advantageous to the kingdom, but if David did not deem it worthy, then he would volunteer for any commission the king suggested.

After he had spoken with the king the night before, he had decided he did not want to present his case to Joab alone. He had a feeling that the king would be more understanding. Of course, the general would probably be present also. It was known to the people of Israel that, except when encamped with the army, the second most powerful man in the kingdom was always at the king's side when he made his decisions. Micah knew it would probably irritate Joab when Micah spoke directly with the king, but he was willing to risk it.

Micah heard the voices of two people entering the garden before he saw them. He recognized the woman's voice at once. It was Ahithophel's granddaughter, and she was with Solomon. The prince noticed him first.

"Look, Shoshanna. It's the man from Ziph. Let's go and talk to him." The boy tugged at her hand to get her to follow. He almost dragged her across the garden. Micah waited for the prince to address him first, as custom demanded.

Solomon drew up before him. "Good morning, sir. You are about quite early. You must not have partaken of the wine as freely as most of my father's guests last night." Micah liked the boy's friendly smile and open manner; so unlike that of Absalom. Oh, Absalom had been charming the few times Micah had been in his presence, but there was an air of petulance and arrogance about him that made Micah distrust him. The attitude of a spoiled royal son was absent in Solomon, even though he was almost as handsome as his older brother.

The tall, slender youth with curling black hair very similar to his mother's still held onto Shoshanna's hand as if he feared she would bolt if he let go. Micah noticed again that she was quite tall. Solomon was a lanky youth, already taller than most women, but he came only to her chin. She didn't speak. Maybe she still held a grudge because he had stepped on her hair. This morning it was braided in a coronet. Too bad. He stood to greet them.

Both Shoshanna and Solomon tilted their heads to look at him. He knew it put them at a disadvantage, but he wanted an advantage over this perfect creature. Funny, he felt much more in awe of her than he did the prince.

Awe. That was the very word Shoshanna was using in her own mind to categorize her response to the man who towered over her. *He must inspire this kind of awe in everyone he meets,* she thought. She marveled that there was not even a modicum of fear mingled with her wonderment.

"Good morning, my prince," Micah said to Solomon, bringing her thoughts back to earth. "I trust you rested well last night. I see you and your companion are busy already this morning."

"Oh, not busy, exactly. I just wanted Shoshanna to see the new species of lily I've added to my collection. See, they are the pale pink ones there. I think they are so much more beautiful than the plain white ones, don't you?"

"I think the lily is not only beautiful, but fascinating," Micah said softly, while he gazed at Shoshanna, not the flower.

Shoshanna felt herself blush. The giant had aimed his remark at her, making a play on words. Why was he flattering her? She was certainly not beautiful, and it was not the proper thing for him to say on such short acquaintance. She shot him a glance and was relieved to see he had turned his attention back to the prince.

"Do you know if I might arrange a meeting with your mother?"

"Shoshanna has an audience with my mother this morning. We were about to go to her. You will come with us, Micah?"

"No, my prince, I would not presume—"

"As your prince, sir, I command you to accompany me," the lad said with a charming smile.

"I suppose I would be wise to obey, hmm? Very well. I will go with you gladly, my lord." Micah made a low bow and Solomon laughed.

Shoshanna had not said a word during the whole exchange. She was intently studying the water lilies in the pond. Micah looked down at the part in her hair. "Do you mind, my lady? I will be intruding on your visit with your cousin."

She slowly raised her gaze and eyed him warily as she answered. "It will be no inconvenience, my lord. You may certainly come with us."

They were shown without delay into Bathsheba's apartments on the third floor of the palace. She received them in a large room with four arched windows, which let in light and cooling breezes. After kissing her son, she turned to greet her cousin. Shoshanna willingly returned her warm embrace, noting that Bathsheba was even more beautiful as a mature woman than she had been in Shoshanna's childhood, when the king had made her his wife. There was a healthy glow to her skin, and her expression was one of contentment.

Today, at home in her private quarters, she wore a plain, sleeveless tunic, and a gossamer white head covering that did little to hide the shining thickness of her black hair. Bathsheba directed her guests to be seated on comfortable cushions surrounding a low, round table laden with fruit, small cakes, and pitchers of water and wine. After insisting that they partake, she asked Shoshanna, as she had last night, about Marah's health. "You did tell her she was invited?"

"She is well enough, my cousin, but as I mentioned before, she prefers not to leave the comforts of home unless it is a necessity. Perhaps next time she will come with me." Shoshanna felt ashamed. For years, she and Bathsheba had kept up this pretense that Marah was not really shunning her niece. They talked as though Marah might come to the palace for a visit any day, although they both knew that she would never consider it. Sometimes Shoshanna feared that the king might seek retaliation for having his favorite wife treated so. But the king acted as though he believed Marah's excuses. Apparently, Bathsheba did not complain of the situation.

"Well again, please give her my regards, and tell her she is welcome here any time." She turned from Shoshanna to address Micah. "I am so glad to meet the son of Jonathan and Ailea. How are your mother and father?"

"Very well, my lady. They send their greetings to the king and all his household."

"It has been years since I have seen Ailea. Your father attends the war council, of course, so I see him periodically."

"Yes. They will no doubt visit Jerusalem soon. My mother remarked before I left that it has been too long since she has been to the city." He decided to get right to the point. "I would not wish to take up much of your time, my lady, but if it would be possible, I would request a private audience with the king. Ordinarily, of course, I would apply to Joab, but . . . I am a bit out of favor with him at present. I'm afraid he would not think my petition important enough to warrant the king's attention, but I would propose a diplomatic mission that should be of great benefit to the kingdom." Micah paused for a response.

Bathsheba's eyes crinkled in wry amusement. "Out of favor with Joab, are you? That can be most unpleasant. I will go with you to my lord's chambers as soon as I have ended my visit with Shoshanna. Solomon's chambers are nearby. Why not let my son entertain you while you wait?"

"Very good idea, Mother." Solomon kissed Bathsheba's cheek before turning back to Micah. Like his parents, he was surpassingly handsome. His keen intelligence made one forget he was still very much a child.

"Do you know the game of chess, Micah?" the boy asked as they made their way to his rooms.

"Oh, yes. My mother was from Damascus, you know, and

brought the game with her when she married my father. She is an excellent player, and she taught my father and me well. Now he and I defeat her more often than not."

"I am most expert, my lord," the boy bragged. "You'll not defeat me so easily."

~ ~ ~

Shoshanna had finished her visit with Bathsheba and silently entered the anteroom of Solomon's quarters. She smiled as she listened to their interchange and then settled down to watch them play chess. The intriguing giant came from a most unusual family, she mused as she studied him. He had told her last night that his grandfather was a Rab from the hill country of Judah. And his mother was an Aramean—an expert at a game of strategy that was difficult even for men to master. His father was one of the *Gibborim*. She wondered what other attributes Micah had beside his striking appearance and size. Was he as gentle as he appeared? As kind? She hoped to find out soon.

"You have defeated me in no time, Micah." Solomon's words turned her attention back to the chess game. "Now you must play Shoshanna. And don't be so certain you can defeat her. She trounces me quite often."

Seeing that Shoshanna was about to decline the game, Micah lent his own voice to persuading her. "Come now, my lady. It is your duty to obey your prince, as it is your duty to entertain this poor guest while he awaits his summons from the king. Do you have the skill to defeat me, or are you afraid I will embarrass you by winning?"

Shoshanna looked into his twinkling eyes and smiled. "I shall show you that my grandfather has tutored me well in the strategy of the game, sir. Let us begin."

The pieces were soon in place and the game began. She took the ivory pieces; he the ebony. It was a fast-paced contest, as chess games go, but a close one. Shoshanna would gain the advantage, then Micah. Only five pieces remained between them when he declared a stalemate. He grinned at her and was surprised to see her scowling at him, her dark eyes shooting fire.

"You did that deliberately!" She almost shouted the accusation.

"Did what?" he asked, his face a picture of innocence.

"You know very well that you had me beat five moves ago. You deliberately passed up a chance to win the game, and that, sir, is an insult to my intelligence as well as my ability. What did you think I would do, burst into tears if I lost?" She pushed away from the table so forcefully that her stool fell over. She blushed in embarrassment as she bent to pick it up. She had lost her temper and overreacted, she knew. Slowly, she straightened up again, determined to apologize. But when she looked up into his face, the exasperating man was grinning at her!

She started to sputter again, but he held up a large hand. "Please, my lady, do not chastise me further. I have learned my lesson. The next time we play, I will oblige you by thoroughly demolishing you."

Solomon, who had found great amusement in the repartee, burst into laughter at Micah's mock apology, and Shoshanna, though she tried to keep a straight face, could not keep her lips from curving into a smile. At least the giant from Ziph now knew that she wasn't as empty-headed as he had believed when he threw the game. They spent the next half-hour admiring Solomon's many collections—rocks and leaves and toy warriors, things any young boy might collect, but more extensive by virtue of his being the king's son. In too short a time, Micah was being summoned for his meeting with the king.

≈ ≈ ≈

Micah was led to one of the meeting rooms on the second floor of the palace. Both the king and the general were there. The king was dressed in full royal regalia this day with a purple robe that covered his embroidered tunic. He wore a gold circlet around his curly hair, which still had more auburn strands than gray.

Joab wore the half tunic of the soldier. The sleeves were short, allowing freedom of movement, and there was a sword strapped to his hip. Though Joab was well over fifty years of age, his arms, bronzed by the sun, were corded with muscles that proclaimed him still to be a formidable fighting man. His hooked nose and black eyes gave him the look of a raptor as he stared, unsmiling, at Micah.

David did smile, and greeted him warmly. "As I told you at last night's banquet, you are most welcome at the palace, son of Jonathan. Your father is one of the mightiest warriors in the land, and I see that he has produced a magnificent son."

Micah felt his face color at the compliment and covered his self-consciousness with a low bow to his monarch. "I am honored to be in your presence, my lord. I would ask permission to speak forthrightly to you and the general."

"By all means, my son, you may speak freely."

"My lords, I wanted to see you both together and face-to-face to declare my unsurpassed loyalty to the king and the kingdom. I suppose the general related to you the trouble of a few months ago." Micah looked to the king for an answer.

"I heard of the incident immediately after it happened, and I expected to see your father before me in a matter of days," the king replied. "Jonathan has never been one to hesitate in speaking his mind freely, and I expected him to be incensed that his son was accused of cowardice, not to speak of treason."

"It took much effort to persuade him not to do that, my lord. But I am no longer a lad. I will handle my own affairs." Micah saw that the statement pleased the king.

"I would expect nothing less of Jonathan's son. You may speak freely on your own behalf."

"Perhaps I showed poor judgment when I released the bandits after confiscating their goods. I thought it was a good thing to show mercy at the time, but it would possibly have been bet-

ter to mete out stern justice. I admit that I have more of a pro-
clivity for mercy than justice."

Micah's gaze had swung between the king and the general as
he spoke. He seemed to have the king's sympathy, but Joab's
expression was inscrutable.

"I assure you both," he continued, "that I would never do
anything to betray or put in peril any of my people, from the
king to the lowliest servant. And let there be no doubt as to
which people I claim. Though my mother is Aramean by birth,
she has been Hebrew by choice since she married my father.
She serves Adonai exclusively, and both of my parents have
trained me to love the Lord as well. I am as Hebrew as any
Hebrew has ever been. I have a mission to propose to the king
that I think might prove that beyond any doubt. I'm not certain
to succeed, but if the outcome were successful, it would greatly
benefit the kingdom."

A long moment of silence ensued before David broke into a
grin and slapped Micah on the back. "You have much of both
your father and your mother in you, young Micah. I remember
Ailea as a young captive, appearing before me with a list of her
requirements in a husband. She displayed courage in her boldness, as do you." The king had to reach up a bit to place his
hands on the younger man's shoulders, and he stretched to give
him the honored kiss of friendship on each cheek.

The general was much less effusive. He grumbled to the king
that Micah was young and had committed a serious error in
judgment, but perhaps should be given another chance. Micah
realized that this was as much support as he could hope for from
his commander. The three sat down to discuss the mission that
would redeem Micah in the eyes of his fellow warriors.

"I would remind you, my lord," Micah said to David, "that
Rezon of Damascus is my uncle." Both the general and the king
nodded. "I understand that he has made himself somewhat of a
nuisance of late." Micah waited for a response.

A look passed between David and Joab before the king answered. "The commander of our garrison in Damascus tells us that he is certain that Rezon is the source of many raids on caravans coming and going from the city. He has noted that Rezon grows more and more wealthy, and yet complains to him often that the taxes levied on him are unfair. There isn't much doubt that we are being robbed by Rezon, both by the losses to our caravans and the fact that he conceals his wealth to avoid higher taxes. In addition, Rezon's popularity is increasing. We believe he may try to oust our garrison sometime in the future and declare himself king of Damascus."

"My father has told me as much, my lord. I thought it might be of benefit to you if I made a visit to my uncle, using our kinship as the reason, and try to find out what he is up to."

"It sounds like a good plan to me," David said. "I will send you as my personal emissary to Damascus. You are to discover to what extent your uncle is exerting influence there. In the early years, after we defeated your grandfather, Rezon was no more than a pesky desert raider, but I think he must have inherited some of his father's ability to lead men. I know that the people of Damascus look up to him as a hero. Our garrison in the city is a small one, and if Rezon has plans to overthrow it, I need to know it now, while there is still time to send reinforcements."

"I am happy that you are giving me this opportunity, but it is only fair to point out that I have never so much as set eyes on my uncle. He disowned my mother when she married a Hebrew. She has sent word to him many times that she would welcome a reconciliation, but he has rejected all her overtures. It is highly unlikely that he will welcome me. He might even hate me enough to wish me dead."

Joab's thick brows lifted. "So you fear for your life?"

Micah clenched his jaw to keep from expressing his irritation. "Not at all, sir. I will do my utmost to accomplish this mission satisfactorily."

David was quick to reassure him. "I have every confidence that you will not only do your best, but will certainly succeed."

Mollified by the king's encouragement, Micah left hurriedly before Joab's cynicism could goad him into losing his temper. He would have to spend one more night in the palace before starting his journey to Damascus in the morning. He would do his best to avoid the general until then.

~ ~ ~

Micah had a disturbing dream that night. It was about the incident that had led to his vow when he was ten years old. At that age he was already a head taller and much heavier than his contemporaries. Being larger put him at a distinct disadvantage, because both his father and his grandfather had taught him that it was not honorable to fight those who were weaker. An older, rather cruel boy named Lemuel had been his adversary, no doubt jealous because Micah, though younger, was larger. He verbally abused Micah with impunity because Micah would not fight back.

In his dream, Lemuel taunted him. "He's a big coward. He won't even join us in teasing the fox." The boy poked a stick at a helpless fox that he and the other boys had tied to a tree. "Let's teach him a lesson," Lemuel goaded the other village lads. He kicked Micah hard in the shin. When Micah reached down to grab his leg, he was hit over the head with the stick. Still, he didn't retaliate. Micah never defended himself. Most of the boys were too intimidated by his size to risk raising his temper. But Lemuel continued to taunt Micah, calling him names.

"I know why he won't fight. He's not a true son of Israel. His mother is a heathen Aramean."

Micah's face turned red with embarrassment and anger. Lemuel hit the core of Micah's insecurity when he accused him of being a foreigner. "I am not! I am a Hebrew, and don't you ever say otherwise!"

Lemuel took a step backward as Micah challenged him, but his hatred for Micah overcame his fear, and he continued to mock. "Micah is an uncircumcised heathen!" The other boys,

encouraged that so far Lemuel was getting away with his tor-
ment of Micah, began to chant the same words. They circled
him, and Lemuel, emboldened by their participation, spit in
Micah's face. Micah's rage finally overtook him, and scarcely
knowing what he was doing, he doubled his hand into a fist and
hit the smaller boy with all his strength.

Lemuel flew backward with the force of the blow, striking
his head against the gnarled root of a tree. He lay very still.
None of the other boys made a sound. They looked at Micah in
awe. Micah was horrified by what he had done. He was certain
he had killed Lemuel. He gathered his nemesis up in his strong
arms and carried him to his mother, who wailed that the big
brute had killed her precious baby. He saw the accusation in
every eye of the villagers who crowded around.

Lemuel had not died, but he had lain unconscious all that
day, and Micah had been certain that he was guilty of murder.
Shageh had looked at him with disappointment in his eyes—a
more painful rebuke than any beating would have been. Jonathan
had merely told him, "Son, you must learn the extent of your
own strength."

From that time on, the village boys had not teased him, but
Micah would not have hurt them if they had. He realized that he
did not want to hurt people. He wanted to help them.

In his dream, the Rab came to him, and it was very real, very
clear. Shageh, who somehow was larger than his grown-up grandson, placed his hand on Micah's head. "You make me proud,
Micah. You have learned not to use your strength to dominate
others. Now that you are a man, you may be called upon to use
that strength to fight for the right, but you will do so sparingly,
and with meekness. You still care about what other men think of
you, but you will not let that sway you into betraying yourself.
You are as Adonai made you, and it is he, not men, who will
continue to shape your life."

Micah awoke at dawn, filled with peace from the Rab's words
that had come to him in the dream. He was now certain that un-

less there was an overt threat to the nation, he would not rejoin the army. His father was right. The Rab was right. He was cut out for diplomacy, not war. If people chose to call him a coward he would just have to accept it. But he would prove that he was not a traitor. He would serve his king well. He dressed and went to gather all he would need for the journey to Damascus.

He joined up with a small caravan that was forming near the city gate. It was always best to travel in a group to avoid the robbers that lay in wait in the lonely, rocky stretches along the road to Damascus. As they were preparing to leave, a shout captured Micah's attention. He saw a group of armed men running in formation. Their lines were five across and about ten rows deep. The crowds at the gate parted as they approached.

"Make way for the prince. Make way for Absalom, eldest son of the king," shouted the center man in the leading row of retainers. Micah had a momentary thought that the announcement was inaccurate. Since the death of Amnon by Absalom's hand, Chileab was now the eldest son of the king. Of course, everyone knew that Chileab was incapable of ever ruling Israel. Still, it didn't seem right that his very existence was ignored in the proclamation.

As Micah looked on, Absalom's chariot sped by. The prince drove it himself, his whip cracking over the backs of two perfectly matched tan horses. The procession halted right in the center of the traffic coming in and out of the city via the Water Gate, not far from the spring of Gihon. The flow of traffic was impeded, which was evidently what the prince intended. As Micah and the others in the small caravan made their way around the chariot and fifty bodyguards, Micah saw Absalom hail several of the more prosperous men who passed through the gate into the city.

"Ho, Ezron, old friend, what brings you to Jerusalem?" Absalom called loudly as he stepped down from the chariot to greet a middle-aged man with a flowing black beard.

"I come to seek protection for my vineyards in Gezer. The

thieving Philistines make raids and then sneak back over their border before we can catch them. I've spoken to your father several times about setting up a garrison in Gezer, but it doesn't seem to be a priority with the king to protect his subjects who are unfortunate enough to live on the borders near the uncircumcised heathens."

Micah expected the prince to take offense at the man's insult to David, but instead, Absalom threw his arms around the man's shoulders and said, "It's regrettable that my father has neglected to protect you. When I come to power, I will certainly do something to alleviate your problems." Micah's group was leaving him behind, so he had to hurry away, but not before he saw that an adoring crowd was engulfing the prince. He shook his head. How could Absalom be so disloyal? He determined to talk to his father at length about it when he returned from Damascus. The thought of Damascus quickly brought his mind back to current business, and he hurried to catch up with his caravan, which had already passed through the city gate.

≈ ≈ ≈

Though he hated being there, Absalom returned to the palace. It was necessary to his plans. He had to pretend, at least for a time, that all was forgiven between him and his father. Besides, if he wanted to see his mother, he had to see her at the palace. He would convince her to go for an extended visit to his grandfather in Geshur. He wanted her out of harm's way until his plans were fulfilled.

Maacah had been so humiliated when she was displaced by Bathsheba that she hardly went anywhere or attended any of the palace functions. David was kind to her and gave her gifts like he gave Bathsheba. But that hardly compensated for being shoved aside. His mother was a princess and should be accorded more respect than the other wives, who were not royalty. When he was in power, he would see to it that Maacah was afforded her due respect.

"Absalom, come and sit at my side for a while. It has been a long time since we talked." David's voice startled the prince for a moment, then he turned toward his father and smiled.

"Father, we see each other at table every day."

David returned the smile, which made the resemblance between father and son even greater. "But we don't really get to talk at meals. There are nearly a hundred people present, so that I get to say no more than a few words to each one. Come."

He left his throne and motioned Absalom to sit down beside him on the cushions that were placed along the wall of the audience chamber.

"What did you do this day, my son?"

David looked so eager to have his affection, his respect, that Absalom could hardly suppress a sneer of disdain. He forced himself to answer warmly. "I went to the market, Father, and talked to some of the common people. I wish to help you take care of them."

David knew Absalom well enough to know that he was far too selfish to care about the common people, and his mind told him that his son was merely telling him what he wanted to hear. But David's heart told him to deny his own logic. David loved this handsome son, who was like him in so many ways, and that love led him to overlook Absalom's faults. Besides, he knew in his heart that he had seriously wronged Maacah's two children by not avenging Tamar. He had driven Absalom to commit murder, and it was unjust of him to hold it against his son. He was trying to be a better father these days, but it was much too late—which David was not yet ready to accept.

"Then tell me," he said as he put his arms around Absalom's shoulders, "how did it go with the people today? Were you able to help them?"

"Oh, yes, Father. I was very pleased with what I accomplished."

Chapter Five

~

*D*amascus was one of the world's most prosperous cities, situated at the confluence of two major rivers and straddling two major trade routes. Its streets were teeming with traders and merchants who mingled with the citizens in a cacophony of noise even greater than that of Jerusalem. Micah stood in the middle of a crowded thoroughfare and took in its sounds and sights and smells. A vendor down the street was roasting strips of lamb on a spit over a brazier, and the smell made Micah's mouth water. He purchased a wooden skewer of the spicy meat, and polished it off in short order as he strolled along the main streets of the city, licking his fingers clean when he finished. A flat-bedded wagon piled high with ivory tusks rumbled by, their gleaming whiteness in contrast to the shining black skin of the African traders transporting the goods. There were a few beggars who mingled with the crowd; most were blind, or had lost a limb, or were obviously witless. But for the most part, the people of Damascus and the caravans that entered the city were a prosperous lot.

It took Micah no time at all to locate his uncle, even amid the confusion, because Rezon was the best-known name in the city-kingdom. In fact, Micah realized as he talked to people that his uncle was looked upon almost as a king here. That Rezon had gained his wealth from robbing others when he and his men had been an outcast group of brigands seemed only to enhance his standing among his fellow Damascenes.

As he made his way into the part of the city where the wealthiest citizens lived, Micah mused about how different his mother's childhood must have been, living in this bustling city, from the life she now lived in the quaint little village of Ziph.

Micah followed the directions he was given and soon came to a massive gate made of beautiful iron grillwork. He looked into the courtyard and saw a large fountain in the middle, with tall, arched columns beyond. Micah did not know what to expect from Rezon, whom he had never met. He took a deep breath and lifted the heavy iron knocker.

The servant who answered his knock took him through the outer courtyard to a large common room that boasted a pool. Standing on the other side was a man whose thick black hair was crimped in the elaborate style of the Arameans and streaked with gray. Micah knew without a doubt that this was his uncle. He was powerfully built and swarthy, handsome in a hard way. He did not cross to greet his guest, but lifted his hand in an imperious gesture for Micah to join him. There was no similarity between Rezon and Micah's mother, as far as he could see, except for the hair.

Despite his rude greeting, Micah's uncle was polite, calling for one of his servants to wash the dust of travel from Micah's feet while another went to fetch wine, cheese, and bread. He inquired about Ailea's health. Micah noticed a reserve in Rezon's manner. The man did not trust this nephew who had appeared so suddenly in Damascus.

Micah decided to go directly to the point. "I was sent here by the king to see what your intentions are," he bluntly informed Rezon.

"My intentions?" Rezon's guileless question did not fool Micah for a moment. His uncle knew exactly why David was concerned about his power in the vassal city.

"He wants me to report to him whether I think the garrison of warriors he has in place here is sufficient to keep order. David also wants to know whether Damascus will continue to pay the levied taxes."

"What choice do we have?" This time the question was laced with a generous portion of bitterness.

"The king thinks you might be ready to lead a rebellion against him. Are you?"

There was a glint of surprise and respect in Rezon's eyes. "You don't fear to come directly to the point, do you, young nephew? Such directness is so refreshing that I will answer you with equal candor. No, at this time my position is not strong enough to lead a rebellion. In a few more years . . . who knows what may happen?"

Rezon could tell by his expression that Micah was wondering whether he spoke the truth. "I fought the shepherd king once, more than twenty years ago. He defeated Damascus and its allied city-states. Your grandfather was killed in that battle. I will come against him again only when I have a fair chance to win."

Micah sighed in relief. "I am glad. I would hate to think that my father or I might have to kill you in battle."

"Then leave your low-born king and join forces with me. A giant like you could win a battle by sheer intimidation alone. David and his men killed your grandfather and confiscated property that by right should have been mine. He took your mother captive. You should not be serving such a man. The blood of Aram flows in your veins, you know."

"And the blood of Abraham, Isaac, and Jacob."

Rezon made a grimace of distaste, but did not challenge Micah's remark. "You will stay here with me while you are in Damascus," he said. "This is the very house where your mother was born, and the one your king confiscated after his army defeated ours. The first thing I did when I had amassed enough wealth was to buy the place back from the rich merchant who lived here. It was the least I could do to avenge the honor of your grandfather, Eliada. Has your mother told you of him?"

Micah nodded. "Yes, and so has my father. They have both told me that he was a great general, and that Hadadezar had foolishly ignored his advice when he fought Israel. My father told me of the battle. My mother told me of his care of her and my grandmother. She has also told me how it was between you two growing up. She said she always followed you around, and that you taught her many things, such as how to climb trees and use a bow and arrow, things other girls did not know."

Rezon laughed at the memories Micah's words evoked. "It used to frighten me, the way she would take on any challenge. She acted as if she had no idea she was just a little slip of a thing. Malik used to call her 'cricket.' He said she deserved the name because she was always making noise and hopping around. Malik was glad when I grew big enough that I was given into my father's care for training as a warrior. Then he only had Ailea to chase around."

Rezon paused and thought for a moment. "Years ago, a friend of your father came to Damascus. He took back with him the old man I've been telling you about—Malik. The young man was to take him to serve your mother. Did he?"

"Yes, most certainly. Malik served our family for ten years before he died. He was very happy with us, and my mother was thrilled to have him. They often spoke of you and your parents. My mother always said it was like having a member of her family once more."

Rezon started to speak, then cleared his throat gruffly. "Malik was a good man." Then, as if embarrassed to have shown emotion, Rezon changed the subject. "I will have Nebai, my steward, show you to your quarters. You may stay in the room that was your mother's. I have three beautiful concubines in addition to my two wives. Shall I call for them? You may choose whichever one you wish, and she will be yours for the night."

Micah kept his expression impassive as he answered. "I am

certain your concubines are of surpassing beauty, Uncle, but I made a vow to my grandfather that I would be as the first man, Adam, and know only one woman, take only one wife. He taught me that it is the will of Adonai, our God."

Rezon could not have been more surprised if Micah had announced that he could fly. "You keep yourself from women? What kind of man are you?" Then he shrugged. "It's no matter to me. Come, and I'll show you your room myself."

That night as he sat on the comfortable bed in his room, Micah heard the sound of feminine laughter drifting across the courtyard. He knew his uncle thought him strange, just as his fellow soldiers did, when he resisted the allure of women. Two faces appeared in his mind's eye—Shageh's and Shoshanna's—and he was glad he had not yielded to temptation.

≈ ≈ ≈

Rezon continued for the next week to try to persuade his nephew to remain in Damascus, but Micah politely refused. "I am a Hebrew. I have been raised as a Hebrew, and I believe in Adonai. I could never live in Damascus and bow down to its idols. But I hope that will not keep us from being friends, Uncle."

Rezon snorted in disgust. "You sound like your mother. She adopted the people of the invisible God without so much as looking back at her former home and her people. She has completely forgotten us, no doubt."

"No, Uncle. You know that is not true. My mother has sent word several times that she wants to see you again, but she never had a response."

"Humph! She chose her life long ago, and I chose mine. That cannot be changed."

"But perhaps you can send word to her by me that you have forgiven her for leaving her people. She really had no choice at the time, you know." Micah watched his uncle carefully for a response, but Rezon brushed the subject aside as if it meant nothing to him.

"I have to meet with someone outside the city," Rezon said. "You will be comfortable here until I return."

Before his uncle reached the door, however, Micah said with a note of authority in his voice, "The king will be pleased if I return with a good report, especially if I set his mind at ease about any 'meetings' that you have."

Rezon turned and looked suspiciously at Micah, his sharp eyes evaluating the face of his imposing nephew. After a long moment, he shrugged his shoulders and grudgingly said, "Very well, you may come along."

Outside, they mounted camels to make the short trip out into the desert. Rezon enjoyed teasing Micah about his inept handling of his animal.

"We have no need for camels in the hills of southern Judah, Uncle," he explained. "And, judging by the disposition of my mount, it is something I should be thankful for. Before I ever mounted him, he spat on me twice and bit me once. And he smells worse than a sheepfold that hasn't been mucked out for a month."

Rezon laughed. "It is likely he objects to carrying so heavy a burden as you, Nephew." They continued in silence until they reached a village of tents at an oasis some ten miles east of Damascus. Everyone, young and old, came pouring out to meet them, greeting Rezon as if he were a conquering hero coming back from battle. Every man among them had a sword secured by his girdle. Most of these were short-handled, with long, curved blades.

The leader showed Rezon and Micah inside a large tent, and Micah drew in a sharp breath at what he saw. The tent was stuffed almost to overflowing with treasure. Items of alabaster, silver, bronze, and gold sat on piles of brilliant-hued rugs. There was a stack of swords, body armor, and shields in one corner. The air was redolent with the smell of cinnamon, aloe, and sandalwood, which Micah assumed wafted from the many intricately decorated jars and boxes around the room. This was a cache of booty from very successful caravan raids. There was no other explanation for such riches in this out-of-the-way oasis.

The conversation was guarded because of Micah's presence. Rezon said only to the leader, "You have done very well this time."

The leader responded simply, "We prosper only because of you, my lord."

The remainder of the day was spent placing the more fragile and costly items in large, innocuous-looking wooden crates. The rugs, Micah noticed, were laid atop sheets of heavy canvas and rolled into cylinders, concealing their lush colors, and placed with the other items on two large wagons. The leader of the band of robbers (there was no doubt in Micah's mind of their occupation) ordered two of his men to drive the wagons. Micah was surprised that they left for Damascus as soon as the loading was done.

They traveled in moonlight and did not reach the city until just before dawn. The streets were deserted, and Micah realized that Rezon had chosen the hour deliberately in order not to draw attention to the wagons. They pulled up at the back of Rezon's mansion.

"Uncle, it would appear that you are depriving the kingdom of Israel of valuable merchandise as well as the taxes that would be due," Micah said as the two men dismounted from their camels.

"A man must feed his family, dear nephew, and your King David has plenty of both 'merchandise' as you call it, and taxes. I would advise you not to look for trouble where none exists. From what I hear, the king should be paying attention closer to home."

Micah pondered his uncle's cryptic remarks as he walked across the courtyard toward his room. Though he was perplexed, he was also tired after the eventful day, and it wasn't long before he enjoyed a deep, restful sleep.

≈ ≈ ≈

At the end of the week, as Micah was preparing to return to Jerusalem, Rezon called for him. He handed Micah a beautiful bracelet fashioned of royal blue lapis lazuli. "This was your grandmother's bracelet, given to her by your grandfather. When your father's men looted the house of Eliada, Shua, your grandmother's old servant, managed to hide this one piece. Your mother should by all rights have it. Give it to her with my greeting." The older man looked embarrassed by what he said.

Micah bid his uncle good-bye and headed for Jerusalem. He joined a caravan making its way down the King's Highway to Jerusalem, passing south of the majestic, snowcapped Mount Hermon and crossing the Jordan at Jericho.

He would tell the king that Rezon evidently had no plans for a revolt any time soon, although he enjoyed an immense popularity with the citizens as well as many of the nomadic people who lived in the surrounding desert. Micah would also recommend an audit of the amount of taxes the city of Damascus should be paying. He was certain that money due to Israel's treasury was finding its way into the purses of Rezon and other leaders of the city. Despite Rezon's veiled warning about starting trouble, honesty required that Micah tell the full story in his report.

All in all, Micah was glad he had finally become acquainted with his mother's only living relative, that he had visited the city of her birth and seen her childhood home. He felt relief that Rezon's flattering offer to employ him had not tempted him even slightly. He had forever answered the question of whether he was truly an Israelite. The answer was a resounding yes. He was glad nonetheless that his uncle had made a gesture of reconciliation with Ailea. He looked forward to giving his mother the bracelet as soon as he made his report to the king.

～ ～ ～

Unfortunately, his trip to Ziph would be postponed. When Micah arrived at the palace, he asked the guard at the door for an audience with the king in order to make his report. The sober-faced fellow nodded and disappeared for several minutes. When he reappeared, the king's secretary was with him.

"Good morning, Jehoshaphat," Micah said. "The Lord be with you."

"And the Lord bless you," the older man replied. "I understand you are returning from a journey to Damascus. Did all go well?" Micah was confused. Did the king intend for him to tell his findings to Jehoshaphat? "Yes, my visit to Damascus went very well, but I don't think I should say more than that. I was to report directly to the king."

Jehoshaphat looked flustered. "Of course, my lord. It was not my intention to pry. I only meant to tell you that Joab has requested that you be brought to him immediately."

Micah was disappointed. He had imagined telling the king about his visit and having the king give him congratulations for a job well done. There was no way the general would give him praise or congratulations. Joab was likely to find something to criticize about his performance, but there was nothing to do but follow Jehoshaphat to meet with the general. To Micah's surprise, Joab merely grunted when Micah finished his report. Ignoring the news about Rezon's involvement with the band of thieves, Joab seem interested only in the military information.

"Then you don't believe Rezon will cause enough trouble anytime soon to necessitate enlarging our troop strength in Damascus?" the general asked.

"No. I believe Rezon is biding his time, increasing his personal wealth and building support. My guess is that he won't make a move until he is certain he can win against us, and he knows that day is in the distant future, if it ever comes at all."

Joab looked relieved at the answer and suddenly seemed eager to broach a new subject.

"Since you have succeeded in the Damascus project, I have another assignment for you, son of Jonathan. This requires the strictest secrecy and the promise that you will report only to me."

"What about the king?" Micah asked, uneasy about any assignment that would be done without the king's knowledge.

"The king knows nothing of this matter, nor will he ever know unless it becomes essential that he be told. I assure you it is in his best interest, and in the best interest of Israel that this mission be undertaken. If you can't agree in advance that you can perform your duty under these conditions, I will choose someone else for the job."

"As long as it is loyal to David's kingdom, I will agree," Micah said after careful consideration.

"Then I will speak forthrightly. I suspect Absalom is planning to overthrow his father and set himself up as king."

When Micah's mouth dropped open in surprise, the general went on to convince him of the truth of his suspicions. "While you were away there was a dedication."

Micah knew the general well enough to realize that this was not just idle conversation. He asked the obvious question. "What dedication?"

"Absalom built a monument to himself in the Kidron Valley. Hundreds of people attended its unveiling. He claims he built it because all three of his sons are now dead, and he won't have anyone to carry on his name. He says he wants to be remembered by the people. I believe he is carefully gathering followers to his cause. The people at the dedication bowed down to him as if he were a god. It was revolting."

"I have seen the runners he sends out before him when he rides through the city in his chariot. But I just assumed that his vanity causes him to draw attention to himself. What makes you believe his goal is the kingdom? After all, now that Amnon is dead, Chileab certainly cannot rule in his father's place. All Absalom must do is wait for the king to die, and undoubtedly he will ascend to the throne. Why would he risk it all in a rebellion?"

"Because of his unbridled ambition, and his resentment of his father," Joab growled. "I have had spies watching him at the city gate for several months. They report that the prince watches for important citizens coming into the city on the days that his father is to sit in judgment. Absalom stops them and asks them if they have a case to present to the king. If they respond positively, Absalom gives them a speech about how his father is likely to rule against them, and how, if he were king, he would treat them so much more justly.

"The king has recently acquired a shipment of ivory from the upper Euphrates and wishes to give each of his children a portion of it. I have informed the king that I will see that Absalom, Chileab, and Tamar receive theirs. I had planned to go myself, but Absalom will be very much on guard around me. He won't suspect anything amiss if you deliver the ivory. When you go to Baal Hazor, you may pretend to be unhappy with your position regarding the army. Let Absalom think you believe that we have slighted you; that when you reported your successful mission to Damascus, we did not completely exonerate and reinstate you, but told you we would consider it. Try to get him to ask you to join in whatever coup he has planned. Take note of who is there. But don't be too anxious to gain Absalom's favor. Let things develop naturally."

"This is a difficult assignment, General. I would not find it easy to lie."

A look of disdain crossed Joab's features, and he shook his head. "Surely, son of Jonathan, you have some real resentment concerning my handling of your case, and if not, you may dredge up some rancor from the past. I am certain your mother has told you that I accused her falsely of being a spy. It doesn't matter how you do it; just make them believe you might be sympathetic to their cause."

Micah had grave misgivings, but he saw no way to refuse Joab's commission. His reputation was tarnished enough already. His parents would bear the consequences if he were permanently discredited. "I will do my best to find out Absalom's intentions," he finally agreed.

The general seemed to warm considerably to Micah after he'd

agreed to the mission. "Come with me, son of Jonathan. I want to see that you are properly outfitted for travel."

~ ~ ~

Joab took him to the king's stables, which had been built some twenty years earlier, after David had defeated the Arameans and brought several hundred of their chariot horses back to Jerusalem. It was a busy place, with a dozen grooms walking or brushing the horses, and builders adding new stalls.

"I see you are expanding here," Micah commented.

"Not as rapidly as I would like," Joab responded. "I have tried to persuade David to let me train a chariot corps, but he vows it will never happen in his lifetime."

"Because the Torah forbids it," Micah said.

"Yes, because the Torah forbids it. But when all the other nations are arming themselves, we cannot be unprepared."

"My father has told me of winning battle after battle with only foot soldiers—against Zobah and Edom, Moab and Ammon. Adonai seems to shed his blessings on an army that trusts in him rather than its chariots."

Joab grunted in reluctant agreement. "Yes, but I am not the Lord. I am only the commander of the army, and my duty is to see that Israel is as prepared for battle as her enemies. To that end, I am expanding the stables for possible use in the future. Let me show you what I've accomplished."

They walked the length of the building, which Micah estimated housed more than a hundred horses, and there were several other buildings of the same size. Joab stopped at the stall of a huge chestnut stallion. The horse's head was up, ears pricked, as the men approached the stall.

"This animal is too large to be handled with ease by most men. You may need a swift mount in the weeks to come if there is a conspiracy. I will be sending you back and forth across Israel to determine the movements of the partisans. You are certainly too heavy a burden for any donkey I have ever seen, so I am giving the horse to you."

Micah was dumbstruck. Horses were almost exclusively the purview of royalty. They were usually imported from the steppes of central Asia, which made them too rare and hard to come by for even the wealthy to own. His father could have afforded several, but sure-footed donkeys could do the same work at a fraction of the price. And a young man like Micah, just starting out, would certainly not consider such an expensive mount.

Why was Joab giving him this beautiful animal? Surely not out of the goodness of his heart. From what Micah knew of the man, he didn't have a heart; or if he did, it was very hard indeed. Joab must think that this gift would make Micah indebted to him, and therefore more willing to do his bidding. Joab should have known that, like his father and grandfather before him, Micah could not be bribed. Still, Joab wasn't likely to understand if Micah refused the horse. Instead, it would make him suspicious of Micah's motives.

Micah stepped closer, to allow the stallion to become familiar with his scent. The clean lines, flaring nostrils, and widely spaced eyes spoke of excellent breeding. The horse's surprisingly soft muzzle snuffled over his shoulder, then butted it. Micah chuckled, and rubbed along the length of its nose. He decided to at least try to turn down Joab's offer.

"I cannot accept such a valuable gift, General. I will gladly pay for the animal and thank you for the opportunity to own him. I would imagine an animal this fine would bring nearly a hundred shekels."

"More like one hundred and fifty," Joab replied. "But you will not pay for the horse. He is necessary for your mission, and the royal stable will bear the expense. Should you not want him after your duties are ended, you may sell him."

Micah could tell by the general's tone that he had taken offense at Micah's words. "No, you are right. This is not the kind of horse that one would sell." Micah eased into the stall. The chestnut snorted and tossed his head, but allowed Micah to run his hand down the smooth length of his back.

Micah took the rest of the day acquainting himself with the animal, and picking up the gifts he was to deliver to Absalom. He named the horse Ramah, because of his long flowing mane. That night Micah slept in the stables and left Jerusalem at first light. He thought of the bracelet once more and wished he had time to take it to his mother, but it was impossible. It stayed secure in the money pouch he always wore strapped to his waist.

Chapter Six

~

Micah turned off the main road at Baal Hazor and patted
his horse as he started up the winding lane to Absalom's villa.
"One more mile, boy, and you can have all the fodder you want.
We're almost there." Micah had always had a habit of talking to
animals as though they could understand. He supposed most
people would think him quite peculiar. Not that the huge stallion looked as though he needed rest. His coat was barely lathered, though the summer sun was very hot.

Micah found an interesting gathering when he arrived at the
top of the mountain. The prince himself did not come out to
meet him, of course, but there was a porter, a stable boy, and
several men of various ages and modes of dress watching him
from Absalom's porch. He turned his horse over to the stable
boy, who had to be reassured that the huge beast was not dangerous. Then he mounted the porch steps to announce his arrival. There were clan chiefs from the tribes of Issachar and
Manasseh, and a few Ishmaelites and Philistines as well. Micah
noted a wariness in several of the men, but none was openly
hostile.

He was taken aback when he saw the tall, dignified form of
Ahithophel descending the steps to meet him. What was he doing

here? Had the king sent him? Surely Joab would have informed him had he known of the counselor's presence. Micah dismissed as absurd any possibility that the elder statesman could be plotting against the king. His presence had to be a coincidence. But Micah realized he was being scrutinized by the man's sharp gaze.

"You are the son of Jonathan," the older man said as he approached Micah. "Do you have business with the prince?" Ahithophel was acting as Absalom's deputy in greeting the new arrival.

Micah bowed to the stately old man with the long, flowing, white hair. "Yes, my lord. I bring the prince gifts from the king's most recent caravan from the east. I also have a message of greeting."

Ahithophel's guarded look disappeared and he smiled. "Let me take you to Absalom right away then. I am certain he will want to hear word from his father immediately." He had accepted Micah's explanation without hesitation. Micah felt guilty to be deceiving such an honorable man, but he reminded himself that his duplicity was only to protect his sovereign.

As he followed Ahithophel from the porch into a huge common room, Micah wondered whether the man had brought his granddaughter. He had not been able to get Shoshanna out of his mind since he left Jerusalem. If the girl was here, Micah knew it would take an extra effort not to be distracted by her beauty and charm.

∾ ∾ ∾

Shoshanna watched Micah from the lattice-covered window of a second-floor guest room. She had seen him ride confidently into the compound with one hand on the reins while he gestured with the other to the half-dozen men who had gone out to greet him.

The horse was as magnificent as his owner, she mused. *What is he doing here?* Had Micah been summoned by Absalom, along with the others, for some kind of parley? Grandfather had told her they were here simply to enjoy the cool mountain retreat. The summer heat was intense at Giloh, and even more so at their home in Jerusalem.

Shoshanna was not convinced that Ahithophel had told her the complete truth. For one thing, they had left Marah in Jerusalem. True, she did not like to travel, but Grandfather had not even attempted to cajole her this time. And when Shoshanna offered to stay in the city with her mother, Ahithophel had forcefully insisted that she accompany him. It was strange, all these guests from different regions just happening to be here at once.

Since their arrival, Ahithophel and Absalom had closeted themselves together for hours of private conversation. The previous night, Shoshanna had retired early to her room, but had not gone to bed. She sewed beads onto the new girdle she was making for her mother. If their visit lasted another week, she might be able to finish the project in time to present it to Marah when they returned to Jerusalem. If so, she would need to purchase more beads in one of the little shepherd villages in the valley below. She decided to seek out her grandfather to ask him how long their stay would last.

When Shoshanna made her way to Ahithophel's room, she was glad to see light coming through the bottom of the door. If the lamps were still burning, then Grandfather was awake. She had just lifted her hand to knock on his door when she heard voices. She thought it was Absalom's voice she heard first, and it sounded like he said, "The time is almost ripe." He must have turned away from the door because she couldn't hear the rest.

She stood with her hand upraised, trying to decide whether to knock, when she heard her grandfather say, " . . . with Amasa as your general." Shoshanna let her hand drop to her side. *Amasa as Absalom's general? Only the king has generals.* She had made her way back to her room, deeply disturbed about what she had heard.

Now she stood, staring out the window, wondering whether the prince was planning to take his father's throne. It was hard for Shoshanna to believe that either Ahithophel or Micah would take part in such a plot. Her grandfather had been David's trusted counselor for many years. Still, she had seen looks and sensed tension in Ahithophel at times when he was unaware she was watching. At those times she had assumed that her grandfather was remembering how David had ruined his granddaughter's reputation and had her husband killed.

Marah's resentment was open and obvious, but had Ahithophel been hiding his own hatred, waiting for an opportunity to seek vengeance? She hoped it was not so. And was Micah a part of a conspiracy to put Absalom on the throne? Shoshanna was confused by her conflicting emotions. Her heart had tripled its beat when she saw Micah arrive, and she hoped that his stay might be long enough for her to get to know him better. But the undercurrents in Baal Hazor made her very uneasy.

≈ ≈ ≈

Micah was ushered into the presence of the prince. "Ah, yes. I remember you from the banquet a few weeks ago," Absalom said as Micah bowed to him. "What brings you to Baal Hazor?" The question was cordial, but the prince's eyes were shrewdly assessing.

"I am sent by the king with a gift for you. It is from Africa." With that, Micah gave Absalom the bag he held in his right hand. The prince opened it and withdrew a large ivory box. Inside the box were several exquisite carvings of exotic animals and an ivory armband. Each gift brought gasps of admiration from Absalom's guests as they were revealed. Even the prince was impressed. "These are beautiful," he remarked, as he set the box on a side table and slipped the armband on. Absalom seemed to accept Micah's explanation for his visit. As any good host would do, he asked Micah to stay for a while. Absalom almost managed to hide his surprise when Micah readily agreed.

Micah spent the rest of the day talking with the other guests, trying to find out why they were at Baal Hazor. The Ishmaelites, with their gold earrings and crescent-shaped swords, scowled at him fiercely when he tried to question them. The visitors from the two northern tribes were friendlier, but gave him no useful information—they were merely here to pay their respects to the king's son, they insisted. Ahithophel was the one he most wanted to question, though he knew he would have to do it carefully. The old man was sharp. He hadn't risen to the position of the king's chief counselor by being easily duped.

As it happened, Micah didn't get an opportunity to talk to Ahithophel that day. He was nowhere to be seen. Neither did he catch a glimpse of Shoshanna. He went to bed early, disappointed at the day's events.

~ ~ ~

The next morning, Micah looked out the window of his spacious room and saw Shoshanna picking flowers on the hillside. Her back was to him, but he knew her by the gracefulness of her tall and willowy form, and by the long rope of ebony hair that hung well below her head covering. She wore a flowing pink tunic the exact color of the wildflowers she was picking. Micah decided to go below and make her a crown of the flowers.

Another woman was with Shoshanna. She was veiled, so that he could not see her features, but he was fairly certain it was Tamar, Absalom's reclusive sister. He felt a stab of compassion for the woman who had suffered so much from a half-brother who should have given his life to protect her. In spite of himself, Micah found he understood Absalom's bitterness against the father who had not punished the evil in his own household.

For Absalom to station himself at the city gates and ingratiate himself with the populace at the expense of his father was one thing, to plan an uprising that would tear the country apart was insupportable, and Micah would not hesitate to do anything he could to stop a rebellion before it could take root. *But instead you are running after the lady Shoshanna,* his conscience chided him.

He reminded himself that his mission was to gather information, and Shoshanna might be able to assist him. The closer he could get to her, the closer he would be to Ahithophel. He didn't wish to deceive or manipulate her, but asking her a few questions couldn't hurt.

In a matter of minutes he was striding across the meadow to join the two women on the hillside. As soon as Tamar saw him approach, she quickly covered herself with her veil and fled, scurrying through the nearest door into the safety of the house.

Shoshanna tried to maintain a disapproving look as she spoke to him. "You frightened her, my lord. That was not well done of you."

"I didn't know I'd frighten her. Maybe she was startled by my appearance. But I am as Adonai made me; there's nothing I can do to change that."

"You are not so very fearsome, though you do take up quite a lot of space. I don't think I've ever seen a larger man." Shoshanna's lips curved in a smile as she studied him.

"And I don't think I've ever seen a taller woman. I think I like that about you. I always get a cramp in my neck when I try to hold a discussion with most women. I still have to tilt my head a bit, but it's not as bad with you."

Shoshanna laughed. Even that mirthful sound had dignity. Who did she remind him of, this girl who exuded such rare charm? He watched her in silence for a moment before it struck him. He laughed. "My mother!"

Her eyebrows lifted. "What about your mother?"

Micah stared at Shoshanna for a moment, nonplussed. He hadn't realized he had spoken aloud. "You remind me of her."

"And why is that so amusing?"

"Because she would scarcely come to your shoulder. But she has your same bearing, and the same dignity. She also stands up to my father, who can cause grown men to tremble. She is fearless, as I expect you are."

"Oh, there are certainly things I fear, but you are correct if you mean I don't fear any man. I revere and obey my grandfather. I know no other man well, and if I did, well, I doubt if there are many men who could earn my obedience."

"*Earn* your obedience! Why, surely you will obey your husband, no matter what his attributes. You will obey him because you are but a woman." Micah did not know why her proud speech had irritated him so. He had come to the field in order to impress her, to gain her trust, yet here he was berating her.

Shoshanna lifted her chin at least three inches as she replied, "I *have* no husband. Nor am I betrothed. But when my grandfather chooses a bridegroom for me, I shall obey him and perform all the duties of a wife with all diligence. I will do that because I honor my grandfather, and would never do anything to shame him."

Micah found himself envious of her loyalty to Ahithophel, but he could understand it. "I felt the same about my grandfather. He was a great man, and I spent much of my boyhood trying to live up to the standard he set for me. It made me a better person." He sat down amidst the flowers and began to pluck them, weaving their stems together. Knowing he would have to ask the distasteful question sometime, he decided to get it over with.

"What brings you and your grandfather to Baal Hazor, Shoshanna?" Micah hoped his query sounded nonchalant.

"Oh, we come here from time to time to visit, often to escape the heat in Giloh. You know that Bathsheba is my cousin and our grandfather is on the privy council. I have played often with David's children, and I am particularly fond of Chileab and Tamar. I try to come here as often as I can to comfort them."

Micah observed Shoshanna keenly as she spoke. She had hesitated for a moment, and a look of doubt had flashed through her eyes before she answered. But he was certain that when she spoke, her answer was completely without guile. He breathed a silent sigh of relief.

"Tell me about your mother, who reminds you so much of me," Shoshanna asked after a moment, taking a seat an arm's length away from him, her eyes smiling and warm beneath the wing-shaped curve of her brows.

"She is quite fearless, despite her lack of stature. Never lets my father cow her at all, even though he is more than twice her size. I remember once, when I was a child, seeing her climb atop a table so that she could look him in the eye as she argued with him. It's funny now, but at the time I didn't think so, nor did I think it strange. She is a very strong woman—no matter that a brisk breeze could blow her away."

"You think of me as fearless and strong? I like that. Is there anything else about me that reminds you of your mother?"

"Yes." Micah knew she was awaiting his reply, but he fastened three more flowers together before he continued. "My mother is also very beautiful."

Shoshanna's mouth formed a perfect "o." She was not being coy. She was honestly surprised. "I am not," she insisted.

"You are," Micah argued as he wrapped the last two stems together to form a crown and placed the garland on her head. "You are very beautiful."

≈ ≈ ≈

She had run away from him. As soon as he had spoken of her beauty, Shoshanna had leaped to her feet, mumbled something about helping her grandfather, and returned to the house with the swiftness of a young gazelle that has caught the scent of a predator in the air.

As he took the evening meal with Absalom, Ahithophel, and several other men whose reason for being present remained a mystery to him, Micah wondered how he would find another opportunity to be with her. He had a mission to accomplish, but maybe he could combine that mission with the pleasure of getting to know the elusive Shoshanna.

"May I speak with you privately, Counselor?" he asked Ahithophel, who was seated across from him.

The older man stroked his white beard and studied him through eyes that were hooded by thick white brows. "Ummm, I have some matters to settle with the prince, but after that I could meet you on the verandah. It is pleasant out tonight."

Micah waited for two hours before the counselor appeared. "I must admit I am curious about what you have to say. I was fairly well acquainted with your grandfather, and know your father by sight, but I cannot imagine what interests we might have in common."

"We have none now, sir, but I wanted to discuss the possibility that we might have rather a lot in common in the future."

"Oh?"

"I met your granddaughter some weeks ago at the palace, and since I came here, I have had occasion to see and speak with her. I must confess a decided interest in her. She is beautiful and seems virtuous and loyal as well. I wonder if there is any betrothal contract or spoken understanding that would keep me from seeking her as my wife."

Ahithophel's surprise was evident as he pondered his response for a while before answering. "I have not chosen a husband for Shoshanna, but I have been speaking with one young man's father. She is the apple of my eye. It is presumptuous of you to speak to her of this matter, or even to approach me directly. If you wish to have my granddaughter, have your father speak with me. That is the proper way to do things."

Micah smarted from the insult. He was of age, and it was not at all improper for him to speak directly to Shoshanna's guardian. While it was perhaps not proper in the strictest sense for him to have seen Shoshanna without her grandfather's permission, they were both here as guests of the prince, where dozens of men and women interacted every day. Their meetings had never been the least bit secretive nor had their behavior been unseemly. Realizing that Ahithophel was simply being protective of his granddaughter, Micah apologized, telling Ahithophel that he would speak to his father concerning the matter.

≈ ≈ ≈

Micah did not catch so much as a glimpse of Shoshanna over the next two days. But he did go a long way toward accomplishing his mission. He accompanied Absalom on a visit to his shepherds in the valley below the villa. Absalom included Chileab in the party, and Chileab was clearly thrilled to have his brother's attention.

"What is your friend's name?" he asked after studying Micah for several minutes. Though he was a man in his mid-thirties, Chileab's affliction was apparent from the unabashed way he studied Micah. His eyes held a look of innocence, and he had a dazzling smile. He was very appealing, and Micah smiled back at him.

Absalom answered his brother patiently. "This is Micah ben Jonathan, Chileab, and he is our guest. You must not ask him too many questions."

Chileab nodded, but in the very next moment seemed to have forgotten his brother's admonition.

"How did you get so big?" he asked Micah with all the ingenuousness of a child.

"Chileab, do not ask such questions." Absalom started to chide his brother, but Micah wouldn't allow it.

"I do not take offense at such questions, and will gladly answer," he told Absalom. Turning to Chileab, he explained, "I am big because my father and grandfather before me were."

Chileab thought for a moment, then broke into a grin. "You look like your father and I look like mine. At least my brother and sister tell me it is so. Have you met my father?"

"Yes, Chileab, I have. And it is true you resemble him very much."

"He is a very handsome man, and so am I," Chileab said, nodding his head. Micah tried to stifle his laugh, but Absalom chuckled and threw his arm around Chileab's shoulders, so Micah allowed the laugh to escape. Chileab took no offense, but smiled, proud of himself that he had brought about the mirth.

When they found the shepherds and their flocks, Chileab went off with some of the boys to see twin lambs that had just been born. "You have an impressive flock here, my lord," Micah remarked. "Not only in numbers, but in quality as well."

"I suppose, because my father was a shepherd, I must have inherited his knowledge," Absalom responded. Micah thought the remark sounded somewhat self-deprecating, and didn't respond to it. They continued to walk together, Absalom asking questions of his shepherds periodically.

Micah explained to the prince that Ziph had very large flocks, and that he had often helped the shepherds while he was growing up. Absalom seemed impressed with Micah's suggestions in regard to improving the breeding of his flocks.

As they walked side-by-side back to the villa, Chileab lagging behind or running ahead if he saw something that interested him, the prince asked Micah about his standing with the army. He had heard of the accusations that had been leveled. Micah took a deep breath before he spoke.

"The accusations were not all false. I did show mercy to those raiders. But I truly believe that they were harmless. I was angered when the general seemed to believe those who accused me."

"Joab can be a hard man. Have you not been able to convince him?"

"He still seems to doubt me, even though my mission to Damascus had a favorable outcome. It seems I have yet to prove myself."

Absalom shook his head in sympathy. After a few moments of silence, he asked, "Have you appealed to my father?"

Micah knew that his answer was of utmost importance in gaining Absalom's trust. He answered with a hint of disappointment in his voice. "I did see the king. However, he seems to be too busy to adjudicate such cases as mine. I believe he will accept whatever Joab decides in the matter."

Absalom shook his head. "A complaint I hear all too often lately. Joab is a great general, but he has no diplomacy, no empathy for the common man's problems. My father should. . . . Maybe some-day I will be able to help in these matters."

Very good, Micah reflected as they reached Absalom's house and paused outside for a moment before going their separate ways. *He's dropping hints, but says nothing that could be construed as treason—yet.* "Is it possible if I am not allowed back into the army, you might have some use for me in your service, my lord?"

Absalom tugged at his full lower lip. "Umm, yes. I'm certain I could find a place for you, Micah. I seek to have loyal men about me. If you could give your oath to be loyal to me above all others, I think you could go far in my service." Absalom waited for Micah's response. With that last statement, the prince had come closer to treason than ever. Every Israelite owed allegiance to the king above all others. Absalom was virtually asking if Micah would be willing to turn his back on David and become Absalom's man. Micah hesitated, then breathed a sigh of relief when an interruption kept him from answering.

Chileab, who had run ahead of them, was trailing his hands in the water of a small pool. He waved to them, then turned and retrieved something from the water. As they drew nearer, Micah saw that it was a miniature boat.

"See, Absalom? I'm sailing the boat you gave me. Come and watch. I will let you sail it too."

Absalom placed his arm around his childlike brother. "Be patient, Chileab. I will sail the boat with you tomorrow. I'm too busy today."

Micah looked on, surprised again at Absalom's tender handling of his afflicted brother. How could a man who was totally self-absorbed and selfish in every other area show such compassion for the only two siblings who could bring him no gain, do him no favors? The prince was an enigma that Micah could not solve.

Chileab interrupted his thoughts. "What is your name?" he asked again, having forgotten what he'd been told earlier.

"I am Micah."

"Would you sail the boat with me?"

Micah saw Absalom open his mouth to deny his brother and spoke quickly. "I would like that very much, Chileab." Absalom smiled, shook his head, and took his leave of them.

"You go over there, see?" Chileab pointed to the other side of the pond. "And I will push the boat across to you. Then you will send it back."

"Good idea," Micah told his new friend as he complied.

"When did you see my father?" Chileab wanted to know after he had launched the little boat in Micah's direction.

"I saw him about a month ago at a banquet in the palace."

"You were invited to my father's banqueting hall?" Chileab's eyes were round with either awe or envy. Micah couldn't decide which.

"Yes."

"I'm not allowed," he said after a moment, his countenance dropping.

"You have never gone to a banquet with your father?"

"No. I can't be seen with my father in public. I'm never allowed to ride out with him either. But maybe I will see him soon. Do you know if he plans to come here?"

Micah felt compassion constrict his throat as he watched the spark of hope in the other man's innocent eyes. But he would not lie to him.

"No, Chileab. I don't know if your father has plans to come here any time soon. He is very busy, you know. But I am sure he will either come, or send for you just as soon as he is able."

"Oh, that's all right. I have Tamar to play with. And Shoshanna too. But Tamar is so often sad, and doesn't feel like playing games. And Shoshanna will only be here for a while. She is my good friend. Do you know her?"

Micah assured Chileab that he did. Then, typical of his nature, Chileab's attention shifted to the boat, and he began to ask Micah questions about boats and sailing. When he finally left Chileab, Micah felt sick at heart that Chileab's life would surely be torn apart in the event of an uprising. He would almost certainly lose either his father or his brother, both of whom he adored. He found himself praying that Joab would prove to be wrong in this matter. But he doubted that would be the case. There was something here that was not quite right, an ambiance that spoke of secrets and schemes. And he was here to get to the bottom of it.

≈ ≈ ≈

When Absalom and Micah were in the village, an invitation had been issued to the prince to bring his guests to the valley for a feast celebrating the end of the flax harvest. Flax ripened in early spring, and this year the villagers had garnered an abundant crop. Next would come the soaking to loosen the fibers; then the women would lay the fibers flat to dry on the rooftops before beating and combing and weaving it into linen. The people wanted to celebrate before the next labors began, and they wanted their lord and benefactor to join them. At dinner, Absalom announced they would all attend the next evening.

"I am too old for such nonsense," Ahithophel announced. "You younger men go on without me. It will give me a chance to retire early."

The women, of course, were not invited. The royals and aristocrats would not allow their women to have contact with common villagers. Their celebrations were often rough and bawdy, and though no one from the village would harm anyone in the prince's household, custom nevertheless had to be followed. Micah did not see Shoshanna that evening nor all the next day. He thought it a shame that he wouldn't see her at the festival either.

As the sun began to sink behind the hills of Ephraim, the prince and his guests made their way down to the village. A large area had been cleared beside the harvested flax, which was already soaking in huge vats. Several lambs and a bullock were roasting on spits; bread was baking in the communal oven, sending forth a mouthwatering aroma.

All the village women roamed freely about. Only a few were veiled, and most of these were married. Several of the girls were quite openly flirtatious, but their fathers and brothers kept a careful eye out to see that nothing more than looks passed between the women and their wealthy guests.

"The people of this village are famous for their dancing," Absalom informed his guests as they were seated on rugs spread out in a place of honor close to the bonfire. "Some of the men will likely challenge us to a contest of jumping and twirling."

"And we will beat you," boasted the village chief, a small man in his forties.

"You would ply us with food until we are too heavy to leap," Micah joked as he was handed a portion of roasted lamb. On a rug in front of the guests, piles of bread were placed alongside bowls of olive oil seasoned with rosemary for dipping. In a large communal bowl a mixture of chick peas and parched grain waited to be shared. Several of the married women kept the pottery cups of the guests filled with wine.

When everyone was feeling full and lazy, a drum started to beat somewhere behind them. All of the young men rose when a piper joined in. The women took up the chorus with their timbrels as the village men began to circle the fire. Faster and faster they went until the first tune was finished.

Then the challenges began. At first it was among the villagers, and gradually the older and slower men were eliminated, until only three of the younger men were left. They called out a challenge to their guests, and it was answered in good humor. Even the prince participated. Most of the women claimed that the guests had won the contest, even though none of them even came close to the prowess of the villagers, who had nothing more to do night after night than perfect their technique. While the participants sprawled breathless on their rugs, the sound of tinkling bells heralded the dance of the virgins. Some of the maidens wore finger bells and ankle bells. Others kept rhythm with timbrels, while some clapped. They began a high descant as they took their turn circling the campfire. All were veiled and barefoot. Some appeared to be very young, while others were grown and obviously ready for marriage. This was an opportunity for them to show off to prospective husbands while still under the watchful eyes of their elders, and they were enjoying it thoroughly, as they performed an entirely different dance than the men.

There was no aggressive challenge in their movements, only lithe grace as they swayed to and fro, their hands moving above their heads like branches in the wind. They began to twirl faster, and Micah's attention was captured by the tallest one as she came so near that her feet almost stepped on the rug where he was sitting. Her ankle bells tinkled and the skirt of her tunic swirled around her. There was something very familiar about her, and Micah watched her in fascination as the dance continued. It was definitely a dance of courtship as the girls seemed to continually step close to certain young men each time they passed.

The tall one had picked him. There was no doubt about it. As she floated by, Micah caught a glimpse of narrow feet with high insteps. Her anklets and the attached bells appeared to be silver. She swirled closer each time the dance brought her by, and a fragrance of citron and jasmine floated around her. She was graceful, beautiful in her movements. And she was tall, just like . . .

Micah's eyes widened as realization dawned. Beside him, the prince laughed and clapped his hands.

"The food and wine have slowed your wits this evening, my friend. I knew who it was the first time she passed. None of the village women are nearly that tall."

Micah watched the rest of the dance in wonderment as he realized why he had felt so strongly drawn to the dancing stranger. After several more minutes, the dance ended, and the maidens floated away into the dark fringes of the crowd. Micah's heart had been racing from the moment he realized the identity of the veiled dancer. He tried to keep his voice from showing emotion as he responded to Absalom's remarks. "You knew, and yet you allowed her to continue?" For some reason Micah was angry with Shoshanna for sneaking down to the village to dance, and even more angry with Absalom for allowing it to go on.

Absalom shrugged off his question. "There is no danger and no harm in what she has done." Micah opened his mouth to argue, then closed it. This was the prince of the kingdom, after all. Besides, much as he hated to admit it, Absalom was right. It was perhaps a bold thing to do, but Shoshanna was in no danger.

"She likes you."

"What?" Micah was taken aback by Absalom's statement.

"She chose you, singled you out to dance for. Are you interested?"

Micah colored in embarrassment, hoping the prince could not see it in the firelight. But Absalom noticed his reaction. Slapping Micah smartly on the shoulder, he threw back his head and laughed. Micah couldn't hold back a grin. There was something infectious about the prince's laughter.

At one point, as the entourage wound its way back up to the retreat, Micah thought he saw Shoshanna silhouetted against the mountain when the moon peeped out from the clouds. She was running. She thought no one was aware of her escapade, but Micah would find a way to tease her about it tomorrow. He smiled as he anticipated her reaction.

$\approx \approx \approx$

Shoshanna was mortified. "What did you say?"

"Why aren't you wearing your anklets today? I like the way the little bells tinkle." Micah stifled a smile. He continued to groom Ramah with the currying brush he had borrowed from the king's stable master.

His idea to use Ramah as a lure to bring Shoshanna to him this morning had worked. He had brought the horse from the stables at the back of the house and had begun to groom him below her second-story window. Soon she had appeared to get a closer look.

"He is magnificent. May I touch him?"

"Certainly. First, hold the back of your hand near his nostrils so he can learn your scent," Micah instructed. She complied and laughed when Ramah, after a moment or two, butted her shoulder. Most women would be afraid of Ramah, but Shoshanna wasn't. *Grandfather, I wish you could see her. You would recognize right away how rare and precious she is.* Mentally, Micah still talked to his grandfather about important things, and suddenly, in the same instant he wished Shoshanna and the Rab could have met, he realized that he loved her. He wanted her for his own. His mother and father and Jerusha would love her; he knew it instinctively. Then he asked her about the anklets. Her hand paused where it had been patting Ramah's nose. She stared at him, her mouth open.

"Are they made of silver? I couldn't tell for certain in the firelight."

He watched the interesting play of emotions across her face—surprise, anger, and amusement. Her sense of humor won out. "Oh, you!" she exclaimed and playfully punched his shoulder. "Ow. What are you made of, iron?" She shook the hand that had hit him.

"I am sorry, my lady." He took her hand and gently stroked the knuckles. Her expression softened, and her big, dark eyes grew even bigger. Then she dropped her gaze and jerked her hand back.

"Yes, they are silver. But I didn't think anyone recognized me."

"You stood out. But don't worry. Only Absalom and I knew it was you, and we won't say a word to your grandfather."

She turned her beautiful smile toward him, and Micah felt his heart leap. "It was very enjoyable. I'm glad I went," she said.

"I enjoyed it too, especially your dance. Do you think you

could enjoy the simple pleasures of village life?"

"Oh, yes. Our family has a home in Giloh as well as Jerusalem, and I always prefer being there. I consider myself a village girl."

Micah, who had been studying her intently as she spoke, was very pleased with her answer. One of his chief concerns was whether Shoshanna could be happy in an out-of-the-way little village like Ziph. It seemed she could.

She took her leave a few minutes later, knowing it was not proper to spend much time with him, even outside in full view of all the inhabitants of the house. Micah reluctantly let her go. Her grandfather was already irritated with him, and he didn't want to anger him further. Micah still hoped that Shoshanna and Ahithophel were innocent visitors. He had no proof otherwise, but he had caught a few looks he didn't like being passed between Absalom and the counselor.

He could get little out of the other guests, though he tried to befriend them. It seemed that Absalom was conferring with them one at a time. All had departed by late that afternoon, and Micah knew it was time for him to leave as well. Absalom had guessed his attraction to Shoshanna, and it was likely he would think that Micah tarried in order to be near her. Still, the prince would probably become suspicious if he stayed much longer, and Joab was waiting in Jerusalem for a report. So Micah announced that he would depart the next morning.

≈   ≈   ≈

That evening the full moon rose to shine directly into the window of his room, waking him. He tossed and turned, thoughts of Joab and Absalom, Ahithophel and Shoshanna chasing each other through his head. After some time, he gave up trying to go back to sleep and decided to take a walk. He slipped into his tunic and long-sleeved cloak to guard against the chilly mountain air.

As Micah passed by the window that overlooked the veranda,

he heard voices and stopped to investigate. He looked out the window, but could not see the people who carried on the conversation. Then he realized that they must be seated in the chairs under the overhang directly below. He could hear their conversation quite distinctly.

"I tell you, the time is not right. You must have patience. Support for you is building, but there is still much to be done." The voice was Ahithophel's.

Micah's stance stiffened when he heard Absalom answer. "And I tell you, I won't wait much longer. You have seen me at Jerusalem's gate, seen how my people respond to me. You have heard what the representatives from Issachar and Manasseh have said this week. And we have no doubt at all that Benjamin will be with us."

"Shh. Never assume you can't be overheard. I will send messages to the tribes of Zebulun and Asher tomorrow, and after we get their response, we will see."

Absalom made a sound of reluctant acquiescence before asking, "You will journey from here?"

"No. I dare not risk it. The king expects me at his side, and I can do our cause the most good from Jerusalem. I will send a courier with pouches that will contain letters to the most powerful clan leaders in the northern tribes. It is best if you don't know the identity of the messenger.

"As long as it is someone who can be trusted."

"It is."

Absalom murmured something and there was a scraping of chairs and the rustling sound of movement as the two ended their conversation and went their separate ways. Micah stood rooted to the spot, his mind reeling with what he had overheard.

He could take this information back to Joab immediately, and the general might think it was enough to condemn the conspirators. But they had been circumspect in what they had said. How would Shoshanna react when she found out that he was spying on her grandfather? He fervently wished he had never been given the assignment, but his anger burned against the man whom the king had trusted all these years—a man David looked up to, whose every word was taken almost as if from heaven. In the entire kingdom, only Nathan the prophet had earned greater respect.

With Ahithophel on his side, Absalom had an incredible advantage. Micah had never before considered that Absalom could bring down the kingdom, but if the king's closest advisor had turned against him, it was a distinct possibility that there would be civil war in the near future, and that David's side might not win.

Micah also knew that if David went down, so would his father. Jonathan would fight to the death for the king, along with the other *Gibborim*. Micah prayed that none of the mighty warriors had turned traitor. That would truly break his father's heart. He thought of Joab's reaction and suddenly his heart was filled with dread. If it could be proven that Ahithophel was the strategist behind the rebellion, not only would he be executed, but it was highly possible that Joab would order his family killed as well. That would include Shoshanna. Micah made a covenant with himself to never let that happen. He would follow the courier tomorrow to find out more of the rebels' plans. Then he would make his report to Joab and try to play down Ahithophel's culpability. It would keep Joab from acting in the heat of anger, and perhaps before long Ahithophel would withdraw from this insane plot.

Chapter Seven

~

*S*hoshanna sat with her grandfather on the terrace, where he had summoned her in order to discuss "an important matter," as he had put it. "I have some very important messages in these pouches that I need you to deliver for me," he told her now. "I would go myself, but I am old, and lately I have noticed my heart pounding heavily when I exert myself too much. Besides, I need to go back to Jerusalem as soon as possible to take care of some matters there. Would you do this for me, my sweet?"

Shoshanna hesitated for a long moment, and saw Ahithophel's brows rise in surprise. She had always given him her complete obedience. She was his only heir, his only heritage, and she felt that very keenly. Not even Marah was as close to her as Grandfather, and she would do almost anything for him. But she was no longer a child, and so she asked her grandfather the questions that had been plaguing her.

"Grandfather, I inadvertently overheard something the other night that disturbed me. You and Absalom were talking. It sounded as if you were discussing a coup. Are you plotting to overthrow the king?" There, it was said, plain and to the point.

At first Ahithophel's shrewd, gray eyes flamed with anger, and she thought he was going to rebuke her for eavesdropping.

Then the flame went out and he sighed. "I shouldn't have expected I could keep you from the truth. I sought to protect you, my child. If the plans we are making do not succeed, the less you know, the better it will go for you."

He leaned forward and spoke very softly. "Even now, I will only tell you that we are sending messages throughout Israel to test the will of the people. I personally believe they will not keep David as their king much longer. There have been many abuses in his reign, as you probably know." He briefly considered telling his granddaughter the full extent of his hatred, that he had plotted and waited all these many years. But Shoshanna would be shocked, and she would worry about him. Better to minimize the extent of the rebellion.

"Do not be afraid to carry the messages. They are merely letters to some friends of mine, and nothing in them will condemn you if anyone were to find out about them. Of course, they won't, because David suspects nothing. Besides, we are only seeking to find out the will of the people at this time. Nothing of importance will happen very soon. If you are apprehended with the notes, nothing will happen to you. But if I am forced to deliver them personally, I will be suspect because of my position as the king's advisor. Now, what is your answer? Will you help me?"

Shoshanna swallowed hard. She had a terrible sense of foreboding, and she wanted no part of these activities herself. But she knew that Ahithophel was correct when he said he would be placing himself in danger to carry the messages in person. She loved her grandfather too much to allow him to do that. Still, she sought to dissuade him from this course. "Grandfather, I will help you, but will you seek the Lord's face about this matter? The king is the Lord's anointed. Maybe we should leave it to him to remove David."

Ahithophel studied his granddaughter's earnest face for a long moment before he answered. "You may seek the Lord's face, my child. I will seek the will of the people."

~ ~ ~

At noon, Micah sat hidden in the midst of a pile of boulders just off the road that led to Manasseh, where the road coming down from the mountains of Ephraim met the major route that ran north and south between the mountain and the beautiful plain of Sharon. His horse was tethered a half-mile away, under a large oak tree. Few people had passed by in the hours he was stationed there, and as the sun made its arc in the sky, there was less and less shade to shelter him. He was hot and uncomfortable. Only a startled gazelle and a few double-crested hoopoe birds sporting their brilliant colors broke the monotony.

Then the clopping hooves of a donkey caravan broke the stillness. As they neared the crossing, Micah stayed hidden, but raised up enough to get a good look at the travelers. Two women rode on donkeys, one led by an elderly servant. Both women were heavily veiled. One of them was stooped, probably as elderly as the man. Her clothing was very plain. She was undoubtedly a servant as well. The other woman was richly dressed and her feet nearly dragged the ground. She wore fine sandals, and with his sharp vision Micah could see as they passed nearby that even her toenails were rouged. It was Shoshanna. He knew it as surely as spring follows winter.

At first he felt relief. Ahithophel was sending her home. He was getting her out of harm's way before he sent his courier north. Then he would follow later, distancing her from himself and therefore the rebellion. Micah would mention in his report to Joab that Shoshanna was nowhere nearby when the courier—

What are they doing? Shoshanna and her servants turned north. *North? Maybe she is going to visit a relative somewhere in the tribe of Ephraim.* He knew it was highly unlikely. Still, he stayed in his hiding place for another hour, hoping and praying that the messenger—a man—would come down the mountain road and turn north. The sun grew hotter and Micah began to sweat from more than just the heat. He finally admitted the truth. She was Ahithophel's courier.

How could she take such risks? he thought furiously, as he stepped out onto the road and began to follow them. He wasn't concerned that they had an hour's head start. He would stay far back anyway. He did not want to be discovered. How could Ahithophel send her on such a mission? Micah had no doubt that she carried packets containing plans for insurrection. His temper seethed all day, and did not diminish when the little caravan stopped for the night. He stood in the darkness and watched their campfire. He heard the roar of a lion some distance away. There was danger in the night. Wasn't the foolish girl afraid? He followed them through much of northern Israel, and after several days, his disposition had only worsened. But he had the names of several likely conspirators.

≈ ≈ ≈

Shoshanna was pleased with herself as she started the journey home. She had delivered her grandfather's packets in three days. She had gone first to Harosheth, nestled at the foot of Mount Carmel, and had no trouble finding the intended recipient. He was a great man in the tribe of Asher, chief of his clan, and everyone knew where he lived—in the largest house in town. He had not appeared surprised to see her, but had told her nothing when she asked whether he had a return message for Ahithophel.

Next, when she entered Shimron, a little town almost in the center of the tribal lands of Zebulun, about five miles west of the Sea of Chinnereth, she was greeted warmly by Jahleel, an old man who lived very comfortably and who insisted that she stay a day in his home. He was a long-standing friend of her grandfather, and he was eager to hear all the family events that had happened in the five years since he had been to Jerusalem. Shoshanna could not refuse.

At the evening meal, she asked, "Jahleel, did my grandfather's letter contain good news?"

"Very good news, important news." He handed her a bowl of almonds. "How is your lovely mother? It was so sad for her after the death of your father. Is she still prone to despair?" Shoshanna sighed, recognizing his desire to change the subject, and answered his question. She would be no more successful in finding out the exact contents of the message here than she had been in Harosheth. Were the missives simply inquiries into the mood of the people, as her grandfather had suggested? She wasn't certain she wanted to know.

Shoshanna took her leave of Jahleel early the next morning. She was determined to reach Jerusalem before nightfall of the following day. Although things had gone smoothly, Shoshanna would feel truly safe only when she was within the walls of her grandfather's house. One night in the deserted darkness of the plain of Sharon was more than enough for her.

As she and her two servants passed through the village market, she stopped to buy fresh figs from a vendor. Beside her, two old men stood talking. "I have never seen such a man, I tell you. He was at least a head taller than any other man in these parts. Had strange eyes that looked right through you. Arms as thick as the trunk of that terebinth tree over there. And he had a mane like a lion. And that great stallion of his was as powerful as his master. The man saw me struggling to move that heavy barrel of grain and stopped to help. The barrel was full and must have weighed at least three talents, yet he lifted it as easily as I would lift a feather!"

The other man laughed. "And did you ask him where he came from? Perhaps it was an angel you spoke with." He laughed again, not believing the story for a moment. But Shoshanna stood like a statue.

"My lady, will these suffice?" Anah, her nurse since infancy, finally got her attention. "Oh, yes, Anah, I think that will be more than enough."

All day, Shoshanna thought of the description she had over-heard in the marketplace. It sounded like Micah. It had to be Micah; there was none other like him. She thought of him: tall, broad-chested, and with that shock of hair streaked by the sun. Certainly he resembled a lion. He even moved with catlike grace.

What was he doing in Shimron? It couldn't be a coincidence. His appearance at Baal Hazor had not seemed unusual given the many other visitors, but now she didn't know. She suspected it all had to do with the packets she had delivered. She didn't like the situation at all. Had her grandfather arranged for Micah to follow her to protect her? If so, why had he not told her?

Was Micah one of the men who were considering replacing King David with his son? Or was Micah a spy for the king? Surely not. If Micah was out of favor with Joab, he wouldn't be working for the king. Would he be happy to know a rebellion was underway? Perhaps not. But he might have followed her in order to make contact with the men in Shimron and Harosheth, intending to offer his services to them if a civil war broke out.

Her heart was sick. She didn't want to find out that Micah was spying on her, because that would mean that all his atten-tion toward her had merely been for the sake of getting closer to Ahithophel. She hoped it wasn't true that Ahithophel was con-spiring with the prince. Had he told her that no uprising was underway merely to put her mind at ease? She did not want to lose her grandfather. And she did not want to lose Micah. What was she thinking? Micah wasn't hers to lose.

Nevertheless, he had spoken to her grandfather about her. Ahithophel had said to Shoshanna, "We will see whether the young man asks his father to speak to me, my lily. I am not sure he is at all what he seems. You must be patient and trust your grandfather to do what is best for you. You mean more to me than ten sons." He had kissed her, and she knew she would gladly die for Ahithophel if necessary.

From the moment she overheard the conversation in the marketplace, Shoshanna continually looked behind her. She had a feeling of being watched, but she tried to tell herself it was just her imagination.

They made their camp in the shelter of an overhang of rock protected on three sides. On the open side, Anah and Gamal worked to build a fire for protection from the animals and to roast the kernels of wheat they had brought along. The sun went down and both servants rolled up in their blankets. They were no longer young and were very tired from the trip. Shoshanna regretted having pushed them so hard, but by tomorrow at sunset they would be in Giloh.

The evening was chilly and Shoshanna pulled her blanket around her shoulders, but she did not lie down, because she knew she couldn't sleep. She worried about her grandfather, about her mother, about Micah. It was a trait she knew she should try to overcome—this feeling of responsibility for everyone in her life. But it was so deeply ingrained that she doubted she could rid herself of it.

She heard the howling of a wolf, somewhere off to the north. It came from some distance away, and they were safe as long as the fire continued to burn. She leaned back against a large rock and closed her eyes. Maybe she would be able to fall asleep soon. The wolf howled again. It was answered by several howls coming from a much closer point to the south, which caused Shoshanna to open her eyes.

The fire was still sufficient, but little wood remained for stoking it. She needed to find more. Shoshanna moved out of the circle of light, looking for dried branches, hoping she would not have to go far from the camp to find enough to last until morning.

"If you continue to roam around in the dark you are likely to make a good meal for the pack." Shoshanna jumped and gave a small shriek at the sound of the quiet voice from somewhere in the darkness. Evidently, Gamal had heard the voice as well, for he called out to her.

"My lady, what happened? Where are you?'

"I am only gathering more firewood, Gamal. Go back to sleep. I won't go far."

During this interchange with her servant, Micah moved closer, and now Shoshanna hissed at him. "You frightened me."

"You need to be frightened! It's dangerous for you to wander alone in the dark of night."

"Keep your voice down. I don't want to wake my servants."

"Then come with me," Micah walked away, obviously expecting her to follow. After a moment she did. She had to find out why he had been following her. The wolves howled again and she stepped closer to Micah. He turned to face her.

"Do you wish to die young, or are you truly foolish enough to be unaware of the danger you put yourself in?"

She could feel his anger, though he spoke in a low voice. "I would not have gone far from the camp and would have called for Gamal's help if the wolves approached."

"I wasn't talking about the wolves, and you know it."

Shoshanna whirled around to start back to the campsite. Micah gripped her arm to stop her. "You can't avoid talking to me about this, so unless you want your servants to hear us, you had better stay." She shrugged free of his hold.

"What I have been doing is no concern of yours!"

"It is my concern if you carry messages advocating rebellion. If you really care about your grandfather, you will persuade him to distance himself from Absalom before it's too late."

Shoshanna felt like crying. Her suspicions had been true. Micah was a spy for the king. He did not truly care for her, as she had begun to hope during their time at Baal Hazor. If he was her grandfather's enemy, out to prove him a traitor, he was also her enemy. Her hurt changed to anger.

"I don't know what you're talking about. The messages were to two of my grandfather's old friends. I didn't look at the contents. Unlike you, I do not meddle in other people's affairs, and I don't pretend to befriend them only to find a means to betray them."

He took her arm again, not too gently. "I never 'pretended' to be your friend. And I am not in the business of betrayal. But I would seek to protect the king from those who seek to harm him. This isn't a game, Shoshanna. Let this be the last time they use you as a courier." The moon appeared from behind a cloud and reflected in his golden eyes, which now glinted with anger and determination. For the first time, she was afraid of him.

To mask her fear, she tried to yank free of him again, but he wouldn't release her arm. "Let me go," she hissed sharply.

He stared hard at her for another moment before letting his hand drop. "I will help you gather some sticks to place on the fire, but then I want you to go back to camp and get some rest. I will be nearby, and the wolves won't bother you."

They gathered sticks in silence for a few moments. Then Micah placed his bundle in her arms. He didn't even touch her, but she felt her heart race at his nearness. "Nothing I said to you at Baal Hazor was a lie, Shoshanna. No matter what happens, believe that, at least." Even in the moonlight she could see the look of supplication in his eyes. She dropped her eyes from his piercing gaze, but nodded her head. Then she spun around and hurried back to the shelter of the rocks and the fire. As she huddled beneath her blanket, sleep eluded her. She told herself it was because she could still hear the wolves calling to each other, and stared into the darkness until she finally nodded off.

When she woke just after dawn, there was no sign of Micah, and she did not see him again on the trip to Giloh.

≈ ≈ ≈

Micah agonized over how he would word his report to Joab. He didn't want to mention the messages that had gone out to Harosheth and Shimron, but he knew he must. He could not betray his mission, nor his king, by withholding the information. Even as he was shown into the common room of Joab's villa, located just outside Jerusalem's walls, Micah wasn't certain what he would say.

"You have a report for me, son of Jonathan?" The general's obsidian eyes stared, unblinking, as he gestured to a chair across from his own.

Micah took a deep breath. "Yes, my lord, I believe I have evidence of a conspiracy. But I am not certain it is enough yet to convince the king."

"Tell me everything."

As soon as he was seated, Micah revealed the most important piece of information. "I have discovered that Ahithophel is conspiring with Absalom." Micah had never seen the general unnerved, but for a moment Joab paled and was speechless. Then he rose and began to pace the room while he muttered curses under his breath. "This is not good. With Ahithophel as their advisor, Absalom's men might gain the victory."

"But surely those who remain loyal to the king far outnumber the malcontents," Micah offered hopefully.

"I'm no longer convinced of that. Many of the common people believe the king taxes them too heavily and that he is unconcerned about their needs."

"But the army . . ."

Joab shook his head. "Of the Pelethites and Cherethites and the *Gibborim* I am certain. The rank and file is another matter. We cannot waste time. We must squelch this rebellion before it boils over. Now tell me everything that happened in Baal Hazor."

In the end, he reported not only the conversation he had overheard between Ahithophel and Absalom, but also their plan to use Shoshanna as a messenger. He emphasized that, in her grandfather's own words, Shoshanna knew nothing about the conspiracy. "I followed her, sir. She took messages to several men in the north. Here is a list of them."

Joab studied the small parchment for a moment before speaking. "You merely followed her? Why not confiscate the messages from the girl, maybe even force her to talk? She may know more than you think."

Before Micah could answer, the general smiled. "You were right not to reveal your purpose to the girl. Instead, pretend an interest in her, maybe pay a visit to Ahithophel's home in Giloh and gain the confidence of both of them. Without more evidence, we can't go to the king and accuse his son and his most valued counselor. It would be your word against theirs. We need something more tangible," Joab explained.

Micah was reeling from the general's words. He had no need to "pretend" an interest in Shoshanna. He already had an interest. But if he asked to be excused from involvement, the general might suspect him as one of the conspirators. He couldn't tell Joab that he cared for Shoshanna. But if he found out on his own, Joab would be furious. He forced himself to listen to what the general was saying.

"You need to observe both men and the girl closely from now on. I have heard that Absalom is planning some kind of gathering. I want you to find out what it is. The prince and Ahithophel returned to the palace yesterday. You can watch them both. I will station men at Giloh and Baal Hazor to report on them when they are not in Jerusalem, and to try to intercept the messages they spoke of sending. If we can get something in writing, we can go to David with it."

Micah didn't want Joab's servants intercepting Shoshanna if she was foolish enough to ignore his warnings. "General, I will look into the matter. I won't rest until I find written proof of a conspiracy. You needn't tie up other men on this assignment."

"Your cunning surprises me, young fox. You are more competent than I expected you to be. Very well, for now I will let you handle this alone. After this matter is brought to an end you may not only be accepted back into the army, you may be placed in a position of great responsibility. But written proof isn't necessarily needed. If events unfold too quickly for you to get word back to me, just do what you can to persuade our fellow Judahites to stand with us. It will be an opportunity for you to prove yourself worthy in war."

"Thank you, General," Micah responded, knowing that accolades of any kind from Joab were rare. As he left, Micah felt unworthy of the general's praise. He had refused help in order to protect Shoshanna when he should have accepted it for the king's sake. He felt terribly guilty that he had implicated Shoshanna, even as an unwitting accomplice. He prayed that his words would not somehow place her in danger. He hoped that Joab had been sincere in assuring him that he could investigate on his own.

≈ ≈ ≈

It took only two days to find out what Absalom was planning. The prince made no secret of it. Micah had followed him in the city market the next morning. The prince had only three of his bodyguards with him when he stopped at the booth of a Phoenician scribe. As soon as the prince left, Micah spoke to the man.

"Do you sell ink and parchment?"

"The very best of both, my lord. I import them from Egypt and Tyre. What quantity did you require?"

Micah ordered a large quantity of parchment, two pots of ink, one red and one black, and an expensively carved stylus. He paid the merchant with a gold coin. The man was duly impressed. "If you need the services of a scribe at any time, my lord, don't hesitate to call on me. I am the best in Jerusalem."

"I assumed that when I saw the prince stopping by. Did he order parchment?"

"No, he did not buy ink or parchment. He hired me to send out invitations to a feast he is holding in Hebron two weeks from now. I am to see them all delivered by the day after tomorrow. See, here is the message and here is the list. It must contain two hundred names. I will be working very hard for the next two days."

When the man went behind a curtain to fill his order, Micah read the invitation. It sounded innocuous enough. The prince planned to make burnt offerings in Hebron in thanks that Adonai had reunited him with his father. There would be a feast following, to which the recipient was invited.

He rolled up the list of names and slid it inside his tunic. The poor man would be frantic when he discovered it missing. He would have to face Absalom's anger when he asked for another list, but Micah couldn't waste time with pity. He had to study the list.

Absalom was sending invitations to more than two hundred of Jerusalem's wealthiest and most respected citizens. Most were Hebrew, but some were members of the original Jebusite aristocracy that had been in power when David captured Jerusalem nearly thirty years before. In a characteristic display of mercy, David had allowed these families to keep their wealth and status in the city. How many of them would now repay him by going over to Absalom?

After studying the list, Micah sought out his father in the *House of the Gibborim*. "You knew I would be here?" Jonathan asked.

Micah nodded. "I knew that Joab was recalling all of the *Gibborim* to Jerusalem. He told me so before he sent me on an assignment."

"What assignment? I haven't seen you in many weeks, though we did get your message that you were going to Damascus. Are you back in favor, then, with Joab and the army?"

Micah had been so preoccupied with recent events that he had forgotten he had not seen his father since before his assignment to Damascus. "I have much to tell you, Father. And I need your counsel. Can we find a private place to talk?"

They went into a small room that contained only a bench and a table, but it perfectly suited their need for privacy. Jonathan took a seat on the bench while Micah perched a hip on the table. Micah shared most of what had occurred over the past weeks—his trip to Damascus and Rezon's unexpected softening toward Ailea, as well as his most recent assignment.

"I knew Joab was worried. He tacitly announced his concern by recalling all the *Gibborim*. In briefing us, he has hinted that we may have to put down a rebellion. I assume these things are not to be spoken of as yet."

"No, they are not, because we haven't gathered enough proof yet to present to the king." He handed the list to his father. "Tell me what you make of this."

Jonathan read in silence for several moments. "It looks like a social gathering. I know many of these men. They are merchants, scribes, traders. They are doing very well under David's administration. I see no insurrection here," he finally said.

"Neither did I. The list is made up of people who have prospered under David's reign. I would have suspected Absalom to court malcontents. Why would Absalom invite these people to Hebron if he is planning a coup there?"

Jonathan's brows drew together as he contemplated. "Maybe the list is meant as a smoke screen to allay David's suspicions, and perhaps Joab's as well. Or maybe he plans to take these men away from Jerusalem so they won't be in residence to offer support to David once the rebellion starts."

Micah nodded his agreement. "I also had considered the possibility that Absalom will woo them while they are in Hebron, offering them rewards if they come over to his cause. The truth is likely a combination of all three motives."

"So you agree with Joab when he says that a rebellion is imminent?"

"I can't help but agree, Father, after what I've seen. Messages have been flying between Giloh, where Ahithophel lives, and Baal Hazor, where Absalom spends much of his time. And Ahithophel sent several messages to small cities in Asher and Zebulun. He used Shoshanna, his own granddaughter, to deliver them! Both recipients wield power in the north."

"You say they are using a girl to convey their messages? Ahithophel must not care for her much, to place her in such danger. Why did you not intercept this Shoshanna and take the letters away from her?"

Micah's face flushed at the question. That was exactly what he should have done. "I wanted to see who they were meant for and what took place after the messages were received. Shoshanna is not part of the conspiracy, Father. I confronted her after the deliveries were made, and she did not know what the messages contained. I want this ended before she gets into serious trouble."

Jonathan scrutinized his son for several minutes. "You care about this woman, don't you?"

Micah didn't answer, but his silence was enough to tell Jonathan all he needed to know. "You care about her and wish to protect her. Just don't let Joab catch her carrying treasonous messages. He would not hesitate to kill anyone, even a helpless girl. Your mother almost lost her life because of him. Don't let Shoshanna fall into Joab's hands if you care for her at all."

Micah paused for a long moment. "You can be sure I will see that no harm will come to her, Father. I have known her such a short time, yet she is already precious to me."

"Son, there is one other thing you must consider. The young lady may be deceiving you, using you in Absalom's cause."

"That is not possible," Micah responded heatedly.

Jonathan held up a conciliatory hand. "I am not accusing her, I am simply raising a question. If you believe you can trust her, then you are probably right. The Lord knows there was a time when I didn't trust your mother, and I later regretted it very much."

Seeking to avoid further questions on the subject of Shoshanna, Micah turned to other matters. "What will you do now that the council has met? Will you stay here in Jerusalem?"

Jonathan nodded. "We are here on alert. But I will try to return to Ziph for a short while, to explain to your mother and try to see that the elders do not rebel against the Lord's anointed if it comes to war. They turned against David once before, you know, when he was hiding from old King Saul. They sent a message to let Saul know his whereabouts. The Rab tried to talk sense to them, but they would have none of it. So your grandfather sent me to warn David. I was fourteen at the time. I've been his man ever since."

"Surely after all these years of loyalty to David, the men of Ziph won't betray their king now, Father."

Jonathan shrugged. "How anyone could prefer that vain, arrogant puppy over his father is a mystery to me, but we should never underestimate the power of Absalom's charm. You have seen him at the city gates, currying favor with the people, subtly undermining his father. Without the Rab to advise them, the men of Ziph could easily be led astray. I must try to head off that possibility."

"Grandfather is sorely missed at a time like this," Micah reflected somberly.

"Adonai will raise up a man to take his place, my son." Jonathan's frank appraisal was not lost on Micah.

"It will be a man older and infinitely wiser than I am, Father." Jonathan did not argue, but asked Micah what his plans were.

"I will go to Hebron, and perhaps attend Absalom's celebration. I have put the word out that I am still unhappy with the king and with Joab about being sent home in disgrace some months ago. And I have suggested that they did not appreciate the work I did for them in Damascus. I'm hoping that Absalom's people believe I can easily be persuaded to join their side. I should be safe enough in Hebron."

"Ha! You will be in the midst of your enemies. Only Isaac can be trusted. Remember that, Micah. Better to be at the forefront of the battle than to be the king's spy in Hebron," he said.

Micah shrugged. "I go where the king sends me, Father; but I will be careful. I left the prince with the impression that I favor him, although I have not been taken into his confidence yet. Perhaps we are all wrong about a rebellion being imminent. Maybe this is simply his way of showing discontent, and nothing will come of it."

"I hope you are right. In the meantime, guard yourself well, my son."

Chapter Eight

~

*A*bsalom's entourage entered Hebron with much greater fanfare than his father had some thirty years earlier when he had first been proclaimed king by his fellow Judahites. David and his men had still looked the part of desert marauders after their years of running from King Saul and his army. The Hebronites resented David for moving his capital from their town after ruling there for seven years. Now they saw a chance to regain their former glory. As soon as they saw Absalom, many began to talk openly of putting the son on his father's throne.

Absalom wore a wide-skirted, pleated tunic, and his attendants were resplendent with the trappings of royalty. Adorning his neck was a heavy gold collar and his right hand flashed with a signet ring set with a ruby the size of a ripe grape. His long-sleeved mantle was iridescent blue, matching the peacock feathers attached to its train. Absalom's chariot was preceded by his usual contingent of fifty footmen.

He was escorted to a villa, the second home of a wealthy Jerusalem merchant who was unable to attend the festivities. The house sat on a hillside in the elite part of the city and offered a view across town to the famous Cave of Machpelah, the burial place of Abraham and Jacob.

Nearby was the home of Isaac ben Ahiam. Absalom had heard him spoken of in the city market as one of the most successful caravaners in Israel. Absalom remembered seeing him at the palace shortly after Isaac's father was killed. Ahiam was one of David's mighty men, fallen in battle more than fifteen years earlier. Absalom was aware that Isaac harbored resentment against both David and Joab for the death of his father. Ahiam had been in the phalanx of soldiers sent on David's orders to fight directly under the city wall of Rabbah. When the battle had turned, Ahiam had died alongside Uriah the Hittite, Bathsheba's husband.

Everyone in Israel knew that David had sacrificed his own men to cover up his affair with Bathsheba. David had admitted as much several months later when confronted by Nathan the prophet. Absalom's own resentment of his father began in earnest around that time, because his father no longer honored Maacah, his mother, as his favored wife, but had replaced her with Bathsheba.

Surely, Absalom thought, *Isaac also must hate the king and would likely join the rebellion against him.* "Send an invitation to the merchant Isaac, son of Ahiam, to join us tomorrow in the offering of a sacrifice and the feast following," he told his servant as soon as he had settled in his villa.

No one overtly mentioned an uprising the following day, but rumors were rife in the city. Absalom, with much fanfare, went to the Cave of Machpelah to pray at the tomb of the patriarchs. As soon as this ceremony was completed, he had one of his servants summon Isaac to his side.

"I have heard of your success in the caravan trade, Isaac ben Ahiam. It is a pity your father could not be alive to see how you have prospered. Killed in battle at Rabbah, was he not?"

Isaac looked into Absalom's handsome face and saw hatred and cunning and ruthless ambition. There was no doubt he was testing the extent of Isaac's grudge against the king. But no matter how much he resented the king, he would not support the prince.

Not now. Not ever. He smiled and gave an innocuous answer, hoping Absalom would not guess his true feelings. Apparently, Hebron would soon be under Absalom's complete control, and Isaac knew that the prince would not hesitate to destroy anyone he believed to be an enemy.

So for the sake of his mother, Judith, his wife, Keziah, and his twin sons, Hanani and Nebat, Isaac made up his mind to feign friendliness to the prince. At the same time, he sent a message of warning to his friend Jonathan ben Shageh. Jonathan would fight to the death for David, there was no doubt about it. Isaac's heart clenched at the thought of the king's forces being defeated.

≈ ≈ ≈

Micah stood on the fringes of the crowd that had gathered for the prince's public offering of ten bullocks. On either side of Hebron's altar of sacrifice stood two priests, each with the help of a Levite to steady the cattle, ready to cut the throats of the animals with a special ceremonial knife that was sharp enough to cause death without suffering. The process was repeated five times, until all ten animals had been killed, their blood collected in the ceremonial bowls, and the meat burned as an offering to Adonai.

By the time the offering was done and the feast of celebration was underway, Micah had spotted three of Joab's men planted in the crowd. He knew who they were, because he had seen them briefly at Joab's house. Micah supposed they had been chosen because Absalom would not know their connection to Joab. He couldn't very well have sent his armor bearers; Absalom's men would have recognized them immediately.

Why were they here? Didn't Joab trust him to observe events and report back? Was he merely being cautious and sending these men to back up Micah if needed? Or did he think Micah might defect? These questions plagued him as the revelry increased. But his main concern was that Shoshanna might be caught by these men with one of her grandfather's dispatches. If she was, these men would show no mercy. He had to protect her and at the same time carry out his mission. It wouldn't be an easy task, because she considered him an enemy now. He prayed that Ahithophel had been cautious and left her at Giloh. She didn't need to be in Jerusalem or Hebron right now.

∾ ∾ ∾

Micah spotted Ahithophel in the crowd and followed him back to the wealthy merchant's villa, taking care not to be seen. It was getting dark by this time, and Micah stood in the deepening shadows outside the house, trying to determine whether Ahithophel had brought Shoshanna with him. He had no idea what he would say if someone caught him skulking here. It was possible that Shoshanna would tell her grandfather he was a spy. She loved Ahithophel, and she had been very angry at their last meeting.

Regardless, he had to protect her. A quarter hour passed before he saw her appear briefly in a window of the second story of the house. Micah was so furious that he would have gladly shaken the remaining teeth out of Ahithophel's head. He had brought his granddaughter along to use her. There was nothing Micah could do. He would do his best to look out for Shoshanna's safety as well as his own. He turned and slipped quietly toward the household of Isaac ben Ahiam, where he would stay.

When he entered the home of his father's friend, the entire family was together on the rooftop watching events unfold. People with torches were still celebrating in the streets. An air of expectancy hovered in the city.

"The family of Isaac ben Ahiam is not celebrating, I see," Micah said after giving the customary greetings from his family and answering questions about the health of his parents, sister, and aunt. Isaac had once been Jonathan's armor bearer, so the families had long been close.

"We see no cause for celebration, Micah," Isaac spoke openly in front of his family. "Things are progressing so rapidly now that they can't be turned back. I sent a message to your father yesterday to warn him that a rebellion is coming, but I had no idea it would be this soon."

"Tell me everything you know," Micah said as the two men stood at the balustrade of the rooftop and watched the throngs mingle and celebrate by torchlight.

≈ ≈ ≈

The next morning, a steady stream of armed men poured into Hebron. The city elders made no secret of their welcome for the growing army. Talk of impending war could easily be heard on the streets, although these comments were still made in lowered voices, the speaker's eyes darting about as if afraid of being overheard.

Micah assumed that the three spies Joab had sent would report these activities to the general. He was tempted to stay in Hebron to see that Shoshanna was not in danger, but knowing it was his duty to return to Jerusalem, he headed for the capital with all possible speed, pushing Ramah to fly through the hills as swiftly as an eagle.

Micah dreaded telling the king of his son's treachery, but he knew now beyond a shadow of a doubt that within a matter of days, Absalom would declare himself king in Hebron. What disturbed Micah most was the extent of the rebellion. According to Isaac, runners would go, maybe even in a matter of hours, to the northern tribes to call rebel forces to join Absalom's army. And according to Jonathan, many in the militia, the civilian troops, would go over to the prince's side as soon as he made his move.

≈ ≈ ≈

Arriving in Jerusalem at midday, Micah went directly to the palace steward and demanded a private audience with the king.

Although his father's investigation had shown that the core of David's best men would remain loyal, Micah wanted to take no chances that anyone other than David and Joab heard his report. Micah had no illusions about the character of the general, but one thing was certain: Joab was first and foremost David's man. His loyalty was total.

The room he was shown into had only one door, and no windows. It was well lighted by wall torches, even though it was daytime. He had never seen or heard his father speak of the room. It was obviously meant to afford the greatest degree of privacy. There were several chairs and couches upholstered in bright colors. In the center of the room, Joab and David were sitting in plush cushions, legs folded, before a low table that held goblets, flasks of wine, as well as fruit and bread.

"Come and join us, son of Jonathan," the king invited, gesturing with a hunk of crusty bread he had just dipped into a small bowl of olive oil seasoned with rosemary. "Joab and I have been so busy today that this is the first chance we have had to eat. You must be hungry as well. You came all the way from Hebron, did you not?"

Micah seated himself, folding his long legs as best he could. "I came as quickly as possible, my lord. I am afraid I bring distressing news."

The king paused in chewing his food. "I know you have been following the activities of my son. If there is bad news in that regard, it will come as no surprise, so tell it quickly."

"The king's son has arranged to declare himself king in Hebron within a day or two. Messengers are set to take the word to all the northern tribes as well. According to my source, most of the militia will follow him."

Joab growled a curse as the king's face went white. After looking to Joab to deny the accusation, David asked, "Who is your source, and how has he come by this knowledge?"

Micah was careful in his answer. Isaac would be in deep trouble unless both the king and the general were convinced that he was truly on their side. Micah knew that, in times past, Isaac had criticized the king. While David was forgiving in nature, Joab most certainly was not.

"It was Isaac of Hebron, the son of Ahiam, one of your most loyal warriors. The rebels came to him, thinking to persuade him to join them. He determined he could best serve the king by pretending to go along with them. We were correct in assuming that most, if not all, the two hundred guests from Jerusalem are not part of the conspiracy. Five of these men are guests of my friend, Isaac. He questioned each of them privately, and is certain of their loyalty, my lord."

"But are we certain of *his*?" Joab's eyes were dark and brooding.

"Isaac ben Ahiam has never been other than honest in his dealings with me, Joab. Years ago, when he had a complaint against me, he brought it to my face. We are no longer in a position to reject the offered help of someone as powerful and rich as Isaac. Thank him for me, Micah. We need no further discussions about this matter." Joab scowled but had no choice but to drop the subject.

The next morning, the king received further reports that entire towns were declaring loyalty to the prince, not only in Judah and Benjamin, but in the farthest northern tribes as well. Jonathan returned from Ziph with the discouraging news that the most he had been able to do was persuade the elders not to declare for either side. But if all the neighboring villages went over to the prince, Jonathan could not guarantee that the men of Ziph wouldn't follow.

He talked to Micah about their village. "What they are lacking is leadership. If I had been able to stay longer, I'm sure I could have persuaded them to change their minds. They need a student of the Torah, like you, to speak to them with wisdom."

Micah blew out a breath. "Father, they are far less likely to listen to me than to you. I am half Aramean and I have no gray in my beard." Jonathan didn't argue, but his face was a picture of disappointment. Micah put a hand on his shoulder. "But to honor you and Grandfather, I will try when I have completed my mission for the king."

"That is all I ask, Micah," Jonathan told him.

David made plans to leave Jerusalem immediately. Micah was to return to Hebron and pretend to side with the rebels so that he could make periodic reports on developments there and in the rest of the hill country. "Take care, Micah," David admonished. "Hebron has become a dangerous place for my supporters. If you must flee, take care to preserve your life, and join us again." Micah left with an aching heart for the sixty-year-old ruler. Though his body looked more fit than his years would indicate, sorrow had etched the visage of a much older man into his handsome face.

≈ ≈ ≈

Ahithophel asked Shoshanna to walk with him in the quiet garden of their host. "I am leaving Hebron today, Shoshanna, but I don't want you to go with me. You are an intelligent maiden, Granddaughter, and I'm certain you have noticed a gathering of troops here over the last few days."

"Absalom is trying to take his father's throne." Shoshanna made it a statement, not a question.

"He will do more than try. All Israel is with us. In a short time he will be declared king in Hebron. You have seen with your own eyes how many men have already joined themselves to his cause."

Shoshanna felt her heart beat faster. She had never questioned Ahithophel's judgment. "You told me that you were testing the mood of the people. I never expected this to happen so soon."

"Neither did I, honestly. I had no idea of the degree of support Absalom has among the people. The dissatisfaction of the people with David is widespread; otherwise, we wouldn't be attempting a rebellion."

"Why do you not support the king, Grandfather?"

He stared at her for a long moment, as if debating whether to speak openly. "I stopped supporting the king years ago, when he debauched my granddaughter, made her an adulteress. And when he murdered Uriah, the only male heir left to me. True, he was only a grandson-in-law, but what a magnificent man he was. Losing him was almost like losing Eliam again. I never forgave David for his death. I never will."

"But all these years you've been his most trusted counselor. You have aided him."

"It is very difficult to avenge yourself on a king. I had to gain his trust, allay suspicions. Your mother's refusal to see Bathsheba hindered my plans. I tried to get her to change her mind, to forgive her niece."

Shoshanna was shocked at Ahithophel's blindness and hypocrisy. He would have Marah extend forgiveness while he himself preserved an unforgiving heart. "So my mother is not a part of this?" She thought she knew the answer, but she had to ask.

"No, my dear. But she will be glad to see David suffer, believe me."

Shoshanna was not so certain. True, Marah held an old grudge, but Shoshanna knew her mother, and believed that she would draw the line at seeing blood shed in a quest for vengeance.

"Shoshanna, I must ask something of you one more time. There are messages that must reach the villages close to Giloh. I would take them myself, but I will be needed in Jerusalem, and I have several places to visit before I go to the capital." He reached in his girdle and withdrew a cloth bag. After opening the drawstring, he withdrew a potsherd. "I have written these messages on pieces of broken pottery so that they might be smashed if you believe you are about to be caught with them. All I will tell you about the messages are the names of the people to whom they are to be delivered. I want you to promise me you won't look at the messages. That way, if you are caught, you can truly say that you didn't know what was in the packets. Will you do this for me, Shoshanna?"

Shoshanna licked her dry lips and cleared her throat before answering. "What would happen if I did not?"

"Then I would be very disappointed, and in great danger, because I would have to deliver them myself. If I am caught, I will surely be executed. If you are caught, nothing will be done to you because you are only a young woman, doing her grandfather's bidding."

Shoshanna had known all along that she couldn't refuse. She reached out her hand for the bag.

≈ ≈ ≈

Micah tethered his horse inside an old, deserted shed that stood beside a farmer's abandoned watchtower, then stationed himself in the tower. Landowners built these towers to keep would-be thieves away from their flocks or fields. The field he chose was newly planted in barley, so there was no need to set a watchman. Micah knew he would not be discovered here and it was an ideal place to keep watch, because he could see both of the main roads that led into Hebron.

If Absalom planned to use Hebron as his base, he would have to send messengers to let the other rebels know when he was ready to openly declare himself. Micah planned to intercept as many of them as possible to question them about Absalom's plans. He ought to turn them over to Joab, but that thought made him ill. All of Israel knew about Joab's ruthlessness. He also feared that one of the conspirators might implicate Shoshanna if forced to appear before Joab. Micah turned his thoughts to the other assignment he had to fulfill. He was supposed to muster as many men from southern Judah as possible and join the king's troops in Mahanaim. But first things first. He wrapped his cloak more tightly around himself to keep out the chill, and settled in to keep watch.

The lamps of Hebron were extinguished one by one over the next two hours until the entire city was dark. It was nearly midnight when Micah saw three men making their way from the north, down the road from Jerusalem. Why were they traveling this late at night? Did they bring a message to Absalom? Had they gotten wind of a rebellion and come to offer their services? Micah had been looking for couriers leaving Hebron. He hadn't thought about messengers entering the city.

As he pondered whether to accost them, the three cut across the field directly toward him and stopped right under his hiding place. "Should we keep a lookout from atop the tower?" Micah recognized the same three loyalist soldiers he had seen in the marketplace. They discussed the issue for a few minutes before the apparent leader said, "No. The general told us to cover the city. We should do that first. Then you and Temah can come back here, and I'll keep watch in Hebron."

Micah watched the three head to the city. Evidently Joab had not trusted him to handle the job alone. Maybe the general thought he might go to the other side. Micah settled in to wait for Joab's men to return. He would not reveal himself unless he had to.

≈ ≈ ≈

Shoshanna secured a pouch inside her girdle, containing the messages she was to carry. She pulled on a woolen hooded cloak, chosen because it was her warmest and was dark brown. She would be able to travel without being seen. She decided against using a mount. An animal would make noise, and she didn't know whether Joab would have spies out tonight. From what she knew of the man, he would not give up without a fight. She told herself that Hebron was now under Absalom's control, and that much of southern Judah had gone over to him. She should be in little danger.

She was to take the communiqués to three villages of southern Judea—Debir, Adoraim, and Lachish. After delivering the last message, she was to return to Giloh and await her grandfather.

After that, she hoped the situation would resolve itself quickly. It appeared that Absalom would indeed become king over Israel. A tremendous number of supporters had joined him at Hebron, and Grandfather believed that similar numbers were waiting for a call to arms in towns and villages throughout the nation.

Her thoughts went to Micah. He had known what was coming, even before she had admitted it to herself. His father would fight for the king, of course. But what about Micah? Which side would he be on? If he indeed fought for David, and she sensed that he would, she hoped he would come through the battle unscathed. Perhaps the prince would be lenient with the loyalists when he came to power.

Perhaps Grandfather would not hold it against Micah that he had remained loyal to David. In time, maybe he would look favorably on Micah as a suitor. Shoshanna sighed. The question, of course, was whether Micah would still be interested in marrying her. Then a worse thought entered her mind. *What if Micah was lying when he insisted he wasn't using me?* But if he were lying, why had he merely followed her? If he had no feelings for her, why had he not confiscated the messages and turned her over to Joab? *He must care at least a little, or he would not have let me go,* she concluded.

She nervously left Hebron, startled when she passed three men in the street. They stared hard at her, but she continued on as though she didn't notice. Surely they weren't David's men. Oh, how she hated carrying these messages. But what could she do? She had to help her grandfather. He would be the one who would lose his life if he were caught. She was certain that the king would be merciful to a woman.

She knelt behind a thick bush for several moments and waited. Soon she saw two men coming along the road behind her. Were these the same men she had seen earlier? *They can't be,* she argued with herself. She had seen three men in town. Now there were two. What if the trio had split up and the third man was circling around to trap her? Her heart began to pound. The two were coming closer. She scurried to another bush and when the clouds obscured the moonlight, she ran into a deserted watchtower.

Micah had been at his post in the watchtower for an hour and all had remained quiet. Not a single animal or human had passed by. Then Micah saw a dark, cloaked figure approaching from the direction of the city. The person did not walk along the road, but stayed within the fields, sometimes crouching for a moment behind a large bush before continuing. Movement on the road caught his attention, and Micah saw two more shadowy figures leaving the city. Something told Micah they were in pursuit of the furtive person he had been watching. Before he could think any further, the fugitive stood up and ran straight for the watchtower.

Shoshanna groped her way up the staircase that wound around the outside of the tower. She was thankful that clouds still covered the moon. When she reached the top, an arm snaked around her waist. Her scream was muffled by a large hand that covered her mouth.

"You little fool. I told you to stop your spying before you got into deep trouble." Shoshanna should have been terrified by the furious whisper and by the size of her captor, but instead she was relieved, because she knew it was Micah who held her. No matter how angry he might be, he would never hurt her.

"If you promise you won't scream, I'll let go of your mouth," he said in a low voice.

She nodded vigorously and he dropped his hand from her face while continuing to hold her firmly at the waist. She tried to spin from his grasp while blustering, "How do you know I am spying? I mean, I'm not spying. I'm merely going back to Giloh."

"Keep your voice down. You're being followed. And never lie to me, Shoshanna. You are up to your neck in sedition, and if you aren't careful, you will get yourself killed."

"I have no idea what is in the messages, so leave me alone!" she hissed.

"Shh. Take off your cloak." Micah put his mouth right next to her ear and whispered this instruction very softly. When Shoshanna hesitated, trying to comprehend, he tugged at the hooded cloak. "Hurry! They are about to find us."

He threw her cloak on the floor and pushed her down on it. Then he opened a skin of wine that he carried, took a swig, then sprinkled it liberally on himself and Shoshanna. "Lie down," he hissed. She obeyed and he came down beside her, pulled her close, pillowing her head on his arm and drew his own cloak around them until she was completely covered. She felt smothered and a little frightened at being held so closely by Micah, but squirming merely caused him to tighten his hold, so she forced herself to be still.

She heard the two men whispering as they climbed the tower steps. They carried a torch. She could see its brightness behind her eyelids. Micah stirred as if just awakening. "What are you doing here?" His voice sounded rough, as if he had been asleep, and slightly slurred, she supposed, to convince the men that they had partaken liberally of the wine and were under its influence.

"We are envoys for the king. What are *you* doing here?" The man shined the light closer to them, and Shoshanna did not know what to do, so she continued to pretend to be asleep. She felt Micah sit up, effectively blocking off the light, and the view the warriors had of her.

"I am resting here with my woman. We have traveled far and are tired." He did not stand up. Joab's men would almost certainly recognize him by his size if he did.

"Did you see anyone pass by? It might have been either a man or a woman."

"No one has been here but us," Micah answered quite truthfully.

The man grunted. "Let's go. He probably took the road to Adoraim."

Shoshanna lay still, her heart continuing to pound as the two went on their way, talking quietly. Micah sat still for several more minutes. Then he reached down to the girdle around Shoshanna's waist and removed the bag.

"Stop it! That is mine. Give it back to me." She tried to snatch it back, but he kept her at bay with one arm while he withdrew one of the potsherds and squinted at it in the moonlight. Then he put it back in the bag and tucked the messages into his own girdle with his free hand.

"Your days as a secret messenger are over, Shoshanna. I am taking you to the home of my friend Isaac."

"I will sneak away as soon as you leave."

"And what good will that do? I thought you didn't know the contents of the messages."

"I don't," she had to admit. The moon had come out and they glared at each other in the pale light. Then sudden tears welled in her eyes. "You don't understand, Micah. My first duty is to my grandfather. He asked me to carry these messages. If I didn't, he would have to do it himself or hire someone else. Either choice could mean ruin for him. I won't risk his life!"

"And what about your own, Shoshanna? What about your duty to your king? Has Absalom's handsome face and winning smile beguiled you, as it has the residents of Hebron? Are you taking sides against the Lord's anointed?"

"No . . . I . . . I don't know. If it is going to happen, I want my grandfather to stay safe. Besides, Absalom isn't completely evil. You have seen for yourself that he has a kind, compassionate side."

Micah snorted. "You mean his care of Tamar and Chileab? They offer no threat to his claim to the throne. But if he takes the kingdom, what do you think will happen to David's other sons? Remember what he did to Amnon. I know you will say it was solely to avenge Tamar, but Amnon was also heir to the throne. All the royal offspring will be in danger if Absalom is successful, especially Solomon, because he is obviously the king's favorite. One of the first people slaughtered will be your cousin's son, Shoshanna. Do you want to see that happen?"

As he spoke, he gripped her upper arms in both hands. She winced. "You're hurting me." He immediately dropped his hands to his sides, then removed two pieces of flint from his girdle and lit a small clay lamp that sat atop the wall.

He pushed up the sleeves of her tunic, first one, then the other.

"I bruised you. I didn't mean to do that." He gently rubbed her arms.

"I'm not really hurt."

"Not this time. But if you continue on this course, you will be. I have to put a stop to it, Shoshanna. Come."

This time he didn't grab her arm. He used gentle pressure at her waist to guide her down the stairs, along the road, and back into the city. As they entered Hebron, the third warrior, whom Micah had seen earlier, stopped them. As Micah had surmised, he had stayed in the city to keep an eye on what happened there.

"Who are you, and what business have you at this time of night?" the warrior challenged.

"I am Micah, son of Jonathan of Ziph, and I was sent by Joab." Micah drew himself up to his full height and spoke in a gruff voice that was full of authority. The other man backed down.

A few moments later, Micah was pounding at the gate of Isaac's house. A sleepy manservant opened it. He took one look at Micah and immediately obeyed his command to wake his master.

Shoshanna had been born to a wealthy family and had been in the homes of some of Israel's wealthiest people, as well as the king's palace and Absalom's home. But the grandeur of Isaac's home was stunning, even to her. The courtyard where they stood contained a beautiful fountain and was paved with vivid mosaic tiles in deep blue and white. Shoshanna noticed the lofty columns that flanked the portals to the living quarters.

Isaac appeared at one of the upstairs windows a few minutes later. He was apologetic. "Ira shouldn't have made you wait out here. Come inside. The night air is cold."

"I apologize for disturbing your rest, Isaac, but I needed to get Shoshanna to a place of safety and I thought of you," Micah explained. "She is the granddaughter of Ahithophel, David's counselor, and there are people who seek to harm her. I will place her under your protection if you will consent."

Shoshanna stepped from Micah's side. "I am under my grandfather's protection, and I demand to be taken to him!" She directed her comments to Isaac, who shifted his gaze back and forth between Shoshanna and Micah. He did not exactly look sympathetic, but she did have his attention, so she continued. "My grandfather is Ahithophel of Giloh, advisor to the king. The house where we are guests is no more than a short walk from here. If you will kindly spare one of your manservants to go with me, I will not impose further on your hospitality." She took another step toward the middle-aged man with the high cheekbones and warm brown eyes, but felt two hands reach out from behind her and clasp her arms, effectively halting her.

"Ahithophel is one of the major conspirators against the king. If she gets to him, she will tell him I have been spying on the rebels, and that I intercepted their messages. Absalom is in control of Hebron now, my friend, and I doubt even you would be able to keep his forces from taking me."

"I wouldn't betray you, Micah, and you know it!" Shoshanna said earnestly. Then, turning to Isaac, she pleaded, "Please, my lord, he is holding me captive. Make him let me go. I won't tell my grandfather what he's done."

Isaac again looked from Shoshanna to Isaac and back to Shoshanna again. "I would like to believe you, Lady Shoshanna, but my friend seems to have his doubts. My family and his are very close. I would never have peace in my house again if any harm came to him. I'm afraid I will have to do what he asks."

"As you can see," Micah interjected, "the lady doesn't appreciate my protecting her from Joab's men. I must also protect myself from her grandfather's wrath. Please keep her here as your guest; do not allow her to leave until I come back for her. I must evaluate the strength of the prince's troops, and recruit more warriors for King David. When I have completed my mission, I will come back and escort Shoshanna to safety, wherever that happens to be."

"Do not concern yourself," Isaac remarked. "I have a guest room that can be secured from the outside. It is very comfortably furnished, I assure you, my lady. You will rest there tonight, and my friend will soon come back for you." He smiled at Shoshanna. She scowled back.

Isaac left the room and Shoshanna tried to break free of Micah's grasp. She might as well have been chained. He pulled her closer and said softly. "Stop your struggling, Shoshanna. You are exhausted and need rest, and I need for you to stay put until I can be sure you're safe and can do no mischief to me or the king."

Isaac returned, followed by an attractive woman. "Shoshanna, this is Keziah, my wife. I have explained to her that you will be staying in our second-floor guest room. She will see that you are settled in your chambers, with the door bolted. You may go with her now." Shoshanna was comforted to note that both Micah's friend and his wife looked extremely uncomfortable with their roles as jailers.

Keziah smiled at her. "Welcome to our home," she said as she came forward and put a guiding arm around Shoshanna's waist. Shoshanna noticed Keziah's beautiful auburn hair as it fell freely over her shoulders, a little mussed from sleep. She had a sweet, wide smile and a soothing voice as well. "Come with me, dear. There is no need for us to stand here shivering while the men go on and on. The bed in your room is very soft, and there is a sheepskin blanket that feels just wonderful on a cool night like this."

Shoshanna glared at Micah, who smiled and nodded his head. She felt her anger stir at his paternalistic attitude. He acted like he was in charge, as though he controlled her life. And he was lying to Isaac. He knew she would never say anything that would put him in danger! But exhaustion overcame resentment, and she went willingly with Keziah. She still had the problem of finding a way to get her grandfather's messages back, but first she had to sleep.

She was awakened by the early dawn light. It streamed through a small window that was well above her reach in the high-ceilinged room. She studied it thoughtfully for a moment before shaking her head. It was too high to reach, and it seemed too small for her to squeeze through anyway. She would think of another way. After rising and washing her face, she went to listen at her door. All was quiet. She tried the latch. It was locked, of course.

Shoshanna knocked softly, and immediately the door opened. An old man was standing there. "I am Abed, my lady. Are you in need of something?"

"No, I just wondered if the household had awakened." Shoshanna looked past the servant and didn't see any other guard. She could push past the old man and try to escape. But, knowing the wealth of Micah's friend, she had to assume that there were numerous other servants, young and robust, who had been given orders to keep her captive. Deciding she wouldn't risk it yet, she gave her attention to the servant.

"Ordinarily they would be up and about, but they stayed up very late last night, so my master told me they were not to be disturbed this morning until the sun was well risen."

"What about their other guest?" At her question, Abed looked puzzled. "The big one," she clarified.

"Ah, yes, the son of Jonathan. He left many hours ago, my lady."

She was not surprised, but a wave of disappointment washed over her. She didn't care if she never laid eyes on Micah again, but now she had no hope of recovering the potsherd messages and making her deliveries. She hoped her failure to carry out her mission would not place her grandfather in any danger. In any case, Shoshanna was determined to find Ahithophel and stay by his side until the conflict was over.

Keziah came to let her out of her comfortable prison an hour later. "I trust you slept well, Shoshanna. I am sorry that this room is rather sparse, but we keep it that way because it is used for different purposes; from storage to guest room. Is there anything that is lacking that I could provide?"

Shoshanna looked around the room. Aside from the bed, there was only a very low chest. There was a shelf that contained a pitcher and bowl. "I would like to have a chair or stool, if it could be arranged. I have need of nothing else."

Keziah showed her some of the exotic items that Isaac had acquired on his caravan journeys. She introduced Shoshanna to her twin sons, Hanani and Nebat, who looked nothing alike. Hanani resembled his mother, with his generous mouth and hair that glinted with red highlights. Nebat was wiry and had the facial features of his father.

A delicious meal was spread on a mat near the fountain, and Keziah motioned for her to sit. They ate in silence. When Shoshanna had taken her last bite, Keziah spoke. "I know you must be very worried about your grandfather, Shoshanna, so I took the liberty of making inquiries about him. He will be leaving Hebron any time now with Absalom's army. They will be marching on Jerusalem."

Shoshanna's face grew pale. "Then he will be in the midst of battle."

Keziah shook her head. "Not necessarily. From what my husband has learned, it is very likely David will surrender, or at least go into exile. Absalom definitely has the majority of the kingdom on his side."

"Are you certain?"

"As certain as anyone can be in circumstances such as these. But that is without taking into account Adonai's intervention on behalf of his anointed."

Keziah carefully watched Shoshanna's reaction. She hoped to discern whether she was truly on the side of the rebels or just trying to help Ahithophel. She had her answer when Shoshanna said, "I know. I have a feeling Absalom won't remain in power long because the Lord will never bless him for deposing his father. Perhaps my grandfather will soon come to realize that. Even if he doesn't, it is my duty to help him. And to keep my mother safe, of course."

Keziah looked disappointed. "I hoped what I told you would help you realize that you don't have to run to Ahithophel. The truth is, Micah is in far more danger at the moment than your grandfather."

Shoshanna paled again. She knew Keziah spoke the truth. Those who had gone over to the side of the prince would kill Micah if they discovered he was trying to muster men for the king right under their noses. She realized then that even though Micah was her enemy in many ways, she cared about him deeply and wanted him to be safe. Was that disloyal to her grandfather? No. But she had to get away from the house of Micah's friends before she did become disloyal.

Chapter Nine

∽

Jonathan realized after his talk with Micah that the political situation was now at a full boil and would erupt in warfare very soon. He was therefore not surprised when, not long after Micah left for Hebron, he received a summons to convene in the council chamber at the palace, along with the other *Gibborim*. But he was taken aback when he saw a distraught David hunched like an old man in the huge chair at the head of the council table. He was shocked to see his monarch and friend so shaken. He had not seen David so grieved since his infant son had lain at death's door as punishment for his sin with Bathsheba.

Bathsheba stood at the king's side now, offering support and strength in this time of crisis. She had been wrong to succumb to David's seduction all those years before, but ever since, she had proven her loyalty as a good wife to him and as a wonderful mother. She stood slightly behind his chair, with a hand placed lightly on David's shoulder. She remained silent during the entire meeting.

As soon as the Thirty were assembled, Joab presented the facts without honey-coating them. "The prince has rallied men from all twelve tribes to his cause. Many of the standing army have gone over to him. Amasa is now the commander of the prince's forces," he announced bluntly. A few gasps greeted that disclosure.

"My *nephew*?" David asked, incredulous. His eyes were glistening with unshed tears. The king loved his family—even his extended family—to distraction. He was ever generous, ever forgiving, of any of his kin. That was the chief reason they were in this predicament now, Jonathan reasoned. If the king had not so outrageously spoiled his children, Amnon would not have dared to behave so wickedly toward his half-sister, and Absalom would probably not despise his father enough to try to wrest the kingdom from him. Joab's words interrupted his thoughts.

"Yes, my lord, your nephew, my cousin. He who was nothing more than a stinking shepherd wandering the hills of Bethlehem until you exalted him to a position of wealth and honor in your kingdom. I shall gladly hunt him down and cut his—"

David held up a hand for silence. "Our concern is not what to do if we put down this rebellion. Our concern tonight is what to do *now*." The muscles in Joab's face twitched as he clenched his jaw. The king seldom rebuked him or went against his recommendations.

Jonathan looked at the grim expressions on the faces of his fellow officers and knew they had taken note, as he had, that the king had said "if," not "when," in his mention of winning the coming conflict. It was the first time he had ever seen David face a battle with less than complete confidence, and it concerned him greatly.

Joab started to speak, but hesitated when the king stood, pushing back his chair. "I have never been fond of sieges, even when I was the one conducting the siege. I don't think we should cower here in Jerusalem, waiting until the rebel forces cut off any chance of retreat. If Jerusalem is lost, then we are all lost. I say we arise and cross the Jordan, and let Absalom's army wear themselves out looking for us. It will be as it used to be in the days of Saul, when we were outnumbered, but never defeated. What do you say, men?" The room was filled with enthusiastic affirmations. The king's fighting spirit seemed restored.

~ ~ ~

At dawn the next morning, all of David's mighty men were assembled in formation before the *House of the Gibborim,* dressed in full battle array. Joab gave the order, and they marched to the palace entrance. As soon as they arrived, they were joined by the palace guard, which was followed by the royal family. Everyone was unnaturally silent—even the king's smallest children. The warriors formed two columns on either side of the king and his family.

They passed almost silently through the streets, this multitude of at least seven hundred. Their sandals touched down softly on the cobbled streets of the still-sleeping city. No one wanted Jerusalem to wake to the sight of their king fleeing his own son's army. For the most part, the inhabitants slept on as the day dawned gray and misty. When the entourage reached the area of the bazaar they encountered tradesmen setting up their market stalls. Many wept openly as the king's dejected retinue passed. A few turned away from the sad sight. No one mocked. The hearts of the city's populace had not been entirely stolen by the prince.

But when the king's supporters and family passed through the city's eastern gate, David stopped just outside and tore his cloak. He scooped up sand and poured it over his head in mourning. Young prince Solomon did the same. The king insisted on keeping the lad near his side. No one doubted what would happen to the boy if he fell into the hands of his older brother.

Years ago, the prophet Nathan had given Solomon a special name, Jedediah, which means "beloved of the Lord." His predictions about the child seemed to declare that he would be the Lord's anointed to rule the kingdom after David. All knew of this prediction, and it was foolish to believe that Absalom was unaware of it. After his disposal of Amnon, no one doubted that Absalom had the nerve to kill a sibling who stood between him and the throne. The entire royal household was in tears, but what made Jonathan's own eyes misty was the pitiful wailing that came from the roof of the palace. The ten concubines of David who had been left behind to care for the royal house, leaned over the edge of the roof and waved their good-byes while crying out their grief. *The innocent always suffer in war,* Jonathan thought as he marched directly behind the king with the other members of the Thirty.

When he had gone a little further, David paused again, and row after row of the faithful passed by him. There were the Pelethites and Cherethites, foreign mercenaries who had been with David from the beginning of his power; and the Gittites, fierce Philistine warriors who had forsaken their own people to follow the Shepherd King and his God. They numbered six hundred and functioned as the king's palace guard. They would protect the king, even if outnumbered by thousands.

As Ittai, the captain of the Gittites, passed by David, the king motioned him from the ranks. The Thirty followed Ittai and David as they withdrew to the side of the path that led down to the Kidron Valley. The remainder of the retinue continued to march.

David put a hand on the Philistine warrior's shoulder. "Why are you going with me? You should stay and serve my son, who will soon be king in Jerusalem. You made yourself an outcast to your own people when you chose to follow me and worship Adonai. Go back to the city and take your Gittite troops with you. You haven't been with me long. It seems like only yesterday that you joined me. You don't owe me so much that you must flee with me to who knows where."

Ittai put his hand on the king's opposite shoulder and swallowed hard before responding. Jonathan was surprised to note that the swarthy Philistine was looking suspiciously damp-eyed. This was an emotional day, to be sure.

"As Adonai lives, and as my lord the king lives, I will be with you wherever you go. And we will be together in death if the Lord of Hosts so wills, but I have sworn allegiance to you and no one else, and with you I shall be, no matter what happens." There was a clamor of voices as each of the *Gibborim* agreed with their mercenary comrade.

David looked at them with tears streaming down his cheeks before commanding Ittai. "Go on, then, man. Lead us across the Jordan." The warrior turned and ran off at a trot to catch up with his men.

As the royal family marched along, many of the citizens who lived just outside the city walls lined the road, weeping openly to see their beloved David forced from power so ignominiously. It was gratifying, this demonstration of loyalty.

Jonathan prayed silently to the Lord Almighty for the safety of the innocent, for protection for Micah. For himself, he prayed only for courage and strength to fight for the Lord's anointed, and for a death with honor if he were to fall in battle. His thoughts went to Ailea and Jerusha at home, and he wondered whether the elders of Ziph would declare for David or Absalom. He thought of the irony that his service to David had begun in the first place because the elders of Ziph, loyal to Saul, had informed the old king of David's whereabouts in southern Judah. Shageh had sent Jonathan to warn the fugitive, and Jonathan had joined his band. Would they again turn against David? He prayed they wouldn't.

They stopped to rest after they had crossed the Kidron brook. Zadok and Abiathar, the high priests, sought out David as he sat on a camp stool, drinking water that had been drawn from the stream. "My lord," Zadok said, slightly breathless from his march. "We have come with you to assure the Lord's blessing, and we have brought the Levites with the Ark of the Covenant." Zadok was just past middle age, with iron-gray hair, and a slight paunch. His open, unlined face spoke of true holiness.

"Bring the high priest a camp stool," David said to one of the armor bearers. It was produced immediately. "Sit down, Zadok. There has been enough sorrow this day. I would not have you dead of your exertions."

After Zadok had seated himself, David reached over and patted the priest's folded hands. "I am touched by this show of fidelity, Zadok, but you really must go back to the city. Take the Ark and all the Levites with you." Zadok began to protest, but David silenced him with a shake of his head.

"If Adonai sees fit, I will again see both Jerusalem and the Ark. But if he is saying to me by this rebellion, 'I have no more delight in you, son of Jesse,' then so be it."

"But, my lord, I would be of service to you. It is not right, this wickedness of your son trying to depose you!"

David patted the man's shoulder. "Zadok, you may be of more use to me in Jerusalem. You will be sought out as a counselor, and may be privy to the plans the rebels are making. Take your son, Ahimaaz, and Abiathar with his son, Jonathan, back with you, and when you know their plans, send your son across the Jordan to warn me. That is the most useful thing you can do. And Zadok, take no unnecessary chances. Your calling is the service of God in the Tabernacle. If my son comes to power, it will still be your calling, and you will continue with no dishonor to me."

When the march started again, the Gittites were well out in front of the procession, but David led the remainder of the retinue. He covered his head, weeping as they ascended the Mount of Olives. The king called a halt when they reached the top, and called for a time of prayer. He scanned the crowd, and Jonathan asked, "Who are you seeking, my lord?"

"I would have Ahithophel, the Gilohite, to intercede for us."

Jonathan felt a surge of anger. Joab should have informed the king already of Ahithophel's treason. Now the responsibility fell to him. "My lord, it is as if there is a knife in my heart to tell you so, but Ahithophel is with the conspirators. In fact, he is Absalom's chief counselor now."

There was a gasp from behind him, and Bathsheba stumbled forward, both hands to her mouth as if to hold back a cry. Jonathan reached out to grab the king, thinking his heart had burst within him, for he swayed on his feet, and his face became ashen. But before Jonathan could steady him, the king pulled himself up to his full height. He pulled his distraught wife into his arms to comfort her. "My own grandfather seeks to destroy you! It is because of Uriah. I know it. He has never forgiven me," she sobbed against her husband's shoulder.

Joab saw that something was amiss and hurried to his uncle's side. "David, I did not tell you. I hope you will forgive me, but I wanted to spare you the pain of knowing until we were well away from the city."

The king sighed. "I know you always do what you think best for me, Joab. We must pray now. And we must beseech the Lord to make the counsel of Ahithophel seem foolish to my son." David stood on the hilltop with raised hands and lifted up his face to the Lord. "El Shaddai, Almighty One, hear the prayer of your servant. Save me from my enemy, my bosom friend, who has betrayed me and plotted against me. I beseech you, O Lord, make the counsel of Ahithophel foolishness in my son's eyes. Do not let the prince prosper from his words."

They were preparing to continue their march into exile when an old friend of David's, Hushai the Archite, appeared. Hushai was a native of Archi, a town southwest of Bethel, on the northern border of Benjamin. Hushai was older than David by only a few years, but looked much less strong. His gray hair was thinning, and his shoulders stooped in depression. He had torn his robe and smeared ashes on his face. "My lord, I will come with you," he said in a quavering voice.

David shook his head. "If you go on with me, then you will become a burden to me and slow us down because of your years. But if you return to the city, and say to Absalom, 'I will be your servant, O king; as I was your father's servant before, so I will now also be your servant,' then you may defeat the counsel of Ahithophel for me. And don't you have Zadok and Abiathar the priests with you there? Whatever you hear from the king's house, you will tell the priests. Indeed, they have with them their two sons, Ahimaaz and Jonathan; and by them you shall send to tell me everything you hear. Truly, my friend, you have been the Lord's instrument to answer my prayer this day."

David turned to Bathsheba to confirm his words. "Did I not just pray that Adonai would make Ahithophel's counsel seem foolish? There is no other man the prince might listen to who would contradict Ahithophel's advice. Only you." When Bathsheba confirmed her husband's words, his old friend smiled for the first time. David's friend embraced him and left for Jerusalem, where Absalom was taking the city.

≈ ≈ ≈

A little past the peak of the Mount of Olives, suddenly Ziba, Mephibosheth's servant appeared leading a couple of saddled donkeys carrying two hundred loaves of bread, one hundred clusters of raisins, one hundred summer fruits, and a skin of wine.

"What do you mean to do with these?" David asked.

"The donkeys are for the king's household to ride on, the bread and summer fruit for the young men to eat, and the wine for those who are faint in the wilderness to drink."

"Is this from Mephibosheth, or do you bring it on your own?"

Ziba managed to look ashamed, as if he hated to betray his master. "On my own, O King. May you live forever."

"And where is your master's son?"

Ziba hesitated, as if he did not want to answer. "He is staying in Jerusalem. He said to me, 'Today the house of Israel will restore the kingdom of my father to me.'" Ziba held his breath, wondering whether the king would see through the lie he told. After all, Mephibosheth was no fool. Even if he aspired to the throne, he would know that supporting Absalom's cause would certainly not further his claim. The cripple had grown up with Absalom, and knew as well as anyone the ambition and ruthlessness that lay behind the beautiful smile.

But David was too distraught from the day's events to think

rationally. He had been betrayed by his son, by his most trusted counselor, by one of his top army officials—a relative, no less. The king clenched his jaw, struggling with the emotion that came with the news that the son of the best friend he ever had had also turned against him. Finally, he found his voice. "From this day, everything that I had given to Mephibosheth is yours. You go back and tell the ungrateful cur that!"

Ziba bowed low and made an obsequious parting speech. "I humbly bow before you, my lord. May I find favor in your sight, my king."

~ ~ ~

Due to severe pain in his crippled legs, Mephibosheth had not been present at David's table the night before. He had been forced to drink poppy juice in his wine to alleviate the agony, and had therefore remained unaware that Absalom was marching on the city until the next morning.

When he had heard the clamor of the king's departure, he had called for Ziba twice before the servant answered his summons. "Ziba, what is happening? It sounds as though there is a great uproar out in the halls."

The servant's eyes narrowed on his master for a moment before he hesitantly answered. "I am not certain, my lord. But I will go and find out."

Ziba was gone for a long while. Mephibosheth made his way to his window with the help of the special crutches the king had ordered to be made especially for him. He saw people pouring out of the palace in great numbers. Most seemed to be in a panic. Finally, Ziba reappeared.

"Master, there is an insurrection in progress. The prince has mustered an army and is expected to take the city before the sun sets. The king says he will not cower behind the city walls to wait for his son to besiege him, but will choose the time and place of battle. He is leaving Jerusalem, and his troops are going with him."

"Then let us prepare to leave immediately, Ziba," Mephibosheth said.

"Oh, no, my lord. I sought out the king himself; that is why I was gone so long. He says you are to remain here in the palace. He is concerned for your health if you were to undertake such an arduous journey. You will be in no danger, as Absalom's attention will be on pursuing his father. But he does instruct you not to leave your chambers until Jerusalem is once again restored to him. There is the slight possibility that those who favor the prince will see you as a threat due to the blood of Saul that flows in your veins. But if you do nothing to attract their attention, you should be safe enough."

"But I must go with the king to show my support . . ."

Ziba had raised his hand to stop Mephibosheth's protest. "I hate to remind you of your unfortunate affliction, my lord, but surely you realize you would only slow the king down. You might expose him to greater danger."

Mephibosheth paled at the thought of causing any harm to the man who had taken him in years ago and treated him as a son. "Of course, Ziba. I see that now. I will do as the king wishes. But, Ziba, please take supplies to him from my own stores, and assure him of my unfailing loyalty."

"Of course, my lord. I will go right away." Ziba had bowed himself out of the room and did as Mephibosheth had suggested, except he changed the message he gave the king.

≈　≈　≈

Once Ziba had departed, the pace of the march picked up as they headed northwest, a route that took them through the village of Bahurim. The path ran parallel to a small ridge. As they passed along it, they saw a man running along the top. When he was even with David and the *Gibborim,* he began to curse and throw rocks down upon them. The first rock thrown, though rather small, glanced off the king's shoulder. Jonathan and his fellow warriors raised their shields to deflect the projectiles.

"Come out from behind your men and their shields, you murderer, and fight me!" The scrawny man's face was red with rage.

"Who is that man?"

"He's mad!"

"He must be tired of living to taunt us so!" David's men looked to Joab, just waiting for the order to punish the treasonous man. Joab started to speak, but David stopped him.

"Hold, Joab. I recognize the man. He's a nephew of old King Saul. He was often at the palace in Gibeon when I lived there. His name is Shimei."

"What does it matter who the man is? I will skewer anyone who dares to address you in such a manner!"

The man began to scream again. "Adonai has brought down upon you all of the blood of the house of Saul, in whose place you have reigned. And Adonai has delivered your kingdom into your son Absalom's hands. You are caught in your own evil, you bloodthirsty man!"

The king grabbed Joab's arm as he drew his sword. "I said, leave him alone!" David walked on as if he had not heard Shimei's accusations. Abishai, Joab's brother, could not hold his peace a moment longer. He made his way to David's side. "Why should this dead dog get away with cursing his king, my lord? Please, let me go and chop off his head!"

David shook his head emphatically. "I am not like you hotheaded sons of my sister. Let him alone, and let him curse me if he will. Maybe the Lord has prompted him to curse me. If so, who should tell him to stop?" And the king motioned for the whole column of marchers to stop.

When he had the attention of all the *Gibborim,* he continued to speak. "If my own son, who came from my own body, is trying to take my life, how much more reason does this Benjamite have to do so?"

Jonathan knew that David felt guilty for allowing the closest relatives of Saul to be slaughtered, except for Mephibosheth. Since the overthrow of Saul's regime, many of the people of his tribe—the Benjamites—had deeply resented David. Was the king now saying he had been wrong to take the throne? Had he forgotten that Adonai had sent his servant Samuel to anoint David when he was still herding sheep in the hills around Bethlehem? And had he forgotten how the Lord had blessed him and given him victory in virtually every battle he had fought? Was the king giving up?

The king's next statement seemed to confirm Jonathan's fears. "Let him alone. Let him curse. Adonai has willed it. It may be that the Lord will look down on my affliction, and that he will repay me blessing for Shimei's cursing this day."

David resumed the march, and his men, grumbling quietly, surrounded him. With their shields they deflected the stones that Shimei threw, but they could not deflect his hateful words. Shimei followed them until they were in Bahurim, where they stopped again to rest.

Chapter Ten

～

*A*bsalom was greeted in Jerusalem by a cacophony of shouts and a celebration. By no means did the entire city greet his coup with joy, but those who did turned out for a vocal demonstration of their loyalty to the prince.

Hushai stood on the second-floor balcony of the palace that overlooked the main courtyard and watched the royal procession. Amasa and Ahithophel flanked the prince . . . *king.* Hushai reminded himself that if he was to help David regain control, he must remember to refer to Absalom as king. He would have to falsely pledge his allegiance to a man he despised, and he must be convincing enough that Absalom would make him privy to all his plans. He hurried down the steps to the main entrance, so that he might be among the first to greet the usurper. The *king,* Hushai reminded himself again.

When Absalom swept into the great hall a few minutes later, his eyes widened in surprise to find Hushai waiting for him. Hushai knew that this was the moment to convince Absalom of his sincerity.

"Long live the king! Long live the king!" he said, bowing himself to the ground.

"Is this the way you show your loyalty to your friends? Why

didn't you go with my father, your friend?" Absalom was openly suspicious.

"Whomever Adonai and his people choose to be king, his man I will be, and with him I will remain. Furthermore, shouldn't I serve the son in Jerusalem as I have served the father? I offer my services to you, just as I did to David."

Absalom gave Hushai a cynical look before responding. "I will consider your words," he said. He motioned Ahithophel and Amasa into the royal council chamber. Hushai was left standing in the hall. Numerous military and advisory people were milling around in a reception area nearby, and Hushai joined them, hoping to hear something that would be of use to his master.

Inside the council chamber, Absalom called for a meal to be brought for himself and his two closest counselors. They discussed the apparent capitulation of David, and all agreed they were surprised at his flight.

"Never underestimate your father's courage, or his cunning as a fighter. He's not done yet," Amasa cautioned.

But Ahithophel was more encouraging. "We need to secure the city, and the people need to see that leadership has irrevocably changed. As soon as that is accomplished, and I believe we can do so before the sun is high tomorrow, we should take the army and pursue David before he can go to ground—while he is still discouraged and disorganized."

Absalom absently plucked at his perfectly groomed beard, as his eyes narrowed on the elder statesman who had been the originator of the coup. The advice sounded good, but he needed to ponder the ramifications, maybe seek another opinion as to military action. After all, that wasn't Ahithophel's area of expertise.

"I will take that under consideration. First, there is the matter of securing the city and the palace. What do you advise?" Ahithophel, who had bristled at Absalom's hesitation, was mollified and ready with his council.

"My lord, I have given this much thought. There are in the harem ten of your father's concubines, who have been left behind to look after the household. You should claim them for your own. And so that everyone will know that you have wrested power from your father, you would do well to lie with each of them in a place where you will be seen. I suggest that before the sun goes down this day, you lie with them on the rooftop of the palace, where you may be seen."

The counsel of Ahithophel had always been filled with wisdom. At the palace, when Ahithophel spoke on a matter, everyone took it as the counsel of God. Still, Absalom was shocked at the suggestion, even though concubines did not have full status as wives. The thought of adultery sickened him. Hadn't his entire family been torn apart because of that sin? Absalom had always pointed to his father's adultery on the rooftop with Bathsheba as the beginning of his family's problems. That was when David had for all intents and purposes put Maacah aside. That was the beginning of his mother's bitterness. And the union of David and Bathsheba had resulted in Solomon, that little usurper who had supplanted Absalom as David's favorite son.

Absalom lifted a perfectly shaped eyebrow. Did memories of that rooftop scandal prompt Ahithophel's advice? Possibly. Despite having been only fourteen years old at the time, he remembered the grief-stricken look on Ahithophel's face when it all came to light. The old man had gone home to Giloh and had not darkened the door of the palace for nearly a year. Absalom shrugged mentally. The old man's reasons didn't matter; the suggestion had merit.

An hour later, in the quarters of the king's concubines, which took up half of the third floor of the palace, there was wailing from some, silent tears from others. But only two of the concubines who belonged to the king went willingly to the three-sided tent that had been set up in the king's rooftop garden. One had only recently come to Jerusalem from Egypt. The other was older and had been in the harem for several years, but had no child by David. She boldly stated that perhaps there would be fruit from joining with the prince. She made herself a permanent enemy of the other women, as did the Egyptian.

Though not many vistas in the city looked down on the palace rooftop, numerous people were witness to the disgraceful scene. Ahithophel saw to it that the servants who were there knew they could spread the word of what happened with impunity. *You debauched my granddaughter on your cursed roof. Now I have seen to it that your son debauches your concubines in the same place. It is justice, at last.* Ahithophel's face broke into a satisfied smile at the thought.

As the sun sank low in the sky, Ahithophel came to Absalom again. "We have twelve thousand men mustered and ready to march even at this hour. We should pursue your father before he has a chance to develop a strategy."

"But night is falling," Absalom said as he gestured to the sky.

"And there will be a full moon. A night march will be easier on the troops than a trek in the sun." Ahithophel paused, and when Absalom didn't respond immediately, pressed on.

"If you will not go, let me lead the men. We will overtake the king tonight while he is weary and weak, seeking his rest. When we come upon his camp at night, we will strike fear in his heart and his followers will run away. I will personally dispatch the king and we can later offer amnesty to his men. The whole thing will be accomplished with a minimum of hardship or bloodshed."

Absalom spoke to the council of elders, made up of the city leaders and men who had come from the far reaches of Israel to represent the interests of their various tribes. They seemed to concur with Ahithophel's strategy.

Still Absalom hesitated. He remembered his earlier conversation with Hushai. Suddenly, it seemed important to get the Archite's advice as well. He called for the man, who, it seemed, had been waiting just outside the council chamber. The dignified foreigner came at once. He was wearing a friendly smile.

"Hushai, this is Ahithophel's recommendation," he said without preamble. "What is your opinion?"

Oh, God of heaven, let them not do this thing, or the king's cause is lost, he prayed silently, at the same time casting about in his mind for some way to stall the pursuit of David. It came to him in a burst of inspiration that could only be divine intervention.

"The advice of Ahithophel is sound, in and of itself, but it is not the best thing to deploy the army in a hasty and haphazard manner. You know that your father and his men are awesome warriors, and at present they are as furious as a bear that has been robbed of her cubs. Also, I believe, from what I remember of his days running from Saul, that David will not camp with the main body of his men, but will be hidden in some cave or other place that will be impossible to find. We would doubtless win the skirmish, but if your father survives, and people hear of it, even the man who is brave, who has the heart of a lion, will lose his courage, because everyone in Israel knows the valor of your father and the *Gibborim*."

Absalom raised an eyebrow, not fully convinced. "And you would propose . . . ?"

"That all the troops from each tribe who are with us be fully mustered, so that the number is like the sand of the sea, and that you go to battle in person. Then when you come upon him and his troops, they will be so greatly outnumbered that all will be killed—not one of them left alive." Hushai did not say them aloud, but the words "including your father" hung in the air, as if he had. He paused for a moment, but Absalom said nothing, waiting to be further convinced. So Hushai continued.

"If by chance the old king finds some city on the other side of the Jordan that will give him refuge, we will besiege the city and cast its stones into the river. There is none that can stand against your might, my lord." Hushai hated speaking disrespectfully of David and flattering the arrogant prince, but he would do anything to get Absalom to listen to him if it would buy time for the king to prepare for the coming battle. He paused again to await the response of the prince.

Absalom's handsome face was furrowed in concentration. He

rose from his ornate chair and made a turn around the room before returning to the conference table. He leaned over it on extended arms and polled each of his councilors. "Do you favor Ahithophel's plan, or Hushai's?"

Hushai could hardly believe what he was hearing. Unanimously, the council voted to follow Hushai's advice. He glanced at Ahithophel and almost felt pity for the elder statesman. Before his eyes the man shrank, his formerly straight shoulders curling inward, his head drooping, his color changing to an unhealthy pallor.

Ahithophel made one last effort to persuade the prince. "My lord, I have been with your cause from the beginning, and always seek what is best for you. If you hesitate because you don't want to strike down your father, rest assured I will gladly be the one to kill David. Please reconsider—"

Absalom held up a hand to halt Ahithophel's words, and the old man knew better than to continue. The prince put an arm around him and smiled. "I am well aware of your loyalty, my friend, and you will soon be greatly rewarded for it. Hushai has recommended that we proceed with more caution to secure our position, and I think time will prove him right. Now go to your quarters and take your rest. You have earned it."

Ahithophel's stance shrank even more at these words of dismissal. The prince was not allowing him to stay and perhaps put in a further word during the remaining strategy session. All hope of victory would be lost if Absalom stuck to Hushai's strategy. And if David put down the rebellion, all his plans for revenge were futile. David wouldn't die a humiliating death—he would. And perhaps even Marah and Shoshanna would die, or at least be punished.

Ahithophel made his way to his spacious quarters on the third floor of the palace, but he did not sleep. He began gathering his belongings to return to Giloh. He had many things to accomplish and not much time. He knew as sure as the sun would rise tomorrow that Absalom's bid for the kingdom was doomed. He was giving David time to strategize and gather his supporters, perhaps even to pick the location of the battle. And Ahithophel knew only too well that given that kind of fighting chance, the warrior king would be victorious.

Before he left Jerusalem, he found a young boy who was a message runner. "I wish you to take a message for me to Mahanaim. You will find one of the *Gibborim* there named Jonathan. He is from the village of Ziph. Listen most carefully to what you must tell him." The lad was bright and repeated word-for-word the message he was to take to Jonathan. His eyes widened at the silver that was dropped in his hand, and he set off at a run for the town of Mahanaim.

Chapter Eleven

~

As soon as he returned to Hebron, Micah went directly to Isaac's house. A servant washed the dirt from his feet as he stood in the courtyard that led him to the common room. It was furnished with several couches. Tyrian rugs in vivid blues and purples were scattered about the floor. He turned to see Shoshanna leaning on the sill of a window, the breeze rippling her black, silky hair. He breathed a sigh of relief. He had not believed she would obey him and stay put. After greeting Isaac, he walked over to the window where she stood.

"You are an obedient maiden, after all," he said with a grin. "I am pleased."

"And you are *wrong,* as usual, Micah. I am not obedient—at least not to you!"

He grinned even more broadly. "I stand corrected."

Why could she never win a word battle with him? Shoshanna looked around her rather desperately. She could not fall under the spell of those amber eyes. Her plan to help her grandfather was paramount, and she must ignore all distractions. But she was afraid that the gentle giant who lately filled her dreams would prove more than just a distraction. Underneath the gentleness lay an iron will. He would undoubtedly do all he could to keep her from joining Ahithophel.

"I am reading your mind, Shoshanna, and it is telling me that you are plotting to run away from me again. Don't you know by now that it is useless to try?"

Her mouth dropped open at his perception. She wondered fleetingly if somehow those uncanny eyes of his really could see into her mind. She mentally chastised herself for being fanciful. She laughed lightly to show her disdain for his words. "I was just retiring to my room. I am sure you have important, *manly* things to say to Isaac that should not be overheard by a mere woman. Good night."

Shoshanna swept upstairs to the guest chamber, her head held high with dignity, proud of having the last word in her encounter with the infuriating man. Some of her pleasure was eroded by the sound of booming laughter that followed her. When she reached her room, she slammed the door behind her.

Micah turned at the sound of the slamming door, and saw Isaac leaning against the doorway, arms folded, with a huge grin on his face. He had forgotten his friend was there. Shoshanna had a way of doing that to him—erasing all else from his mind when he was with her.

"You have a way of irritating her, my friend. With everyone else she is a picture of meekness and submission." At Micah's raised eyebrow, Isaac held up his hand in surrender. "All right, she has not been all that meek. Several times she has tried to elude the servants I have set to watch her. But she is an intelligent woman, and after three attempts to . . . ah . . . leave the hospitality of my house, she has become as sweetly biddable as any tender maiden ever was."

Micah snorted at the thought of Shoshanna being biddable. She was the most stubborn creature Adonai had ever put on the earth. But he did not want to discuss Ahithophel's alluring granddaughter with his friend.

"So, what is afoot in Hebron?"

"Most of the young men have gone to Jerusalem in support of the prince. I made it a point to keep abreast of the situation for you. Ahithophel was at Absalom's side—no great surprise, given his recent behavior. But I hated to finally confirm it, especially after I met Shoshanna. I have mentioned nothing about it to her, of course. As far as I know, she still believes he is in Hebron."

"Thank you, my friend. I suppose I will have to tell her tomorrow. I will take her to my mother. She will be safe in Ziph. But enough about personal matters. What else can you tell me about Hebron?"

I believe that many who are over the age of thirty still secretly support David. It is my belief that if David manages a decisive victory against Absalom's forces, there will be no pocket of rebellion left in Hebron. But if the prince wins the day, I believe the older men will reluctantly uphold his claim to the throne. In other words, the Hebronites are a fickle, vacillating lot."

Micah grunted agreement. "As the rest of Israel seems to be at present. And where do you stand in all this, Isaac?"

"Probably with the rest of Israel. No, that is not true. The nation has prospered under David's reign, and while I deplore some of the things he has done, I would not be happy to see him deposed by such a one as Absalom. He is, I believe, the Lord's anointed." Isaac's smile flashed white in contrast to his darkly tanned face. Many years plying the caravan routes had darkened his complexion. But he was still as lithe and strong as ever. Isaac never seemed to age, though he must be nearly forty now. Keziah also retained a youthful look, though some gray showed in her auburn hair.

Over the years, Micah had noted the devotion between the couple who were his parents' closest friends. Isaac and Keziah were truly one, as were Jonathan and Ailea. The Rab had always held out that standard to Micah: that Adonai had created one woman for him who would be his soul mate. He had been taught to save himself for her, so that no shame would mar their union as man and wife, and so that he could completely trust his wife with the deepest secrets of his soul. He knew in his heart of hearts that that woman was Shoshanna. He did not know how they could completely trust each other now, when they found themselves on opposite sides in this turmoil, but somehow they would find a way if they were truly made for each other.

He deliberately interrupted his thoughts and continued his conversation with Isaac. Before an hour had passed, they had both agreed they needed to seek their rest. Micah would be underway at first light. On his reconnaissance mission, he had already estimated Absalom's troop strength to be upward of ten thousand. He would endeavor to rally as many men as possible to fight for the king. He would have to travel with caution, lest he find himself in the clutches of Absalom's men, but he would visit as many villages as possible on his way to Manahaim, to feel out the sentiment of the people, so that he could report accurately to David what would be needed to put down this rebellion.

Micah woke, fully alert after only four hours of sleep. In the predawn darkness he made his way to the second-story landing, moving quietly, so as not to disturb the resting household. He paused before the door of the guest room, debating whether to see Shoshanna just one more time before leaving. Perhaps he could look in on her and she would never know. If she woke, she wouldn't be happy to see him, of course, but he would be very quiet and go no further than the doorway.

He succumbed to the temptation. Who knew what lay in store in the coming days of upheaval? He eased back the bolt that locked the door from the outside, and pushed the door open. A shaft of moonlight fell across the bed. It was empty! A quick check of her room revealed no items belonging to Shoshanna. He immediately searched the common rooms of the villa, but already knew that he wouldn't find her. *How in all creation did she get out of that locked room?*

A few minutes later he was on the road to Giloh, chafing at having to stop at each village along the way to gather the information he needed for the king. He prayed that Shoshanna had headed there rather than following her grandfather to Jerusalem.

Surely she had enough wisdom to stay away from Jerusalem until the conflict was settled. He hoped she would join her mother in Giloh and wait to hear further word from Ahithophel.

≈ ≈ ≈

By the time he reached Giloh, Micah realized that the defection of southern Judah was every bit as thorough as he had feared. He had also confirmed that it had indeed been Ahithophel who had turned the men of Judah against their king. Without his complicity, Absalom would have had little chance of bringing this rebellion about.

Though angered by the irrefutable evidence of Ahithophel's treason, Micah was heartsick at the report he would have to give Joab. He knew there would be no mercy, and he knew that Shoshanna would be devastated when she lost her grandfather. He wanted very much to be there to comfort her when the inevitable loss happened, if only he could find where she had gone. "What am I thinking?" he said out loud to himself. Shoshanna would not be likely to accept any comfort from the man who would be Ahithophel's chief accuser.

He reached Giloh before the setting of the sun and headed directly for Ahithophel's house. As he made his way up the wide stone steps leading to the entrance, hoping to find Shoshanna there, he was greatly surprised to see Ahithophel himself, sitting on a bench beneath a spreading terebinth tree that cast its shade over the gate to his courtyard. Micah hesitated. Why wasn't the old man in Jerusalem, still celebrating Absalom's victory?

As Micah considered what to say, Ahithophel glanced up with a look of unconcern, and motioned him forward.

As Micah gingerly approached, he realized as never before that the Gilohite was an old man. Ahithophel seemed infinitely tired as he greeted Micah. "You pause on your business for David." It was a statement, not a question. Micah noted that Ahithophel had not referred to David as king.

"I am about the king's business," he said, not willing to let the slight go unchallenged. "But I am also searching for Shoshanna. I gave her into the care of my friend, Isaac ben Ahiam, but I discovered this morning that she had slipped away."

"My granddaughter is a clever girl. She outsmarted you." By the smile on his face, Ahithophel was proud of what his grand-daughter had done. It angered Micah.

"Anything could have happened to her, running off alone like that, but she was unconcerned, as always, for her own safety in her desire to help and protect you. How could you be so reckless as to use her in your plans to overthrow the king? I realize that you believe the prince will prevail, but he will not. Even within the walls of the palace are those who would give their own lives to restore the kingdom to David."

"I am well aware of that," Ahithophel stated calmly. "Our plans will all come to naught now. You are correct when you say I have endangered Shoshanna. But I have taken steps to rectify that."

Micah shook his head as if to clear it. Ahithophel was conceding defeat? After all these months of planning and plotting? He wanted to find out why, but Shoshanna was his first concern. "Is she now safely under your roof?"

"As I told you, son of Jonathan, I am seeing to the safety of my granddaughter. She is here, safely inside the house, even as we speak."

"If her safety is truly your concern, then you would send her away. Giloh is no place for her to be. When this is over, the king will demand your head, and your family will lose theirs as well if they are found with you." Micah expected Ahithophel to argue that Absalom's army would surely prevail. Instead, the man merely stroked his long beard several times in a distracted fashion and instructed Micah to sit at his feet.

"Shoshanna made it here safely just after midday," Ahithophel said after Micah sprawled on the ground. "She was very distraught when she told me that you had robbed her of the missives

I entrusted into her care. But I assured her that their delivery makes little difference now. However, I don't think that those words lessened her anger at you, young man.

"I also told her that she must not remain with me any longer, and that I would arrange for her and her mother to leave Giloh. She cried and told me that her place was by my side and that if I should send her away, she would run away to be with me." Micah's anger at her stubbornness warred with his pride in her fierce love and loyalty to her grandfather. What would it feel like to have that love and loyalty transferred to him? It seemed impossible. If Shoshanna believed she had to choose between them, there was no doubt she would choose Ahithophel every time.

Ahithophel's next words almost stopped his heart. It almost seemed as though the old man were addressing his secret thoughts. "When we last spoke, you expressed an interest in having Shoshanna as your wife. Do you still wish it?"

The hammering of his heart made Micah sputter. "I . . . after we talked, I thought there was no chance. She doesn't want me, . . . I . . ." He hesitated, but Ahithophel just waited for his answer. "Yes, I still wish it," he finally managed to choke out.

Ahithophel nodded. "The situation has changed completely since the last time I spoke with you. Then, I was certain that my future, and Shoshanna's, would follow a much different path. But I must tell you that I was wrong. Absalom will not be able to hold on to power. He will not defeat his father on the battlefield."

"How can you be so certain? Most people believe that the prince will easily win. What has happened to change your mind since we last talked?"

Ahithophel related all that had happened in Jerusalem. It shocked Micah that the man who had masterminded the revolt would confide in him, but by the time Shoshanna's grandfather had finished his story, Micah realized that he kept no more secrets because he truly believed Absalom's cause was lost. Micah felt a surge of hope that it was so.

His concern for Shoshanna came to the forefront. "Joab will

send men for you as soon as the battle is over. You must send your family away and throw yourself on the king's mercy. Maybe for the sake of Bathsheba and your long service, the king will spare your life. But you cannot risk the lives of Shoshanna and her mother."

"I told you that I would see to her protection," Ahithophel replied testily. Then something at the side of the house caught his attention, and Micah turned to see what it was. His eyes widened in surprise. It was Ailea and Jerusha.

"Mother, what are you doing here?"

"We have come for the wedding, of course," Jerusha piped up. "Mother said we were not to mention it until you had talked to Shoshanna's grandfather. She is very beautiful, Micah, like a princess. And she is tall enough for you. You have made a good choice."

The child pronounced this solemnly, as if her opinion were of utmost importance. Micah shook his head to clear it. Events were speeding by at a pace that made his head swim. He looked to Ahithophel for explanation.

"I wish you to marry her before you leave for the battle. When she told me of her encounter with you at Isaac's house, I hoped you would follow her here, and that you had not changed your mind about marrying her." He handed Micah a small parchment. "This is from your father, expressing his wish that you and Shoshanna marry with all haste." Micah took the document but did not open it. He was still trying to collect his thoughts.

"But I haven't time to wed. I have delayed too long as it is."

"You can marry her tonight and send her and her mother to your home in Ziph when you leave Giloh. I wish her to be under your care before . . ." Ahithophel's voice trailed off, and Micah assumed he was contemplating his inevitable arrest.

Micah cleared his throat. His heart seemed to be lodged there from the moment Ahithophel had told him he might have Shoshanna. "But Shoshanna will not consent to this hasty union. Does she even know?"

Ahithophel was unperturbed. "Don't concern yourself about

her reaction. Shoshanna will do as I wish, of course. She is a loyal and sweet-natured child."

Micah laughed and replied, "If you say so, then I suppose it is so."

Ahithophel suggested they go inside and find Shoshanna, motioning Ailea and Jerusha to go in ahead of him. Before they entered the house, Micah stopped the older man. "You realize that this union will not have any effect on the future as far as you are concerned."

"I do not seek this for myself; only for my daughter and grand-daughter. I believe you are strong enough to see that no harm comes to them."

"You have my solemn vow that I will protect them both."

Ahithophel nodded. "That is all I ask."

Once inside the house, Ahithophel went to fetch his grand-daughter while a young servant girl washed the dust off Micah's feet. His mother and sister disappeared into their guest chamber. Why did his mother leave him alone to face this ordeal? He glanced down at the little girl as she dried his clean feet. She trembled slightly, and Micah sighed. She was probably afraid of him be-cause of his size. Children often reacted that way to him at first, and he was always saddened, for he liked children very much. She had just dried his feet and was replacing his sandals when he saw Ahithophel and Shoshanna coming toward him.

Shoshanna held her head high, as she always did. But when she was close enough that he could see her eyes, Micah saw that she was distressed and near tears. He had an almost irresistible urge to reach out and draw her into a comforting embrace, as the Rab used to do with him. That was out of the question of course, not only for its impropriety, but because Shoshanna's pride would demand that she reject any such gesture.

"I have explained to my daughter and granddaughter that I wish you and Shoshanna to be wed immediately. Her dowry is a casket of gold and a herd of twenty donkeys that I keep in the next valley. You may send servants to collect them now, or leave them to pasture where they are until you can claim them."

"I suppose the best thing would be to leave them for the time being." Micah felt that this mundane discussion would drive him mad. He wanted so much to talk to Shoshanna alone. At the same time, he dreaded having to speak to her. As Ahithophel explained where the man lived who kept the donkeys, Micah took the opportunity to study his prospective bride.

Shoshanna's tunic was simply made, but of fine linen cloth. It was embroidered with blue and silver thread at the neck and hem, and hung perfectly on her tall, slender frame. It struck him, once again, that she was just right for him. Her face was pale, but she did not drop her gaze from his. Evidently she had not been paying attention to her grandfather's words either, because she interrupted with an observation. "So that is why your mother and sister are here," she said simply. Micah wished her expression did not convey such resignation. He would have preferred to see her angry.

"Their presence is the result of an understanding between my father and your grandfather. But the idea of marriage is not a new one for me. Were you are aware that I spoke to your grandfather about a betrothal?" Micah quite forgot Ahithophel's presence.

"You only said that because you had to. You needed to find out about the messages." Shoshanna did not try to hide the resentment in her voice.

Micah shook his head. "No, Shoshanna, I never lied to you." He paused for a long moment, but she said nothing else. He realized she didn't know the depth of his feelings for her—she still thought he had been using her.

"Shoshanna, you agree to this? You will have me as your husband?" In many ways it was a foolish question, of course. She really had no choice. Women never did. But in asking the question, Micah wanted to give her some modicum of power, some chance for her feelings and wishes to be heard. He had given her an opportunity to rant at him, to tell him she wanted none of him, and perhaps he would regret having done so.

She was silent for several moments, seeming taken aback by being asked for her opinion. Micah held his breath while he waited to hear what she would say. Her grandfather was not as patient. He started to speak, but stopped at the sound of her voice.

"My grandfather has explained to me that he wishes this marriage. He has chosen you because it is for the best for . . . for all of us. I would never go against his wishes. And I hold it an honor to be sought after by a man of integrity. I will consider myself blessed of Adonai to belong to you, my lord."

The speech was quite a declaration of love and familial loyalty. But that loyalty and love was for Ahithophel and Marah, not for him. He would have to be satisfied with her feeling "honored" and "blessed" to be espoused to him, and that she considered him "a man of integrity."

Micah tried not to feel disappointed. After all, this was more than he had ever dreamed, even in the desert that night, when he had warned her of the danger she was in, when they had come close to revealing their feelings to each other, even though each knew they could be betrayed by the other. That is when he had known he loved her. Or maybe his heart had been lost from the first, when he had seen her at the banquet, so self-contained, so animated in her conversation with Solomon, so graceful in her movements.

He was not certain when he had started to love her, but he recognized that time had only deepened his affection. He hoped that when the rebellion was behind them, he might have a chance to win her love. Now here she was, coming to him at least somewhat willingly, if not happily, telling him she would be honored to be his bride. He felt his chest swell with pride.

"But I have to report back . . . I mean, there is not much time." He addressed Ahithophel, embarrassed at his fumbling speech but unable to capture his racing thoughts.

Ahithophel responded calmly, "I have already sent my servants throughout Giloh to invite our neighbors to the wedding celebration, which shall take place this evening. Thankfully, your father sent word to Ziph in time for your mother and sister to be here. Your mother will take your new bride back to Ziph with her tomorrow afternoon, after you have left for Mahanaim."

"But Grandfather, I wish to stay here with you."

Ahithophel merely shook his head and addressed Micah. "It is a good plan. Shoshanna will take you to the guest house so you can ready yourself for the wedding."

"I need to speak with you, Grandfather," Shoshanna said pleadingly.

Ahithophel spoke almost harshly to his granddaughter. "It is time now to prepare for the wedding. We will talk later." He turned on his heel and strode purposefully out of the room.

The two were suddenly standing together alone. Shoshanna's thoughts were in turmoil. She looked at Micah, who stood bewildered watching Ahithophel's abrupt exit.

"I will call a servant to show you to your room," she said quietly.

"No, wait," Micah said, shaking his head as if to clear the cobwebs. "There's something I need to ask you."

Shoshanna blushed as she looked up at his strong face, her eyes moving slowly up until they met his amber gaze. He appeared startled and quickly began to stumble over his words. "What did . . . I mean how . . . how did you manage to get out of that locked room?"

"What?" Shoshanna came to herself. "Oh, I climbed out through the window."

"But that was surely not large enough for you to pass through!"

"That's what I thought as well—until I tried it."

"But how did you reach it? It was much too high to reach."

Her lips quirked slightly, and Micah thought for a moment she would smile, but her expression became bland. "Oh, I think I should leave that a mystery. You have bested me too many times already, my lord. You would find me no challenge at all, were you to learn all my secrets."

"You needn't worry, lovely lily. You will provide me with more than enough challenges through the next fifty years, by Adonai's mercy. And I shall make it my main ambition to discover all your secrets." He lifted her hand and kissed it.

When he raised his head, their gazes locked for a long moment before Shoshanna remembered the circumstances. She blushed again. "Uhh . . . I'll go and let you have your privacy. Just ask the servants if you have need of anything."

"I understand. You will have preparations of your own to make. Thank you for your hospitality." *My, but that was a brilliant observation,* Micah thought as Shoshanna swiftly disappeared. Maybe it was for the best. His mind seemed to go begging when he was around her. Yet when they were apart, all he could think of was wanting to be with her again. He wondered how he would keep his mind on battle when the time came. Maybe after he had claimed her for his wife this obsession with her would cease. He hoped so.

Shoshanna returned to the house and went straight to her room to prepare herself for the ceremony. She was glad, for the moment, that neither her mother nor Anah was waiting for her, because her head was spinning with the rapidly unfolding events. Just a few days before, she had heard the news that Absalom had declared himself king in Jerusalem. Grandfather had gone there to celebrate his victory, but then suddenly returned to Giloh, telling her and Marah that everything had changed. He had refused to tell them anything else.

Then Micah had come. He hadn't even seemed angry with her, though she had expected him to be furious that she had disobeyed him. Perhaps he was as stunned by the turn of events as she. It was all so confusing that her mind could scarcely take it in. Micah had been her enemy, because he was the enemy of Ahithophel. Yet now, both men seemed set on this course of uniting their families.

No one had asked her opinion. But she really had no other

choice, anyway. She had to marry Micah because the rebels were not going to win, and her grandfather and mother would be in danger. If she married Micah, he could appeal to the king to spare her grandfather's life. For the sake of Micah's father, David might allow Ahithophel to remain in exile at Giloh.

Shoshanna told herself she was marrying to save her family. Deep down, though, she knew that she wanted to be Micah's wife for other reasons: his unbending faithfulness to the Lord and the Lord's anointed, his gentleness despite his giant stature, and the fact that whenever she was with Micah, she felt she was in the presence of a rock of strength, a shelter in which she could take refuge.

Chapter Twelve

~

Micah dressed in finery that Ailea had brought from Ziph: a long-sleeved purple undergarment topped with a sleeveless violet tunic that was pleated and embroidered with gold and silver thread. Around his neck hung a massive pendant that matched the armband he always wore. How had she found the ornament on such short notice? A heavy gold circlet provided by Ahithophel held his purple headdress in place.

Micah slipped through the back-door of the main house and went to seek out the family to see how events would proceed. In an ordinary situation, a bride and groom who lived in the same village would each prepare for the wedding by taking a ritual bath, and dressing in their wedding garments. The bride would wear bracelets, anklets, rings, necklaces, or earrings that were made of precious metal, maybe encrusted with jewels if the family were wealthy. This was her dowry. The groom would wear a circlet of gold on his head if he were rich, or a garland made of laurel leaves or flowers if not.

The groom's friends would meet at his house, where the wedding feast would take place. The bride's attendants would join her at her father's house. The bridegroom and his friends would go with much celebration to the bride's home to fetch her and her guests to his father's house. Once there, the wedding feast would begin. In some instances the feasting would last a week.

Customarily, the fathers would pronounce a blessing on the couple, perhaps offering a prayer of supplication that the Lord would bless the union with many children. Then the bride and groom would retire to the bridal bower for the consummation. But in this case, with the wedding so hastily planned, Micah wasn't certain whether protocol would be followed.

He found Ahithophel waiting in the common room. "Sit down, my son," the old man said. "All the women of the household have gone to the home of my brother to await our coming. At dusk we will go and fetch them. But for now, I would assure myself that you are worthy to guard my greatest treasure. If you do not love her enough to persevere and overcome all the obstacles you will face in your life together, then I would have you tell me now, so that I can make arrangements to see to her welfare, and her mother's."

"I love her enough, my lord. I will protect her; you needn't worry. But I am afraid that she feels that in going with me, she is deserting you, and that may prove difficult to overcome."

"Nonsense. She will adjust very quickly to her new life in Ziph. She won't grieve too long when I . . . when she leaves Giloh. Besides, I will speak to her again before she departs, and try to explain that though you and I are on opposite sides in war, for the sake of her happiness we will put that conflict aside."

"I know that you are a persuasive man, my lord. I trust your efforts will be successful."

≈ ≈ ≈

Dust was kicked up in the streets as many citizens made their way to the home of the town's most prestigious resident. Dogs barked and children laughed in their excitement for the feast that would follow the ceremony. This wedding was a distraction from the anxiety of an impending war for the whole town.

Micah and a dozen of the young men of Giloh, each under the age of twenty because all the others had gone off to fight for Absalom, went to fetch Shoshanna at her uncle's house at the other end of town. Micah wondered how friendly the young men would be if they knew he was one of David's men. They naturally assumed he was a rebel because he was marrying Ahithophel's granddaughter. Would they forgive Ahithophel for leading them into insurrection once word came back that their brothers and fathers had died in a futile cause? Ahithophel didn't seem to be worrying about it.

All such thoughts deserted him when he reached the modest home of Ahithophel's youngest brother. Shoshanna was waiting for him, surrounded by several female cousins, and some of the girls from the town. Her dress was made of white linen with a long outer coat of variegated colors. The backsides of its sleeves had gold tassels that trailed nearly to the floor. Her veil was held in place by a circlet of braided cords, also in many colors. Micah could not see his bride's face clearly, for the veil was too opaque. He wished he could. He wanted to see in her eyes whether she was pleased or unhappy about what was taking place.

Micah took her hand and the wedding party proceeded back to Ahithophel's house. He hoped that somehow Shoshanna would understand in days to come that he could not save her grandfather from the fate of a traitor. He probably would not, even if he could. Ahithophel and Absalom would have the blood of many on their hands before this rebellion was over, and they must suffer the consequences. Ahithophel seemed to have changed completely since the prince had decided not to take his advice. Of course, he had done the most expedient thing to protect his granddaughter by marrying her into the family of a *Gibbor*.

At the home of Ahithophel, they were led to a raised seat of honor, where they would preside over the wedding feast. Ahithophel beckoned Micah to lean down and whispered in his ear, "I had the servants lay by stores of food because I thought I would be having a celebration of an entirely different kind. It is good that it won't go to waste."

Micah was confused and rather shocked that the old man could jest about the prospect of Absalom's lost cause. Did the man not realize that the king would certainly execute him?

After Ahithophel made everyone welcome, making no explanation of the hasty union, nor mentioning the conflict that divided the kingdom, he asked Micah and Shoshanna to stand and announced they were to be man and wife. Shoshanna heard his words, but none of this seemed real. It was as if she were in the midst of a dream.

Micah turned to Shoshanna and, though it was not prescribed, made his vow to her, raising the long cloak he wore to cover her shoulders. "From this day on, I will cover you; I will shelter you and keep you from all harm. I will cleave only to you, and care for you as long as we live." Shoshanna was deeply touched, and thankful that as a woman she was neither required nor expected to say anything in response. She would have found it impossible to speak around the great lump in her throat.

Ahithophel stepped forward and placed one hand on Micah's head, one hand on Shoshanna's, and prayed, "Blessed are you, Adonai our God, ruler of the universe, who created man and woman to fill the earth and subdue it. Look with favor now on Micah and Shoshanna, and may their offspring be many and fear your name." With this blessing, the ceremony was complete.

Micah's mother gave her blessing and welcome into their family. Shoshanna had to lean down in order to be embraced by the dainty woman. The bride smiled for the first time that day when Micah received his mother's embrace, and lifted Ailea's feet off the ground as he hugged her.

Jerusha, who sat on the other side of Shoshanna, was almost exhausting in her unrestrained enjoyment of the occasion. She kept trying to coax her to taste some of the delicacies Ahithophel had provided for the feast, but Shoshanna barely touched her food. Her stomach lurched each time she took a bite of the roasted kid or seasoned lentils, and she altogether refused the sweet almond cakes. She noticed, however, that Micah ate a great quantity of everything. The suddenness of their union and the uncertain aspect of their future did not seem to affect him. *How much food does such a huge man consume?* she wondered.

"You must have used a chair or stool with a rope tied to it so that you could lift it up after you reached the windowsill." When Shoshanna's mouth dropped open, he popped in a plump apricot. He grinned at her as she chewed, pleased at the annoyance he saw in her eyes. It was much better than the apathy she had been displaying all day.

"Well, am I right? You pulled up the chair you used for climbing so any servant who came in would not see it beneath the window and know you had left. It was a clever idea to arrange the cushions like you did, to make it look as if you were asleep with the covers pulled over your head."

"And when did the servants discover my ruse?"

"They didn't. I did. I came to your room around dawn. I wanted to have one last glimpse of you."

"You had no right to come into my room!" For some reason, Shoshanna felt frustrated, as if he had bested her once more in a contest.

Micah rolled his eyes. "It wasn't your room. It was my friend's room. And there was nothing wrong with looking in on my wife."

"I wasn't your wife."

"No, but I knew that some day you would be. I just didn't realize how soon."

She gave up and pretended to be absorbed in her meal, forcing down tiny bites, so that she wouldn't have to converse with him.

≈ ≈ ≈

Only her mother escorted Shoshanna into the bridal chamber. Her attendants and new mother-in-law and sister-in-law stopped outside the door and left after many kisses and well wishes. Actually, Ailea had to pry Jerusha's little arms from around Shoshanna's neck. Shoshanna hoped that none of them were offended that she hadn't asked them to stay. In truth, she was relieved to be alone with her mother.

"You must do everything you can to please your new husband. Do not speak back to him in that impertinent way you sometimes have, Shoshanna. When the moment is right, perhaps tomorrow, you must ask Micah to speak to the king on behalf of your grandfather. You are his last hope now. At first I believed he was simply anxious over the outcome, but he has told me that there is not a single doubt in his mind now that Absalom's cause is a complete loss." Marah made these admonishments as she helped Shoshanna remove the braided headpiece and veil, then take off the heavily embroidered outer robe and fold it away. The bride stood in her sleeveless, white linen tunic.

"Mother, I am not sure that Micah could even get an audience with the king. Surely my cousin will ask the king . . ."

Marah shook her head vehemently. "You do not know Bathsheba very well. She loves David more than anything else on earth. Now that she knows her grandfather has betrayed him, she won't intercede on his behalf." Marah snorted. "More likely, she will insist on being present at his execution. Be assured, Shoshanna, only you can save your grandfather's life."

Their conversation ended abruptly when Micah entered the chamber—alone, thankfully. Micah stood, drinking in the sight of his new bride. Her mahogany-dark eyes were large and round in the ivory oval of her face. *She is mine. Mine! Oh, Grandfather, I wish you had lived long enough to meet her. She is everything you taught me to search for in a wife—loyal, brave, chaste, intelligent . . .*

He stood just inside the doorway—rather like a mountain, Shoshanna thought—massive, muscular, and immovable. He was unsmiling, his eyes fastened on his bride, merely nodding when Marah said good night and left the room.

How had anyone cast aspersions on Micah's masculinity? His

mere presence was intimidating, and now he was her husband. The thought brought an involuntary shiver.

The movement snapped Micah out of his reverie. "You are cold?" he asked.

She shook her head slowly. "I am only . . ." she shrugged helplessly.

"You will not be afraid." Shoshanna suppressed the smile that came to her lips at the confident arrogance of the command.

She lifted her chin proudly. "I'm not afraid of you, Micah. But this is all so strange and new . . ."

He smiled. "It is new to me too, being a husband. And, Shoshanna, I have never touched a woman. I've been waiting for my wife. Waiting for you."

Her eyes widened in surprise. "Most men, especially warriors, do not keep themselves only for their wives."

"I am not most men."

"That I believe."

"Take down your hair for me, Shoshanna."

The abrupt order surprised and frightened her a little, but she did as Micah said, removing the four large pins that held the silky mass atop her head. It came tumbling down to its full length. Micah picked up a section and wrapped it about his large hand; his face softened and his eyes were warm as he held her in his gaze. How he had dreamed of reaching for her hair, feeling its silky texture, letting it run through his fingers.

"When I first saw you at the king's banquet, this was the first thing I noticed about you, the glory of your hair. It angered me that other men could look upon it. Now only my eyes will see it like this."

It was true, of course. As a married woman, she would never again wear her hair uncovered in public. But again, the sheer male arrogance of the statement struck her. At the same time she felt strangely pleased by his jealous comments.

He wound more of her hair around his hand, in effect, reeling her in. When she stood very close to him, he studied her for long moments, as if to memorize her features. His thumbs brushed across her cheekbones. "Shoshanna, my beautiful, beautiful lily." He feathered kisses lightly across her face.

"I'm not beautiful."

"You are."

He lifted her effortlessly and placed her on the bed. Shoshanna looked up at the canopy, wound about with grapevines that held small clusters of grapes. She kept her eyes fastened on it, too shy to look at her bridegroom.

He came to her. "You are trembling," he said.

"So are you."

He laughed ruefully. "That is because you make me feel weak . . . and strong at the same time. Shoshanna, there should be nothing between us," he whispered in her ear.

"Please . . . I don't want you to see me."

"But Shoshanna, you are beautiful. My beautiful wife."

"I'm afraid," she managed to stammer.

"I told you not to be afraid."

"Yes, but . . ." He smothered the remainder of her protest with kisses, and soon Shoshanna wasn't afraid anymore.

≈ ≈ ≈

When the gray light of dawn crept into the room, both husband and wife were already awake, but neither wanted to face the danger and separation that awaited them, so they hadn't spoken. Shoshanna's hair was spread over them like a cover as her head was pillowed by Micah's shoulder.

It was so strange, she reflected, as she felt the steady beat of her husband's heart beneath her palm. In just one day, her life was totally changed, and it had her mind spinning. As she clung to Micah, she felt safe and protected for the first time since the intrigue had begun. She wanted to hold onto him and never let him go. Yet she felt vulnerable at the same time. At the root of her fears was the realization that she loved him more than she ever thought possible, and that love might require her to turn her back on her grandfather. She couldn't do that.

As though he read her thoughts, Micah kissed the top of her head and hugged her closer for a moment before rising. "I'll return to you as soon as I can," he promised as he dressed and prepared to leave.

"Micah, please take care."

He crossed the room to her and tilted her chin on the tips of two fingers as he bent to kiss her. His lips were as soft as a butterfly's wings against hers, and she marveled again at how gentle her giant could be. "I will take care, Shoshanna. I wouldn't wish to make you a widow when you haven't been a bride even for a whole day."

"Don't jest about it. I wish it were all over." After a long pause, Shoshanna continued. "Micah?"

"Ummm?"

"About my grandfather." She took a deep breath. "Will you speak to the king on his behalf?"

"No."

Tears welled up suddenly in her eyes. "No? That's all you have to say?"

"Yes. That is all I have to say. The discussion is over, Shoshanna. Your grandfather and I have an understanding, so please don't ask again."

She could not believe she had heard right. "But you have to help, Micah. Grandfather is too proud to beg your help, but if the king wins, he will surely seek my grandfather's life. You must—"

"Enough!" Micah said, his voice soft but implacable.

"But I can't just let my family . . . ."

" *I* am your family now, Shoshanna. Get dressed. My mother wishes to leave before midday. After I have taken my leave, you will return with her to Ziph, to my father's house. If your mother can be persuaded to leave Giloh, she will also go with you. I cannot escort you because I have already taken too much time seeing to your safety. It is past time for me to join the king."

She was confused. Why was he behaving this way? "No! I want to stay here with Grandfather. He needs me."

Micah crossed the room in two strides. He took her chin in one of his huge hands and lifted it until she was forced to look at him. "Hear me well, Shoshanna. Your days of being involved in your grandfather's schemes are over. That's the way he wants it. That's the way I want it. That is the way it will be. Now hurry. Time is slipping away."

Shoshanna fought back tears as she prepared to leave for Ziph. Micah was not even going with her. What would her new life in Ziph be like? Above all, she was worried about her grandfather. How could she leave him to face the king's wrath alone?

When she entered the courtyard, Micah and Ailea were deep in conversation. He was asking her what the mood was in Ziph. "Will they stay loyal to the king?" he asked his mother.

"I wish I could say yes, Micah, but I am not certain. I know that some of the young men have gone off to follow David, while others are joining up with the prince. I certainly miss your grandfather at a time like this. I don't suppose you could take the time to go back there to talk with them?" It was obvious by her tone that she believed the answer would be a negative one. He surprised her.

"With the horse that Joab gave me, I might have time if I push myself and him. Besides, part of my assignment is to rally as many men as I can to the king's cause and bring them with me when I join the army at Mahanaim."

"You will be able to escort us home?"

Micah shook his head. "No, I must press on. It will take time for Shoshanna to pack her things. I will have met with the elders and left Ziph before you arrive."

Shoshanna stood watching and listening to their conversation. She felt sharp disappointment that Micah would go to Ziph but would not be there when she arrived. She was unsure of what to do. Her grandfather approached her and took her in his arms. "Child, you will go to the home of your bridegroom this day. This marriage is what I wished, what I believe best for you. You will go with my blessing and be happy."

"But Grandfather, I want to stay with you until the battle is over. Then Micah could come and get me. Maybe if you ask—"

"Hush, my lily. Your mother-in-law will take you to your new home, and you want to make a good impression on her. You mustn't start out this marriage by arguing or defying your husband. Now go and bid him good morning."

Shoshanna bid her husband God's blessing on the day. She was still confused and angered by his rejection of her request, and her tone of voice showed it. Micah's mouth thinned in response, but he made no comment on her behavior, merely asking her whether she thought she would be prepared for her journey to Ziph by midday.

While Micah was saddling and loading his horse, she again spoke to Ahithophel, offering to stay with him until Micah returned from battle, but her grandfather refused to allow her to stay. He seemed different somehow, as though his plans to see Absalom take the throne were no longer important. In fact, he refused to even speak of the rebellion. Nor would he explain his reason for agreeing to her union with a man who owed his loyalty to the king.

Shoshanna had assumed when she arrived and found that Ahithophel had returned, dejected, from Jerusalem, that his decision to marry her off to Micah was for her safety. If he now believed the rebel cause was lost, he also feared that David would retaliate against his family. Shoshanna wanted the king's forces to prevail, because she knew in her heart that he was the Lord's anointed, but she feared for her grandfather. And if David's forces were defeated, what would happen to Micah? There was no outcome that would not harm someone close to her.

There was no time to talk to Micah. When he finished preparing for his own journey, he helped the women load pack animals with provisions for the trip. Marah had refused Ailea's offer of hospitality, but it had been arranged for her to stay with her cousin who lived at the other end of Giloh. Because she had not been aware of the conspiracy, she assured her daughter she would be safe if the king's guards came to take Ahithophel. She promised Shoshanna that she would look in on Ahithophel every day.

While the morning was still new, Micah's mother and little sister were ready to depart, but it seemed that, even with old Gamal and Anna helping, Shoshanna would never be ready. Shoshanna was fascinated by the dainty beauty of Ailea as she stood beside her son. She tried to hide her shock at the thought of such a tiny woman being the mother of a giant such as Micah. But her husband read her expression and laughed. "No need to be embarrassed at your thoughts. No one would ever believe my mother could possibly be my mother, but she is."

Shoshanna studied her new husband for a moment. "Yes, I can see the likeness in your eyes now." She turned to Ailea, who had heard the exchange, and gave a respectful bow.

Ailea came forward and kissed her on both cheeks. "You are just perfect for my son, and we will be very happy to have you in Ziph."

"You are so tall and beautiful," Jerusha remarked as she studied the new member of her family.

Shoshanna smiled down at the child, who was the perfect image of her mother, petite, green eyes with the same shape, and shiny black hair that curled around her face.

"Thank you, Jerusha. You are very lovely yourself."

"No, no, I am quite plain. My teeth are too large, and I am afraid I will never be tall, but it does not matter, really. I am a shepherdess, and will always be one. And Reuben, who is a shepherd, will marry me when we are old enough. He likes me well enough just the way I am, and—"

A large hand came down atop the little girl's head. "Jerusha, stop your rambling on. It can drive a person insane! Now kiss me good-bye, because I have delayed my departure too long as it is." Micah lifted his sister up until she was face to face with him. She grabbed his full mane of hair and kissed him heartily, asking him to stay a while longer. But he was determined to begin his journey, so he took his leave of them just a few moments later. He called Shoshanna aside to instruct her.

"Obey my instructions and wait for me at Ziph. Listen to my mother's counsel, Shoshanna. She is a wise woman. She will take good care of you." Without kissing her good-bye, he turned to leave. Shoshanna felt bereft as she watched him mount the great chestnut stallion and ride away.

Before leaving for Ziph herself, Shoshanna walked with her mother to her cousin's house. "I will stay here to be of help to your grandfather," her mother told her when they reached the cousin's home. "Go to your new life, daughter, and do not worry about either of us."

The last person she said farewell to was Anah. "I am leaving you here to look after my mother, Anah. When this is all over, I will send for you. No, don't cry now, or you will make me cry, and that won't impress my new mother-in-law." Shoshanna forced a smile and gave her old nurse a final pat on the shoulder before setting off with Ailea and Jerusha.

$\approx \ \approx \ \approx$

Micah stood in the center of the circle of Ziph's elders, trying to get them to see the folly of declaring for Absalom. "Have you forgotten the lessons of the past, when you supported Saul and reported David's whereabouts to him? Had it not been for my father's warning, the old king might have caught up with David. It was only through the pleading of my father and grandfather that David did not punish you when he ascended to the throne. Can you not see that for all his faults, David is the chosen of Adonai?"

"But the prince's forces outnumber David's more than four to one. How can the king hope to overcome that?" The man who spoke was Eliezer, one of the oldest of the city fathers, and unofficially their leader since the death of the Rab Shageh. Unfortunately, he also tended to be the most cautious. He must be won over, but how?

"Eliezer, you were a lifelong friend of my grandfather. What would he say if he were among us?" Micah held his breath as he waited for the old man's answer.

"What your grandfather might have said is not important. He is not among us any longer. And if you think you can take his place, you are sadly mistaken. Is that not true, men?" Eliezer looked around the circle congregated at the village gate.

"No one could ever replace the Rab," one of them offered mournfully.

"Especially not the offspring of an Aramean," Micah heard someone murmur.

Someone else commented in a louder voice. "That's right. His mother was sent back to her people, and months later came back with a baby. How do we know from whom he sprang?"

Micah's face turned crimson at the insult to his mother's virtue. For a moment his eyes sparked with anger, and the man who had made the remark shrank back. Then Micah's expression changed to one of deep sadness. In that moment he looked very much like his grandfather. And in that moment the elders knew that like the Rab, Micah would never retaliate for the insult.

"Don't be foolish, Nadab," the man standing beside him said. "One only has to look into Micah's eyes to see the Rab looking right back. He's the true son of Jonathan and descendent of the Rab. No doubt about that. The question is, does he have the wisdom of the Rab? It will be years before that question is resolved."

Micah felt defeat threatening. The city fathers would never listen to him. But then he thought of his grandfather. Shageh would not have wished him to give up so easily, so he tried again. "It is true that I am the son of an Aramean woman, but I am also of the tribe of Judah. I worship only the Lord of hosts, and I am on my way to give my life, if necessary, to see that his chosen one is returned to the throne. I am asking you to stand with me, to send your sons to fight with me. What do you say, men of Ziph?"

"I say we should not risk Absalom's vengeance by supporting his father. He already sits on the throne in Jerusalem, and we know that his forces greatly outnumber David's," one man offered.

"David's men are renowned warriors. I believe they can easily defeat Absalom's untrained men," another said. The discussion continued this way for more than an hour as Micah tried to hide his impatience. If they took much longer to decide they would miss the battle altogether.

Eventually it was decided that the elders of Ziph would remain neutral, supporting neither David nor Absalom. They would allow the young men of the village to choose to fight for either side, or not fight at all. Micah felt deep disappointment that the elders had not stood solidly for the king, but their decision was not a total loss; some of the young men of Ziph left with him two hours later when he set out for Mahanaim.

As Micah and his small contingent left the village, he paused and scanned the road from Giloh. There was no sign yet of his mother, sister, and wife. His wife. It was difficult to believe Shoshanna was truly his. He wished he could see her for just a moment before he left for battle. He regretted that he had not kissed her good-bye. But she had been angry with him, and he had been afraid that she would turn away from him and embarrass him in front of their families and the servants.

But she was his wife now, and he was headed into battle. And now he would have no memory of a farewell kiss to sustain him. Well, it was too late now to remedy that. He would have to make do with memories of the time they had had before the issue of Ahithophel's fate had come between them.

Chapter Thirteen

~

*H*ushai made his way from the palace to the tabernacle, located in the heights of Mount Zion. It was midday, and he knew that both Zadok and Abiathar would be there, directing the priests and Levites in the worship rituals. He waited until he could get their attention, then motioned them to the far corner of the Tabernacle compound so that their conversation would not be overheard.

"Absalom is not going to attack immediately. I've persuaded him to continue to muster his troops, in contradiction to Ahithophel's advice. But it is still essential that David get as far away from Jerusalem as possible before the prince's army comes in pursuit. Send word to the king immediately."

Both men agreed, and as soon as Hushai had left them, Zadok went to his house. "Send me Nehusha," he told his wife as soon as he entered. The young servant came immediately, her sandals slapping on the smooth marble floors of Zadok's villa.

"Nehusha, I have a very important errand for you. It is most confidential, and will perhaps determine if we may see the king returned to his rightful place. You wish to see that happen, don't you?"

The dark eyes of the plump young woman shone earnestly as

she answered. "Oh, yes, my lord, more than anything!" Several years ago, the king had passed a caravaner who was bringing slaves to the market in Jerusalem to be sold. The man had been very cruel to each of the five slaves he had for sale, but had particularly abused Nehusha. The king saw the evidence of their abuse and had immediately bought all of them.

The king had arranged for her to become a servant in Zadok's household, one of the most esteemed in Jerusalem. Zadok himself divided his time between Jerusalem and Gibeon, where he presided over the priests and sacrifices offered in the tabernacle of Moses, which was still functioning there. Nehusha's life as a servant of Zadok's wife was luxurious beyond what she ever could have dreamed. The master's wife, having no daughters, treated Nehusha almost as if she were one. And all of this because of the king's act of mercy. She would do anything for him.

"Then listen carefully," her master continued. "You must go to En Rogel tonight and take this message to my son, Ahimaaz, who is staying at the home of Jonathan son of Abiathar. But let no one see you or overhear what you tell him."

Several hours later, Nehusha slipped through the Hinnon Valley into the enclave of En Rogel, being very careful not to be seen. She delivered the message that David was to keep his forces moving away from Jerusalem.

Nehusha hurried back to her master's house in Jerusalem, her heart filled with pride at furthering the king's cause. She did not see the twelve-year-old boy who sat atop a wall at the edge of the village of En Rogel. The boy had been begging at the city gate one day when he had come to Absalom's attention. The prince had smiled at him and given him a silver coin, and in return, the boy had promised to be Absalom's eyes and ears in his village. From time to time, he reported to the prince and was always generously rewarded.

He did not know whether the girl who had come to En Rogel was a friend or foe of the prince, but he had seen by her furtiveness that she was up to some intrigue. He followed her to the house where the high priests' sons were staying. Soon, Ahimaaz and Jonathan came out of the house. From where he was hiding in the darkness, he could hear one say to the other, "We will find him near the river." They left En Rogel on swift mules, headed down the highway toward Jericho, in the direction of the deposed king's retinue. The boy ran as quickly as his legs would carry him to the city gates of Jerusalem. There, he spoke urgently to one of the guards, and before long a troop of soldiers was headed out to investigate this possible act of treason.

On their way to find the king at the river ford, Ahimaaz and Jonathan entered the environs of Bahurim. Ahimaaz reined his mule to a stop, jumped off, and scrambled up the high rocks that marked the route between Jerusalem and Jericho. "What are you doing?" his companion demanded. Ahimaaz did not answer, but no sooner had he reached the summit of the hill, than he came skidding back down.

"We're being followed—Absalom's men!" Jonathan did not argue with him as he remounted. They were off immediately. A few minutes later, the young men were pounding on the door in the wall of a compound Ahimaaz had identified as belonging to his cousin.

The rebellion had the people of Bahurim very nervous, and no one was about. "Who is there?" demanded a fearful voice from within.

"It is Ahimaaz, your husband's cousin. Let us in, please, Rachel."

The door creaked open a few inches, and Ahimaaz shoved his way into the courtyard, with Jonathan right behind him, leading their mules. He quickly closed and locked the door. "You have to hide us. Absalom's men are not far behind. If we're apprehended, the prince will have us killed."

The young housewife looked at her cousin doubtfully, then pointed to a shed at the far end of the courtyard that held a donkey and two sheep. "Put your animals in there." After they had tied their mounts to a post in the shed, Rachel led them to the cistern to her left. "Here, get in, both of you. It's dry." They jumped into the five-foot-deep cistern, thanking God it was the dry season. Rachel struggled with the heavy wooden cover her husband had made to keep their young children from falling in. The men inside helped her put it in place. There was already the sound of voices outside in the street, and in the next moment, a furious pounding on the door. Rachel paused for a moment to heft a large basket filled with winnowed wheat. She dumped the kernels on top of the cistern so it appeared they had been spread there to dry. Then she hurried to open the door, unable to hide her fear as she faced a half dozen angry men.

"Where are Ahimaaz and Jonathan? We know they came in here!" Even as their leader questioned the young woman, the other men searched the house. They looked in a large wooden chest that held precious firewood. It sat right by the cistern, and Rachel's heart clinched as she fully expected them to lift the cover off it and discover the fugitives at any moment. But miraculously, they didn't.

"Answer me, woman, where are they?" The man was very angry, and it was all Rachel could do to keep her voice from quavering.

"Ahimaaz and the fellow who was with him took bread and passed through my back door. They said they were going to cross over the brook that is back there. I think they were going to try to circle back to Jerusalem. It was only a few minutes ago." Rachel could not control her strident breathing as she waited to see whether the leader of the troop, a very hard-looking man, would believe her.

She jumped as he shouted to his men. "Come! Remount and circle behind the house. They've crossed over the water brook back there."

For long moments after they left, Rachel stood frozen, terrified that they would come back. Finally, she ran up the stairs to her rooftop and looked. In the moonlight she could see the search party beating the low bushes that grew by the brook. They were getting farther and farther away, headed in the direction of Jerusalem. Apparently, they had believed her story. Faint with relief, she went to let her guests out of their hiding place.

≈ ≈ ≈

Within minutes after the arrival of the sons of the high priests with their warning, David's company was crossing the ford over Jordan, just east of Gilgal. They would march all night and not stop until they reached the city of Mahanaim, just south of the Jabbok River. The young men's assessment had been that Absalom would continue to follow Hushai's advice and gather more troops before he pursued David, but there was always the chance that he would reflect on Ahithophel's sound advice and decide to come after David immediately. Jonathan of Ziph and all the other *Gibborim* had agreed.

The *Gibborim,* the Cherethites, and the Pelethites continued straight to Mahanaim. On their arrival, they were greeted more warmly than they could ever have anticipated. Mahanaim was a fortress town and a city of refuge. It was on the border of the territory of Gad and the half-tribe of Manasseh.

Here, the night before his reconciliation with Esau, their forefather Jacob had slept and dreamed of the angels of the Lord, and exclaimed, "This is God's army." He had therefore named it Mahanaim, meaning "two camps"—God's and Jacob's. It was the city where Saul's son Ishbosheth had declared himself king. But the prosperous city held no remaining loyalty to the Benjamite kingship, and came out to welcome David and his men.

Shobi, the son of Nahash, the deceased Ammonite ruler who had been a friend of David, was now living in exile in Mahanaim. He came to meet David's army, bearing supplies and gifts. "We come to offer you our welcome and support, friend of my father," the younger son of Nahash said, offering David the traditional kiss of greeting.

Jonathan looked at him and the king in wonder. Here were two men who, in spite of the traditional enmity between their people, had a friendship that could not be shaken. When Nahash had died and his elder son, Hanun, had succeeded him as ruler of Rabbah, the Ammonite's capital city, Hanun's treatment of the diplomats David sent to convey his condolences had set off a long and bloody war between Israel and Ammon.

Shobi had been angered by his elder brother's provocation of the war and had opposed it, even though he had fought against David's forces out of loyalty to his people. When the Hebrews won the conflict, David had been very conciliatory toward Shobi, even though he punished Hanun and other military leaders severely.

This had made Shobi suspect among many of his own people, and he had been forced to take his household and followers into exile in Mahanaim, or else live in fear of a dagger in his back. He now offered his personal army, which consisted of several hundred men, to David's cause. The king, it appeared to Shobi, could use all the manpower he could get.

Machir, the son of David's old friend Ammiel, accompanied Shobi. He had come from his home at Lo Debar, not far from Mahanaim. His first words were of Mephibosheth, as David knew they would be. For years after King Saul's death, before David had brought him to live in the palace, Mephibosheth had lived as a son in Shobi's household.

"My lord, is Mephibosheth with you? Did his health allow him to make the journey?" Machir took a step back at the look of anger that flashed in the king's eyes.

"According to reports I received before I left Jerusalem, Mephibosheth chose to remain at the palace and become a follower of Absalom. It seems he did not feel he owed me any loyalty for what I have done for him since I fetched him from your house many years ago."

Machir's mouth dropped open. "No, my lord, surely the reports were wrong. The young man is ever grateful to you. Whenever he returns for a visit to my household, he has nothing but praise. Why, you may ask his servant what he—"

David shook his head in dismissal. "It was his servant who told me of Mephibosheth's defection, Machir. They can't both be telling the truth, but I'm afraid there is no way to determine who is the liar, at least not anytime soon. Now let us talk no more of the matter. There are more important things to consider."

The king's words conveyed unconcern, but the hurt in his eyes was deep. Machir knew that believing the son of David's best friend had turned on him was a devastating blow at this low point of his reign.

"As you wish, my lord. But please investigate the matter thoroughly when you return to Jerusalem. This report is not consistent with the character of young Mephibosheth."

David smiled. "When I return to Jerusalem. . . . You believe our cause will prevail, then, Machir?"

"Without a doubt, sire. Come and see the supplies your allies from Gilead and all the surrounding regions have brought you." David went with Machir to examine the stores of food that were being unloaded from camels and donkeys. Besides Shobi and Machir, Barzillai from Rogelim, a town in Gilead, had come with men and gifts, which included cots for the officers to sleep on, utensils for cooking and serving food, wheat, barley, beans, lentils, and toasted seeds. Barzillai was a magnificent old desert chieftain who offered to throw in his forces to put down the rebellion.

Looking regal himself in his multicolored robe and pristine white turban, Barzillai bowed low to David. "I have brought such provisions as I thought you might need, my lord," indicating the special items he had set aside for David's own table. There were honey and curds, cheese and milk, and a herd of sheep to supply the king's table with meat.

A tempered celebration took place as David's allies made him welcome in Manahaim. Jonathan and his comrades felt their spirits rise as they realized that not all of the nation had turned away from David or been seduced by his handsome, charismatic son. David had been a loyal friend, and now that loyalty was being rewarded by the support of his friends during his darkest hour.

Over the next several days, thousands of loyal fighting men from every tribe, after giving careful consideration to Absalom's call to arms, chose instead to join the king's forces in Mahanaim. Now David would face the prince's twelve thousand-man army with some four thousand of his own troops.

The king and his *Gibborim* had chosen Mahanaim as their base of operations because its location on the highest elevation overlooking the river offered a strategic advantage. They would be able to see Absalom's army approaching and choose the field of engagement. Though still vastly outnumbered, their spirits rose by the hour.

Had they not won victory after victory in days gone by, when circumstances had indicated they did not have a chance? They had defeated the Philistines, who had superior weapons; and they had conquered the Arameans, despite their elite chariot corps. The victory had been Adonai's. Mahanaim was a Levitical city, and David asked the Levites to offer prayers daily for their protection. They had gained enough time to be prepared. They were ready for battle.

≈ ≈ ≈

Shoshanna woke disoriented on her first morning in Ziph. She was in a spacious room, on a very large and comfortable bed. Sun was streaming through an open window. It took a moment for her to remember that she was a wife, newly ensconced in her husband's home. She yawned and stretched widely, and still didn't reach the edge of the Micah-sized bed.

She felt a moment of panic, unsure whether she would be happy in this new life of hers. Ziph would likely be her home for the rest of her life. She would live here with Micah's parents and sister, at least until Jerusha married and moved to the family home of her husband. Inside the compound, which encircled an open courtyard, she and Micah would add rooms as their family grew. Micah's mother seemed to be very kind, very friendly. But she had heard enough tales told between married women about conflicts between wives and their mothers-in-law not to have a tiny reservoir of apprehension.

Then there was Micah's father. She had never met him, though she had in all likelihood seen him during ceremonies involving the *Gibborim*. She tried to call to mind as many of the faces of the thirty great warriors as she could, but only a general impression came to mind. They were big. They were hard. They were dangerous. A little shiver went through her at the thought of someday angering her father-in-law. Then she thought of burly Benaiah, and she smiled. He was gruff, but he had a wonderful sense of humor and a tenderness in the way he treated children, or the weak. Just like Micah. Surely his father would be the same kind of man that they were. Sons were usually like their fathers.

Leaning back against the plush pillows on her bed, Shoshanna daydreamed about the children she and Micah might have. She closed her eyes for a moment, trying to imagine what they would look like. Tall. They would probably be quite tall. Then again, they might take after Ailea and be tiny and dainty. She hoped that the girls and not the boys would take after their paternal grandmother. It was strange to be thinking of such things—herself as a mother, living here the rest of her life.

Suddenly, she regretted that Micah had had to go away immediately after the wedding. She walked over to a table that sat beside the window. There were two scrolls, tied with red cord. She unrolled one of them. It was a copy of the Torah. Shoshanna's eyes came to rest in the middle of the scroll. She read the words of Adonai to Joshua: *"Have I not commanded you? Be strong and of good courage; do not be afraid, nor be dismayed, for the LORD your God is with you wherever you go."*

These were the very words she needed as she faced these unfamiliar circumstances. It was as if Adonai had spoken words of encouragement directly to her, and she thanked him once more that her grandfather had taught her to read. A copy of the Law was a rare treasure. Ahithophel owned one, and had often allowed her to read from it. She wondered whether Micah would grant her the same privilege. Shoshanna had a feeling that the old Rab, Micah's grandfather, had given this copy to him. She carefully rolled it up again and tied it with the cord. Then she went to seek out the other members of her new family.

"Good morning. Where is Jerusha?" she asked Ailea when she had descended to the common room. Her mother-in-law looked up with a smile from the sewing she had in her lap, a tunic for one of the men in the family, by the looks of it. "Hello, Shoshanna. I hope you rested well. As for Jerusha, she rose hours ago. She always gets up before dawn to join the shepherds in the field."

Shoshanna blushed with embarrassment. Even Jerusha had been up and busy for hours. "I'm sorry I overslept."

"You didn't. You must rest and adjust to your new home. I imagine you're feeling rather homesick this morning." Ailea patted the place on the couch beside her. "Come and sit by me, and tell me all about yourself. But grab a piece of fruit from the bowl there. You're probably hungry."

For a few minutes Ailea sewed in silence, allowing Shoshanna to finish eating the handful of dates she had chosen from the wooden fruit bowl. When she had finished the last one, her mother-in-law folded the tunic and placed it on one of the shelves that ran along three walls of the room, then returned to sit closer to Shoshanna. She took the younger woman's hand and patted it.

"Now, my dear, tell me how you met my son, and how it involved this conflict in the kingdom." The rest of the morning was spent with Ailea showing Shoshanna her new home, telling her amusing stories about Micah as a child, and generally putting her new daughter-in-law at ease. Shoshanna found Ailea easy to confide in, and her many stories made Shoshanna feel that she knew her husband better. It appeared that one of her fears, at least, could be laid to rest. Ailea would not be a difficult person to live with.

She encouraged Shoshanna to talk about her own childhood and the events that led up to her marriage to Micah. "I am very much afraid for my grandfather's life," she found herself admitting to a sympathetic Ailea.

Ailea patted her hand. "I know, dear. We must pray for the safety of all our family members in this matter."

"Oh, my lady, I never meant to imply that I am not also very concerned about Micah's safety and that of your husband."

"I know that, my dear. You needn't measure your words with me." Shoshanna was touched by her kindness, but still felt guilty as she remembered Micah's words. *"I am your family now,"* and she felt she had somehow been disloyal.

Later that day they went down to the stream where the women of Ziph did their wash. They were disappointed to discover that the elders of Ziph had ignored Micah's counsel. Instead of remaining neutral, most of the young men had gone off to fight with Absalom's forces, according to a woman named Matred.

"We tried to tell our men to listen to Micah, but he is so young. The elders don't respect him the way they did his father or grandfather. If the Rab were here . . ."

"He would have told the men the same thing Micah told them. King David is the Lord's anointed. Adonai will not bless Ziph if her inhabitants turn away from his anointed in his time of trouble." Ailea had interrupted the woman, but she didn't seem to mind. Shoshanna could tell how much the other women respected her mother-in-law, despite her size and her foreign accent.

A very young woman started to cry at Ailea's words. "I begged my Joel not to go. I told him it wasn't right for the prince to try to steal his father's throne. But he listened to Lemuel, and this morning my baby has a fever." She looked around the group a bit desperately. "Do you think the Lord has stricken my babe because he's angry at Joel?"

Ailea immediately went to the woman and comforted her. "Don't you remember what the Rab taught us? 'The Lord your God is a merciful God; he will not abandon or destroy you or forget the covenant with your forefathers, which he confirmed to them by oath.' Those are the promises he gave to Moses. Don't be afraid, Kirah. The Lord isn't angry with your child. I will go with you to look in on him when we have finished the wash. Now come and meet my new daughter, Micah's bride. She is about your age."

It was impossible not to love such a kindhearted person, and Shoshanna found herself drawn to Ailea as the days passed. She felt some guilt when she realized that she could talk to Ailea about things she would never be able to share with her mother. She missed Marah and Ahithophel still, but her new family members helped her overcome her homesickness.

≈ ≈ ≈

Shoshanna quickly came to feel at home in Ziph. It was not the poor and primitive town that Shoshanna had imagined. Micah's family had brought wealth and prosperity by investing in sheep and in the pottery works that employed several of the local families.

Shoshanna thought her mother-in-law was the most beautiful, exotic-looking creature she had ever seen. She could not get over Ailea's dainty delicateness. At first, she felt like an ungainly giant in her presence. But Ailea soon put her at ease.

"Come, Shoshanna, let's go draw water from the well," she told her daughter-in-law on her second day in Ziph.

"But the storage jars are already full." Shoshanna pointed to the twenty-gallon stone jars that stood on either side of the main doorway.

"Oh, I know that, dear, but most of the village women will be there, and I want them all to see what a beautiful choice my son has made."

In a very short time, Ailea introduced Shoshanna to every woman in the village. She spoke of Shoshanna as her daughter, not her daughter-in-law; and she made every effort to overcome the natural distrust the isolated villagers felt for a stranger in their midst.

Another time she said, "Shoshanna, dear, would you get that pitcher down from that high shelf for me? It is sometimes frustrating not to be able to reach things. Even Jerusha can reach things I can't. Oh, well, the Lord has now blessed me with a daughter of perfect proportions who can help me." Spoken by anyone else, the words might have sounded contrived, but Ailea truly meant them. They came from her very large heart.

Jerusha also helped Shoshanna's transition into her new life. She was a whirlwind of activity and provided almost endless entertainment with her exploits. Each day, the child rose at daybreak and put on the coarse, simple tunic of a shepherd. Then she wrapped her head in a turban to cover the shiny black curls that she had inherited from her mother.

With the turban framing her face, her exotic green eyes were even more striking. They, too, were inherited from her mother. Jerusha would then go out to join her friend Reuben, the grandson of Habaz, Ziph's chief shepherd.

When Shoshanna looked into the eyes of Ailea and Jerusha, she was reminded of Micah. Though his eyes were amber, not the intense green of his mother and sister, the feline slant was identical. It was certainly a handsome-looking family she had married into. Modest as she was, she did not recognize the striking beauty that she herself added to the family.

~ ~ ~

Gamal made his way with shuffling steps up the pathway to Ahithophel's home. This morning, Ahithophel had awakened him early. Gamal was ashamed that lately he would oversleep if someone didn't wake him. He was fortunate that his master did not seem to mind his lapses of duty.

Ahithophel had said, "Gamal, you are to go with Lady Marah to the home of my nephew today. I don't want her to be a burden to her cousin. Offer your services for any work they might have for you."

Gamal had risen as quickly as his arthritic bones would allow. "Yes, my lord, I will go. Allow me to prepare a meal for you before I go."

Ahithophel had said solemnly, "No, Gamal. I shall be fasting today and I need to be alone."

"I will come back at sundown and bring you some of Anah's delicious venison stew to break your fast."

"Bring it tomorrow, Gamal. That will be soon enough." Then Ahithophel had done something he rarely did. He embraced his old retainer and kissed his cheek. "You have served me well, Gamal. I am ever grateful. You will look after Marah?"

Later, Gamal chastised himself severely for not understanding the true import of his master's words and actions. He had been with Ahithophel since they were both young men, and he knew something was different that morning. But to do his master's bidding was deeply ingrained in Gamal, and he assured Ahithophel that he would see to Lady Marah's needs.

He had been instructed not to return until the next day, but once Marah was comfortably settled, his nagging conscience compelled him to set out for home. The sun was setting as he approached his master's house, the lengthening shadows spread over the grounds and the villa. His old eyes could no longer see in the twilight darkness, and he paused as soon as he stepped inside the house. He felt for the square table that sat just inside the doorway. After carefully placing the basket of food on it, he picked up the lamp that was kept there and fumbled to light it.

Finally, the lamp flared to life and Gamal held it aloft. "Master?" There was no answer. Gamal listened, but heard no sound at all. The house had a feeling of emptiness, of desertion. The old man's hand began to tremble as he walked through the house.

He made his way to the master's study. There was a large window in the room, and enough light came in so that Gamal could see that Ahithophel was not in the spacious chamber.

He continued to search the house, calling out twice more, with no answer. When he got to Ahithophel's room, the door was closed.

He knocked. No answer.

Slowly, he pushed open the door. He looked around quickly, but his master wasn't there. Gamal let out a sigh of relief. *Perhaps he returned to Jerusalem,* he said to himself. He turned to leave the room, but the feeling of foreboding that had enveloped him as soon as he entered the house remained. His eye was drawn to the alcove, which Ahithophel used as a dressing room. He hadn't looked there. Slowly, he approached the curtain that set the little nook off from the rest of the L-shaped room.

As he pulled back the heavy fabric, he noticed an overturned stool on the floor. When he looked up he dropped the lamp. In the gathering darkness, he saw Ahithophel, suspended by his neck from a beam. Gamal ran all the way back to the home of Ahithophel's nephew.

≈ ≈ ≈

Shoshanna had begun her second week in her new home. She was sweeping the brick-lined courtyard when she heard the commotion of someone arriving at the gate. She glanced up, expecting to see a group of neighbor women come to visit, and was surprised to see a young cousin from Giloh, riding one donkey and leading another. Her immediate thought was that Marah had sent her some of her personal belongings. But she noticed that the second donkey was not carrying anything.

Immediately, she knew something was amiss, because the

boy's eyes were filled with pity. She dropped her broom to rush over to him. "What has happened, Joel?"

"Your mother needs you, Shoshanna. She said to tell you not to come, but she is very distraught. I brought the extra donkey in case you want to return to Giloh with me."

Shoshanna's heart was pounding. "Tell me quickly, please. I know something terrible has happened. Have they arrested Grandfather?"

Joel's eyes filled with tears. "He is dead, Shoshanna. Your grandfather is dead."

Shoshanna shook her head in rejection. "No! He can't be dead! Was he executed without appearing before the king? How could this have happened so soon? We haven't even heard word from the battle yet."

"He hanged himself, Shoshanna." He spoke in a low voice barely above a whisper, but Shoshanna heard the words perfectly. Still, she made her cousin repeat what he had said. "Your mother was staying at our house, as you know. Anah was with her, as your grandfather had insisted. Old Gamal found him in the alcove of his room. He had looped a rope over a beam and . . ." Joel could not finish the sentence.

Shoshanna could not believe it. She sat, deeply shocked, and stared at her cousin, vaguely aware that she should be seeing to the comfort of her guest after his journey. She felt numb, unable to move. Her grandfather had committed a terrible sin. He had murdered himself. Ahithophel had always stood for what was right. People even said that his counsel was so righteous that the words of Ahithophel were straight from God. Yet his hatred for David had driven him to this awful act.

Suddenly, Shoshanna was very angry with Grandfather for involving her in the rebellion, for marrying her off and sending her away so that he could accomplish this final, terrible deed. Then, in her mind, she saw his lifeless body hanging from that beam, and for the first time, terrible pain shot through her, so deep that she thought she couldn't bear it. She cried out.

"When did this happen? When is the burial? I'll get some things, and we will start back to Giloh immediately. Grandfather must be buried before sunset if he died yesterday." Shoshanna knew she was babbling on, but couldn't stop herself.

"As for the burial, it was done quietly two days ago, the same day we found him. The circumstances of his death required it. The people of Giloh mourn him, cousin. Despite what he did, they hold his memory dear. We can take comfort in that."

Ailea, who had been inside the house stuffing a new mattress with lamb's wool for her son and daughter-in-law, heard voices and came to investigate. She saw the lad she recognized from Giloh and the look on Shoshanna's face, and asked in a hushed voice what had happened. The boy told her everything. Ailea's tender heart went out to both Shoshanna and her mother. She knew that Ahithophel had meant everything to both his daughter and granddaughter, and she felt a hot burst of anger that the man had brought this shame on those who loved him.

Shoshanna insisted on leaving at once for Giloh. She felt she should have done something to prevent what had happened. At least, she thought, she should have refused to leave Giloh. She could only rectify that mistake now. Joel and Ailea both argued that she should wait at least until morning to leave, but she wouldn't listen. She gathered a bundle of her things and was ready to go almost immediately.

"My dear, I'm concerned for your safety if you go back to Giloh," Ailea said, even as she watched her daughter-in-law mount the little donkey Joel had brought.

"I have no choice. I must go to my mother. She needs me."

"Marah sent her strongest admonition for you not to come. She says she will visit you in a week or two." Joel shrugged as his words were dismissed as quickly as Ailea's had been. He had grown up around Shoshanna and knew how hardheaded she could be.

"But what should I tell Micah when he returns? When will you come back to Ziph?"

"I have no plans to return to Ziph," Shoshanna replied, and watched Ailea's eyes widen with shock.

Shoshanna knew that she was being curt and unkind, but she couldn't help it. She felt anger at Ahithophel, and a growing anger at Micah. He should have done something before he left, she told herself. When he had married Shoshanna, it had become his duty to protect her grandfather. He had refused to do so. He didn't deserve her loyalty or any explanation. She just wanted to get away from his village, his family—anything that reminded her of her husband. She refused to wait until Jerusha returned to say good-bye to her, and before the sun had reached its zenith, Joel was accompanying her out of the village of Ziph.

Shoshanna's head was crowded with thoughts as they made their way back to Giloh. Thoughts of her grandfather were too painful, so she fanned the heat of her anger toward Micah by remembering the cold way he had refused her plea to speak to the king on Ahithophel's behalf. If only he had told Grandfather that he would do so, that would have given the old man some reason to hope. Instead, Micah had made it plain that he believed her grandfather to be a doomed man. He hadn't cared about Ahithophel. Nor had he cared about her own feelings. He was coldhearted, and she would never forgive him. Never.

Shoshanna wondered if Micah would even bother to come for her when he returned from battle. If he did, she would greet him coolly and let him know she held him responsible for Ahithophel's death. More than two weeks had passed. Surely the battle was ended, the outcome decided, but no word had come yet.

Wouldn't it be ironic if the prince's troops had won, after all? Shoshanna immediately felt guilty. Despite her anger at her husband, she could not hope that King David had been overthrown. She wanted him back in Jerusalem, restored to his throne.

Chapter Fourteen

~

*J*onathan waited anxiously for Micah to appear in Mahanaim. What was keeping his son? Had Absalom detained him? Had he been found out? During such a time of upheaval, it was unlikely the prince would bother with a trial. In all likelihood, he would simply order his men to execute Micah on the spot, if he were caught intercepting messages or recruiting warriors for the king's cause.

Do not entertain such thoughts, Jonathan told himself sternly. He would assume the best—that Micah was gathering men for the king's cause in every village he passed through, and that he would arrive soon, hailed with honor. Jonathan wanted Micah to fight in the coming battle in order to prove his mettle to all who thought him cowardly or disloyal. After that, Jonathan hoped his son would take up the mantle of his grandfather and never have to fight again.

~ ~ ~

On their fourth day in Mahanaim, Micah finally arrived with more than two hundred recruits. Barzillai owned a large house in the city, and had offered its use to David and his *Gibborim* as residence and military headquarters. Barzillai moved into his brother's home for the duration of the conflict. Jonathan was standing on the wide portico of the house when his son appeared, leading his great horse. With his stallion and his own wild mane of tawny hair, Micah had the attention of the entire camp. His muscles rippled as he towered over the other men. Jonathan looked on his son with great pride.

Jonathan's joy was mitigated by anxiety as he waited for Micah to reach him. When he was finally close enough to read his expression, Jonathan could see that Micah was smiling broadly. Jonathan let out a breath. He had been fairly certain that his son would approve of the arrangements he had made with Ahithophel to expedite his marriage with Shoshanna.

Still, there was the possibility that he had found her to be a traitor to the king and a betrayer of his love. If that were the case, he would have the right to be angry with Jonathan for practically forcing him to marry her without consent. But here was Micah, smiling a warm greeting as he bounded up the broad steps of the portico. The two men embraced with unashamed affection. "You took your time about getting here," Jonathan said gruffly.

"Much has happened, Father. I would like to speak with you alone after I present my men and my report to the king. I should not be long."

David was impressed with the number of men Micah had been able to call to arms from southern Judah. Micah sadly reported the defection to Absalom of many towns and villages in the hill country, including Ziph. "But I have with me twenty men from my village, who trained with my father in the past and are ready to give their lives for you, my lord," he told David as he bent the knee in homage to his king.

"You are an honorable man, Micah ben Jonathan. You will lead the men you have brought with you in battle. You will be under Abishai's command. Now go and speak with your father. He has been full of worry for you."

Micah rejoined his father, and they went to a wooded rise near the edge of town to speak. "I have not only been gathering recruits and information about Absalom's plans, Father. I also spoke to the elders of Ziph, but they wouldn't listen to me. Do you think they will ever accept me as a leader?"

Jonathan had expected Micah to speak first about his wedding, and it took him a moment to register the question. Finally, his mind switched courses, and he responded to Micah's concerns. "You mustn't be discouraged, Micah. It may take some time, but eventually, I believe that you will be as great a leader as your grandfather."

"You are the natural one to take the Rab's place, Father."

Jonathan shook his head. "In matters of war, maybe. But you have a special wisdom about people that I will never have, an ability to evaluate, and the patience to withhold judgment. It takes such wisdom to be a Rab."

"I can only be a leader if other men will follow me. We will wait to see if that is the case. I have yet to tell you my most important news, Father. I have also been to Giloh and have taken Ahithophel's granddaughter as my wife, as you instructed." Micah raised his eyebrows as he said the last part, but the twinkle in his eye told Jonathan that his son was not unhappy with his father's intervention.

Jonathan's eyes searched the face of his son. "So your mother arrived in time? I was shocked to receive Ahithophel's message, telling me that you had previously asked for Shoshanna and been refused, but that now he had changed his mind and was willing for the wedding to take place. I would not have acted on his message alone, though. But I remembered the look on your face when you spoke of Shoshanna. I was certain you cared for her—"

Micah interrupted. "What else did Ahithophel tell you?"

"He informed me that the wedding must take place quickly, due to the war, that he would see his granddaughter safely married before the battle, and if he didn't hear from me, he would marry her to someone else. I assumed you still felt the same about

Shoshanna, so I followed his suggestion to send your mother and sister to Giloh as a sign that the wedding had my approval. You aren't angry with me for expediting the wedding, are you?"

"Not at all, Father. I have loved her since we met in Jerusalem months ago. I never thought it possible she would be my bride so soon. This rebellion placed us on opposite sides. She is not really a traitor to the king, Father, only loyal to her grandfather. Ahithophel . . . Ahithophel has changed. When Absalom chose not to accept his plan to follow and engage you immediately in battle, he returned right away to Giloh. He was setting his affairs in order when he sent you the letter. He knows I will protect Shoshanna. I think he knows he will die as soon as David is done with this battle.

"When he sent you that message he was counting on the fact that I had not changed my mind about wanting Shoshanna. I had talked to him about it months ago when I was in Baal Hazor. I know I have no right to ask it, but I hope you will plead for the king to punish only Ahithophel and not his family members for this rebellion."

"You have every right to ask it, Son. Shoshanna is my daughter now. I will lend all my influence to protect her. But you told me some time ago that Joab suspected she was being used as a courier for messages between Absalom and Ahithophel, and if he has proof, I warn you, he will seek to destroy your wife. I speak from bitter experience."

≈ ≈ ≈

David planned the battle strategy himself. The area around the Jabbok River, known as the Forest of Ephraim, contained thick woods and steep canyons. Rugged terrain was David's favorite geography for battle and would afford his warriors, led by older men who had fought with him as guerrillas years ago, an advantage over Absalom's young troops. The king at first insisted on personally leading his army, but his commanders and captains argued that David was the prize piece in this battle. If they lost him, it would not matter how many of the enemy they slew; their entire cause would be lost. David would command the battle from the safety of Mahanaim.

The king divided his forces into three units. The main force was to be commanded, of course, by Joab. His brother, Abishai, would lead the second, and Ittai the Gittite would be the third commander. His other *Gibborim* were captains under these three.

"This is what we will do," he told his officers as he knelt in the packed dirt in front of his headquarters. "Ittai and Abishai will hide their troops in the forest, while Joab stations his to the front of them, in the open, thus." David illustrated by drawing with a pointed stick in the dirt. "Amasa will engage Joab, who will have his men fall back toward the forest as they fight. Amasa will think our forces are being driven back, that we are in retreat. Then, when he is drawn into the forest, Ittai and Abishai will flank his army, and he will be defeated."

"Brilliant, my lord. Absalom's army will then not be able to use the advantage of their horsemen or chariot corps, and the inexperienced troops will panic at the surprise attack!" Joab told the king. Then he did something very rare for the general—he laughed. A full-throated, unrestrained belly laugh. Nothing made him happier than the anticipation of battle.

Jonathan was relieved when he was placed in Ittai's unit. He would rather be under the command of the Philistine mercenary than Joab any time. In fact, since the time nearly twenty years ago when Joab had ordered Jonathan's best friend, Ahiam, to certain death along with Uriah the Hittite, Jonathan could barely stand to be in Joab's presence. The feeling was mutual. The animosity between the two men had started when Joab accused Ailea, Jonathan's captive bride, of spying for the Arameans. Jonathan had believed the general and had sent her away.

Jonathan and Ailea endured harrowing months of separation. But when Jonathan found Ailea, he had proof that Joab had set up the whole scenario for Ailea to be accused of treason. Joab had not been able to do any further harm to her for fear Jonathan would go to the king with his proof. The rift between the two men had never really been healed. The only thing they had in common was their loyalty to David. For his sake, they put their personal differences aside. Still, the air crackled with animosity whenever they were in a room together, and they never fought side-by-side.

"I could tell by the grim look on the king's face that he was not happy about it, but he reluctantly agreed to command the battle from the safety of Mahanaim," Jonathan told his son that night as they made themselves comfortable in Jonathan's tent. The officers' tents had been set up near Barzillai's home, and Jonathan's was roomy enough that he invited his son to spend the night there. Jonathan spoke of the king's reasonableness.

"He possesses a meekness that is seldom found in men of power. Perhaps it is because of his humble beginnings. In spite of the fact that he is one of the greatest warriors—possibly the greatest strategist Israel has ever known—still, he places the good of his men above his own pride. Such a contrast to the attitude of his arrogant son, eh?"

Micah snorted. "The prince showed his lack of reason or military savvy when he let Hushai flatter him into taking the wrong advice."

"That was the intervention of Adonai. As we were leaving Jerusalem, the king prayed that Absalom wouldn't listen to Ahithophel's counsel. A short time after he had finished that prayer, Hushai came to join the king in exile. But David sent him back, saying that Hushai could perhaps be the means of weakening Absalom's strategy, that he might be the Lord's answer to the king's prayer. Without Ahithophel guiding him, Absalom will make all kinds of mistakes. That young puppy has never soiled his hands once in battle. Mark my word, he will face the battle with more concern about his appearance than about battle readiness."

~ ~ ~

Jonathan's prediction proved true. The next day, Micah stood on a rise and watched Absalom's troops approach from the north, led by Amasa. Absalom's cousin, who was now his commander, had advised an attack from the northern, more difficult approach, in order to take the king's forces by surprise. Of course, David wouldn't be taken by surprise. He had sent several reconnaissance parties out, including Micah's.

He watched as the prince, riding a white mule that was resplendently bedecked with fine trappings, silver bit and bridle, and colorful saddle, led his army toward battle. He wasn't even wearing a helmet, Micah noted with a shake of his head. Perhaps Absalom felt that his beautiful hair was some kind of symbol, a banner of sorts for his men to follow. Had there ever been a man more arrogant and vain?

With that observation, Micah turned and went to seek out Abishai. Their forces would hide in the forest tomorrow for a surprise attack when Joab's men drew the enemy to them. Although Joab's troops would be the first to see combat, it would be gratifying to launch a surprise attack on Absalom's forces.

$\approx \approx \approx$

The king's army was ready to meet the enemy long before dawn the next morning. They were arranged in their ranks, their swords and spears sharpened, their brass helmets and the greaves of their armor polished. David took up his position in the predawn light, mounting a raised platform placed right outside the city gate. He wore not a crown, but all the accouterments of war: a breastplate of overlapping bands of bronze, a battle kilt made of hanging strips of leather, and a great sword strapped at his side. Except for his gray hair, the king looked like a much younger man. His form was tall and straight, and he looked as fierce as any of his younger warriors. His three commanders stood at his side as he addressed the troops.

"My generals tell me that it is best for my people if I stay here, but it is my failures that have brought us to this battle. I would lead you out in the name of the Lord." A great cheer went up as David held aloft the sword of Goliath, symbolic of his greatness as a warrior and as a leader who had won impossible battles before and could be trusted to do so again. The veterans who made up the core of his forces were also past their prime, but their experience and confidence compensated to a great degree for their waning physical strength.

Abishai raised his arms and the ranks of warriors fell silent. "My lord David has spoken from his great courage and love, but we, the Three, and the rest of the *Gibborim* have discussed the matter, and we feel it would be unwise for the king to personally lead us this day." There was an audible groan of disappointment before the troops controlled themselves and gave Abishai their attention again. But this time he addressed the king. "If my lord goes out with us this day and we lose you in battle, then our cause is lost, and we will be under the thumb of Prince Absalom. You are too valuable to put yourself in the way of a rebel sword. On the other hand, even if a thousand of us fall, we may still win the kingdom back for our rightful monarch."

David looked for a moment as if he would overrule Abishai's counsel. He studied the faces of the Three—the most renowned warriors in the land, and his commanders. His face fell, and he lowered the huge sword. "Very well, then, I will not go out with you. I will stay here at the gates of Mahanaim as long as the battle rages, and if there is need of me, I will go forth at your call. May Adonai be with you and keep you safe from harm."

"For the Lord, and for David!" the men chorused as one.

As Joab, Abishai, and Ittai turned to leave the platform, the king stopped them. "Go gently with Absalom, for my sake. Go gently with the young man." Jonathan, who was standing directly below the wooden platform with the rest of the Thirty, could see the anguish and pleading in David's eyes, and strong emotions clogged his throat. The king was not wise concerning his children, but there was no doubt that he loved them. Jonathan breathed a prayer that it would not be his sword that struck down the comely prince, but he knew he would do it if he had to.

He was conferring briefly with his lieutenants as the divisions began to march toward the north, when he heard the king, who was now seated in a large chair for the purpose of keeping his vigil, call out.

"Micah ben Jonathan, pull your unit to the side for a moment, please. I would have a word with you."

Micah, who was now just a few feet from his father at the foot of the platform, shot Jonathan a questioning glance before joining the king, who was smiling at him. David raised his voice to be heard by Micah's men. Jonathan felt gratified that the king was possibly planning to put his personal stamp of approval on the young warrior who had been discredited months before. Micah needed the full confidence of his men. But he was thunderstruck, as were the many others who were near enough to hear David's remarks to Micah when the king spoke.

"Young man, you have not only proven yourself in performing a delicate diplomatic mission for Israel, but you have recently placed your life in danger in order to find out what my enemies were up to. I have considered several rewards that might be appropriate, but just now I have thought of one that might help you this day. The sword of Goliath has been used by no one but me since I took it off the giant more than forty years ago, and truthfully, I find it too large and heavy to have used it often or effectively. I will not have occasion to use it myself today. I would like you to take it and use it with my blessing. You are a man big enough in every way to merit the honor."

As the king held the massive weapon out to him, Micah could only stare. He was snapped out of his reverie by the loud cheer that went up from the men in his unit. He took the sword from the king and knelt in homage. "I vow to do my utmost to use the sword with honor, my lord."

David placed his hand on Micah's head. "Go with my blessing, and the Lord's. But remember it is not the sword that you are to put your trust in. That was Goliath's great mistake. Rather, let the sword remind you that no matter how great or small our human strength, the battle is the Lord's."

Micah secured the huge sword by its scabbard at his waist and rejoined his men, who looked at him with heightened respect. He cleared his throat loudly and took his place at the head of his troops. "Let's move out!" he barked, and returned his father's wide grin as his unit passed Jonathan's company of regulars.

≈ ≈ ≈

From his vantage point, the king could see the progress of the battle. The pasturelands surrounding the city stretched out for several miles before him. He could see the bend of the Jabbok, and the dense forest that grew around it. Between the city and the battlefield, the fields were empty of sheep, cattle, or men.

He could tell that his men were acquitting themselves well, because he would see his units go into the forest, pursued by Absalom's cavalry or foot soldiers, and in most cases Absalom's men would come out sometime later in obvious disarray, their numbers considerably diminished. Often the horses would come running out, riderless.

He did not move from the spot all day, except to eat a meal in the cool room located above the gate. Rains came several times, and still the king stayed at his outdoor position. He kept the young princes with him. His sons who were old enough had gone into the battle. If Absalom won the day, David would be able to see his army advancing and would have his servants take his wives and children and flee into the desert.

Above him, in the room where he had dined, the watchman also waited, and several times the king called up to him during the tedious hours. "Watchman, what do you see?" And the watchman would call down, "Nothing, my lord."

Chapter Fifteen

~

Joab had sought to intercept Absalom as soon as he heard the prince was on the field of battle. He was determined that the ungrateful prince would not live to see tomorrow's sunrise, no matter what David said. He was filled with disgust at the last words David spoke as his brave and loyal troops had marched out of Mahanaim. To ask that they spare the life of the man who had betrayed them all, who had forced the rightful king from Jerusalem, was nearly incomprehensible. Some, like Jonathan, had looked back at their monarch with compassion and understanding. They had nodded their heads affirmatively. But many were shocked and hurt that the king would be more concerned about the enemy than those who had stood faithfully by him.

Joab had spat on the ground and ignored the request, determined not to dignify it with a response. Several others did the same. The king's soft spot for his children and others who did not deserve his love repulsed Joab. He was convinced that his uncle would have lost the throne years ago had it not been for Joab and others who had no such feminine weakness.

He saw Jonathan of Ziph and thought of Micah's similar weakness, no doubt fostered by his father and that foreign woman he had married. Such a man was not a true man at all, in Joab's opinion, no matter his impressive size and strength.

≈ ≈ ≈

The terrain was nearly impossible—thickly forested and rough. It precluded any organized battle plan, which very much favored David's outnumbered forces. Ittai, Abishai, and Joab all had experience in the kind of hit-and-run combat that was necessary in the rocky terrain of these wooded hills. Micah and his men, along with the other units, launched arrows and slung rocks from the cover of the trees when Absalom's troops, drawn there by Joab's men, entered the forest. The inexperienced forces were lured deeper into the thick forest where they became disorganized and disoriented.

The sun went behind clouds, and the forest became quite dark in some places. Men from both sides were lost when they came upon the deep gullies and canyons formed by the Jabbok and its tributaries and fell to their deaths. Others slid down them and were injured and unable to climb back up again. The battle was fought in small skirmishes because units were cut off from each other by the forest. Sometimes men came upon their own comrades and slew them before they realized who they were fighting because only a minimum of light penetrated the thick canopy of leaves.

Micah ordered his men to fan out in order to find and engage the enemy in the dim forest. He instructed them to every few minutes give a call like that of a dove. If they heard no responding call, they were to stop where they were and continue to signal until they did. The method worked well, and all morning Micah's unit was able to stay together in the eerie green light of the forest.

Micah, leading his men in skirmish after skirmish, easily brought down the enemy with the sword of Goliath. His stomach revolted at the first kill he made, but he forced himself to fight on. He found that it was easier to kill when he was forced to do so to protect his men. After a particularly violent encounter in which Micah dropped his shield in order to use both hands to wield the sword, young Igal appeared at his side.

"I notice that you fight without an armor bearer, my lord. I would be honored to fulfill that function, if you would permit."

Igal was the younger brother of Lemuel, and that made Micah pause for a moment. But as he studied the face of the thin young man, he saw in his countenance none of the shiftiness or cruelty of the older brother. And Igal must have had the courage to go against Lemuel or he wouldn't be here. Besides, Igal was one of the youngest, smallest men in his unit, and if Micah kept him close he could see to his protection. Micah smiled and nodded at Igal and handed over his javelin, bow, and quiver, which had been strapped to his back. In battle it would be Igal's responsibility to hand the armor to Micah when it was needed. Also, it was now Igal's job to protect Micah's back.

A short time after Igal joined him, in a spot where the trees thinned out, Micah and his men came upon a large unit of Absalom's troops. During the ensuing battle, Micah saw one of his men take an arrow in the back that seemed to come from the surrounding oak trees. As Micah searched for the source of the missile, another arrow thudded into the ground right beside him. "Igal, hand me my bow and an arrow," Micah instructed. He aimed at the place where he estimated the sniper was hidden and fired the arrow into the tree.

There was a slight thud, followed by a gasp, then a man came crashing down. Micah could see the arrow protruding from the fellow's leg and rushed over to the place where he lay, sword raised. It was not a man who looked up at him, but a boy. He looked at Micah with huge, frightened eyes, and Micah didn't have the heart to kill him. He looked at Igal, and saw that the boy had his eyes tightly closed to avoid seeing the lad killed. Micah shrugged. "Come, Igal!" he said, turning his back on the injured youth. When Igal glanced back over his shoulder and saw that Micah had spared the boy, he smiled and nodded.

All day, units were separated from each other because of the thick forests, the steep drop-offs, and rocky terrain. Micah kept his troops together by assigning two to scout ahead and warn the other men of hazards as well as the placement of enemy warriors. Slowly, the experience of the veterans—the *Gibborim,* the Pelethites, and the Cherethites—turned the tide of the battle to David's side. Micah was proud of his men, who, though unseasoned, fought wisely and did not panic.

As the hours passed into early afternoon, Micah's unit engaged a troop of Amasa's best-equipped warriors and were gaining the advantage, even though outnumbered. Micah seemed to be everywhere at once—at the forefront of his men, encouraging them to fight on; in the middle of the fray; at the rear of the vanguard, making sure they weren't attacked unawares. Igal stayed beside him all the way, seeming to sense what Micah's needs were at any given moment. When this was over, Micah thought, he would personally tell the general about the young man's valor.

No sooner did the thought pass than he heard a scream and turned to see that Igal had been thrust through the back with a javelin. Enraged, Micah turned to fend off the attacker and found that it was the same boy whose life he had spared earlier! The young man drew his sword from his scabbard and ran at Micah, who easily knocked it aside with Goliath's sword. The young man's eyes widened in fear, and in the next instant grew glassy in death as Micah ran him through.

As his opponent dropped like a stone, Micah fell to his own knees, sickened at the carnage. Here lay two young lads who had scarcely begun to live. He was responsible for the death of both. Had he acted as he should have earlier, at least one of them would have returned to his mother. But because of his weakness, Igal's mother would see her son no more. And now Micah had killed in hatred, for revenge. He felt like a murderer.

"Sir, what's wrong? Are you injured?" Another young man from Ziph was at his side. When Micah did not answer him, he turned over the body that lay next to him. "It is the brother of Lemuel."

"Yes. It's Igal, murdered by a rebel I didn't have the stomach to kill. It is my fault Igal is dead. His blood is on my hands." The other young warrior looked at Micah in disgust. Having heard the rumors that Micah was a coward, he assumed that Micah had been afraid and that Igal had taken the wound that was meant for him. He was a friend of Lemuel's, and he purposed to repeat Micah's own damning words to his friend as soon as he got home.

~ ~ ~

Absalom was pleased with the way the battle was going. Amasa, at the point of the main body of the army, had forced Joab's army to retreat further and further into the Forest of Ephraim. The prince did not command a battalion, but rode back and forth between his divisions to offer support and give commands. Although he had never been in battle before, he took to it naturally. He was, after all, David's son. He made a commanding sight on the back of his white mule, his hair in all its glory flying like a flag behind him as he rode. Without a helmet he was easily recognizable, so that his men might gain courage from the sight of their new king.

The trees were thick in the forest, and it was difficult going, even on foot, but particularly treacherous on the back of a mule. Absalom continually ducked to avoid low-hanging branches. After a particularly close call, the prince glanced back at a nearly missed branch. Before he could turn again he felt a searing pain in his scalp as his flowing mane became tangled in yet another low-hanging branch. Absalom was jerked off his mount as the mule ran on, leaving him suspended above the ground with his hair hopelessly ensnared.

He struggled for several minutes, but unable to free himself, he called out for his men. He saw a cadre of his soldiers moving quickly through the forest in his direction, but it soon became apparent that a unit of Joab's men had overpowered them and they were running away.

But someone had heard Absalom's cries. One of the king's men was riding toward him, sword drawn. He was a young man, not a veteran, and he was awestruck when he saw the prince's predicament. The soldier gaped at Absalom. "I . . . I'm . . . going to have to get some help to . . . to get you down from there." The young man jammed his sword into its scabbard, turned, and rode away without using his sword. As painful as his position was, Absalom gave a half-smile. His father must have given an order that he was not to be killed. *Softhearted old fool.*

The young soldier galloped in the direction he had last seen the general. He wasn't sure what Joab's reaction would be, but the young man had heard King David's order to go gently with the prince, and he was not about to disobey an order from the king. He was relieved when he spotted Joab with his armor-bearers up ahead. The general could take responsibility for the situation now. He shouted and waved to get Joab's attention, then bent over for a minute to regain his breath while the general approached him. "Sir, I saw him! He's caught in the branches of a tree. You must hurry before his men free him."

"Who did you see, and how is he caught?" Joab asked impatiently.

"It is the prince, Absalom, my lord. He is caught by his hair in the branches of a large oak tree, over there, in the thickest part of the forest." The young man pointed to the place.

Joab's eyes widened, then he laughed. "Caught by his hair! That is justice, justice indeed." Then his eyes narrowed and darkened with displeasure. "And why did you not kill him when you had a chance? I would have rewarded you with ten shekels of silver and thrown in my fine leather belt as well."

"My lord, though I were to receive a thousand shekels of silver, I would never raise my hand against the king's son. I heard the king instruct you and Abishai and Ittai not to harm the young man. I would never get away with killing the prince."

Joab gave the young soldier a look of contempt and spat on the ground. "Show me where he is." He grabbed three spears and motioned to his armor-bearers to follow him. Joab had made many enemies over the years, some of them his own countrymen. These ten young men were his constant companions and bodyguards.

≈ ≈ ≈

A look of fear crossed Absalom's face when he saw the wily general riding toward him through the woods, but he did not demean himself by begging for mercy.

"Sir, we must take him prisoner and bring him before his father the king," the young man who had found Absalom insisted.

"We are going to execute him, as you should have done," Joab shouted.

"Sir, hold a moment, please." One of the general's armor-bearers leveled his javelin across the general's path to stop him. "We will all take part in his death," he said, "so that the king will not be able to accuse you." A wicked gleam came to Joab's eyes and he nodded his approval. The soldiers joined him in surrounding the hanging prince. Absalom growled but refused to cry out. Joab readied one of his spears, and with a sudden thrust pierced Absalom's chest. Absalom kicked and screamed.

Twice more Joab struck, until all of his spears were depleted. The rest of the soldiers quickly thrust their lances into the prince's body until he no longer struggled. The captain of the guard stepped forward and cut the prince's body down from the tree. The young man who had discovered Absalom fell to his knees and retched.

"Get up and call for the trumpet blast. We have won the day!" Joab ordered him. "Tell our men to spread the word that the prince is dead. See that Amasa gets the word. Without the prince their uprising is pointless. Amasa is smart enough to realize that. Go now."

The young man staggered to his feet. "Do you wish for me to bring back a litter to bear the prince's body to his father?"

"That won't be necessary. Just do as I've commanded," Joab said sternly. The young warrior nodded and started off at a trot to obey.

Joab turned to his armor-bearers. "Cut him down. There is a sinkhole not far from here. We will bury him in it."

An hour later, Joab and his men stood wiping sweat from their brows. They had thrown Absalom into the hole and filled it in with rocks. "If the king asks where we buried his son, none of us will be able to find this place. Is that understood?" Each of the men nodded affirmatively.

At the camp near the edge of the forest, the king's soldiers assembled at the trumpet's call, and word quickly spread that Absalom had been killed. The men cheered their general as he strode into camp.

Ahimaaz, who had stayed on to fight after delivering Hushai's dispatch, ran up to Joab. "My lord, may I run now to Mahanaim and take the news to the king that he has been avenged on his enemies?"

Joab hesitated. Now that the blood lust had worn off, he was wary of David's reaction. He remembered David's response to the Amalekite messenger who, years ago, had brought him news of King Saul's death. The foolish man had believed that David would welcome the death of his adversary, and had claimed to be the one who had finally dispatched the old king, albeit out of mercy. David had immediately ordered the Amalekite executed. He knew that the life of any messenger bearing news of Absalom's death was also at risk. "Ahimaaz, you have proven your worth as a messenger, and you will live to run another day."

Joab summoned another messenger, an African mercenary from Cush, and instructed him to go to Mahanaim and tell the king everything that had happened.

Ahimaaz stood nearby, swallowing down a protest. He knew the risks of bearing bad news, but he was exhilarated over his successful mission to warn the king of Absalom's plans, and he wanted another opportunity to prove his courage.

"General, please do not be angry with me, but I would ask that you allow me to follow the Cushite with the news of our victory."

Joab studied the thin, young man for a long moment. "Why do you want to run? You haven't got the final word on this battle."

"I'm aware of the risks, my lord, but I pray you, let me run."

Joab shrugged. "Very well, then, go. But you will never catch the Cushite." These last words were said to the back of Ahimaaz, who had already started off in a different direction than the African runner.

Chapter Sixteen

~

*T*he king had spent one of the longest days of his life waiting for word of the battle. At last, when the sun was well past its zenith, the watchman called down to him. "My lord, a runner comes up by way of the river valley. He is alone and his feet are very swift. You will be able to see him for yourself in a moment."

"If he is by himself, then he isn't fleeing from the battle. He must be a messenger. Yes, I see him now!"

"My lord, I now see another man running by a different route, over the hills. I don't recognize him, but I believe the first man is Ahimaaz, by the way he runs."

"That young man is of excellent character. I believe the news he brings will be good." David's voice held not a hint of uncertainty.

A few minutes later, Ahimaaz, thrilled that he had outrun the Cushite, gasped out the message, "All is well," before collapsing at the feet of the king. In just a moment, he had gained enough breath to continue. "Blessed be Adonai, our God. He has delivered up to our hands the men who dared to raise theirs against the Lord's anointed."

A smile crossed David's face, then disappeared. After a pause, the king asked the question that had been heavy on his heart. "Is it well with the young man Absalom?"

Ahimaaz resented that the king showed so much concern for the prince who had tried to kill his own father and his followers. Suddenly Ahimaaz was afraid—very much afraid. He had been foolish to outrun the African. His answer to the king's question might bring him to grief. He chose his words carefully.

"When Joab sent me from the battle, there was much confusion. I'm not sure who were among the casualties." A half-truth, but Ahimaaz dared not risk more.

The king wasn't suspicious. His eyes were on the other runner. "Well, then," he said, "stand with me here until the other runner reaches us."

The watchman shouted down. "The second runner is the Cushite who is in the service of Ittai of Gath." David walked to the edge of the platform. Dignity would not allow him to rush out to meet the runner, and the minutes that passed seemed like hours until the messenger flung himself at the king's feet. His black skin glistened like polished ebony with the sweat of his exertion. David's heart gave a leap of hope when he saw that the young man was smiling.

"Tidings for my lord the King," he said. "Adonai has brought vengeance this day on your enemies."

Immediately David repeated the question he had asked Ahimaaz. "Is it well with the young prince, Absalom?" Poor fellow, Ahimaaz thought. As a mercenary, he has no idea of the precarious position he's in at this moment.

The African didn't hesitate to give an answer. "My lord, may all your enemies and all those who would rise up to do you harm, be as that young man is."

The king staggered backward, his face crumpling in grief. He couldn't seem to catch his breath for a moment, and Ahimaaz wondered if, after such a great victory, they would lose their king after all—to a heart attack. Then David sucked in a deep breath and turned away. Ahimaaz heard him whisper, "O Absalom."

≈ ≈ ≈

As Jonathan and the other *Gibborim* marched into Mahanaim, they were greeted by cries of joy from the citizens, but the king was nowhere to be seen. Upon hearing the heartwrenching news about the death of his son, David had torn his tunic and retreated to an apartment located over the gate of the city.

Through the open window, everyone could hear the king's weeping, and his voice repeating the hopeless words, "Oh, Absalom, my son, my son. If only I could have died in your place. Oh, Absalom, my son." The king refused requests to greet and congratulate the *Gibborim,* which he had always done after battle. The veteran warriors were offended, and Joab acted quickly to restore the morale of his troops. He ascended to the king's chamber and confronted him as he lay facedown on the floor, weeping.

"We saved your life today and the lives of your sons, your daughters, your wives, and your concubines. Yet you are acting as if we have done something wrong, turning our joy into shame. I do not understand. You seem to love those who hate you and hate those who love you." The king grew silent as Joab rebuked him in the tone of a father to a son; he spoke more as an equal than as a subject to his monarch. So great was Joab's ire that he did not even try to speak diplomatically.

"You have made it clear today that we mean nothing at all to you. Would you have been happy to have Absalom live and all of us dead? Now go out there and congratulate your troops, because if you don't not a single one will remain with you. Then you will be worse off than you have ever been!"

The king lay perfectly still on the floor for several minutes. His weeping had ceased. Finally, he stumbled to his feet and called for a basin of water. After washing his face, he went down to the city gate and sat down on his elevated seat to review the troops.

The morale of his people was instantly restored, and they cheered him, and though the lines in his face seemed to have deepened since the day before, making him look every one of his sixty years, he managed to smile as his warriors recounted their victory. No one mentioned Absalom or the way he had died.

≈ ≈ ≈

"I still say it is a big mistake to dawdle here on the wrong side of the Jordan when we ought to be reestablishing the king in Jerusalem." Benaiah scratched his bushy beard as he stood talking to Micah and Jonathan. The two of them were preparing to return to Ziph, along with the volunteers from the hill country. In the week since the end of the battle, the dead had been buried, the wounded had been tended to, the weapons of war repaired. Last evening in council, Jonathan and others had been given leave to go home for a short period of time if they wished. David had announced that he would continue his stay in Mahanaim for the time being.

"I can see the logic of the king's argument that we need to take a little time to see if all the trouble is really put to rest. No sense going back to Jerusalem only to find it necessary to fight again. Besides, his point is well taken. Since he left the city in such a clandestine and shameful way, some planning must go into bringing him back with much ceremony and fanfare. That will take some time." As he spoke to his friend, Jonathan finished saddling the mule he would ride.

Benaiah grunted. "I don't know about fanfare. I think like a warrior, and I say it doesn't feel right to let you and half the army go back home before the king is solidly reestablished on his throne."

Micah, eager to get underway, broke in to try to end the debate. "We are going back to Ziph to make certain the elders there are committed to bringing back the king. If there is any trouble at all, we will be back here fully prepared for combat. Otherwise, we will be back when the king sends word he is ready to cross the Jordan once more. Now let us go on our way, or else it will be time to come back before we even see the hills of Judah."

Benaiah laughed. "Spoken like a newly married man. Take your son home, Jonathan, before he pines away to nothing missing his new bride."

"That would take a while, I'm afraid. But we should have pity on him, I guess." With that statement, Jonathan mounted up and they soon left Mahanaim behind them.

≈ ≈ ≈

Though Micah tried, he could not hide his impatience to return to Ziph and Shoshanna. Jonathan teased him mercilessly for two days as they made their way south. When they were just outside of Hebron, Micah used the excuse that Ramah was restless and wanted a good run to ride on ahead of Jonathan and the young recruits and go directly to Ziph. He galloped ahead to the sound of laughter and shouts that he was completely under the spell of his new bride, but Micah didn't care. It seemed like forever since he had seen her, his love.

When he arrived at the gate of his father's house, he saw Jerusha, who was more enthralled by the sight of Ramah than by her brother. She stroked the horse's nose and commended his strength and beauty. Micah handed the reins to his sister, with instructions to rub the horse down and feed him. The girl was still patting the muzzle of the stallion and promising him a feast of the finest hay as she led him away. When Micah entered the courtyard, he saw his mother coming toward him. "Micah, what happened in battle? Where is your father?"

He wanted to ask her about Shoshanna, but first Micah knew he had to wipe the worried look off his mother's face. "Father is well, Mother. He did not receive a scratch in the battle. I rode on ahead, but he will be here soon enough. Where is my wife?"

A look of dismay crossed Ailea's lovely face. "Oh, Micah, something dreadful has happened."

Micah's mouth went completely dry. "To Shoshanna?"

"Yes. I mean, no, not exactly. It is her grandfather. He's dead, son. He hanged himself when he realized that the king's forces would prevail. Shoshanna went to Giloh as soon as she received word."

Micah frowned. "She shouldn't have done that. I'm not sure what reprisals will be brought against the rebels. The king has no more stomach for bloodshed, but Joab might send word for vengeance to be taken on anyone who had any connection to the uprising. Shoshanna would be safer here."

"But my dear, she had to go and comfort her mother."

"Marah also needs to leave Giloh. I will go and fetch them. We'll return by sunset tomorrow." He turned abruptly and spoke to Jerusha, who was just removing Ramah's saddle. "Leave the saddle on. I'm leaving now."

"You should stay at least long enough for Ramah to rest and eat," the little girl scolded. Her brother remounted and rode off without answering.

≈ ≈ ≈

It was late afternoon before Micah arrived at Ahithophel's home. Ramah was lathered in sweat, and Micah was hot and very tired. Still, his pulse raced when he thought of finally seeing Shoshanna again. He was greeted at the door by Gamal, who, if possible, seemed even more ancient and stooped than before. The old servant looked so sorrowful that Micah sought to comfort him. "Good day, Gamal. I am so very sorry about your master's death. I came as soon as I heard."

"It was a great shock, my lord. I am the one who found him, you know—in his private study. I never should have left him alone. I should have known. It doesn't seem possible that he is gone. I served him for forty years. What is to become of us?"

"I will take care of you, Gamal. I will take care of all of you. Take me to the women and we will make plans. Try not to worry."

Gamal led him to a small garden behind the house, where Shoshanna and Marah were sitting on a stone bench. Marah was leaning against her daughter. Both looked up in surprise, but it was Marah who rose and came to him, her hands outstretched. He took them in both of his. They felt quite cold. He kissed his mother-in-law on each cheek and said, "I am so sorry, Marah. No matter what happened in the last months of his life, your father's wise counsel served the king well for many years, and I respected him for that. That is the legacy you should remember."

"I know you are right, Micah. But to hang himself!" She shuddered. "I don't know if I'll ever get over the shock. And I think it's even worse for Shoshanna. She blames herself because she wasn't here in Giloh. She believes she could have prevented it, somehow." As she said this, she turned around, as if to speak to her daughter, but Shoshanna had left the garden. "She must have gone to the guest house. She can't bear to stay in the house since. . . . Please be patient with her, Micah. She is still deep in grief." But Micah was already striding toward the guest house.

When he reached the door, a poignant memory of the one night they had spent there struck him, erasing the resentment he had felt that she had not greeted him. Shoshanna had come to him so willingly, so sweetly, and had returned his kisses and expressions of love without hesitation. Perhaps her feelings toward him weren't negative at all, despite the way they had parted. Maybe Shoshanna was merely so distraught that she did not want to speak with him in front of her mother. In any case, she deserved his patience, the benefit of the doubt.

When he entered, she was sitting on a couch near the window. He knew by her set expression that she had not chosen this place to meet because of its memories of their wedding night. As he moved toward her, she looked away. "Shoshanna, I am so—"

She interrupted him. "Sorry that my grandfather is dead? Is that what you were about to say? At least speak honestly, Micah. You were my grandfather's enemy, and you refused to intercede to save his life when I asked you to. Don't pretend to mourn him now!"

"As you would have heard me tell your mother if you had stayed in the garden, I respected your grandfather very much. His contribution over the years cannot be wiped out by the events of the past few months. Of course I cannot mourn him as you do. I did not know him well. But I am saddened by the manner of his death, and I am especially sorry for your loss and grief." Micah sat down beside her and tried to reach out to her, but she jumped up from the couch and started toward the door. He followed her and grabbed her arm to stop her.

"Don't run away again, Shoshanna. You are my wife, and we will talk about this. I know you are angry, but none of what happened is my fault."

"Yes, it is. You spied on us. You reported to Joab about my grandfather. You refused to listen to my plea that you intervene with the king on his behalf. You wished him dead, and now he's gone."

"I never wished your grandfather dead, Shoshanna, but he chose to side with Absalom. There was nothing I could do. And I don't believe there was anything I should have done. He committed treason against the Lord's anointed. That was *his* decision."

Her eyes filled with tears and her chest rose and fell with emotion. He was struck by her beauty even as she struggled to elude his grasp. When he realized that he would bruise her arm if he continued to hold her, he let her go. She turned her back on him. "Leave me alone, Micah. I cannot forgive you. Go back to Ziph."

He felt his anger rise at her unjust condemnation. Through clenched teeth, he said, "Oh, I *am* returning to Ziph—and so are you. Your mother will also go with us, as will Gamal and Anah. I will leave you alone tonight. In the morning, you will rise and pack your things, and you will behave as a new bride should toward her husband. We will leave this place at midday. I am certain that your grandfather's properties will be confiscated, and I am not at all sure that you will not be sought for treason. You and your mother will be safe in Ziph."

"I won't go!"

Micah clamped down on his anger as he studied his wife's mutinous expression. If he stayed here, their argument would escalate, and he didn't want that. He had envisioned an evening in the arms of his bride. *How naive,* he now realized. "I will leave you to sulk alone, Shoshanna. But know this. You will travel with your mother, your servants and me to Ziph tomorrow." Satisfied at the great dignity and authority his words conveyed, Micah quickly left before Shoshanna could think of a gibe in response.

It certainly hadn't been a very auspicious reunion. But they had both been through a lot. The hasty marriage. Their separation because of the battle. The death of her grandfather. Perhaps things would be better in the morning after a good night's rest, he thought as he returned to the main house.

He found his mother-in-law packing their things and helped her with the chore as an opportunity to offer comfort. "I hope you will make allowance for Shoshanna," Marah said as they wrapped breakable things in clothing and placed them into two large baskets. "She has had a terrible shock. In some ways she was closer to my father than I ever was."

He studied Marah's sad, uncertain expression, and his heart went out to her. Life had not dealt kindly with his mother-in-law. She had lost her husband, then her father. And now, because she had no son, she would go to the house of strangers to live with the family of a son-in-law she barely knew. She didn't have the strength that her daughter displayed. Micah decided Shoshanna had taken more after her grandfather than her mother.

"I know you have both been through an ordeal, but there is nothing to worry about. Shoshanna and I will deal very well together once all this turmoil is over. And you both will be made welcome by my family and the people in my village." This speech earned him a quavering smile from the older woman, and he felt he had gained an ally.

Things would improve once he got his bride back in Ziph, where she belonged, he assured himself as he climbed into bed at last.

∼ ∼ ∼

The next morning Micah was up very early, despite having slept very little. He instructed Gamal and Anah to make final preparations and went to the guest house to check on Shoshanna. He had decided in the early hours before dawn to woo his bride, cajole her out of her anger. Marah had been correct. She hadn't had an easy time of it, and he had perhaps expected too much of her.

He quietly opened the door and looked inside the darkened room. She was sleeping, completely rolled up in a blanket. He decided that he would load the pack animals for their journey and awaken her later. He reluctantly admitted as he went back to the main house that he was a bit relieved that a confrontation with his bride would be postponed a little longer.

Before long, everything was packed, and Micah decided he could not allow Shoshanna to sleep any longer. He brought her a tray with ripe figs, a small loaf of fresh bread, and milk that had been cooled in the cistern. He had observed that a man's humor often improved when his hunger was filled. Surely it was the same for a woman. Balancing the tray in one hand, he first knocked, then entered the guest house.

After setting the tray on the table, Micah went to open the shutters. "I hope I haven't married a slothful woman, Shoshanna," he said in a teasing manner. "The sun has been up for hours, and here you are, still in bed." He reached out to pat her still form and immediately knew he had been tricked. He threw back the covers and saw three pillows lined up to resemble a sleeping form. The same ploy she had used before, and he had fallen for it! Storming out of the house, he instructed the two elderly servants to go on to Ziph, assuring them that he and their mistress would soon follow.

Assuming that she had probably left Giloh, he hurried to the stables. But where would she go? Surely not to Jerusalem. He hoped she realized the great danger she would face there. Perhaps she had gone to Ziph, after all, leaving early just to irritate him. He shook his head. Who could understand the mind of a woman? When he entered the stable he saw at once that Ramah was missing. Only the mule that Shoshanna was to have ridden remained. He grumbled as he saddled the animal. If she was riding Ramah, she was far ahead of him—if she had managed to keep the huge mount under control. He fretted and fumed as he made his way to Jerusalem, alternately worried that Ramah could have thrown her or bandits could have harmed her, and angry that she was causing him such trouble.

Chapter Seventeen

～

Shoshanna let herself into the house in the upper city of Jerusalem. She was uneasy about being here, but hoped that in the confusion surrounding the rebellion she would be safe for a few days before the king's forces returned.

She had run away from Micah because she wasn't ready to give up her anger yet, and she wanted to further mourn her grandfather. She could barely stand to be at the house in Giloh with its ghastly reminder of Ahithophel's suicide. Here the memories would be pleasant. She wanted to go through his things and keep those that had special meaning. The rest she would give to the poor. She did not want the crown to take possession of Grandfather's personal things.

For a while she went from room to room, placing things she planned to take with her in a large basket. She had not slept at all last night, and had sneaked Ramah out of his stall well before first light. She was exhausted, physically and emotionally, and soon went upstairs to her sleeping chamber to rest. The house was eerily quiet, and for a few moments she felt uneasy, but exhaustion soon claimed her.

～ ～ ～

She awoke with a start. Someone was in the house! She could distinguish two male voices and froze for a moment before reaching for her clothing. Her hands shook as she dressed. She knew it must be the king's men, or more likely, Joab's. She crept to the door and listened for a moment, but heard nothing. Maybe the intruders had left or gone to the back of the house. She had to take this opportunity to escape. She opened the door and was snared by a powerful arm. "Aha! I told you someone was up here. I knew it the minute we saw that basket filled with things." The man who had her around the middle was squeezing her so hard that she couldn't have screamed if she tried.

"I checked the other sleeping quarters. No one is in them." The man who spoke was as tall and cadaverous as his companion was short and burly. She recognized the tall one as the same man who had accosted her and Micah in the watchtower. They worked for Joab. Micah had warned her that they would be totally ruthless.

The burly one wrestled her back into her room and into a chair. He removed his leather girdle and used it to tie her. He yanked her head back by her long braid. "Where is your grandfather, your servants?"

"My grandfather is where you can never harm him." Her tall captor, who had looked on while his friend manhandled her, suddenly reached out and slapped her so hard that her head snapped back, sending a jolt of pain through her neck and down her shoulders. Her stinging cheek felt as if it were on fire, and her eyes watered, but she was determined not to give them the satisfaction of seeing her cry.

"I won't be at all disappointed," he said with a smile, "if you decide not to answer my questions. I would very much like the challenge of persuading you to talk. Now, where is your grandfather?"

"In a grave in Giloh. He hanged himself two weeks ago."

Her captor's cold black eyes studied her face for a moment. "I think you might be telling the truth. Then where is your family, your servants?"

"My grandfather closed down this house when he went to Giloh for the last time. I came here this morning, alone."

Again he struck her, his hand darting out so fast that she didn't see it coming. "We will have to hurt you, girl, if you don't tell us the truth," the thin one said while rubbing his hands together.

Shoshanna hated that her voice sounded so weak when she answered him. "I am telling you the truth. I came here alone. I rode the horse that is in the stable. Check the stables, the house. There are no other animals, servants, or family members here. Only me." As soon as she spoke, she regretted it. *I should have said that the entire family will be arriving at any moment.* But these men seemed prepared to confront anyone related to Ahithophel. It probably would make no difference in their treatment of her.

The thin one sent the other man to verify her statement. He was back in just a few moments, but it seemed like an hour to Shoshanna, who had to endure the cold-eyed gaze of her captor. "It seems she may be telling the truth," the other one reported when he returned. He looked disappointed.

"Well, you know how to tell the truth. Now you will give me a list of all the clan chiefs who planned the insurrection."

Shoshanna remained stoically silent, even when the brute slapped her a few more times. She felt a trickle of blood run from her lip to her chin, but still she wouldn't speak. To show fear to these men would only encourage them to greater cruelty.

In anger, the thin man took her hand and secured it with the pressure of one arm while he grabbed her little finger and bent it back. The pressure caused enough pain to convince her of his serious intent.

"You will give me a name, or I will break this finger," he said mildly. "And I will break them all, one by one, each time you refuse to name a traitor." He looked surprised when she didn't respond.

"Give me a name," he repeated. When an answer wasn't immediately forthcoming, he slowly bent her little finger until it broke. She couldn't suppress a gasp, but bit down on her lip to keep from crying out. Without any hesitation, he took her other hand in his grip, and again bent her little finger. "Now tell me who betrayed the king."

"Absalom," she said, then cried out as the man snapped her finger like a dry twig.

"Now we will try again. Tell me the names of the men you persuaded to betray the king. You have ten fingers, and we have all night."

No sooner had he spoken than the heavy door to the chamber slammed open with such force that it swung completely back on its hinges and resounded against the wall.

In a heartbeat, Micah had both men by the necks of their tunics. Pulled off the floor, both choked and clawed at the cloth that was cutting off their breath. Ignoring their struggles, Micah pushed both of them outside into the courtyard, where he threw them to the ground with great force. Before they could recover, he stood towering over them.

"Go back to Joab and tell him that Micah ben Jonathan allows no man to harm his wife! Tell him that I await his apology for his unfortunate error in believing my wife, the queen's cousin, could possibly commit treason. Tell him that anyone who tries to take her will have to come through me. Can you deliver the message word for word, or shall I repeat it?"

Nodding their heads vigorously as they got to their feet, the two miscreants backed away from the young giant who threatened them. They tripped over each other in their hurry to get away.

Micah rushed back upstairs. Shoshanna had not seemed seriously injured, despite the scream he had heard. He had noticed that her cheeks were swollen and her lip was bleeding, as though she had been slapped, but now that her attackers had fled, his heart clinched in fear that they had injured her in a way that was not immediately apparent. He took the stairs three at a time and again burst through the door. Shoshanna sat hunched over in the chair, her hands turned palms up in her lap. When she looked up at him, he saw that her complexion had turned a pasty white, and that her eyes were glazed with pain. "They broke my fingers, Micah," she whispered hoarsely.

When he looked more closely at her hands, he could see that her little fingers stuck out at odd angles. They had been broken at the first joint. He wanted to take her in his arms to comfort her, but was afraid of hurting her, so he picked up a linen scarf that was atop a clothing chest and began tearing it into narrow strips as he sat down beside her. "Are you hurt anywhere else, Shoshanna?" She started to raise her hand to her face, then, wincing in pain, lowered it. "They only cut my lip when they slapped me."

"Then you should be fine as soon as I get your fingers set. I want you to stretch out on the bed here. Can't have you fainting and falling over while I'm in the middle of things. Don't worry; it's the same as setting a bird's wing or a lamb's leg. I've done it many times."

He kept up a steady chatter as he gently straightened each finger, binding them tightly to the rest of her fingers. "We can splint these properly when we get home to Ziph. You will need to keep them bound together for several weeks. Don't bite your bottom lip, Shoshanna. You're making it bleed more. It's much better to cry or yell." Micah hated causing her pain, but just as when he helped his wounded animals, he forced himself to think only of the benefit of his ministrations.

Shoshanna obediently stopped biting her lip, but she didn't cry out. Micah noticed tears edging her lashes as he asked her where the wine was stored. "Lie there while I get you some." In a few moments he was back with a cup and a skin of wine. He refused to let her rise, instead lifting her head so she could drink. "Finish the cup. It will help you rest. There now, rest your hands near your cheek. It will keep the blood flow away from the fingers and keep them from swelling and throbbing as much."

All this time Shoshanna said nothing. She was too tired and

in too much pain to think clearly. She knew that Micah had a right to be angry with her, but she was still angry at him, and did not like to think of having to apologize for her own behavior. "I will gather your family's most personal belongings, but I am certain that the house and most of its contents will be confiscated, and there is nothing I can do about it," she heard Micah say as he started to leave the room.

Shoshanna mustered enough energy to murmur, "Nothing you want to do about it." She knew her response had reached his ears when he closed the door a good deal harder than necessary.

≈ ≈ ≈

The morning sun, shining in her eyes, wakened her. She had slept through the night. Had Micah drugged the wine, or had her exhaustion caused her to sleep through the discomfort of her broken bones? She rose to wash her face, but soon sat back down in frustration. With her hands bandaged and her fingers throbbing, she was unable to lift the ewer to pour the water into the basin. When she tried again to tip the pitcher, it slipped from her hands and shattered on the floor. She half expected Micah to come crashing into the room to rescue her, but she heard no sound of him in the house. Still frightened by the events of the day before, she hurried downstairs to look for him.

He was packing two donkeys with items he had gathered from the house. Shoshanna made a quick search and returned to tell him about additional items that she wanted to take. "There isn't room, Shoshanna," he said sharply. "We don't have a third pack animal, and Ramah will have all he can do to carry both of us." He didn't look at her as he spoke and she knew that he was still very displeased. Well, so was she!

He quickly mounted and reached down to lift her to ride in front of him. "I can ride behind you," she grumbled. She didn't want to ride for hours sprawled across his lap.

He snorted in disdain. "You couldn't hold on five minutes

250

with your hands bandaged like that. Besides, the journey is too long and too rough for you to ride behind me. You'll just have to endure the closeness of your husband for one day at least." Micah click-clicked and Ramah started off for Ziph with the pack mules, secured by ropes, following along behind.

At first Shoshanna tried to hold herself upright and stiff, refusing to relax in the embrace of her grandfather's enemy. But only a few minutes after leaving Jerusalem, her aching muscles gave out and she sank back against the hard wall of his chest. She pretended not to hear his low laugh at her capitulation.

As they rode along, he tried several times to converse with her. "Shoshanna, what did you think of Ziph?" She merely shrugged her shoulders. "Were my mother and sister kind to you?"

"Very kind," she answered. But she did not embellish her reply. After trying twice more, Micah finally settled for silence. Before long, Shoshanna fell asleep.

Micah situated her comfortably in the crook of his arm, crossing her hands above her heart so that they would not dangle down and swell as they rode. Several tendrils of new hair growth curled around his wife's face, peeping from under her headcovering. It made her look very young, he thought. He noticed the dark circles beneath the long fringe of her lashes. Things would not be normal between them until she had had time to grieve for Ahithophel, and he knew he needed to give her time to do that. But in the meantime she continued to act in such unpredictable and reckless ways that she drove him crazy. He had always been such a patient person; why could his wife so easily make him lose control? This business of being married was not as easy as he thought it would be.

≈ ≈ ≈

Shoshanna did not awaken until she heard a child's shout of welcome as Ramah passed through the gate of Micah's home.

"We're home," he whispered before dismounting and lifting his arms to help her down. If not for her damaged hands, she would have refused his help, she told herself as she tried to clear the cobwebs from her brain and greet the family members who were welcoming them.

"Ramah looks winded, Micah. You have ridden him too hard. Look at the lather he has worked up, having to carry both of you. I will see to him now." These words from her little sister-in-law rather amused Shoshanna. Jerusha was certainly not afraid to scold her overgrown brother. He merely smiled at the child and patted her head. "You'll have some explaining to do to Mother about those bandages on Shoshanna's hands, you know," the child tossed back over her shoulders as she led the stallion away. "A man is supposed to protect his bride. That's one of the things you're useful for!"

Ailea and Jonathan rushed into the courtyard along with Marah, who ran into Shoshanna's arms and began crying softly. "I was so worried about you, my baby. Why did you go to Jerusalem when there is such danger there? And what happened to your poor hands?"

Micah and Jonathan exchanged a look over the heads of the women. They would talk later. For now it was up to them to calm the other members of the family. Ailea stepped forward and gently guided Shoshanna into the house. "Come, my dear. I set some food aside, just in case you arrived today. Micah, you come too. You can tell us how we can best help Shoshanna. Marah, stop your weeping now; they are safely returned to us, just as I told you." Ailea had such presence and dignity that it did not seem strange to see her take charge of people who towered over her. She led Shoshanna into the common room and ordered Anah to bring food, knowing that the faithful old servant needed to feel useful to her young mistress.

"You did a fine job with the bandages, Micah," Ailea said a few minutes later, after he had told the story of what had happened to Shoshanna. "They won't have to be changed again until tomorrow or the next day. But you must be careful, Shoshanna. If these broken fingers don't heal properly they could trouble you for the rest of your life."

Turning to Marah and Micah, she explained, "Shoshanna was such a help for the little time we had her—worked from daylight to dark. We must see to it that she does no work with her hands until they have healed."

"I will try, Mother," Micah said, "but I must warn you that my new bride has not yet learned obedience to her lord and master. I expect that you and Marah will instruct her in the proper behavior of wives." He barely suppressed a smile as Shoshanna flushed in embarrassment.

"Oh, my daughter, your husband has been very kind. He was so worried when you ran away. You mustn't be a trial to him, truly—"

Marah fell silent when she felt the large hands of her son-in-law on her shoulders.

"My dear Marah, I spoke only in jest. Please don't think that I am not pleased with my bride. I am certain that as time goes on we both will learn much about how to go on. But now, I think we must seek our bed because it has been a particularly hard day for us. Come, Shoshanna, let us bid our family good night."

Shoshanna stared at her husband for a long moment, then decided to acquiesce. She was too tired to challenge him.

A short while later, as Shoshanna removed her headdress and outer tunic, she noticed that Micah was doing the same. His movements seemed to fill the room, and she realized that her husband had complete power over her. He was larger, stronger, and—she suspected—smarter. She would never get the best of him, so she might as well stop trying. To her chagrin, the thought made tears come to her eyes. She quickly ducked her head, but Micah had already seen.

"Don't be distressed, Shoshanna. In time your grief will lessen and you will become accustomed to your new home—and me as well." He stooped down and pulled back the covers from the bed. "Come to bed, and try not to worry. Just sleep." She wanted to stay angry, to reject his offer of peace, but his voice was so soothing that she found herself doing his bidding. Soon he cradled her in his arms. She tensed at first, but when he did no more than say good night and kiss the top of her head, her qualms melted away and sleep overtook her.

Micah waited until he was certain Shoshanna slept deeply before slipping from the room to seek out his father. Jonathan was using a mallet to straighten his badly dented round shield. He tapped patiently on the metal, not hearing Micah approach.

"Father, I have some concerns to discuss with you." Jonathan jerked in surprise, causing the mallet to hit his thumb. "Ow!" He shook the injured digit while motioning Micah to have a seat on the bench beside him.

"You heard what Joab's men did to Shoshanna. I am very concerned that he will come after her. Do you think the king will stand for it?"

Jonathan shrugged. "I would think not. King David made it very clear that he wants no further bloodshed, no punishment for the rebels as long as they cease the rebellion. His relationship with Joab has always been strong. Much as he deplores some of his nephew's actions, David finds it hard to oppose him. But don't worry. We won't let anything happen to Shoshanna, even if we have to defy the king. I plan to leave for Mahanaim again in a few days. I'm growing nervous, not knowing when the king is going to be reinstated in Jerusalem. From Mahanaim, I should be able to keep an eye on the general. I will send you word if he does anything that could mean danger to your wife."

"You go to Mahanaim and I will keep her here, where she will be safe."

Jonathan grinned. "From what I have learned of your bride, Micah, she isn't an easy woman to 'keep.'" Micah had to agree.

≈ ≈ ≈

At first it seemed to Shoshanna that neither of Micah's predictions would come true. The pain of her bereavement continued, and the strain between bride and groom was unabated. Still, despite Shoshanna's seeming indifference to his attention, Micah patiently set about to win her over with gentleness.

And the gentleness was not for her alone. Micah patiently answered Jerusha's endless questions, helping her tend to the small, wounded creatures she brought home to heal. He treated Marah with reverence, cutting a pomegranate for her and scooping out the delicious but hard-to-get-at seeds. He helped renovate her room and made a partition in it so that Anah had a place to sleep that was separate but nearby in case her mistress needed her.

Ailea was just as attentive as her son to the new members of their household. She allowed Gamal to cook when she learned that he had performed that function for Ahithophel. Both Micah and Jerusha had told Shoshanna that Ailea had never had a cook in the past because she loved to prepare the meals herself. But to make an old man feel useful, she had given up that pleasure. Sometimes Shoshanna's throat closed up and she fought tears when Micah and his family were so kind. She still held herself aloof because of her anger toward Micah, but she began to feel guilty for shunning the others.

The day after their arrival back in Ziph, Ailea declared that there would be a formal time of mourning for Ahithophel. "But his suicide was a disgrace," Marah said in a quavering voice. "No one in Giloh would have come if we had sat in mourning for Father."

"Well, this is not Giloh. Eventually everyone in Ziph will learn about your father's death and the events surrounding it, but for now we will honor his life and remember his days as advisor to the king. The villagers will all come to visit when you sit in mourning. You will be able to properly mourn the father you loved." That said, Ailea proceeded to make plans for seven formal days of mourning.

Jonathan sought out Shoshanna as she sat alone on the rooftop, grieving the loss of her grandfather. "I am very sorry that I can't stay in Ziph and join in your time of mourning," he said as he perched on the barrier around the edge of the roof.

She turned her head to look at him, and he saw the naked pain in her eyes. "But he was your enemy," she said. "He planned the rebellion and forced the king out of Jerusalem. You would still honor him?"

"Yes, Shoshanna, I would. Because he was your grandfather, and you are now my daughter. Make no mistake about our feelings—Ailea's and mine. You are as much a daughter to us now as Jerusha is. We will always stand with you, no matter what. And if you have need of anything, just come and ask me. Will you do that?"

Her father-in-law's kindness made a lump come to her throat so that she couldn't answer. She wiped her eyes and nodded. He patted her shoulder. "I have to go back to Mahanaim tomorrow, my dear. But I will look forward to returning and becoming better acquainted. In the meantime, you must feel free to talk to your mother-in-law about anything that is troubling you. I know you don't want to burden your mother in her time of grief. Despite her size, my wife is a very strong woman and will be honored to help you." After patting her shoulder once more, he left her alone again.

The next day, after they had seen Jonathan on his way, Shoshanna joined Marah, Gamal, and Anah in mourning for the dead. They tore the ends of their tunics, smeared their faces with soot, and sat on the ground in the courtyard. Jerusha and Ailea had told the villagers about it, and they came to offer their condolences and bring food for the family. Micah also came and sat with them for a while. He tore his own garment and put soot on his face. As he sat between mother and daughter, he wrapped Marah in his strong arms and comforted her, crooning as if to a child. Shoshanna fought back tears, but she decided that if her husband tried to treat her in the same manner, she would rebuff him.

Micah ignored her all morning, however, and finally she couldn't stand his nearness. She left in search of Ailea and Jerusha and offered to help with the household chores. Ailea wouldn't hear of it. "Your mother sits in the courtyard, and so shall you. Your grandfather may have done wrong, but you and Marah loved him, and you need your week of mourning. Now go. Our neighbors will be coming to pay their respects. You have no other responsibilities today."

Shoshanna returned to the courtyard and was relieved to see that Micah was no longer there. She joined her mother and finally was able to weep for her grandfather.

When the mourners were served the midday meal, Shoshanna took a large bite of the roasted lamb Ailea offered her. She was surprised to find that she was very hungry after her one-day fast. She had always thought it a bit strange how family and neighbors always plied grieving survivors with food. Perhaps it was a tribute of sorts to life—a ritual that asserted life's victory over death.

After the week of mourning, Shoshanna insisted on taking an active role in the housework. Her hands were still tender, but with strong splints on her injured fingers, she was able to do most chores with little discomfort. Though Shoshanna still was quiet and withdrawn, Ailea seemed to understand and to welcome the help. Jerusha could not curb her natural exuberance, and continued to try to get Shoshanna to talk to her, ignoring her mother's commands to leave her sister-in-law alone.

Finally, in desperation, Shoshanna agreed to accompany Jerusha and her little shepherd friend, Reuben, into the hills to follow Ziph's herds. *Maybe it will raise my spirits,* Shoshanna thought as she agreed. Jerusha was thrilled to have her company. The young girl never fell quiet all day. She pointed out every vista, every point of interest, seeming to know and love every hill in southern Judah.

She took great pride in explaining the shepherds' equipment to Shoshanna. "Do you know what the shepherd's crook is for, Shoshanna?" she asked.

"I have seen it used for dragging a wandering sheep back into the fold," Shoshanna replied.

"But there is another use."

"I give up. What else is it used for?"

"Well," Jerusha replied patiently as if she were teaching a child. "The crook is used during lambing time to lift a newborn lamb and hold it out to its mother if the ewe has rejected her baby. You see, a mother knows her baby by its scent, and if the smell of the shepherd gets on the lamb from his handling it, then the mother will never accept it. But when the lamb is held next to the mother's nose by the shepherd's crook, most of the time the flighty ewes, usually first-time mothers, will recognize and accept them."

Shoshanna smiled. "That is very interesting, Jerusha. Maybe at lambing time I could come and see the new lambs."

"I will be glad to bring you," Jerusha said. When they returned with the sheep in the late afternoon, Jerusha told the other shepherds to continue on to the sheepfold while she showed her sister-in-law one more thing.

She led Shoshanna to a very large sycamore fig tree. It appeared to Shoshanna to be the oldest tree she had seen around Ziph. Under its spreading branches was a rock that was naturally scooped out in the shape of a bench. It was most unusual. "This is the teaching rock, where my grandfather taught the Law. He taught me to read and write." Jerusha preened with pride. "Do you know how to read?" She clearly expected a negative answer. Not many people knew how to read and write, and for a female to possess the skill was truly unusual. Jerusha's eyes widened when Shoshanna answered affirmatively.

"Who taught you?"

Shoshanna smiled at her. "Guess."

It took but a moment for the child to come up with an answer. "Your grandfather!"

Shoshanna chuckled. "You're right. Grandfather spent much time teaching me many things. He was a very learned man."

"So was my grandfather. The whole village listened to him.

Micah was his best pupil. I'm afraid I was too young and too restless to sit for very long at his feet, but the Rab didn't mind. He loved us all. But he loved Micah best of all."

Shoshanna ran a hand along the smooth stone of the rock, then sat down on it. She could picture generations of children being taught here. And she could picture the Rab. She knew that Micah missed him very much. Her eyes teared as she was reminded of Ahithophel. She felt a small hand slip into hers. "I miss my grandfather too," Jerusha said.

Chapter Eighteen

~

Several weeks later, as the women combed through raw wool that had been set aside after the spring sheep shearing, Ailea told a story Shoshanna had never heard.

"I understand how you both feel about . . . about the way Ahithophel died. My mother died the same way."

Marah gasped at Ailea's statement. "She was hanged?"

"No. No, I didn't mean the method. I meant that she did it herself. Killed herself. She let herself be stung by scorpions. I found her body in her own chamber." The words evoked such a disturbing picture that neither Marah nor Shoshanna knew what to say. They just looked at Ailea as she continued.

"For a long time I felt guilty. I believed that I could have prevented my mother's death. I had known how despondent she was after my father's death. But worse than that, deep in my heart, I was angry at her for leaving me all alone at the mercy of the invaders." Ailea stopped combing the wool for a moment and smiled. "I thought the coming of the Hebrews to Damascus and their invasion of my home was the worst thing that ever happened. In order to deflect the guilt I felt about my mother's suicide, I chose to blame them, and specifically Jonathan. I'm afraid I gave him a very hard time. But the hand of God was on me, even through those difficult days, because my mother's death was one reason that Jonathan decided to keep me with him, and later, to marry me. Now here I am, serving the God of Abraham, with a loving husband and a wonderful family. All the pain is just a dull ache now. When I think of Mother, I remember her as she was before grief stole her mind, and I choose to dwell on the love we shared, rather than the way she died."

The three women hugged each other and cried. Now they shared a closer bond. When Marah began to talk about returning to her home in Giloh, Ailea insisted that she make her home with them. She brushed aside Marah's protests that it was an imposition. "I'm enjoying Shoshanna's companionship so much that I will be thrilled to have you as well. Besides, I have been the only woman in the household since Jonathan's sister Ruth married a wealthy widower from Maon and moved there. I have missed her sorely, and her room stands empty, just waiting for someone to fill it. The Lord graciously arranges such things, does he not?"

When Marah tried once more to protest, Ailea insisted, "You haven't been here long enough to know how much help I need to keep up with my daughter, but Shoshanna can tell you. I would love to put Anah in charge of Jerusha and see if she can bring a little civilization to that girl."

Marah laughed in spite of herself. She had already observed Jerusha's liveliness. Only the day before, the child had come home bringing both a lamb and a wolf pup. She had explained that the mother wolf had killed the lamb's mother. Habaz had killed the wolf and two of her pups before Jerusha grabbed the third. She refused to listen when Habaz insisted that any wolf was the enemy of shepherd and sheep alike, and that the pup had to be killed.

Jerusha had hurried home carrying the lamb in one arm and the wolf pup in the other, with every intention of raising them both together. Habaz was not far behind, insisting that Ailea talk sense to her daughter. Ailea took one look at the small, trembling animal and told Habaz they would await Jonathan's return and leave the decision up to him.

Jerusha was a handful, and looking after her would make Anah feel useful. She had been in low spirits ever since Shoshanna had left home. Neither Marah nor Shoshanna was able to summon the will to refuse Ailea's kind offer, so they set about trying to make themselves useful in their new home.

Shoshanna was growing to love her new family, and it seemed that Marah and Micah were also growing close. But the newlyweds' relationship still held mistrust and constraint. After his father left, Micah seemed to give up on trying to woo Shoshanna and began to mirror her distant behavior. It was the time of year for the vineyard keepers to make wine. They had mashed the grapes into a paste and allowed them to ferment naturally for several weeks. Now they had the chore of adding just the right amount of water to the paste and placing the mixture in new wineskins to age. For ordinary consumption at meals, the mixture was nine parts water to one part fruit of the vine. Micah was gone from daylight to sunset as he helped with this process. When that was finished, he helped in the village pottery.

Shoshanna sensed that her husband was avoiding her, and she knew why. When they were together in public, she was polite but distant. She responded to any question Micah asked her, but she never started a conversation with him on her own. Secretly she hoped to goad him into a reaction, but he never referred to her coldness. Only in their room at night were they as close as a husband and wife should be. One night he told her, "This is a splendid thing we share, Shoshanna. Let's both promise to leave our differences at the door when we enter this room."

"And take them up again when we leave it?"

"Only if that is what you wish," he said.

≈ ≈ ≈

Micah had other problems to deal with besides Shoshanna. The young men who had fought with him had returned to the village with the story of how he had been their leader, fighting with Goliath's sword until the enemy was vanquished. They praised his bravery and skill as a warrior. The recruits spread the word about Micah's feats of courage in the battle. Those who had withheld judgment after the scandal that had resulted in his dismissal from the army now decided that the son of Jonathan was worthy of honor, after all.

But the young man who had seen Igal die had come home with a different story. He went straight to Lemuel with his account of how his younger brother had died by the hand of a man Micah had failed to kill. One of the first things Micah had done when he returned to Ziph was to seek out Igal's parents to tell them how bravely the young man had fought and to express his own sorrow at Igal's death.

While Igal's father seemed willing to accept Micah's condolences, both Lemuel and his mother blamed Micah for the death and yelled at him to get out of their home. From that time on, Micah heard whispers of "Aramean coward" and similar insults from Lemuel and a few other people in the village. Micah was coming to believe that no matter what he did, he would never gain the respect of the villagers; certainly not enough respect that they would choose him as a leader.

One market day, he accompanied Shoshanna to buy food and household articles. Lemuel was sitting with a merchant who had brought rugs from Maon. When Shoshanna and Micah passed by, Lemuel stuck out his leg and deliberately tripped Micah, who sprawled ingloriously on the ground.

"Big, clumsy lout," Lemuel said under his breath, but loud enough for both the merchant and Shoshanna and Micah to hear. Shoshanna lost her temper, even as Micah rose and dusted himself off. "He is not clumsy! You tripped him on purpose. What a childish thing to do!"

"That is enough. Let's go." Completely ignoring Lemuel, Micah took her by the arm and started to lead her away.

"But why do you not defend yourself? Why did you let him get away with that?"

"Lower your voice, Shoshanna. The whole village can hear you." She tried to dig in her feet to make him stop, but he pulled her along with him.

"And what difference does that make when the entire village wonders aloud if you are really the coward Lemuel says you are? If you don't care what they say, then think about the embarrassment to your family, and do something to shut Lemuel up!" With that, Shoshanna yanked free of her husband's hold and continued shopping on her own. She pushed away the guilty feeling that she hadn't expressed confidence in her husband. She knew very well that he was the bravest of men, but she had sounded like she doubted him. She wanted to apologize, but her pride stood in the way.

~ ~ ~

When Jonathan arrived in Mahanaim, he found that King David still had no immediate plans to return to the capital. That evening in the house where they were quartered, he joined a group of about ten of the *Gibborim*.

"What's the problem with the king?" Jonathan asked Benaiah, his deeply furrowed brow displaying his concern. The grizzled veteran shook his head as he cracked four large almonds in the palm of one powerful hand.

"I don't know, my friend. But it makes me uneasy that we tarry here. Who knows what trouble could be brewing in the capital without the king to take a firm hand? I'm not certain that the northern tribes welcomed our victory. What is the mood of the men of Judah?"

Jonathan shrugged. "More were against us than were for us. Micah tried to convince the elders of our own village to come out strongly for David. Instead, they sent their sons to fight on both sides of the conflict. They are like many other towns of the hill country. They will follow the man who seems the strongest. If the king appears to have regained his former power, then they will serve him. However, in the days before my departure, I heard some mumbling about the insult David was dealing the Judahites by staying in the north, and on the wrong side of the Jordan. They can be so petty sometimes."

"When I think of all the Philistine raiders we battled to save those little towns and villages, and all the casualties we took trying to protect them, I sometimes wonder why we bothered," Benaiah said. "David was their hero then, when he fought on their behalf. Now that he needs them, why can't they stand by him?"

"Micah did a lot to convince them they should be ashamed not to send their young men to the king's aid. I hope he will stay in Ziph now and become the clan chieftain. He is powerful enough to have earned their respect, but is gentle enough, kind and reasonable enough to persuade them to follow the right path. He has much of his grandfather in him, and I think the elders see that."

"He also has his father in him. He has proven himself a formidable warrior. Are you certain he won't desire to make a career of the army?"

"I am certain, Benaiah. He is a man of peace, a man of healing. The events of the past months have proven that Micah will fight for his country, for his king, but he only does so out of necessity. I want him to do his duty, but I want him to be happy as well."

"The lad is fortunate to have a father such as you, Jonathan. Many men would insist that their sons follow in their steps. It is a matter of pride with them."

Jonathan took a large swallow of water from a jug that sat on a side table. "I'm proud of Micah no matter which course he takes, because he has grown to be a man of integrity, which is all I have ever asked of him. The Rab taught me that, and I have passed it down to my son."

"As I said, Micah is extremely blessed."

≈ ≈ ≈

That evening, there was a long, agonizing meeting of the *Gibborim* and their king. They all pleaded with David to leave Mahanaim, but at first, they made no headway. Joab finally lost his temper.

"What is this that ails you, my kinsman? Do you no longer have the will or the heart to rule?"

The Thirty were accustomed to hearing cutting remarks pass between David and Joab, so they were not shocked to hear the general's disrespectful comment. After all, Joab had said worse to David the day of the battle, when the king had been told of Absalom's death. They were shocked by the king's response to Joab's goading.

"You are right about one thing, nephew. I am brokenhearted. My son, after all, has been put to death. But you are wrong if you think I don't have the will to lead my people. I am still your monarch, and because you have repeatedly questioned my leadership, I choose to remove you from your position as general. You will still hold equal rank with Abishai and Benaiah, but I will appoint another man as general in your place."

Joab stared at David for a long moment, his jaw clenched. "You speak in anger. Surely you will reconsider. My own words were hasty. I—"

David cut him off with a chopping motion of his hand. "There is nothing to reconsider. This rebellion has taught me there must be changes, and I have just made the most important one."

"Who would you have to take my place, then?" Joab's tone was supercilious, as though he was certain that no one else was capable of leading the army.

David folded his arms, and a steely look came into his hazel eyes. "I have given it considerable thought, and have already come to a decision. I had intended to wait until I returned to Jerusalem to announce it, but you have changed my mind. There is no need to wait. I choose Amasa to lead the army in your place, and your duties will come to an end as soon as he arrives here. When that happens, I will return to Jerusalem. Not before."

There were mutters and gasps throughout the room, and some looks of outrage, but no one spoke any objection aloud to the king. The *Gibborim* knew of the many times Joab had displayed brutality that went far beyond what David intended. It wasn't surprising that in killing Absalom, Joab had finally gone too far. But to appoint Amasa, the leader of the rebel troops, was incomprehensible to most of them. True, Amasa was the son of David's half sister, Abigail, but how could they ever trust the man?

Joab stormed out of the meeting without another word, but David went on as if nothing was amiss. "Now, what shall we do about the problems in the south?" he asked.

It was decided that a delegation would go to Judah and persuade the Judahites to participate in a great ceremony to return the king. David chose the high priests, Zadok and Abiathar, to fulfill this mission. He also instructed them to find Amasa in Bethlehem and tell him that, far from being punished for his part in the rebellion, he was now to be general over all the armies of Israel in place of Joab.

They found Amasa hiding out in the caves near his home of Bethlehem, but it took hours to convince him that this was not some scheme to trick him into showing himself. Finally, after reading a personal letter sealed with David's own seal, Amasa realized that the offer was real. He agreed to go with the two priests to Hebron to speak to the elders there about sending a large delegation to escort David back to Jerusalem. After they got to Hebron, Abiathar decided to go to Ziph and some of the other villages so that the news would spread faster.

≈ ≈ ≈

Jerusha stood on the crest of a hill where she and the other shepherds had taken the sheep to graze. She saw a gray mule, ridden by a man in fine clothes and a white turban. His mule was led by a servant. Even from a distance she could tell that this was an important man.

"Reuben, I'm going to find my brother and tell him about the stranger who is coming to Ziph. Take care of the sheep." Reuben, who was ten years old and her constant companion, smiled and nodded. He always did whatever Jerusha asked of him.

A few minutes later, Jerusha breathlessly entered the pottery where her brother was helping construct a new, larger kiln. "Micah, hurry and come with me. There is someone coming, someone important. He might even be coming to our house. We have to tell *Ahmi* and Shoshanna."

"Whoa, little one, what are you talking about?"

Jerusha took his hand and began tugging it to get him to come with her. "I told you, he will be here in a matter of minutes. You need to put on a fresh tunic and be ready to meet him. You look a mess, Micah." Micah gave in and went with her.

Shoshanna was on her hands and knees cleaning the flagstone paving of the courtyard. Although her fingers were still often stiff and painful, she had undertaken the arduous task to make certain that Ailea, Anah, or her mother would not have to. She dipped a large sponge in the pail beside her and scrubbed the next flagstone with it and the fine sand she had put down. Ailea had several large sponges from the Great Sea that Isaac, her friend's son, had brought back from one of his trade expeditions. It made the cleaning go faster. When she heard Micah and Jerusha coming, she plopped the sponge into the pail and looked up.

Micah grinned at her. "You have transferred the dirt from the flagstones to your tunic and your face, my lily."

"Oh, Shoshanna, you have to go at once and wash up. We are about to have an important visitor. You'll want to look your best." Jerusha dropped her brother's hand and began tugging on Shoshanna's arm. As usual, she wasn't worried at all about her own appearance, which was much more disreputable than her brother's or sister-in-law's. Jerusha wore a sheepskin tunic that crossed under one arm and was tied at the waist with an old length of rope, and she was barefoot.

Shoshanna was flustered by the news that a guest was coming. "Why didn't you inform me that you had invited a dignitary for a visit?"

"Because I didn't invite anyone home. And I'm still not sure that—" His sentence was interrupted by Jerusha. "He's almost here! I'll go get *Ahmi*," she said. Shoshanna and Micah both rushed to their room.

A very short time later, a knock came on their door. It was Anah. She had a clean tunic for Micah. "The high priest Abiathar graces our home today. Your mother makes him welcome now, my lord. But hurry. You don't want to keep such an important man waiting." The servant left after delivering this directive.

Shoshanna blotted her face dry with a clean cloth. "Are my smudges all gone now?" she wanted to know.

"Yes, they are. I rather liked them, though." Micah cupped his wife's face with his big hand. "You look lovely, as always."

As they left their room Shoshanna asked, "What is he doing here, Micah?"

"I don't know. I would imagine he brings us news from the king, or he is here on some political mission. Strange he should come to such an out-of-the-way place as Ziph."

Micah welcomed Abiathar and offered him bread and wine. He was eager for the man to get to the point, but it would be rude to insist. So they spoke of commonplace things for a few minutes.

Then Micah said, "You will sleep this night in my home, my lord. The blessing of Adonai will certainly fall on my family and our house because the high priest has graced it."

Abiathar waved the compliment away. "I would love to avail myself of your wonderful hospitality, but I will sleep in Hebron tonight. I have left Zadok to convince the elders of that city to give a show of support for David. I'm here to do the same for Ziph. Could you convene the elders? Your father tells me you are the leader here now."

Micah's eyes widened in surprise. "He said that? I'm afraid he is mistaken. But I will convene the elders and pray that they have the wisdom to heed us both."

Micah called the elders to meet at the teaching rock just outside of Ziph. A crowd of spectators followed along to see the high priest.

Abiathar, a man in his midforties, did not smile when the elders greeted him. He came right to the point. "Do you men of Judah support the king?"

There was a long, drawn-out silence before the oldest man spoke. "We would first wish to know what concessions will be given us."

A look of disdain flickered across the high priest's face before he stroked his beard and delivered his message. He stood upon the rock where the Rab had taught for so many years. "I bring you words directly from the king's mouth. It is not I who speaks to you, but King David." He paused a moment before continuing in a louder, more authoritative voice. "'Why are you the last ones to reinstate your king? I am hearing from all Israel that they are ready once more to embrace me. Yet Judah, my own kinsmen, still holds back. You are my own tribe, my own flesh and blood.'" Abiathar paused once more in order to gauge the effect of his words. None of Ziph's elders would meet his gaze. Micah hoped it was because of shame rather than recalcitrance. Micah looked at Abiathar and nodded his head in approval. The priest was encouraged and continued.

"Additionally, your king says to tell you that his nephew Amasa is this day with Zadok in Hebron. He has been newly appointed general in place of Joab." A murmur of interest swept through the crowd. They hated Joab. He had, after all, killed the prince, whom some had supported. Second, they knew that if David was granting Amasa amnesty, after he had served as Absalom's general, he would not seek revenge on them either.

As soon as Micah himself had absorbed the surprising, and, to him, very welcome news of the demotion of Joab in favor of

Amasa, he quickly took advantage of their changed attitude. "We should send a delegation to meet our king at the Jordan and escort him home to Jerusalem."

"Son of Jonathan," old Eliezer said, "I am too old to lead such a group, but you are young and strong. Will you go in my place as Ziph's leader?"

Micah was speechless with surprise. Always in the past he had been too young to be taken seriously, or he had been suspect because he was the son of a foreign woman. More recently, there were the accusations of Lemuel passing around the village. Now they were looking to him for leadership. He was thrilled to be honored, and he felt a sense of union with his grandfather, who had prophesied that this would happen.

On the other hand, he was stricken with a sense of anxiety, a sense of fear that he might prove unworthy to be a leader of men. After all, he was not even near the age of thirty, the age commonly thought of as the minimum for the position of elder. Of course, there was no rule about it in the Law of Moses. They wanted him to go. He knew how important it was to present a united front with the king in order to restore peace to Israel. He would accept the offer. He had to.

He took a deep breath and slowly exhaled. "I will go," he said. The men cheered. More than a dozen men from Ziph agreed to go with him. Within hours, Abiathar and Micah visited the smaller villages of Maon and Debir, and the elders committed to send men as representatives.

The sun was setting when Micah and the high priest reached Ziph once again. Reluctantly, Abiathar agreed that he should not journey on to Hebron in the dark. He accepted Micah's hospitality. When they entered the house, Micah could not suppress a smile when he looked at the women of his household. They were all sitting in the common room, dressed in their finest attire. Except for Jerusha, each had her head covered, which was unusual in the privacy of their own home—even in the presence of guests.

Shoshanna was busy embroidering the neck of a tunic. Marah was filling each oil lamp with olive oil. Ailea was instructing Anah and Gamal in placing cushions around the low table from which they would take their meal.

The entire scene was staged to appear as though the house sparkled with this degree of cleanliness every day and that the whole family had many rich garments to choose from. Even Jerusha was dressed in her best, and wonder of wonders, there were even sandals on her feet. Micah smiled and introduced the priest to his family.

The meal was a sumptuous affair for such short notice—late-summer fruit, cheese, beans, onions and cucumbers. When Anah brought out a platter with roasted quail, Micah raised his eyebrows at Shoshanna in question. Meat or poultry was not everyday fare in most homes. Micah's family had it maybe once a week. At his look, Shoshanna nodded her head slightly in Jerusha's direction. She answered the question of where it came from by chattering to the high priest. "Reuben set a snare for the quails. He and I are friends. We take care of the flocks together. When I found out you were coming, I ran to Reuben's house and told them we needed them for a special guest. He had already dressed them, but he gave them to me."

Abiathar listened to Jerusha's monologue with patience. "Please convey my thanks, then, to your friend. And to the cook as well. The birds are done to perfection." In a very grown-up, important tone, Jerusha assured him she would.

To crown the meal, Ailea topped the bread with honey and cinnamon, a rare delicacy.

"You are a fortunate man to enjoy such food, Micah," the high priest told him after stuffing himself on the rich fare. "No wonder you grew so big and strong, eating like this every day." Micah nearly laughed out loud at the looks Ailea, Marah, and Shoshanna shot him. They were afraid he would tell the high priest that their daily fare was nothing like what they enjoyed this night. They all gave sighs of relief when he merely agreed with Abiathar.

Alone in their room later, Micah told Shoshanna about Joab's fall from power. "It may well mean that you will have nothing more to fear from him, but we mustn't assume. Joab has been out of favor with the king more than once and clawed his way back into power." He took the comb from her hand and took over the task of pulling it through the long strands of her hair. Shoshanna knew such acts of affection were melting her heart toward her husband, and told herself she was a weak woman to be won over by such blandishments. Then Micah spoke to her in his voice of authority and ruined the pleasant tone of the evening.

"You are to stay in Ziph this time, no matter what happens. This is a command I am giving you. Do you understand me, Shoshanna?" She snatched the comb back from him and yanked it through her hair as she responded. "You have made it very clear to me, *my lord!*"

Micah, Abiathar, and the ten delegates from Ziph left at dawn the next morning. Micah rode Ramah. He had offered the priest the use of his horse, but the man claimed the powerful beast made him uneasy. He would be glad to ride his own mule. Before they left, Micah kissed his wife. "When I return, we will put away the issues that keep us apart."

Shoshanna did not deny the estrangement that had hindered their adjustment in the marriage. She knew that it had mostly been on her part. She would have to forgive Micah for not doing more to save her grandfather. She promised herself she would apologize to her husband for being unreasonable on this issue. She would do so as soon as he was back home, she promised herself. For now, she clung to her husband for an extra moment to try to convey to him how she felt. They swayed together, arms around each other until he slowly unwrapped her arms from around his neck and stepped back. "May Adonai keep you, my lily."

"And you, my husband."

Chapter Nineteen

~

As Micah and his companions from Ziph made their way to Gilgal, some of the men who had fought with him during the revolt expressed relief that the turmoil was almost over. Once they had installed David in his capital, they could go home and no longer worry about fighting. Only one of the young men had become smitten with the idea of being a warrior. The others would welcome being civilians once more.

"I'm glad I don't have to serve under that traitor," declared one lanky young man with more boldness than sense, referring to the new general, Amasa.

The man to his left scoffed. "Amasa is a hundred times better than Joab. It takes a vicious man to stab someone who is helplessly hanging from a tree. And don't forget Abner years ago. Joab did him in while pretending to give him the kiss of greeting."

Micah cleared his throat and turned to the two, who had been marching behind him. "I would advise you to keep your tongues between your teeth or you may find them missing some day. Amasa now holds the most powerful office in the land. I would not call him a traitor if I were you. As for Joab, he seems to have eyes and ears everywhere. He does not wait for the king's permission to punish those he considers enemies. And in spite of the fact that he has been demoted, don't be surprised if he manages to climb right back into the seat of power before many months go by." The two men, hearing the wisdom in Micah's words, fell silent as the march continued.

When they reached Gilgal, they found the town overflowing with men from every tribe who had come to show their support for the king. Micah thought that David would have already forded the river, and that he might find his father in Gilgal, but the main body of the army was still camped on the east side of the Jordan, some five miles away. Micah's group clamored to continue on and join them. Of course, that would mean fording the river twice, but the younger men looked upon it as an adventure. "We will find no place to sleep in Gilgal anyway," they argued. Micah was looking forward to seeing his father and was not hard to persuade. They left the old men to find lodging as best they could and hurried to cross the river before dark.

It was the beginning of the fall rainy season, and the water was running higher than usual. They reached the east bank cold and shivering, but found the warmth of a hundred campfires awaiting them. Beside the *Gibborim,* the Cherethites, and the Pelethites, Micah saw that many of his countrymen had the same idea as his group—to escort the king across the river.

Micah found Jonathan with the other *Gibborim*. They were talking to an elderly man, trying to convince him to accept the king's invitation to accompany him to Jerusalem. Jonathan introduced him as Barzillai from Gilead. "He came out to meet us when we were in retreat and brought us food and supplies. Now the king wishes to reward him by making him a member of the court, but he will not hear of it."

The old man, with a very large, hooked nose and sharp eyes under bushy white eyebrows, laughed. "I am eighty years old, young man," he said to Jonathan, who hadn't considered himself a young man for many years. "I would no sooner arrive at Jerusalem than you would all be asked to attend my funeral. I want to spend my last days in the comfort of my own tent, and a spacious tent it is, too. But my son, Chimham here, will make a fine member of David's court. It is he who will enjoy the favor of the king and reap honor to the house of Barzillai. The king has graciously promised him some land near Bethlehem as well as a generous pension." Micah smiled at Barzillai's son, a striking man in his thirties who was dressed in white with a white turban wrapping his head.

Micah and Jonathan left the group and walked to Jonathan's tent, which he offered to share with his son. "Do you think we will both fit in there?" Micah asked with a smile. His father surveyed the small field tent he had set up and shrugged. "We will sleep close and keep each other warm." As it happened, they were glad for the cozy confines, because a steady downpour began during the night.

At dawn, the king's entourage, made up of the Thirty and the members of his family, crossed over the Jordan, preceded by the Cherethites and followed by the Pelethites. They wanted to cross quickly, before the rain swelled the river to dangerous proportions. Micah saw his father off.

"Don't tarry too long in crossing, or the flooded river will keep you on this side for a week," his father instructed. Micah promised he would gather his men quickly.

"I will see you on the other side," he promised before turning back to camp.

"How will we get our men across?" Micah asked the question of Bani, an old army veteran, as they surveyed the rising Jordan an hour later.

"That is why I came by," Bani explained. "Joab says it would be best to spread out to the north and south—each unit can attempt to cross at the spot of their choice. That way we avoid confusion and have a better chance of everyone getting across safely."

"I think we will look to the south. You are welcome to cross with us." The dozen young warriors echoed their approval of the invitation. It would be an honor indeed to have one of the *Gibborim* accompany them.

"I can't go right now because I need to take word to the rest of the men. If you are willing to wait until I complete that duty, I will go with you."

So it was that Micah's group was one of the last to attempt to ford the rapidly rising river. They found a place a bit to the south of the major crossing, and though the river was wide here, there was a sandbar about two-thirds of the way across with a few scrubby trees. Micah and Bani decided that the men could rest there if the crossing proved arduous.

Micah gave the command for his men to follow him. He was mounted on Ramah and trailed a rope behind the horse for the weaker swimmers to hold on to. "I am going to stay mounted unless Ramah gets into trouble and can't swim with my great weight. In that case, I will attempt to tow you to the sandbar myself."

All appeared to go well at first, though the water reached the midsection of most of the men. Ramah held steady against the current, working his way slowly forward. Several yards from the sandbar the river bottom suddenly dropped off into a trough and they became caught in a deep eddy. Micah could feel Ramah struggling, so he untied the rope that tethered the four men to the horse and wrapped it around his own waist before slipping from the saddle. He tried for a few moments to hang onto Ramah's bridle, but the current was too strong. Finally, he pushed off from his horse as hard as he could in the direction of the sandbar. Ramah immediately swam downriver, while Micah swam with all his might toward the sandbar. A whirlpool took him under once, but he used all his strength and finally was able to reach the bar and grab a scrubby bush. He hauled himself and the men tethered to him onto dry land, and lay panting for a moment.

Micah looked up and saw one of the stronger swimmers, who had tried to make it alone, being pulled under at the same whirlpool that had almost defeated him, so he swam out to the man. He took a long piece of driftwood with him and extended it to the man. He would not make the mistake of being taken under a second time. The ploy worked, and Micah was able to tow the exhausted man back to where the others waited. A couple of other men had been swept downstream, and Micah prayed they would be all right.

They had little time to rejoice that their small party had reached safety. The water continued to rise alarmingly. Torrential rains to the north were causing a flood that increased moment by moment. Large trees, dead cows and sheep, and all manner of debris were being swept past the rapidly disappearing sandbar. The noise became so deafening that the men had to shout in order to be heard. They knew that they, too, would be swept away if they didn't get across very soon. Thankfully, the sandbar was closer to the west side of the river than to the side from which they had come. But where there had been a gradual buildup on the other side, there was a deep drop-off on the side they had yet to cross. He was concerned that more of his men would be swept away by the powerful force of the raging river. There was no choice but to attempt it.

"Men, if we hesitate much longer, we are lost. Are you all ready to try for the bank?" Micah looked every one of his ten remaining men in the eye, trying to instill courage in each. He felt a strange calmness as he remembered the word of the Lord to Joshua, which the Rab had taught him many years ago: *"Be strong and of good courage; do not be afraid, nor be dismayed, for the LORD your God is with you wherever you go."* Even as they paused for a moment, the water covered the sandbar, and they were up to their ankles in water. As swift as the river was, by the time it reached their knees, most of the men would be swept off their feet.

Two of the men could not swim and had no chance unless Micah took them across. "Put your arms around my neck and wrap your legs around my middle, but try not to choke me or we will both go down." He turned to the second nonswimmer. "Wait here, and I will come back for you. Bani, you and the other strong swimmers follow me."

Five men followed Micah into the roiling current. The young man clinging to his back tightened his hands painfully around Micah's neck for a moment, then realized what he was doing and loosened his grip. Micah dodged the debris that went sweeping by and made it to the bank, where the young warrior scrambled to safety. Bani and three of the others were right behind him, but one man was in trouble and was slowly being swept downstream as he splashed about desperately. Micah swam to him and wrapped an arm around his neck. He was very tired when he reached the bank again.

Bani reached out for the half-drowned man and yelled at Micah. "Stay here. You will never reach the lad in time anyway." He pointed to the sandbar, which was now submerged under about four feet of water. The young man who was left clung to the largest bush he could find, but the current was so powerful that soon the man and the bush would be swept away. Bani was right; the poor fellow would surely be gone before Micah could reach him. But he had to try. He had promised he would come. He prayed for strength from Adonai as he again battled the powerful current. Just as he reached out for the man, the scrub bush gave way, and he was yanked out of Micah's grasp. Micah swam after him, but the man was swept under by one of the powerful eddies the flood had caused. Micah reached down and pulled him free.

The power of the flood had increased even more in the last few moments, but Micah told himself not to give up. Bani had tied the rope around his waist, which the four other men held onto. He had waded into the river and waited with outstretched arms to pull the victim in. Those last few yards seemed like miles to Micah, but finally Bani took his burden from him. The men holding the rope cheered. Then their voices changed to frantic cries of warning. Micah saw their faces. They were looking at something behind him. Micah didn't waste time looking over his shoulder. He lunged for the bank, but too late. An uprooted tree was careening swiftly toward him, and the root end struck Micah with great force in the back. His men groaned as they saw their leader disappear beneath the water.

≈ ≈ ≈

Confusion reigned in Gilgal, which was swollen to overflowing with delegates from every tribe. Jonathan and the other high-ranking officers were given quarters in private homes. But the majority of the army had to find makeshift shelter, or sleep in their tents.

As soon as David set foot on the west bank of the Jordan, Shimei appeared suddenly to greet him. This time he carried no rocks in his hands, nor was he spewing invectives. He threw himself at the king's feet and begged his forgiveness. "I have sinned in the words I said to you," he admitted. "But look, now I am the first of all the house of Joseph to welcome you. Now please don't take my former actions to heart."

Abishai, the brother of Joab, sinewy and fierce, stepped forward with a drawn sword. "I should have killed you before for cursing the Lord's anointed. Now I will put you to death."

David wrapped a restraining hand around his nephew's forearm. "What am I going to do with you, sons of Zeruiah, my sister? You make yourselves my enemies this day by your insistence on revenge. There will not be anyone put to death today in Israel, but all will celebrate my return as king."

To demonstrate his words, the king reached down and helped Shimei to his feet. "I swear an oath to you this day, Shimei. You shall not be put to death." With those words, the king resumed the march toward Gilgal.

But no sooner had David arrived at that city than conflict and jealousies broke out concerning him. Delegates from the other ten tribes were resentful that the contingent from Judah now outnumbered them. They should not have been surprised, because Judah made up more than half the population of southern Israel. But it offended them that the men of Judah had joined up with the king's entourage on the other side of the river and escorted him to Gilgal. The men of Judah responded by reminding the others that the king was their kinsman. In turn, the ten tribes chided Judah for being the last of the errant tribes to come back to the king's side.

A Benjamite named Sheba was so angry at the Judahites that he called for a renewal of the rebellion. "The son of Jesse will do nothing for us. Let's all go back home and ready ourselves to overthrow him!" This rhetoric was so unexpected that no one moved to stop the treasonous talk. A great many of the men from the ten northern tribes indeed chose to go home in disgust, which gave the Judahites even more influence in the celebrations that surrounded David's return to Jerusalem.

Jonathan's attention was distracted from these political posturings by the fact that he hadn't seen any sign of Micah. He inquired throughout the town, but his son had not been seen. Finally, he saw a bedraggled group of men arriving late from crossing the river. At their head was the man who had been with Micah when Jonathan last saw him. Jonathan's heart turned to stone when he saw the grim look in the man's eyes. He didn't even have to ask the question before Bani told him.

"He's gone."

"What do you mean, 'gone'?"

"He was swept away by the flooding river. After saving all of us, he was taken under by an uprooted tree."

"Where is his body?"

"It was impossible to recover the body. It was swept downstream. But no one could have survived the impact of that tree, much less the river's current. Your son is surely gone, but he died as a hero."

"No! I won't accept it! I don't care about his being a hero. I want my son at my side." These words were wrenched from Jonathan as he sank to his knees in pain. Old Bani merely stood by with his hands on the big warrior's shoulders.

In a few moments Jonathan was once again in control of his

emotions. "I will not go home without my son. If he is dead, I will find his body, but I won't face his mother without at least that comfort."

"I understand," Bani said. "But you weren't there and wouldn't know where to look. Escort the king back to Jerusalem, then come back and join me in the search. I will start looking tonight."

Jonathan knew that what Bani suggested made sense, but he didn't want to leave the area without searching for Micah. He agonized over what to do. Finally, he decided that he couldn't desert the king at a time like this, when the country was so unstable. "Very well," he told Bani. "I will go with the entourage back to Jerusalem. But as soon as I can get away, I will join you. If not tomorrow, then the next day."

A young man came to his side. "It was for me he died, sir. He came back for me. He saved my life. I will go with Bani to search for him."

Jonathan, consumed with grief, merely nodded.

Chapter Twenty

~

*T*he next twenty-four hours were as a bad dream to Jonathan. Not only was he deeply grieving for Micah, but the return to the capital was anything but the grand occasion they had hoped for.

When they neared the city, Mephibosheth, the only surviving grandson of Saul, came out to meet the procession. The poor, crippled man looked terrible. He hadn't trimmed his beard. His feet, which were hopelessly twisted and deformed, needed constant attention to keep sores from forming. It was obvious by their oozing, bloody appearance that they had been neglected. Mephibosheth's eyes were red and swollen, as if he had been weeping.

He stopped his donkey right in front of David, so that the king had to stop or go around him. David halted and gazed on the young man, the son of his best friend, Jonathan, son of Saul. "Why didn't you go into exile with me?" David's voice betrayed no emotion as he asked the question.

"Oh, my lord, my servant deceived me. He told me you didn't want me, and then refused to help me saddle my donkey that I might come after you. Then I found out that Ziba slandered me by saying I went after the prince. But I would not do such a thing. How could I, after you spared my life when my other kinsmen were put to death, and you brought me into your own house? From that time, my lord the king was like the angel of the Lord to me. So what right have I to complain? Do with me what you will."

David looked at the imploring, dark eyes that burned into his. They were so like the eyes of his father. For the sake of his old friend, he must give Mephibosheth the benefit of the doubt. He gave a weary, pained sigh. "Don't worry. You and Ziba can share the land that was your inheritance. Now don't bother me anymore."

It was obvious to Mephibosheth that the king was not able to trust his version of the story. Fighting tears, the young man said, "No, my lord, please let Ziba have it all. I am only glad you have returned safely."

It struck Jonathan then that things would never be as they were years ago, when David had first taken the city and brought the Ark to Jerusalem. How happy they were then, how young and naive. They had loved the Lord, and Adonai had been faithful. But there had also been sin—on the part of all of them—and they were now reaping the tragic consequences.

The saddest moment of all took place when the king's retinue reached the palace. There, on the top story, looking over the retaining wall, were the ten concubines whom David had left to keep the palace. They did not send up a happy cheer of greeting, but rather the shrill wailing of grief. They knew that their relationship to the king was forever altered. Most chieftains or kings with a harem would put to death any concubine who had lain with another man. The ten loudly mourned their fate.

But when David entered the palace—still surrounded by the Thirty and the palace guard, who would not leave the king's presence until every nook of the palace had been searched for assassins—the first place he went was the garden roof. Eight of the concubines came and wept at his feet. Two cowered in the corner. The eldest woman in the harem, a lady about thirty years old, spoke for the group.

"My lord, we fought the prince when we saw he would dishonor us. But he forced us. None of us came willingly, except for those two harlots over there. They did not resist the king's son. We will have no more to do with them! Surely they deserve death! But please, my lord, don't cast us aside."

David had to raise his voice to be heard over the weeping women. He instructed Jehoshaphat, who was again in charge of the palace, to find new lodging for the women, on the other side of Jerusalem. He kissed each one on the cheek, even the two errant ones, who were to be housed together in a different place to avoid the contempt of the others. "You bear no fault in this, any of you," he said. "But you know that now I can never lay with you again, nor can you stay here, else rumors will abound. You will be well taken care of as widows in Israel, for I am truly dead to you from this day."

It was a wrenching sight as these beautiful, pathetic women were pulled away, weeping and begging, by Jehoshaphat and the harem servants. None could marry another, for they had belonged to the king. Those without children were condemned to remain childless, the greatest curse possible in the eyes of an Israelite woman. *Dear God, will the pain never come to an end?* Jonathan prayed that it would.

As if David's heart wasn't heavy enough, word came that Sheba the hotheaded one who had stalked away from Gilgal, had called to arms hundreds of men from the northern tribes and was now planning a new rebellion. Jonathan knew that in a matter of days he would be called upon to fight again. But in the meantime, he would look for Micah.

He went to find Joab, who was still his direct superior. He would have preferred to speak to Amasa, who seemed to have a more compassionate nature than his cousin, but as a military man, Jonathan was trained to follow the chain of command.

He found Joab in the *House of the Gibborim*. He was in the process of moving his possessions out of the three-room suite intended for the use of the commander of the armies. *It must be a bitter thing,* Jonathan thought, *to be pushed out of a position you have held for more than forty years.* He wasn't surprised when Joab looked at him with a scowl and asked what he wanted.

"My son was swept away at the river crossing," he explained to his commander. "I would ask a leave of two to three days to search for him."

"Permission not granted," the general growled at him. "If the river took him, he will not be found alive. It is unlikely that you will ever find his body. You have your duty to the army."

"A man's first duty is to his family, cousin. If more family fealty was shown, we would all be better off." It was Amasa who spoke from the doorway. Joab didn't try to hide the malicious look in his eye as he turned toward his cousin. Amasa was untroubled by Joab's hatred. He continued, "I will grant you the leave you request, Jonathan. You have been a faithful warrior all these years, and there is no pressing need for your services at the moment. I am certain that whatever pockets of rebellion still remain, we will put down in short order. And feel free to continue your leave if you find your son and need to . . ." Here the rugged warrior hesitated, as if reluctant to bring up the possibility of death . . . "to take him home."

Jonathan thanked Amasa and immediately left the two rivals. He didn't want to give Joab a chance to sabotage Amasa's orders. Let the two of them work out their differences. Jonathan cared about only one thing at the moment: finding Micah.

He walked along the banks of the Jordan for several hours before he came upon Bani. The older man shook his head. "I have covered every inch of ground between here and the ford and have found nothing. I think maybe we should look further downstream. The river was so rapid that it would have carried him a long way." Jonathan nodded, swallowing the disappointment he had felt when he saw that Bani had not found Micah. On the other hand, if he hadn't found Micah's body, hope was still alive.

~ ~ ~

We'll never find his body, Jonathan admitted to himself as he stopped to wipe the sweat from his face. The noonday sun, combined with the moisture left by the deluge, created a swampy, stewing, oven-like heat. Debris from the storm was piled along the riverbank, making the search extremely difficult.

They had found a body, which appeared to be that of an elderly man, perhaps a farmer who had been caught unaware. But there was no sign of Micah. Jonathan almost wept when he thought of having to tell Ailea that her only son was dead, and they didn't even have a body to bury. It would be hard on her. She still grieved for the Rab. It had only been a year since Shageh's death, and now they had to face another loss in their family. *Dear God, how are we going to get through this?* Jonathan realized the thought was a prayer, and he continued it as he turned over branches and dug into piles of leaves. *Adonai, king of the universe, help me. Please help me.*

"What is moving there, up ahead of us? See, it's where those rocks jut out into the river. Is it a horse?" Bani interrupted his prayer with his question and Jonathan looked at the spot where he was pointing. It was a quarter of a mile further downstream, and it did appear to be a horse, a very large one. It was a rich red-brown color. Suddenly Jonathan thought he recognized the animal, and a thrill of hope shot through his body. He started to run.

When he drew near the horse, he saw that he had been correct, and called out. "Here, Ramah. Don't be afraid of me. I won't hurt you." Ramah whinnied and tossed his head. He took a few steps forward and nudged something on the ground. It was a pile of clothes. No, it was a body!

"Bani, come quickly, I've found him! I've found him!" He turned Micah over and at first thought he was too late. His son's face was ashen, his eyes closed. Jonathan knelt down and placed his ear to Micah's chest and felt a rush of relief to hear the steady thud of his heartbeat. Bani came up beside him and Jonathan barked out instructions as he examined Micah for injuries. "Hold the reins of the horse while I get Micah up. Ramah can take him back to Gilgal." Bani obeyed, but privately thought there wasn't much use in hurrying. The young man would most likely die anyway. People seldom awoke from such injuries, even if their heart continued to beat. It was a pity, but that was the truth of it.

≈ ≈ ≈

Be still, Micah. The pain will pass. You're safe now. Micah groaned, but obeyed the Rab's instruction. He was being jostled and his back hurt him terribly. Where was he? He tried to ask the Rab, but did not have the strength to form the words.

Grandfather . . . how could he be here? Grandfather was dead. The grief struck him as if it were fresh. Grandfather's voice had seemed so real. It occurred to Micah that if he had heard his grandfather's voice, perhaps he was dead too. But the dead feel no pain.

Micah struggled for several minutes to open his eyes; then when he finally managed to, he wished he hadn't. The ground swung crazily beneath him. He recognized the hooves of a horse and realized he was lying across the animal's back. It was torture. Maybe it would be better if he did die. *It isn't time for you to die, Micah. Your parents need you. Shoshanna needs you, and so do the people of Ziph. You can bear the pain.* Micah tried to turn his head to see if it was truly the Rab speaking to him, but the movement caused such pain that he slipped into unconsciousness once more.

Over the next two days, the Rab spoke to him several more times. He would smooth back Micah's hair and speak soothingly. *Don't give up, son. Fight for life!* At dawn of the third day he heard the voice again, and opened his eyes to see his father bending over him. There were tears in his eyes, and his face was lined with worry. Micah wanted to reassure his father and also tell him about how Grandfather had come to him, but he only managed to breathe one faint word—"Father."

"He's awake, Bani. Bring me the soup from the fire. Cool it first. We have to get some food in him so he can fight the weakness." Micah's stomach had revulsed at first, partly from all the dirty water he had swallowed and partly because he hadn't eaten since before the crossing.

He did not lose consciousness again as they made their way home, though he wished for that blessed oblivion many times. He was too weak to speak, and his father and Bani, knowing that he had little strength, did not ask him any questions. But as the older men talked, Micah learned that the king was once more in Jerusalem, and that they could go home. Once when they stopped, he managed to ask after his wife. "Shoshanna . . . is safe now?"

Jonathan bent over his son's pallet to answer. "I have reason to believe that everyone at home will remain safe. Joab has been removed from his position as general, and Amasa has taken his place. Abiathar spoke the truth when he said that there is to be no retaliation against the rebels, so Ziph will not be set to the torch or any such thing, thank the merciful Lord." Micah fell asleep, relieved by the news.

He asked no further questions after that because he was in such pain that he wished to avoid conversation. His lower back hurt so badly that whenever the horse stumbled or caused him to be jostled, he had to bite his lip to keep from screaming. His legs were completely numb. He could not move them at all. Occasionally, he would experience a terrible cramp in one or the other of them, but other than that, his legs were useless.

Micah wondered if the condition would be permanent. He could not bear to think of the possibility. Was this his punishment for causing the death of Igal? What would happen to Shoshanna if it turned out she had a crippled husband? She didn't deserve such a fate. Micah made up his mind to feign unconsciousness so that no one would find out about his legs. He wanted time to see if the paralysis was temporary, and he didn't want his father or anyone else asking him questions. Due to his weakened condition, it was easy to sleep most of the time, anyway. Then a fever overtook him, and he didn't have to pretend.

"Who is this Rab he cries out to?" Bani asked as they made their way tediously over the hills of southern Judah. They would reach Ziph soon—none too soon, Bani thought as he listened to Micah's ravings. He had decided to stay with the brave young warrior until he either died or got better. He feared that death was inevitable.

"The Rab was my father, Bani. He was a great teacher and the wisest man in these hills."

"Was? But the young man speaks of him as though he were still alive."

"The Rab has been gone a year now, but if you had known him, you would realize that he will never be far from our thoughts and hearts," Jonathan explained.

Chapter Twenty-One

∼

*W*ord reached Ziph a full four hours before Jonathan arrived with his wounded son. He had sent a runner ahead to forewarn the women about what to expect, and to tell them to prepare to help Micah.

Ailea wept the entire time they were making up the room he would lie in and checking their store of healing herbs. Shoshanna remained dry-eyed, with only her pale face and cold hands revealing her distress. She went to a neighbor to borrow aloe to treat her husband's wounds.

"Poor thing. If your husband has taken a fever, it is surely hopeless," the woman commiserated, unaware of the insensitivity of her remarks. "Here, take this myrrh to put in his wine. It will ease him." Shoshanna hurried back to the house, hoping and fearing at the same time that the litter bearing her husband would be there. But it was another half hour before they arrived.

The litter was borne by three men because of Micah's great weight—two at the head and one at his feet. Shoshanna was shocked by the sight of her formidable husband lying helpless. He was in the throes of a fever and tossed his head back and forth, mumbling incoherently from time to time. The thoughtless words of the neighbor came to her mind. *If he has a fever, he will surely die.*

She forced the thought out of her mind and directed the men to carry Micah to his room, the one she had made her own since coming here. Ailea was weeping in her husband's arms, her self-control dissolving in her relief that Jonathan was unharmed and her concern over her seriously wounded son. Shoshanna had no doubt that if she weren't there, Ailea would have held herself together to care for her son. She felt pride in the confidence Ailea had placed in her to look after Micah.

"He burns with the fever since the day before yesterday, my lady, and his worst wound is to his lower back," Bani told her as she led the way to their room.

As soon as Micah had been laid, face down, on the new mattress that had just been finished the day before, Shoshanna called for strips of linen and a basin of cool water. She saw the large swelling near the base of his spine, which Bani told her had most likely been caused when the tree branch struck him. The wound was open and had become infected. It was a disturbing sight, and Shoshanna fought back tears as she ministered to her unconscious husband. She told Anah to boil some figs to make a poultice, and after smearing the concoction on a square of clean linen, placed it over the suppurating wound to draw out the infection.

She had been working over him for some time when she heard a soft voice at her shoulder. "What can I do for him, Shoshanna?" Her mother-in-law still appeared to be near tears, though she had made a good effort to compose herself.

"Have Anah bring us another basin of cold water and more linen, please, Ailea," Shoshanna instructed as she secured the poultice with a long strip of cloth. "Your son is so big that it will take the both of us using ten basins full just to cool this fever." She spoke the words gruffly to hide her dismay. It was disturbing to see Micah so helpless. When the fresh water arrived, Ailea took her place on the other side of the bed and began bathing her son's arm. His shoulders twitched and he mumbled something unintelligible.

"Has he said anything that you could make out?" Ailea asked.

"No. It is just the fever speaking. Bani, you were telling me how my husband came by his wounds," she addressed the warrior who had stationed himself at the foot of the bed with every intention of staying there. "Would you repeat it once more for his mother?" Ailea wept again as Bani recounted the flood and the spectacular way Micah had saved his companions. She smoothed her sleeping son's hair away from his face and whispered, "My brave boy, my brave son."

Shoshanna agreed to leave her husband for a short while to take her supper and rest, but she insisted on sitting up alone with him for the night. Bani was even harder than Ailea to banish. He insisted on staying in case "my lady should need him turned."

Jonathan, who had just entered the room, wouldn't hear of it. "You may seek your pallet now, Bani. I will see to turning my son, and Shoshanna can call me later if Micah needs me." Jonathan looked sad and haggard, but just the sight of his rock-solid strength gave Shoshanna hope. He would fight to keep Micah alive. She hurriedly forced some bread down and ate a few figs that Anah pressed upon her, then retired to Jerusha's room to rest for a while. The child had informed her that until Micah was well, she would sleep in Anah's room, so that whoever nursed Micah could stay nearby in case he needed them.

Shoshanna stayed on Jerusha's narrow bed for an hour, staring at the ceiling, before returning to her husband. Jonathan was sitting, bent forward on a stool beside Micah, his elbows on his knees, and his steepled hands supporting his chin. He sat up straight when she entered. "The physician who treated him in Gilgal told me that such injuries as the one Micah sustained often leave a man crippled. I have not told that to anyone else, not even Ailea. But as his wife, you should know. We mustn't tell Micah or anyone else. He will be whole again. He has to be." Shoshanna turned her eyes away to give Jonathan privacy as tears filled his eyes.

After a few moments he said, "I believe I will prop him on his side. The change in position should make him more comfortable. His fever is down now, so I will leave you to care for him. But please call if you need me."

She assured him she would, and pulled up a comfortable curved-back chair to sit by Micah. He slept for a while, then grew more feverish. As she leaned over him to bathe his forehead, her lone braid swung down and brushed his face. Instinctively his hand reached out to capture it. "Mmmm," her husband mumbled and rubbed the braid against his cheek. Shoshanna tried to gently remove her hair from his grasp, but he held on tighter. "Micah, you are too possessive even when you're out of your head with fever," she said as she finally regained control of her braid. She pressed a kiss on his hand and tucked it under the covers.

≈ ≈ ≈

Micah grunted as he was rudely interrupted in his conversation with the Rab. He had been telling Shageh how afraid he had been when he and his men had been stranded on the sandbar. *I was more afraid that I would fail them than I was of dying, Grandfather. Is that not strange?*

No, the Rab had replied, *it is not strange at all.* Then someone with hot pinchers was prodding his back and he could no longer see his grandfather.

"Easy, Son, we are just cleansing your wound. Shoshanna will be finished in a moment." It was his father's voice.

"He feels pain. That is a good sign, isn't it?" He knew it was Shoshanna asking the question.

"Yes, it is surely a good sign." Even in his fevered state, Micah could hear the insincerity in his father's voice. A vague memory of his father saying something about such injuries crippling a man flashed through Micah's mind. Had Jonathan said that, or was it one of his fevered dreams? And why couldn't he move his legs? He was too tired to think of it right now. Besides, Shoshanna was pressing a sponge to his mouth. He tasted wine with something bitter in it. He would worry about his legs later.

In the night, he woke to see her bending over him. Her hair fell like a dark curtain across his chest. He wrapped his right hand in it and brought it to his nose to smell the fragrance. "Let go of my hair, Micah."

"No," he said quite clearly.

"Are you truly awake now, or are you rambling again?" Shoshanna tugged at her hair as she queried him. "If you are awake, let go of my hair."

"Smells . . . like lilies." When no amount of struggling would get him to release her tresses, she lay down beside him and waited for sleep to cause him to release his hold on her hair. Inwardly, Shoshanna rejoiced in the fact that she could bring some comfort to him.

≈ ≈ ≈

The next morning Micah discovered that he had not dreamed his father's words. He was a cripple! He had awakened on his stomach and tried to turn over. He tried to lift his leg to accomplish the small goal he had set for himself, but it was dead, useless. He tried to move the other leg. He felt some prickles in it, but it was otherwise as dead as the other one. Using his powerful arms, he finally managed to turn himself over, lifeless legs and all. His heart beat in fear. What would life be like if he never regained the use of his legs? He pictured his parents and Shoshanna burdened with lifting and feeding and carrying him about. It was unthinkable.

He calmed a bit when the thought occurred to him that maybe his legs were numb because he hadn't used them in so long. The prickling sensation he felt in his left leg was not unlike the sensation of having his leg fall "asleep." He remembered making the same discovery about his paralysis while they were bringing him home. It had been many days now. But surely it wasn't true!

Frantically, Micah began to massage his legs, thanking Adonai that at least his hands still obeyed his will. He felt desperation choke him when five minutes of rubbing produced no results. He heard someone approaching and pretended to be asleep. It was Shoshanna. Fortunately, after calling his name softly, she left the room. He squeezed his eyes tightly shut to keep from weeping.

He pretended to be unconscious or delirious whenever anyone was in his room. He knew it was cowardly, but he couldn't deal with their pity. He had to find a way to face this disaster before he let anyone he loved share it with him. His pride would not allow him to do otherwise.

He fooled them all. His mother, father, Shoshanna, even Jerusha, thought he had been knocked senseless. At first they tried to get him to respond, sometimes almost shouting in his ear. Both his wife and mother had caught him with his eyes wide open, so he couldn't pretend to be unconscious, but he refused to respond to anything they said, though they continued to try.

Finally, his mother and father stopped speaking directly to him. They came to visit him together, as if they needed to call on each other's strength to face the ordeal of seeing him this way. He hated himself for deceiving them, but he didn't have the courage to face them yet.

≈ ≈ ≈

Micah remembered how he had always complained about his size and strength, always felt that it in some way isolated him. Was Adonai angry with him for complaining? Was he being taught a lesson on how it felt to be weak and at the mercy of others? He began to spend much of his time crying out to the Lord, asking forgiveness for his pride and arrogance.

He recited in his mind passages his grandfather had taught him from the Torah. He also repeated a song David had written years ago, during the time he and his men had served the Philistines. His father had taught it to him as a lad.

> I sought the LORD, and He heard me,
>> And delivered me from all my fears.
> This poor man cried out, and the LORD heard him,
>> And saved him out of all his troubles.
> The angel of the LORD encamps all around those who
>> fear Him,
>> And delivers them.
> The righteous cry out, and the LORD hears,
>> And delivers them out of all their troubles.
> The LORD is near to those who have a broken heart,
>> And saves such as have a contrite spirit.
> Many are the afflictions of the righteous,
>> But the LORD delivers him out of them all.

Micah tried to hold fast to these words, because he knew they were true. And yet they seemed to have no meaning in his own life. God did not seem to have delivered him from all his fears. He broke out in a cold sweat when he thought of the possibility that he might not walk again. As for his troubles, they were many. First, there was the constant pain. Then there was the fact that he had a wife who blamed him for the death of her grandfather, a wife whom he had barely begun to know. And now they might not have children. Micah wondered about that, because surely Shoshanna's life would never be complete without them.

As days went by and no improvement could be seen, Micah stopped praying and reciting the Torah and singing that song of praise in his mind. He felt hopeless and isolated. As much as he wanted to have the comfort of those he loved, he couldn't face them, so he continued the pretense that he was unconscious, which only added to the feeling of being trapped.

Soon, the only prayer he lifted to Adonai was the question, "Why, Lord? Why has this happened to me?" He thought of his effort to obey the Law, just as the Rab has taught him. He thought of the ridicule he had faced from other young men when he kept himself from prostitutes, or from strong drink. Why hadn't something like this happened to one of them? Slowly, anger replaced despair in Micah's heart. He was seething inside. But on the outside, he continued his charade.

≈ ≈ ≈

Shoshanna continued to behave as though her husband could hear and understand everything that went on around him, even though his eyes were closed most of the time. When they were open, they showed no sign of recognition, but merely stared. Shoshanna would let no one speak of his serious wounds, or the possibility that he might die, when they were in his room.

His condition was hard for Jerusha to bear. Every day she would come to visit him and chatter about all her escapades. Shoshanna was certain that the child exaggerated her accounts, hoping they would stir Micah to respond with a scolding, but he never displayed any awareness that she was there.

During the first five days her husband was home, Shoshanna seldom left his side. But one evening Jonathan came to sit with him and insisted that she get some rest. "I will come for you if there is any change," he assured her. "You must get some rest, or else we will have two people to care for."

Shoshanna knew it was true; she was at the end of her endurance, so she agreed to get some rest. From that evening forward, Jonathan or Ailea stayed with their son during the nights while Shoshanna cared for him during the day.

As soon as Shoshanna left the room, Jonathan pulled a stool up to the bed and sat down. "Son, I've been waiting for you to finish playing this game you've been indulging in, but I have grown weary to the bone with it. I know you can hear and understand perfectly well. Why Shoshanna and your mother continue to be fooled, I don't know. But we will have a talk now, and I will know why you've been so cruel."

Micah felt a strange sense of relief along with the alarm his father's stern words brought to him. Finally, he could talk to someone. He closed his eyes to avoid his father's piercing gaze and took a deep breath. "I haven't said anything because there is nothing anyone can do. I am a hopeless cripple and will be nothing but a burden to you all. I thought to spare you the necessity of trying to cheer me up."

Jonathan snorted. "How touching. Your thoughts have only been for your loved ones—no self-pity at all. Do you really think I am foolish enough to believe that? You've been lying here feeling sorry for yourself, and I am sick of it. You think you won't walk again? How can you possibly know that, since you haven't tried?"

Jonathan jerked the covers back and lifted one of his son's lifeless legs. "Son, it is always best to face your fears directly. If I never taught you that, I know the Rab must have." He began to massage the calf of the limp leg vigorously. "If there is yet any life left in these limbs, we will find it, and fan it, and nourish it until it is as strong as it ever was. I won't give up, Micah, no matter how long it takes. Promise me you won't either."

Micah felt ashamed that unmanly tears were welling up and about to overflow. It was enough that he was helpless as a baby. He wouldn't let his father see him cry like one. He turned his head away and closed his eyes again. After a few minutes, his father left the room.

Later, when the only light was the one left burning on the table by the window, Shoshanna came to him, as she did each night before retiring to bed. Often she would press bread that had been soaked in water or wine between his teeth and he would swallow, because he couldn't stand to hear the disappointment in her voice when he didn't. Tonight she stood silently by the bed, holding his limp hand in one of hers. After a few minutes, he felt something drop on his hand. Something wet and warm. Then another drop, followed by another.

She was crying! It was all Micah could do to keep from squeezing her hand, or begging her not to cry. But if he did, then he feared there would be two of them crying. After an interminable time, she bent and kissed his forehead and left the room. Micah prayed to die. He would rather be dead than cause Shoshanna heartache and pain, than burden her with his pain-wracked, ruined body. Micah tried to hold back the torrent of weeping that burst from him. He failed. He bunched the covers in his fists and pressed them over his mouth to muffle the sound. No one heard his cries.

≈ ≈ ≈

Micah followed the Rab to the teaching rock. It was strange because Grandfather looked so much larger than what Micah remembered. The old man took a seat and motioned Micah to sit at his feet. A cooling breeze was blowing the Rab's white hair and beard as he looked down on his grandson. His eyes were pools of sorrow.

I am deeply grieved, Micah, that you have crumbled under adversity. I always believed you would grow up to have courage and strength. The Rab sighed as his hand ruffled through Micah's thick mane of hair. *Now you must listen carefully. There are many lessons to be learned.*

"Micah!"

He woke with a start. "I'm sorry, Grandfather. I must have fallen asleep," Micah said as he rubbed his eyes.

"I'm afraid it's only me, my son," Jonathan told him as he sat down beside him on the side of the bed. "I wish your grandfather were still with us. We could both use his wisdom."

Micah swallowed hard before he nodded agreement. He was

fighting a deep sense of loss as he realized his conversation with the Rab had been only a dream.

"What do you think the Rab would say to us if he were here?"

"I know what he'd say. He'd tell me not to be a coward."

"You're not—"

Micah held up his hand. "Don't make excuses for me. The Lord knows I've made enough for myself. If you are still willing to help me, I'm willing to try."

The look of joy on his father's face was almost overwhelming. "Then I say we get started today!"

"I don't suppose you could be persuaded to keep quiet about this to Mother and Shoshanna?"

"By no means!"

Micah sighed deeply. "Then, will you tell them? And tell them that only you and I will work on my recovery. I don't think I could stand their flittering and hovering around me."

"You're asking a lot of your old father, asking me to face the women alone. You will owe me much for doing it, but I suppose, out of deference to what you've been through, I will agree. Both your mother and your wife will be very angry. I won't be able to keep them from coming after you."

His father was right, Micah admitted a while later, when Shoshanna came storming into the room, marched over to his bed and chastised him. "You are the cruelest man alive, Micah. How could you do such a thing to your mother? She has wept a river of tears for you." Angered further that Micah still did not speak, and in no mood to grant that she hadn't given him a chance, she picked up one of the plush cushions on the bed and began to pummel him.

As worried as he had been about his wife's reaction to his deception, somehow her actions struck him as funny, which infuriated her further; she tried to hit him hard enough to get him to stop laughing. Micah brought an end to her attack by grabbing her upraised arm and pulling her down to him. Even in his weakened state, she was no match for the strength of his arms.

"Hold, Shoshanna. Hold, now. You might hurt yourself. Ow! Stop it." She felt some satisfaction as she pulled his beard hard enough to make him yelp. "Such a wife!" he remarked as he subdued her by imprisoning her other hand.

"Such a husband!" She snapped right back at him.

Micah, who just a few hours ago could not imagine himself ever laughing again, roared with amusement. "I haven't seen you so angry since the first time I beat you at chess. It makes you even more beautiful. Your eyes are brighter and your cheeks are as rosy as a pomegranate."

Shoshanna stared at him, held captive as much by his intimate words as by his hands on hers. He reached up to caress her face. "Won't you welcome your husband home? Kiss me, Shoshanna."

"You think to make me forget my anger, Micah, and you have not even asked my forgiveness for letting me think you were . . . were . . ."

"Witless, I believe is the word you are looking for. I am very sorry. Now kiss me, wife."

"You do not seem contrite at all. I don't think you deserve to be kissed."

"I probably don't, but kiss me anyway, my lily. It has been a very long time."

His uncanny eyes crumbled her resistance, and she felt herself melting inside as she touched her lips to Micah's. What had happened to her anger, not only at his deception, but at his cold-hearted refusal to help her grandfather? She was very much afraid it had dissolved under the onslaught of her love and attraction to him. She could not seem to help it. His kisses were too sweet to resist. She stopped trying.

Their idyllic reunion did not last long. Jonathan entered the room and cleared his throat loudly to gain their attention. Shoshanna drew back, her face flaming in embarrassment. Her husband laughed, and she could tell that her father-in-law was trying not to. She couldn't flee the room fast enough.

"I hope you enjoyed that interlude," Jonathan told his son. "I fear there won't be time for many of those in the near future. I have some very difficult training planned for you, more difficult than any you received in the army. As soon as you are ready, we will get started."

"I am ready now, this very moment." Shoshanna's affection and Jonathan's optimism gave Micah hope for the first time.

"I was hoping you would say that," his father replied.

$$\approx \quad \approx \quad \approx$$

During the next two hours, Micah discovered that Jonathan was true to his word about the difficulty that lay ahead as he tried to bring life back to his legs. Their first session was pure agony, as Jonathan helped his son sit upright on the edge of the bed. As long as he lay prone, the pain in his back was moderate. But as Jonathan helped Micah to sit up, the pain shot up and down his legs and lower back with such ferocity that he had to bite down hard on his lip to keep from crying out. Ailea and Shoshanna inadvertently interrupted the torture session when they came to pay Micah a visit. They both saw the agony on his face and the sweat that had broken out on his forehead from the effort and the pain, and both women started to speak—to tell Jonathan and Micah to stop.

"Get out!" both men yelled in unison, and the women hastily complied.

Shoshanna was distraught. "What if this makes him worse?" she asked, unable to keep her voice from quivering.

Ailea took her hand. "I'm almost certain it will make it worse, at least temporarily. But if it is the means of Micah regaining the use of his legs, it will be worth it. They have to try. They have to try if Micah is ever to walk again."

"Then I won't protest, but I will have to stay away," Shoshanna said. "Will you help me be strong?"

Ailea went up on tiptoe to kiss her daughter-in-law's cheek. "I will keep you occupied so that you won't fret," she promised.

~ ~ ~

That evening, Shoshanna stayed up late. She wanted to wait until Micah was asleep before she went to bed because she didn't trust herself not to ask questions about his therapy session with Jonathan or show how much it disturbed her to think of him in pain.

She carried a small lamp when she finally entered the room, and shielded the flame with her hand so that the light wouldn't wake her sleeping husband. As she quietly got ready for bed, she noticed that Micah slept fitfully, his head moving back and forth and his legs twitching. They were paining him. She got the bottle of olive oil mixed with aloes from the windowsill and went to him.

At first he didn't wake when she began to knead his twitching leg muscles. He groaned as she gradually increased the pressure of her hands. From thigh to calf to the soles of his feet, she worked them until her arms ached. When she stopped to rest, she saw that he was awake now and watching her.

"I didn't mean to wake you, but I thought this might help the pain."

"It does. It's wonderful."

She was embarrassed for some reason by the praise, so she poured more oil into her palm and began the massage again. After a few minutes, Micah said, "That is enough, Shoshanna. You may go to bed now." His tone of voice sounded almost angry. Her hands paused for a moment before she stood up.

She had snuggled up on her pallet before he spoke again. "Thank you, Shoshanna. It really helped the pain. Good night."

~ ~ ~

By the end of the week, the only thing that changed about Micah's condition was that the pain went from bad to excruciating. Each morning, knowing it had been his lifelong habit to read the Torah scrolls, Shoshanna had brought them to him. The first few days he had taken much comfort from them. They made him think of the Rab and the strange dreams he had had when he was first injured. He knew the Rab would approve of his efforts to do something to combat his paralysis.

By the seventh day of therapy, when there was no improvement and the pain was unendurable, Micah pushed the scrolls away when Shoshanna brought them to him. "Poor Micah," she said, wiping the sweat from his forehead and taking a seat beside him on the bed. "You are in pain, I can tell. I will read the scrolls to you." She expected him to show surprise, maybe even pride that his wife had the skill to read the Law.

She was shocked when he turned his head toward the wall. "Go away. It pains me worse when you sit on my bed. And don't bring me the scrolls anymore. I don't want to read them, and I don't want you to read them to me." When she left the room, Micah succumbed to tears. He was going to be a bedridden cripple for the rest of his life.

He felt hopeless and helpless, and he did not admit it, but he felt angry with Adonai. He had fought for the Lord's anointed and this was his reward. He withdrew from everyone, and for several days refused all food and conversation.

Jonathan was determined not to give up. So he brought Micah his meals and badgered him until he ate. He also continued to insist, forcibly at first, that his son continue to exercise his legs and strengthen the rest of his body.

Those first few days of his depression, Micah had literally, physically, fought his father. Jonathan lifted his son's legs; Micah pushed his hands away. Jonathan tried to get Micah to sit up, and Micah resisted. Ordinarily, Jonathan would have been no match against his son, but in his weakened state, Micah was powerless to make his father stop. At one point, it made him so angry that he tried to hit Jonathan. Jonathan easily ducked away, and the blow only landed on his shoulder, making almost no impact at all.

"You might as well admit it, Son. You are weak as a kitten, helpless as a child, and I can do whatever I wish with you." As Jonathan expected, his statement so enraged Micah that his face turned red with his rage. Jonathan took a few steps back. "You would like very much to hit me again, wouldn't you?"

Micah almost felt as if a stranger had invaded his body. One part of him was appalled that he could even entertain the thought of striking his father. But at that moment, he was mad, not only at his father, but at the Rab, and at God as well. He answered his father's question truthfully. "Yes! I would like to fight you, to knock you down, to make you stop tormenting me!"

"Well, then, you are going to have to work at regaining your strength and making your legs obey your will once more, because until you do, I will be your tormentor. Nothing will make me give up and leave you in this state." Tears of frustration streamed down Micah's cheeks as he lay back, panting. When he glanced at his father, he saw that Jonathan's cheeks were also wet. But his father dried his eyes with one swipe of his arm. "Now, let's get you up," he said.

≈ ≈ ≈

Jerusha had also been told to stay away, but she was made of stronger stuff than either her mother or her new sister. When they had ordered her out of the room, she had turned and ran out the door, so the men assumed they were alone. But the inventive child decided she could see her brother's progress very well from the branches of the large almond tree outside his window.

They didn't discover their observer until the second week, when Micah, after an hour of effort, finally managed to stand —just for an instant. Before Jonathan could congratulate his son, they heard a loud whoop of joy coming from just outside the window. Micah was so surprised that he fell back on the bed.

Jonathan yelled at his daughter. "Get in here!" Jerusha swung from her perch on the branch to the windowsill, then hopped in the room. "Not that way, Jerusha. I meant for you to climb down from the tree and enter the room through the door."

"But it was so much faster this way, Ahbi," she explained.

Micah rolled on the bed in laughter. The men didn't even try to win the battle. From then on, they let Jerusha come and go as she wished during the sessions. And Micah admitted to Shoshanna later that his little sister always seemed to distract him from the pain by the outrageous things she said and did.

≈ ≈ ≈

Despite his progress, in fact, because of his progress in increasing his movements, Micah's back continued to pain him so badly that he was terse and foul-tempered with everyone. Only with Jonathan did he seem to have any patience. He resented his weakness in front of the women. Even Jerusha, who was about as sensitive as a goat, stopped coming in to visit him because she was hurt by his rejection.

He continued the battle to stand and walk, despite the excruciating pain he felt whenever he put any weight on his legs. The terrifying numbness that had at first rendered his legs useless was now replaced by a tingling and burning sensation that ran between his lower back and his feet and was agonizing. During the day, Jonathan forced his legs to flex and bend, putting all his strength into the treatment. At night, Micah allowed Shoshanna to knead the pain away with her treatment of ointments combined with hot and cold dressings. But in the light of day, he did not want her help.

"Send Father in to me," he would order Shoshanna. If she accompanied Jonathan back to the room, Micah would say, "You may go now," and Shoshanna knew she was not wanted. But she would pick up a reed broom and begin to sweep the passage outside the bedchamber. She suspected that Micah would try to get out of bed, and she wanted to be near if he hurt himself. It was hard for her not to hover. Amid growls and groans, with Jonathan's support, Micah began to make progress. Within a few weeks, once he was on his feet, Micah was able to stand alone without support.

Then Jonathan was called suddenly to Jerusalem. The hot-headed Sheba was making good on his promise to oppose the reinstatement of the king. "It shouldn't take long to deal with this problem," he told his family.

He turned to Micah. "I expect to see progress on those legs when I get back." Micah assured his father that he would not be slack in his absence. Deep down, though, he wondered if he could do much without Jonathan's help.

≈ ≈ ≈

That afternoon, after Jonathan's departure, Micah decided to try his exercises alone. Ailea and Jerusha were napping, because it was the month of Tishri and the early autumn heat was sti-fling in the middle of the day. Shoshanna was pressing figs into cakes, adding a bit of honey to add flavor and make them hold together. As she finished laying the pressed cakes onto a long strip of linen to dry, she heard a loud crash from the nearby bedchamber. She jumped up, wiping her sticky hands on the end of a cloth strip before running to see what was wrong.

Micah lay on the floor, his jaw clamped tightly shut, and his face pasty white and beaded with sweat. "Micah, what are you doing out of bed?" she asked in alarm.

"It should be perfectly obvious that I've been trying to walk," he snapped. "Now help me get up."

Shoshanna knelt down beside him and he placed an arm around her neck. But when she tried to help lift him, his weight was too great. He removed his arm, and sank back to the floor. "You aren't strong enough to help me. Just let me stay where I am until father gets back."

"But I can't just leave you on the floor!"

"Of course you can. Just leave me a few cushions. I'll be comfortable enough."

Shoshanna gave him a doubtful look but quickly heaped cushions behind him. As she did she tried to wipe the sweat from his forehead, but he grasped her wrist. "Don't coddle me," he growled.

Her eyes narrowed in anger as she reached the limits of her patience. "I wouldn't think of it," she spat as she flounced out the door. She didn't return for the rest of the day.

By sunset, Micah had pulled himself back into bed. He was rather proud of his accomplishment. In fact, he had been waiting all afternoon for Shoshanna to come and check on him so she could see that he had managed by himself.

Ailea brought him his evening meal. "Where is my wife?" he asked as his mother placed his tray across his knees and sat down on a stool beside the bed.

"She's resting. I insisted. She is exhausted from trying to please an extremely uncooperative and difficult patient. Eat your bread and cheese." Micah knew he had better obey his diminutive mother or find himself going hungry. The women didn't understand how hard it was for a man to be helpless and at their mercy.

That night Shoshanna waited until very late to return to their chamber. She carried a small lamp, which she set down on the chest that stood beside her sleeping mat. Micah had already extinguished the one beside the bed. "Shoshanna, come here and bring the lamp."

"I'm tired, Micah. I have no strength to rub your legs tonight."

"I know you are tired. That is why I want you to come over here."

Shoshanna hesitantly did as he asked. When she had set the lamp on the windowsill beside the bed, Micah drew her down to him. "You will not sleep on the pallet tonight. The bed is more comfortable." He scooted over to give her room.

"You are not well," she managed to squeak.

"I will rest better with my wife beside me. Kiss me good night, Shoshanna."

She paused and then landed a quick peck on his cheek. "That is not a proper kiss, and you know it. Have pity on your poor, helpless husband and give me a really loving kiss."

In the glimmer of the lamplight, she saw his eyes dancing with devilment and decided to try to get the best of him. Grasping his hair with both hands she placed a wet kiss right on his mouth. She ended the kiss only when she had to come up for air. By that time, her husband was as breathless as she was. He stared at her for a long moment, then broke out in a grin.

"Woman, you have healed me!" He pulled her closer and kissed her again. "I'm healed!" It was the end of her nights on the pallet.

≈ ≈ ≈

Jonathan tried to put aside his worries about Micah when he arrived in Jerusalem. He found the king ensconced again in the palace, where he belonged. Joab was by his side. Somehow David's nephew had managed to win his way back into the king's confidence, if not his favor. David had turned his back many times on Joab's crimes, pretending he didn't see. But Jonathan knew that he would never forgive Joab for Absalom's death. Of course, David wouldn't do anything about it. The army wouldn't stand for Joab being punished for killing the man who had tried to steal the throne. And Joab's armor-bearers had shrewdly taken part in the killing, so that no individual would be blamed. David had meted out the worst possible punishment when he stripped Joab of the position of general and gave it to Amasa, thereby making the victor serve the vanquished. But why was Joab seated in a place of honor in the royal chamber?

"Where is Amasa?" Jonathan asked as soon as the meeting convened.

"I sent him south to raise the militia in Judah to join us so that we can put down this rebellion by Sheba before it grows," the king replied.

"He was sent south, but he didn't *go* south," Joab interjected. "He went north instead."

"Not very far north," David said.

"But north, nonetheless, and he has sent no word of what he is doing. It seems suspicious to me." Joab looked at each of the *Gibborim* as he said this. The king's greatest warriors did not like the idea of being commanded by a general who had once fought against them. But almost to a man, they had no love for Joab. They had not been unhappy to see him go.

"Exactly where is Amasa?" Benaiah asked.

"He is in Gibeon." The king took charge of the meeting once again, giving Joab a stern look that told him to keep his mouth shut. David seldom reined in Joab, but when he did, the general knew better than to complain.

"It seems it would be easy to take the standing army and go to Gibeon. If Amasa is up to no good, we will catch him at it." This suggestion came from Abishai, Joab's younger brother. Jonathan liked Abishai well enough. He wasn't bad when he wasn't under his brother's influence.

"Then you and Joab, *jointly,* will command the troops until such time as you meet up with Amasa. If he is merely going about fulfilling the mission I assigned him, then you are to place yourselves under his command. Is that understood by everyone?" Every warrior in the room nodded his consent. "Then get some sleep. You will leave at first light." David rose and left the room without speaking another word. *He is still very grieved about all that has happened, and no wonder,* Jonathan thought.

By midmorning the next day, the army commanded by Joab and Abishai entered the city of Gibeon, located five miles north of Jerusalem. It seemed suspicious that Amasa would come here, because Gibeon was in the territory belonging to the tribe of Benjamin, the tribe of the rebellious Sheba as well as the family of old King Saul. The soldiers had discussed the situation as they marched along. "Perhaps Amasa has already gathered the militia and is now in Gibeon to put down the rebellion with the troops he has. He might want to prove his mettle by winning without our help," Jonathan suggested. There were a few grunts of assent and a few of dissent. They would just have to wait and see.

The city was located atop a great limestone outcropping at the eastern end of the Valley of Aijalon. Because the Tabernacle was located there, it was a sacred place, designated as "the mountain of the Lord." But Joab held nothing sacred. As they marched up the winding way to the city, Amasa came out to meet him. Jonathan was marching a few steps behind Joab when the general told his brother to give the command to halt. Then Joab went forward.

There was a smile on Amasa's face. Later, Jonathan would remember thinking that it was surely not the smile of a man who had been up to no good and was about to be caught at it.

Joab greeted his cousin with outstretched arms, but when Amasa's hands went to Joab's shoulders as part of the traditional kiss of greeting, he suddenly slumped in Joab's arms. Joab stepped back, and Amasa fell to the ground, writhing in pain.

Joab turned his back on the fallen man and signaled Abishai to start the march once more. It was a grisly sight that greeted them when they drew near. Amasa was making terrible noises, and for a moment, grasped Joab's foot. Joab kicked him, and the hand dropped away. Amasa's insides were half in his abdomen, and half on the ground. There was foam at his mouth, and his eyes were beginning to glass over in the gaze of death.

"You four men, stay here and keep the columns moving." Joab barked the order, leaving Jonathan, Benaiah, Maharai, and Helez, all members of the Thirty, standing beside Amasa's body. Joab and Abishai soon disappeared over the summit of the hill.

"This is terrible for the morale of the men," Maharai muttered under his breath. They had to keep yelling at the horrified troops to keep them moving. The fallen man was, after all, their newly appointed general.

"Let's get the body out of the way or we'll never get out of here," Helez suggested after a quarter hour of pushing and shouting at the advancing soldiers. The four *Gibborim* dragged the corpse into a field and rejoined the marchers.

This was not the first time Joab had gotten rid of his competition by pretending friendship and then stabbing the hapless victim. He had done the same to Abner, a righteous man who had been Saul's general in the old days. When Saul had fallen in battle, Abner was ready to embrace David as the Lord's anointed. Joab had feared that David might choose the older veteran as general over him, so he had met him at the entrance to Hebron and murdered him in the same way he dispatched Amasa.

Jonathan promised himself he would return to Ziph with all speed. Micah was in no condition yet to protect the family. Joab was so ruthless and unpredictable that Jonathan was afraid he would come after Shoshanna, and perhaps even Micah, because of her grandfather. It would be awhile before Jonathan could return to Ziph, but in the meantime he would keep a close eye on Joab.

≈ ≈ ≈

Sheba had hurried across Israel to try to mobilize his clan, the house of Bicri. At the town of Abel he took refuge behind the walls of the city. Joab laid siege and ordered a battering ram to knock down the gates. The attack continued for several days until an old holy woman from the city called down from the ramparts. "Joab, son of Zeruiah, come close so that I might talk to you."

The old crone looked pitifully small as she stood atop the wall of Abel, and Jonathan feared that if the breeze picked up, it would surely blow her off.

"What do you want, old woman? I have no time for foolishness," Joab growled at her.

"Are you truly Joab?"

"I am."

"Listen carefully to me, son of Zeruiah. There once was a proverb that said, 'If you want to settle a quarrel, ask advice in the city of Abel.' I am one who is peace-loving and faithful in Israel, but you are about to destroy a loyal city. Why do you seek to destroy what belongs to Adonai?"

Joab climbed up on the apparatus that supported the battering ram to get a better view of the woman. It made the hackles rise on Jonathan's neck to see Joab place himself in such danger. Right beneath a city wall was the most dangerous place a man could be during a siege.

The general now could be heard without shouting, and he spoke in a much more conciliatory tone. "Believe me, lady, I don't want to destroy this city. All we want is the son of Bicri who is named Sheba. He is from the hill country of Ephraim, and has revolted against King David. If you will hand him over to me, I will order my men back to Jerusalem, and we will leave your city in peace."

The crone stared at Joab long and hard before answering. "Very well, we will see that you get Sheba. But we will not open our gates to you. Wait there, and I will throw his head to you over the wall."

"Do you think the city elders will listen to her?" Abishai asked the question that was on all their minds. Before long, the old woman was back atop the wall, holding a severed head by its hair. "Here he is, General. Now leave us alone." With that she heaved the head down toward Joab. One of his armor bearers caught it, becoming spattered with blood for his efforts. He brought it to Joab.

"It is Sheba, all right. Thank you, old woman," he shouted up at the wall. "Do not forget that the king's army showed mercy on you and your city." The army was on its way back to Jerusalem in less than an hour.

Chapter Twenty-Two

~

As the days turned into weeks, Micah's family and most of his friends in the village were so caught up in helping Micah recover from his injuries that at first they paid no attention to an old problem that was resurfacing in the village. The problem was Lemuel. While others gratefully accepted amnesty and were once more loyal subjects of David, Lemuel remained bitter— not only because his brother had died, but because his side had lost. He had always hated Micah. Now he disparaged those who would make a hero out of him.

He began telling everyone that if Micah were not a cripple, he would challenge him to a duel, a contest of courage so that everyone might see that despite his great size, the son of Jonathan was nothing but a coward. As ill news is bound to do, especially in a small village, these slanderous words were listened to as avidly as the words of praise. But a great majority of Ziph's citizens, having known Lemuel since boyhood, knew that courage was not the man's strong point, and assumed that his vitriolic attacks would cease as soon as Micah regained his full health and strength.

~ ~ ~

"I am telling the truth, Micah. They are calling you the 'Lion of Ziph.' You are a legend now." Jerusha had just come back from a day with the herds and smelled exactly like one of the sheep. She was standing in the doorway of the common room because Ailea had forbidden her to come near the adults until she had bathed. She unwrapped her turban slowly as she informed her brother of what Ziph's shepherds were saying about him. "They say you fought with Goliath's sword, which no other man could have done, and that you struck down more rebels than the rest of your unit put together. And besides that, you saved your men from the flood, then survived being swept away."

"That's ridiculous. I'm no legend. I have fought in exactly one battle. How could I be?"

The family was gathered in the living area of the house. Micah was able to make it that far every day with the help of two wooden staves the size of weaver's beams. "Oh, I don't know," Ailea remarked. "I think the 'Lion of Ziph' is an appropriate title. You certainly roar like one when we don't come fast enough to do your bidding."

Shoshanna bent her head over her sewing to hide her smile and added, "Yes, he does rather bring to mind a wounded lion with a thorn in its paw."

"Son, I see I am going to have to rescue you from these contentious women before they vex you to death." Jonathan looked up from replacing the wooden handle on a small rotary mill Ailea used for grinding flour and smiled at his son.

"Yes, my dear, do take Micah with you and see how his sweet humor cheers you." Ailea was not going to back down from goading her son to mend his grouchy ways. Shoshanna was too new to the role of being a wife to take him to task for his obnoxious behavior, but a mother was never too old to instruct her son.

"When you go out, Micah, remember that when people call out 'Lion of Ziph,' they are talking about you," Jerusha said. "And I want to go with you. Father, when you take Micah out, could I come with you?"

While Jonathan thought about it, Ailea added a gentle admonishment, "If you don't bathe, Jerusha, and help Shoshanna with your share of the sewing, it will be a year before you go anywhere again. You keep ripping out your stitches and starting over. The chore would go much more quickly if you worked more carefully." Though her words contained a rebuke, she smiled at her daughter. She was well aware that Jerusha felt that it was a torture to do inside chores at all. She much preferred running free over the wooded hills surrounding Ziph.

Micah saw that his young sister was crestfallen and took pity on her. "Work very diligently to complete your sewing, and I will let you come with me when I venture out. But I am very much afraid that people will look upon me as a cripple rather than a hero."

$$\approx \quad \approx \quad \approx$$

A few days later the outing took place on market day. Inhabitants of Ziph and the smaller villages that surrounded it brought all kinds of goods to trade and sell. Micah had been both correct and mistaken in his prediction. The majority of the villagers looked upon him as a hero, stopping him time and again as he made his painstaking way to the center of the market. He heard the word *lion* a number of times as people poked their friends and commented as he passed by.

He also heard some mutterings of "coward" and "son of a foreigner," and once he heard clearly a remark made by a woman, "He got that nice young man killed at the Jordan." Micah tried not to take notice of any of it. He concentrated on using his staves to keep from falling on his face.

He shopped the market with Jerusha and Jonathan. His little sister had not let him forget his promise. She also caused him no end of aggravation, for she would pipe up with answers whenever anyone asked for a retelling of the battle. "My brother held off an entire regiment single-handedly. He was injured when he used his own body as a human bridge for his men to escape a flood." That was her story, and she told it many times. Micah suspected she exaggerated deliberately so that he would correct her, and thus talk about his exploits himself.

"This bread smells wonderful," Jonathan noted after about an hour had passed. "I told your mother not to fix a meal for us. Let's sit down under the awning over there. Tola owns it. He won't mind."

Micah hobbled over and sat down heavily on a big pile of rugs that Tola the merchant had for sale. The sun was hot, but Micah's face perspired from pain as much as from the heat. Jerusha tipped a skin of water into his cupped hands so that he could bathe his hands and face. When the three of them had washed, they passed the waterskin again for a drink.

"Are my eyes deceiving me, Tola? The mighty 'Lion of Ziph' condescends to grace your tent this day. Have you heard of his great prowess in battle? How he lets younger, untrained recruits go before him into battle so that his very large hide may be protected?"

Micah looked up into the face of the man who had hated and envied him from childhood. Lemuel, his tormentor. The man he'd almost killed as a lad when he unleashed his temper. He was determined not to let that happen here today. The Rab would expect him to use reason. But before he could speak, his little sister stepped between him and Lemuel.

"Your lies stink as much as your fetid goat's breath, Lemuel ben Shoham. My brother would never willingly let any other creature, man or beast, suffer if there were anything he could do about it. And he fears no man! Why he—"

Micah put a hand on his little sister's shoulder. She was so fearless, this little one, with such a big heart, but a temper hotter than the noonday sun. "Stop, little one. I can speak for myself."

"Listen to your brother, Jerusha, or I'll send you back to your mother," Jonathan intervened when the child looked as if she would ignore her brother's instruction.

Lemuel mocked, "You need a small girl to defend you, Micah. You must be very proud of yourself."

Jonathan answered, "He needs no one to defend him, Lemuel.

As soon as his legs have healed, I am certain he will be glad to answer any challenge you want to bring. In the interim, why don't you throw some insults my way? When I call you a liar, you can fight me to defend your honor. Surely you aren't afraid to face an old man like me." Jonathan's face was set in a scowl and his hands were fisted at his sides as he spoke to Micah's adversary. Micah had to stop this before it got out of hand.

"Lemuel, don't heed either my sister or my father. They don't understand that you speak out of grief for your brother. I do. I would be glad to give you a full accounting of what happened that day in the Forest of Ephraim."

"I've already heard all of your 'lame' excuses. I will wait for your legs to heal, if indeed there is anything wrong with them, and when you are ready to come out of hiding, I will meet you before the whole village and let everyone see what a pathetic 'lion' you are." He turned on his heels and stomped away.

Micah looked around. A crowd had gathered, curious about the angry, raised voices. They would spread the word all over Ziph and the surrounding countryside that there was to be a showdown between Lemuel and Micah. And as was true of any small town, the gossip would increase and the excitement would build until there would likely be a mob if the altercation ever did take place.

≈ ≈ ≈

"It is time we talked, Shoshanna." Micah was able to walk with the aid of only one crutch now. The pain in his legs was bearable, and he could feel his full strength and quickness beginning to return. His wife had continued the soothing massage of his legs at night, and it had given him great relief. Although their relationship continued to grow stronger along with his legs, they had never been able to talk about Ahithophel without starting a fight. Micah knew that this unresolved conflict was holding Shoshanna back from giving him her whole heart.

He had insisted on coming with her to the stream to draw

water for the household. It was the month of Tishri and the cistern in the courtyard at home had dried up. The autumn rains would not begin for another several weeks.

Micah watched his wife as she walked in front of him. She was trying to outpace him, but he was able to keep up with her. He watched the gentle sway of her walk with her glorious hair braided into one long, thick braid that fell below her head covering to her hips and bounced as she walked. She was slim and agile and beautiful as a young hind in the hills. He loved her more each day.

"What troubles you, Shoshanna?"

"Nothing troubles me."

"I believe it does, and I think I know what it is."

"Be careful, Micah. It is so rocky between here and the spring. You should wait here while I go." Shoshanna did not want to talk about problems. She was beginning to feel that she fit in with her new family and her new town. And everything would be all right between her and Micah if only he didn't expect too much.

"I am coming all the way with you, Shoshanna. There is nothing you can do to dissuade me," Micah said gently. Shoshanna knew that he was not speaking of drawing water.

She said nothing more to him, but waded knee-deep into the spring to fill her jug. It was a large pot, and she struggled to lift it back onto the bank. Micah, leaning on his staff, reached out a long arm and took it from her. He lifted the heavy vessel with one arm. Shoshanna never ceased to be amazed at her husband's strength.

Micah handed her the large waterskin jug with a strap that he had carried over his shoulder, and she filled that as well. When she was finished, he took it and set it beside the water pot. "Come and sit down beside me, my lily."

He tugged on her hand and she sank down beside him on the sun-warmed rock. "Tell me about your grandfather." He took her chin with the tips of his fingers and made her look into his eyes. "Tell me what happened."

"You already know, Micah, and it upsets me very much to

speak of it. I think we should be getting back." She tried to rise, but he stopped her by placing his hand on her shoulder.

Tears stung her eyes. It made her angry that Micah was forcing her to do this.

"Shoshanna, listen to me," Micah said firmly but gently. "It is time for you to release yourself from guilt over your grandfather's death. I know you miss him. I understand your grief and I am truly sorry for your loss, but Ahithophel's death was not your fault, and it was not my fault either."

"But you could have at least—"

"No, my sweet lily, there was nothing I could do, at least not while the war was still being fought. I talked to Ahithophel about the likelihood that he would be arrested, and he seemed resigned to it. He made it clear that he did not expect any help or want any. I think he had made up his mind before he ever left Jerusalem, and there was nothing anyone, including you, could have done to prevent what happened."

Micah lifted the long braid that hung over her left shoulder and toyed with it as it lay in his palm, smoothing it with his thumb.

"Shoshanna, I am so sorry that your grandfather died. Even though his treachery was worthy of a death sentence, I know that he was a good man in many ways, and I hope you will not remember the way he died, but the way he loved you."

She sat there at the edge of the stream, studying him for a long time before she spoke. "I am sorry too, Micah. The things I said before you went away the last time . . . a wife shouldn't say such things to her husband. And I didn't mean them. I know you aren't afraid of Lemuel. You are the strongest man I know."

Micah smiled and kissed her nose. "Now that we have both apologized, can we start over—together?" Shoshanna nodded agreement.

As the couple made their way back home, there was a closeness between them that hadn't been there before. They had been through so much turmoil in the months they had known each other, and their bond had been strengthened by adversity.

~ ~ ~

"It is Lemuel. He has come to see Micah. Oh, Shoshanna, what are we going to do?" Ailea was almost in tears as she entered the common room and told her daughter-in-law about their visitor. Shoshanna's heart sank. Micah was on the rooftop, resting on a couch after walking completely around the village several times to strengthen his legs. He was always more exhausted than he admitted after such exertion, and Shoshanna wanted him to rest. It made her angry that Lemuel was trying to make trouble.

"I suppose it will do no good for us to send him away," she sighed. "He would just go and spread the lie that Micah is afraid to face him. Stay here, Ailea. I'll take him up to Micah."

Lemuel stood sneering at Micah a short time later, having refused an invitation to sit. "I challenge you to prove your valor publicly, Micah ben Jonathan. I have a witness who heard you admit that your cowardice got my brother killed, and I won't rest until the whole village knows you are not the champion they think you to be."

"I have nothing to prove, Lemuel. The king knows I have done loyal service for him. My family knows I am no coward, and the troops I led, with the exception of your witness, who is mistaken about what he saw, will testify to the fact that I did my best for them."

Lemuel's upper lip curled into a snarl. "I thought you would say that."

With that, he turned and stalked away. Micah was left shaking his head. Why had Lemuel always hated him so? And what was he going to do about this foolish contest?

When they retired to their room that night, Micah told Shoshanna, "There has always been a question in this village concerning my character. Perhaps it is for the best if I lay it to rest once and for all."

"You aren't doing this because of what I said before, are you? You don't need to prove anything to me, Micah."

"That matter is forgotten. You apologized, remember? No, this isn't for you or the family. It is for the village. And for me."

~ ~ ~

The next morning, Jerusha jumped up and down and clapped her hands. "I'm so glad you are going to answer the challenge, Micah. You are going to win, and Lemuel and his friends are going to have to take back their lies about you."

The rest of the family did not share her opinion. "What is this challenge?" Ailea asked without a pause from the grinding of grain for her bread.

"Lemuel did not say, Mother. I can't believe it is an honest test of strength. He knows I would easily win such a contest. I suppose it is some kind of test of courage or endurance," Micah told her calmly.

"That horrid man will probably cheat and make it impossible for you to win. I don't want you to do it." Shoshanna went to her husband's side and looked at him in a beseeching manner, but Micah refused to be persuaded.

"I won't have my friends fighting my battles, Shoshanna." And he wouldn't change his mind, not even when his father came to him later in the day and asked him to reconsider.

"The Rab always said that a man's honor lies within him, son. I don't believe that if you do this thing, it will make much difference. You already know within yourself that you are no coward," Jonathan pointed out.

Micah shook his head. "Father, before the Rab died he told me that someday I would learn to reconcile the warrior and the teacher within me. I think I am beginning to understand what he meant. Now is a time for the warrior. If I refuse to fight, my friends will fight for me, and I can't allow that. I want this issue settled for all time."

"I'm proud of you, my son," Jonathan said as he embraced Micah in a full bear hug. "Do what you must do."

Chapter Twenty-Three

~

*T*he day of the contest dawned cloudy and much cooler than the day before, a sign that the fall rains were on their way. Shoshanna prayed that it would pour buckets so that this foolish contest would be postponed. Why couldn't Micah simply pound Lemuel into the ground and be done with it? Or better yet, just ignore him. No one in their right mind would believe the things Lemuel said, anyway. Men! What foolish, prideful creatures they were.

Micah had already left the house, as had Jonathan and Jerusha. Shoshanna went up to the rooftop apartment and found Marah and Ailea there, sitting on a padded bench that had been placed against the low wall that surrounded the rooftop. They were eating bread and cheese as they looked down on the village street. The street was already crowded with more people than usual. Evidently, they weren't going to let the threat of rain deter them.

"Have some wine and bread, dear," Ailea said as she offered Shoshanna a cup and a thick, fragrant chunk of bread.

"I think I had better go find Micah. It looks as if this event is going to happen today after all."

"There is plenty of time yet, Shoshanna. You need to eat first, then Marah and I will go with you. And don't worry. What test could Lemuel possibly devise that Micah could not succeed at? My son can do almost anything."

Shoshanna wished she could share Ailea's confidence. It wasn't that she didn't think Micah could meet any honest physical challenge thrown his way, but she knew his enemy to be an evil man, and he would not hesitate to try by some nefarious means to hurt Micah and discredit him in the eyes of all Ziph.

Reluctantly, she agreed to take the proffered meal. Then she let the two older women accompany her to the center of the village. There, Jonathan and Micah sat on a bench with Jerusha between them. They were laughing at something the little girl said, and Shoshanna wondered how they could find humor in anything this day. Then they heard the challenge.

"Micah, son of Jonathan, do you accept my challenge today? Or will you run away as you did when we were children, and as you did when you left my brother alone to die in the Forest of Ephraim?" Lemuel swaggered forward and spit right beside Micah's foot.

Mocking disrespect was written all over his face, and Shoshanna wanted to fight him for her husband's sake, even though she knew it was a ridiculous thought. Lemuel had the confidence of a man who had planned his challenge well. In a loud voice, he continued, "Some have begun to call him the Lion of Ziph. I think we should have a contest to determine the real lion of Ziph."

As if on cue, a loud roar sounded from the edge of the crowd. A number of women and children screamed, and the crowd parted to reveal a cart with a wooden cage on top. Inside the cage was a lion, who was letting his unhappiness at being a prisoner be known with thundering roars.

Three men pushed the cart into the center of the square, stopping right in front of the bench where Jonathan and Micah sat. Father and son showed no fear, but studied the full-grown male cat that paced and snarled in the confines of his cage. Lemuel seemed to be enjoying the commotion he had caused. He turned to a lad in the crowd, who handed him a young lamb.

Lemuel turned with the little animal, holding it very near the cage. The lion's paw swiped out between the bars, his extended claws grazing the lamb's side. The creature let out a pitiful bleat. Lemuel only laughed and held it over his head so that all could see the bloody scratches along its side.

"Poor lion, he is very hungry. I've seen to it that he hasn't eaten for several days, and at the moment he would do almost anything to have this little morsel." As Lemuel paused to let suspense build in the crowd, Shoshanna felt ill at the thought of Micah tangling, bare-handed, with the cat.

"We all know that our friend Micah likes nothing better than to take in any helpless or starving creature he comes across. Will he take mercy on the starving lion, or the helpless lamb? What better challenge than to see him solve this dilemma."

Shoshanna expected to hear several people protest, but instead a wave of excitement swept through the crowd. They were going to enjoy seeing this! She had to stop it.

"No! Don't do it. Walk away from this right now!" She clung to Micah's arm as Jonathan tried to talk sense to him.

"Micah, this is no way to defend your manhood. You must tell Lemuel to forget the lion, stand up like a man and meet you in a fair fight. The coward will back down. You know that."

"Micah, listen to your father, please. You can't fight a lion. You still don't have your full strength." Shoshanna continued clinging to him, tears streaming down her face. He patted her back, but refused to heed her pleas.

"I will do this and then the matter will be over—settled. I am weary of it and I want it to end. Just trust me, Father, Shoshanna. I will be all right."

"But Micah, a lion—you can't overpower it! Please don't do this to me."

"I am doing this *for* you, my lily. And for me. It will be over soon." He put her away from him and turned toward the cat. The frustrated beast sprang at him, but Micah didn't flinch. Instead he leaned against the wagon, very near the lion.

"Come here, Lemuel," he challenged, with seeming good nature.

His enemy hesitated for a moment, his eyes sweeping the crowd. He figured that they would mock him if he showed his fear, so after handing the lamb back to the little boy, he walked over to Micah. He stopped several feet away from danger.

Micah was not going to let him get away with it. "Closer," he demanded.

Lemuel stepped closer, but kept his eyes trained on the lion, who snarled at him. "Let me see if I understand your challenge. You want to give me the lamb to hold, turn the lion loose, and see what happens. Is that correct?"

Lemuel nodded, still not taking his eyes off the lion to glance at Micah.

"Foolish man!" Micah exclaimed. "You would endanger all these people by releasing this dangerous creature, just to challenge me? If you want me to fight this beast, then take him to the pit the potters have made in digging their clay. That is the only place where he can be released without risk to the others, and I will face him as you suggest." The confident gleam in her husband's eye frightened Shoshanna even more than the lion, and she felt despair as she realized he was set on this course, and nothing she could do would deter him.

Lemuel ordered the young men to pull the wagon, and the crowd surged behind them through the gates and down a winding pathway toward the pit that was located just outside of Ziph. As the adversaries walked along in front of the wagon, Micah growled a question to Lemuel.

"And just what is the purpose of this exercise, Lemuel? I am to protect the lamb, that much is clear. But just what am I supposed to do with the lion? You know I would rather not kill him, because I do not like to kill any animal unless there is a very good reason, and pleasing you and this crowd is not reason enough. So tell me, what am I to do with the lion?"

"I think a better question is, What is the lion going to do with you?" Lemuel threw back his head and laughed, then stepped back into the crowd and called, "Now, enough stalling. Here's your pit, Micah. Tobias, open the cage!"

"Wait!" Micah called out. Shoshanna thought he was about to refuse to go through with it, and she breathed a sigh of relief. But instead, he addressed the crowd. "All of you are to keep well back from the pit, and out of danger. You are not to harm the lion or goad him."

Tobias dropped the startled lamb into the pit, then swung open the cage door. Vaulting into the pit, Micah scooped up the injured lamb just as the lion leaped from the cage. The crowd gasped and drew back, but the lion went straight for the bleeding lamb.

Then a strange thing happened: Micah roared. Holding the lamb tucked firmly under his arm, he roared a lion-like challenge at the beast. The animal roared back, but did not attack.

Shoshanna's heart was pounding so hard as she watched that she feared it would burst. She felt something soft and furry brush her legs and looked down to see Jerusha's little wolf pup run to the edge of the pit, snarling and yipping, its little ruff standing straight up. Fearing the pet might jump into the pit, Shoshanna scooped the little animal into her arms. "Shh, Wolf. I know you want to help him, just as I do, but we can't." She squeezed the small creature so hard that it yelped in pain as her eyes were once more riveted to the scene in the pit.

The spectators fell silent in wonder as the two magnificent creatures faced each other down. As the lion advanced, Micah carefully gave ground. The beast stopped and issued an ear-splitting roar. Nearly every spectator took a step back from the edge of the pit in fear. But Micah's response was not to retreat. Instead, he threw back his head and gave another roar of his own—every bit as loud as the lion's.

The crowd was struck silent at the sight of man and beast, each with head thrown back, mane blowing in the wind, muscles rippling, and golden eyes intent on the other. Shoshanna felt a tremendous surge of pride in her husband at that moment. And, for the first time since the lion had been brought into the town square, she felt a rush of hope.

Then the lamb bleated in terror, and the hungry lion crouched ready to spring. Micah quickly dropped the lamb and stationed himself between it and the lion, his massive arms poised in a defensive posture. Shoshanna breathed a prayer she had already repeated many times: "O Lord God of Israel, give Micah cunning and strength and save him from the jaws of the lion."

Suddenly the cat sprang and Micah knocked it down, midair, with a blow to its chest, but not before its claws raked the length of the warrior's left arm. Man and beast retreated and circled, roaring their defiance at each other. The lion feinted, then circled behind Micah in pursuit of the lamb. Almost too quickly for the spectators to follow, Micah jumped on the lion's back and grabbed it by its mane, pulling its head backward before it reached its prey. The furious lion fought, but Micah held it from behind, its mane still in the grasp of his right hand, the other arm around its middle. The cords on his arms and neck stood out as he struggled to walk the thrashing creature away from the lamb. The enraged beast twisted and snarled, but Micah would not let him go.

"Let it go! Get away!" Shoshanna heard herself scream. Instead, Micah released the lion's mane and quickly, to avoid the terrible claws, he wrapped his forearm around the animal's throat and slowly cut off his supply of air. As he continued to apply pressure, the creature seemed to relax, then fell unconscious.

Micah slowly backed away, well aware that the lion still posed a threat, and searched about him for some means to capture it. Without hesitation Jonathan grabbed a large piece of canvas and a rope from a vendor who had them in his hand as he had followed the crowd. He climbed into the pit with Micah, and the two men wrapped the canvas securely around the still-unconscious lion and tied it with the rope.

"Now we can take this beast back to the wilderness and release him where he deserves to be!" Micah shouted to the crowd as he stood over the bound creature. "Quickly, let's get him back into the cage before he awakens." Several of the men from the crowd climbed warily down into the pit and helped the two men lift the creature.

"Tobias, open the cart." Tobias quickly pulled back the door to the cage, and Micah and the men hefted the lion into the cage, then pulled away the rope and canvas. The crowd roared its approval as the creature began to stir.

Shoshanna pushed her way through the crowd. She tried to sound calm, but she could not keep either her voice or her knees from shaking. "You are injured. Come, I will bandage your arms."

"First, the lion has to be taken to the wilderness and released," Micah said through his teeth, which he had set against the pain.

"Tobias and I will see to it," Jonathan told his son. Micah didn't argue, but went with Shoshanna and Ailea. Jerusha begged but was not allowed to go with her father to release the lion, so she reluctantly followed her brother home.

As Micah moved slowly by them, both arms dripping blood, the crowd began to cheer him. "Lion of Ziph, you're our champion!" and other phrases Micah couldn't hear clearly. There was a buzzing sound in his head. He made it to the house before his knees buckled under him. His wife and mother guided him to a bench not a second too soon.

$\approx \approx \approx$

The entire family of Jonathan ben Shageh was gathered under the arbor that covered half the area of their rooftop. The other half was taken up by the private chamber of Jonathan and Ailea. The arbor was constructed with four poles lashed together with a canopy top fashioned of woven palm branches. Twined around the four poles were grapevines with grapes still attached. The Feast of Booths, or Ingathering, was a joyous festival to celebrate the end of harvest and to commemorate Adonai's care for the Hebrews when they dwelt in booths—or tents—in the wilderness. It was the second day of the week-long celebration, and the family was relaxing after the huge celebratory meal that Ailea and Marah had prepared. Ailea, who years ago had embraced the Law of Moses wholeheartedly, always went to great lengths to see that the family observed every one of the seven days of this, her favorite festival.

The rooftops of Ziph were crowded with people in the spirit of the feast, and it was common practice for the villagers to visit one another in their rooftop retreats. This year, almost everyone in the village had climbed the stairs to Jonathan's rooftop to recount the details of Lemuel's challenge and Micah's victory. Four days had passed since Micah's battle with the lion, and his arms were on their way to healing, though the deep scratches were still inflamed. As the sun set, the family was enjoying one of the few moments that they did not have visitors to entertain.

The day before, they had even entertained a visitor from Jerusalem. Beneiah had come to inform Jonathan that this time Joab had seemed to realize he had gone too far in his vengeance. Though the king had reinstated him as general, David's eyes grew cold whenever he looked upon his nephew, and so far as Beneiah could discern, Joab was stepping very warily and ordering no more reprisals. The whole family had breathed a sigh of relief, though no one had spoken their concern for Shoshanna and Marah aloud.

Micah seated himself on a cushion beside Shoshanna and settled Jerusha onto his lap. After a moment, he suddenly jumped up, dumping his sister on the floor.

"Where are you going, Brother?" Jerusha called after him, starting to follow as he ran down the stairs.

"Stay there, little one. I will be right back. There is something I had forgotten." Jerusha heaved a sigh of disappointment, but sat down beside her sister-in-law to wait for Micah's return.

"Do you know what it is?" Jerusha asked this of Shoshanna, but Shoshanna shook her head.

"Do you know what it is, Father?"

"No, Jerusha, I don't." Jonathan thought for a moment. "Unless it's . . ."

"Unless it's what?" all four females asked him at once, then all laughed that they had spoken together. But Jonathan remained silent.

In a short time, Micah was back with a small drawstring bag in his hand. He went to his mother's side with the instruction that she hold out her hand, palm up.

"Mother, I forgot to give you this," Micah said as he undid the drawstring of the tapestry bag that he had carried with him ever since he left Damascus. He emptied the contents of the bag into Ailea's hand and smiled as she gasped.

"My mother's bracelet! Where did you find this?"

"I didn't. It's a present from your brother."

"Rezon sent me this? Rezon?" She stared at the beautiful piece. Micah knew she was trying to hide tears.

"He bought it back from the rich merchant who bought your family home, and he also bought the house back. He lives there now."

Ailea looked up at her son. Tears were coursing down her cheeks—tears of joy, and of nostalgic sadness. "Thank you, Micah. This is the best gift and best news I have heard in a long time." She turned to Jonathan and squeezed his hand. "Jonathan, Rezon has forgiven me. He has finally forgiven me after all these years."

"There was nothing to forgive, Love, but I am glad the scoundrel has finally swallowed his pride. In the spring we will go to Jerusalem for Passover, then journey on to Damascus to see Rezon. Do you think he will allow me in his house?"

"I think he had better, or I'll cosh his thick head," Ailea replied with a quavering laugh. "Just think, Jonathan, I will be able to see my home again. I have many good memories."

"Such as the first time you saw me," her husband laughed.

"I wouldn't call that a good memory!"

Shoshanna was surprised at her mother-in-law's answer. She

knew Ailea loved Jonathan very much. "Why is it not a pleasant memory?" Her father-in-law grinned as if he had hoped someone would ask that. The other family members knew the answer, of course, because the story had been told many times.

"Because he threw *Ahmi* in a pool. Then he dragged her by her hair!" Jerusha announced this with such glee that Shoshanna looked to Ailea to deny such a thing.

"I'm afraid it is true, Shoshanna. Jonathan tried to drown me, then pulled me by my braid and slung me over his shoulder like a sack of barley. And I was just a young, helpless girl." Ailea said this with a twinkle in her eye as she looked at Jonathan for his response.

"Helpless? Ha! She had laid half of my men low. And I only shoved her under the water after she had done this. Look, I still carry a scar from her attack." Jonathan held out his hand for Shoshanna to see, and pointed out a small, crescent-shaped scar on the fleshy area between his thumb and forefinger.

Shoshanna tried not to laugh at the warrior looking to her for sympathy for such a small mark on his hand. There was a truly appalling scar that ran the entire length of his right forearm. She supposed that after she had been in this family for a while she would find out the story behind that scar as well.

Not receiving the pity he expected from his daughter-in-law, Jonathan turned to Marah and embellished. "She bit me!"

"I put my mark on you," Ailea amended, as husband and wife shared an intimate look.

The festive feeling continued as the sun sank below the horizon and a full moon took its place. Ailea's face was radiant with her newfound link to the past. Then Marah added to the family's joy by a revelation of her own.

"If you don't mind, Jonathan," she said, "I would like to accompany you and Ailea to Jerusalem. I think it is well past time for a visit with my cousin at the palace."

"Mother, you would go to see Bathsheba? Truly?"

Marah turned to her daughter, whose lovely face was wreathed in the biggest smile she had ever seen. "Yes, dear. I should have offered her my forgiveness years ago. If she will forgive me for being so coldhearted, I am more than willing to leave the past where it belongs and start anew."

"What made you change your mind, Mother?"

Marah's mouth quivered as she turned to Ailea. "It was your joy that made me decide to put my bitterness away. You had every right to harbor bitterness at Rezon. You told me the story of how you came to marry Jonathan, how he captured you when Damascus fell. None of what happened was your fault, yet your brother blamed you for it and disowned you. But you have continued to try to contact him all these years, even though he kept rejecting your overtures.

"That pricked my conscience. I realized how mean-spirited I've been to reject every invitation my cousin issued to me. I even wonder if . . ." At this point, Marah couldn't continue. She lowered her eyes to hide the tears that pooled there.

"You wonder what, Mother?" Shoshanna asked softly.

"I wonder if your grandfather might not have forgiven David and Bathsheba if I had done so. I wonder if he would be alive today but for my resentment. My anger at them fueled his own hatred."

Shoshanna squeezed her mother's shoulder. "No, Mother. He kept his hatred secretly in his heart while pretending to forgive them. That is why it grew until it completely took over, until it killed him."

"Poor Father. He was a good man in so many ways."

"Of course he was, and those are the memories you and Shoshanna will cherish." Ailea smiled at her friend, determined to cheer her and make her forget her guilt. "You will send a message to your cousin to tell her you will visit the palace in the spring. Jonathan and I will take you when we go for Passover. I know that Shoshanna would like to be there when you are reunited, so she and Micah will just have to go with us."

Micah laughed. "So, Mother, you have made plans for us all. Well, I am not complaining, because I agree with you. I not only wish to attend Passover, but I intend to return to Jerusalem for the Day of Atonement. It will be around the anniversary of the time I was injured, and I want to bring my sin offering to the tabernacle. I sinned when I failed to trust the Lord and became bitter against Him. You are not the only one, Marah, whose heart needed to change. We will go with you in the spring, won't we, Shoshanna?"

All eyes turned to her, but the immediate agreement they had expected was not forthcoming. Instead, Shoshanna looked a little perplexed. "In the spring? I . . . ah, perhaps it will be possible."

"Perhaps? Shoshanna, what could possibly keep you from a journey to Jerusalem?" Micah studied his wife's face. Something was wrong.

Shoshanna's face flushed and she looked away from him. "Micah, I think we should talk later, privately."

"But we want to know now," Jerusha piped up. "I want you to go with us. Why can't you?"

"I didn't say for a certainty that I couldn't, Jerusha. It may be that I can, but I need to discuss it with Micah."

"Then let's discuss it right here. I don't mind if the family hears it."

"Oh, very well, if you all insist. I don't know whether the baby will be old enough to travel by Passover, though it would be wonderful to present him at the tabernacle with the whole family there."

Shoshanna's announcement met with stunned silence for a moment. Jerusha, bright child that she was, caught on first. "The baby . . . you mean you will have a baby by next spring? Oh, I can't wait! It will happen right at lambing time too." Her prattle continued even as the adults, one by one, reacted.

Marah kissed her daughter's cheek. "Oh, my little girl is to be a mother. We won't travel anywhere until we are certain you are over your confinement. I'm so happy for you, so happy."

Shoshanna almost had the breath knocked out of her when Jonathan pounded her on the back. "I am to have a grandson before another year passes. I have to leave now to go to evening circle. I will tell all the men of Ziph that the line of Jonathan ben Shageh will be continued as proudly as it was begun. Do you want to go with me, Son? I will allow it only if you let me make the announcement first." He slapped Micah on the back twice as hard as he had done to his daughter-in-law. Micah just sat with a stunned look on his face.

"Now, don't let the women frighten you with stories of their travail. Why, it is the most natural thing in the world, and you will get through it wonderfully. I have never told you the story of Micah's birth, have I? You see, I was traveling all alone when I—"

"Later, Mother." Micah cut off Ailea's story as he jumped up, swept Shoshanna into his arms and strode toward the stairs. "Just wait till I get you alone, making an announcement like that with the whole family present," he grumbled into his wife's ear as he headed for their room.

Shoshanna saw the melting heat of the love in his eyes and wrapped her arms around his neck. "You are the one who insisted I tell everyone."

He sank down with her into the comfortable cushioned chair that Isaac had brought him last year from Egypt. After giving his wife a long kiss, he cupped her face in his hands. "You make my life complete, my lily. I will be as thrilled if we have a little girl like you as I would be with twin sons."

She laughed and kissed the dimple above the bow of his lip. "Don't mention twins, please. We will have one child at a time. And they will grow up to be as strong and wise as their father."

Don't miss the first two adventures in the Heart of Zion Series

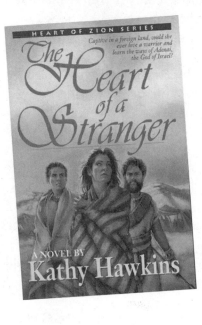

The Heart of a Stranger

Ailea is captive in a foreign land. Grieving over the loss of her parents, could she ever love the warrior Jonathan and learn the ways of Adonai, the God of Israel? Against the backdrop of King David's reign, Ailea and Jonathan find themselves pawns in a treacherous game of war. Ailea must choose between her desire to escape and her growing affection for her captor. (0-8254-2867-x, 304 pp.)

The Desires of the Heart

Keziah's one desire is to experience unconditional love. Isaac, an armor-bearer for Jonathan, is consumed with a desire to seek vengeance for his father's murder. Set against the backdrop of David and Bathsheba's story in 2 Samuel 11–12, Keziah and Isaac learn that trusting God—and each other—will give them the true desires of their hearts. (0-8254-2871-8, 304 pp.)